**W9-ALN-610**

*dancer*

# dancer

A NOVEL

## Colum McCann

METROPOLITAN BOOKS

Henry Holt and Company    New York

Metropolitan Books
Henry Holt and Company, LLC
*Publishers since 1866*
115 West 18th Street
New York, New York 10011

Metropolitan Books™ is a registered
trademark of Henry Holt and Company, LLC.

Grateful acknowledgment is made to Getty Images for permission to
reprint the photograph on p. 5, copyright © 1976 by Hulton
Archive; Warner Books for the excerpt on p. 263 from *The Andy
Warhol Diaries*, by Andy Warhol, Pat Hackett, ed., © 1989 by the
Estate of Andy Warhol; Gary Matoso for the photograph on p. 311 ©
1985 by Gary Matoso.

This is a work of fiction. With the exception of some public figures
whose real names have been used, the names, characters and incidents
portrayed are the work of the author's imagination.

Library of Congress Cataloging-in-Publication Data
McCann, Colum, 1965–
Dancer : a novel / Colum McCann—1st. ed.
    p.   cm.
ISBN 0-8050-6792-2
    1. Nureyev, Rudolf, 1938– —Fiction. 2. Ballet dancers—Fiction.
3. Male dancers—Fiction. I. Title.

PR6063.C335 D36 2003
823'.914—dc21                                                    2002071879

Henry Holt books are available for special
promotions and premiums. For details contact:
Director, Special Markets.

First Edition 2003

*Designed by Paula Russell Szafranski*

Printed in the United States of America

1   3   5   7   9   10   8   6   4   2

*For Allison,*

*for Riva Hocherman*

*and for Ben Kiely,*

*with my deepest thanks for your faith and inspiration.*

What we, or at any rate, I, refer to confidently as a memory—meaning a moment, a scene, a fact that has been subjected to a fixative and thereby rescued from oblivion—is really a form of storytelling that goes on continually in the mind and often changes with the telling. Too many conflicting emotional interests are involved for life ever to be wholly acceptable, and possibly it is the work of the story-teller to rearrange things so that they conform to this end. In any case, in talking about the past we lie with every breath we draw.

WILLIAM MAXWELL,
*So Long, See You Tomorrow*

*dancer*

What was flung onstage during his first season in Paris:

ten one-hundred-franc bills held together with an elastic
band;

a packet of Russian tea;

a manifesto from the Front de Libération National repre-
senting the Algerian nationalist movement, protesting
the curfew imposed on Muslims after a series of car
bombs in Paris;

daffodils stolen from the gardens in the Louvre causing
the gardeners to work overtime from five until seven
in the evening to make sure the beds weren't further
plundered;

white lilies with centimes taped to the bottom of their
stems, so they were perfectly weighted to reach the stage;

so many flowers that a stagehand, Henri Long, who swept up
the petals after the show, had the idea of creating a pot-

pourri, which he sold, on subsequent evenings, to fans at the stage door;

a mink coat that sailed through the air on the twelfth night, causing the patrons in the front rows to think for a moment that some flying animal was above them;

eighteen pairs of women's underwear, a phenomenon that had never been seen in the theater before, most of them discreetly wrapped in ribbons, but at least two pairs that had been whipped off in a frenzy, one of which he picked up after the last curtain, delighting the stagehands by sniffing them flamboyantly;

a headshot of Yuri Gagarin, the cosmonaut, with a message at the bottom reading *Soar, Rudi, Soar!*

a series of paper bombs filled with pepper;

a precious pre-Revolutionary coin thrown up by an émigré who had wrapped it in a note saying that if Rudi kept his cool, he would be as good as Nijinsky if not better;

dozens of erotic Polaroids with the names and phone numbers of women scrawled on the back;

notes saying *Vous êtes un Traître de la révolution;*

broken glass thrown by Communist protesters, stopping the show for twenty minutes while the shards were swept up, and provoking such a fury that an emergency meeting of the Parisian Party branch was held because of the negative publicity caused;

death threats;

hotel keys;

love letters;

and on the fifteenth night, a single long-stemmed gold-plated rose.

# BOOK ONE

| I |

SOVIET UNION · 1941–1956

Four winters. They built roads through drifts with horses, pitching them forward into the snow until the horses died, and then they ate the horsemeat with great sadness. The medics went into the snow-fields with vials of morphine taped beneath their armpits so the morphine wouldn't freeze and, as the war went on, the medics found it harder to locate the veins of the soldiers—they were wasting away, dying long before they had really died. In the trenches they tied the earflaps of their ushinkis tight, stole extra coats, slept in huddles with the injured at the center, where they would get most warmth. They wore padded trousers, layers of underclothes, and sometimes they made jokes about wrapping whores around their necks for scarves. After a while they didn't remove their boots too often. They had seen other soldiers—frostbitten toes dropping suddenly from their feet—and they began to feel that they could tell a man's future by the way he walked.

For camouflage they fastened two white peasant shirts together to fit over their greatcoats, made drawstrings from bootlaces, pulled the cowl tight, and in that way they could lie in the snow unseen for hours. The recoil liquid in their artillery froze. The striker springs in their machine guns shattered like glass. When they touched bare metal the flesh tore away from their hands. They lit fires with charcoal, threw stones into the embers and later picked out the pebbles to warm their hands. They found that if they shat, which was not often, they had to shit in their pants. They let it lie there until frozen, pitched it out after they found shelter, and still nothing smelled, not even their gloves, until a thaw. To piss, they hitched oilskin sacks under their trousers so as not to expose themselves to the weather, and they learned to cradle the warmth of the pissbag between their legs and sometimes the warmth helped them think of women, until the bag froze and they were nowhere again, just a simple snowfield lit by an oil-refinery fire. They looked out over the steppe and saw the bodies of fellow soldiers, frozen to death, a hand in the air, a knee in a stretch, beards white with frost, and they learned to steal the dead man's clothes before he became forever stiffened in them, and then they leaned down to whisper, Sorry comrade thanks for the tobacco.

They heard the enemy were using the dead to make roads, laying down the bodies since there were no trees left, and they tried not to listen as noises came across the ice, a tire catching on bone, moving on. There was never silence, the air carried all sounds: the reconnaissance crews on skis, the hiss of electric pylons, the whistle of mortars, a comrade calling out for his legs, his fingers, his rifle, his mother. In the mornings they warmed their guns with a low charge so that when the first volley of the day rang out the barrel did not explode in their faces. They wrapped cow skin around the handles of the antiaircraft batteries and covered the slits of the machine guns with old shirts to block the snow. The soldiers on skis learned to drop to a moving crouch to pitch their grenades sideways so they could still advance and maim at the same time. They found the remains of a T-34 or an ambulance or even an enemy Panzer, and they drained the antifreeze through the carbon filters of their gas masks and got drunk on it. Sometimes they drank so much that after a few days they went blind. They lubed their artillery with sunflower oil, not too much on the firing pins, just enough on the springs, and they wiped the excess oil on their boots so the leather would not crack and let the worst of the weather in. They peered at the ammunition boxes to see if a factory girl in Kiev or Ufa or Vladivostok had scrawled a loveheart for them, and even if she hadn't she had, and then they rammed the ammunition into their Katyushas, their Maxims, their Degtyarevs.

When they retreated or advanced they blew a ditch with a 100-gram cartridge in order to save their lives if their lives were something they felt like saving. They shared cigarettes, and when their tobacco was finished they smoked sawdust, tea, lettuce, and if there was nothing else they smoked horse shit, but the horses were so hungry that they hardly shat anymore either. In the bunkers, they listened to Zhukov on the wireless, Yeremenko, Vasilevsky, Khrushchev, Stalin too, his voice full of black bread and sweetened tea. Loudspeakers were strung through the trenches, and amplifiers were put on the front line, facing west, so they could keep the Germans awake with tango, radio reels, socialism. They were told about traitors, deserters, cowards, and were instructed to shoot them down. They stripped red medals off the chests of these dead and pinned them to the undersides of their own tunics. To hide at night they put masking tape over the headlights of the cars, ambulances, tanks. They stole extra tape to put on their hands and feet, over their portyanka socks, and some of them even wrapped it around their ears, but the tape tore their flesh and they howled as the frostbite set in, and then they howled further against the pain and some just put their guns to their heads and said good-bye.

They wrote home to Galina, Yalena, Nadia, Vera, Tania, Natalia, Dasha, Pavlena, Olga, Sveta, and Valya too, careful letters folded in neat triangles. They didn't expect much in return, perhaps just one sheet with the perfume left on the censor's fingers. Incoming mail was given numbers and, if there were a series of numbers missing, the men knew that a mail carrier had been blown to bits. The soldiers sat in the trenches and stared straight ahead and composed letters to themselves in their imaginations, and then they went out into the war once more. Pieces of shrapnel caught them beneath their eyes. Bullets whipped clean through their calf muscles. Splinters of shells lodged in their necks. Mortars cracked their backbones. Phosphorus bombs set them aflame. The dead were heaped onto horse carts and laid in huge graves blown out of the ground with dynamite. Local women in shawls came to the pits to keen and secretly pray. The gravediggers—shipped in from the gulags—stood off to one side and allowed the women their rituals. Yet more dead were heaped upon the dead, and frozen bones were heard to crack, and the bodies lay there in their hideous contortions. The gravediggers shoveled the final dirt on the pits, and sometimes in their despair they pitched themselves forward, still alive. More dirt was thrown upon them so that afterwards it was said that the ground quivered. Often in the evenings the wolves came from the forests, trotting high-legged through the snow.

The injured were lifted into ambulances or onto horses or put on sleds. A whole new language appeared to them in the field hospitals: dysentery typhus frostbite trench foot ischemia pneumonia cyanosis thrombosis heartache, and if the soldiers recovered from any of these they were sent out to fight once more.

In the countryside they looked for newly burnt villages so the ground would be soft for digging. The snow unearthed a history, a layer of blood here, a horse bone there, the carcass of a PO-2 dive-bomber, the remains of a sapper they once knew from Spasskaya Street. They hid in the ruins and rubble of Kharkov and disguised themselves in piles of bricks in Smolensk. They saw ice floes on the Volga and they lit patches of oil on the ice so the river itself seemed aflame. In the fishing hamlets by the Sea of Azov they fished instead for pilots who had crashed and skidded three hundred meters along the ice. Gutted buildings lined the outskirts of towns and, in them, more dead in their havoc of blood. They found their comrades hung from lampposts, grotesque decorations, tongues black with ice. When they cut them down the lamps groaned and bent and changed the spread of their light. They tried to capture a Fritz alive to send him to the NKVD, who would drill holes in his teeth, or tie him to a stake in the snow, or just starve him in a camp like he was starving theirs. Sometimes they'd keep a prisoner for themselves, loan him an entrenching tool, watch him try to dig his grave in the frozen ground and, when he couldn't, they shot him in the back of the head and left him there. They found enemy soldiers lying wounded in burnt-out buildings, and they pitched them out of windows to lie neck-deep in the snow, and they said to them, *Auf Wiedersehen, Fritzie*, but sometimes they pitied the enemy too—the sort of pity only a soldier can have—discovering in his wallet that the dead man had a father, a wife, a mother, maybe children too.

They sang songs to their own absent children, but moments later they put the stub of a rifle in an enemy boy's mouth and, later again, they sang other songs, Raven oh black raven why do you circle me?

They recognized the movements of the planes, the half rolls, the chanelles, the sudden twists, the pancake falls, the flash of a swastika, the shine of a red star, and they cheered as their women pilots went up to hunt the Luftwaffe down, watched the women as they rose in the air and then fell in flames. They trained dogs to carry mines and they guided the dogs, with shrill whistles, to walk beneath enemy tanks. Crows patrolled the aftermath, fat on the dead, and then the crows themselves were shot and eaten. Nature was turned around—the mornings were dark with bomb dust and at night the fires cast light for miles. The days were no longer named, although on Sundays they could sometimes hear, across the ice, the Fritzes celebrating their god. For the first time in years they were allowed their own gods—they took their Crucifixes, their beads, their prayercloths out into the battlefields. All the symbols were needed, from God to Pavlik to

Lenin. The soldiers were surprised by the sight of Orthodox priests, even rabbis, blessing the tanks, but not even blessings enabled them to hold their ground.

In retreat, to deny the enemy, the soldiers blew up the bridges their brothers had built, ripped apart their fathers' tanneries, took acetylene torches to pylons, herded cattle over ravines, razed milk sheds, poured gasoline through the roofs of silos, hacked down telegraph poles, poisoned water wells, splintered fence posts and tore up their own barns for wood.

And when they advanced—in the fourth winter, as the war turned—the soldiers marched forward and wondered how anyone could have done such a thing to their land.

The living went west and the injured went east, packed into cattle cars, pulled by steam trains, which moved slowly across the frozen steppes. They huddled together, drawn to whatever light came through the wooden slats. In the center of each cattle car was an iron pail with a fire burning. The men reached into their armpits or groins to take out handfuls of lice, and then pitched the lice into the fire. They held bread to their wounds to stop the bleeding. A few of the soldiers were carried off, put onto carts, taken to hospitals, schoolhouses, clinics. Villagers came down to greet them, bearing gifts. The men who remained on the train heard their comrades leaving, all vodka and victory. And still there was no logic to their journeys—sometimes the trains passed right through their home-towns without stopping and the ones with legs tried to kick out the wooden slats; they were shot dead by the guards for insubordination and later in the night a family would trudge out through the snow, bearing candles, having heard that their son had died just a few kilometers from home, disgraced, left frozen by the tracks.

They lay awake in their blood-stiffened coats while the railroad cars rocked to and fro. They passed around the last of their cigarettes and waited for a woman or a child to shove a package between the slats or maybe even to whisper a sweet word. They were given food and water, but it tore through their intestines and made them sicker. There were rumors of new gulags being built to the west and south, and they told themselves that their gods had loved them this long but might not love them very much longer, so they furtively slipped their charms and icons through the floorboards to lie on the railroad tracks to be picked up by others in days to come. They pulled their blankets to their beards and threw more lice onto the fire. Still the trains poured steam into the air and carried the men through forests, over bridges, beyond mountains. The men had no idea where they would end up, and if the train broke down they waited for another to nudge up behind them, roll them forward, toward Perm, Bulgakovo, Chelyabinsk—where in the distance the Ural Mountains beckoned.

And so, in the late winter of nineteen hundred and forty-four, a train sped daily through the landscape of Bashkiria, emerging from the deep forest along the Belaya River to cross the wide stretch of ice into the city of Ufa. The trains made their way slowly across the trussed bridge, a quarter of a kilometer long, the steel giving out thuds and high pings under the stress of the wheels as if mourning in advance. The trains made their way to the far side of the frozen river, past the wooden houses, the tower blocks, the factories, the mosques, the unpaved roads, the warehouses, the concrete bunkers, until they reached the railway station, where the stationmaster sounded his whistle and the city's brass band blew their battered trumpets. Muslim mothers waited on the upper platform clutching photographs. Old Tatar men went up on their toes to look for their sons. Babushkas huddled over buckets of sunflower seeds. Vendors solemnly rearranged the emptiness of their kiosks. Tough-faced nurses in brown uniforms prepared to transport the wounded. The local guards stood weary against pillars under red metal signs for rural electrification that swung in the breeze—*Our Great Leader Is Bringing Electricity to You!*—and a smell penetrated the air, foreshadowing the soldiers, sweat and rot, and each winter afternoon a six-year-old boy,

hungry and narrow and keen, sat on a cliff above the river, looking
down at the trains, wondering when his own father would be coming
home and whether he would be broken just like the ones they were
lifting from beneath the steam and the bugles.

❊

We cleaned out the giant greenhouse first. Nuriya gave the tomato
plants to the farm boy who hung around the hospital. Katya,
Marfuga, Olga and I shoveled most of the soil onto the ground outside. I was the oldest and my shoveling duties were light. Soon the
greenhouse was clear, as big as two houses. We dragged in eight
woodstoves, stood them next to the glass and lit the fires. After a
while the greenhouse didn't smell so much of tomatoes anymore.

The next thing was the big metal sheets. Nuriya's cousin,
Milyausha, was a welder at the oil refinery. She had gotten permission to take away fifteen sheets. She borrowed a tractor, hitched the
sheets to the back of it, dragged them through the hospital entrance,
down the narrow road to the greenhouse. The sheets were too big to
fit through the doors so we had to remove the back windows to slide
the metal in. The farm boy helped us lift the heavy sheets. He kept
his head down—maybe he was embarrassed by all us women working so hard, but it didn't matter to us, it was our duty.

Milyausha was a splendid welder. She had learned just before the
war. She wore special glasses and the blue flame lit up her lenses.
After two days it was there: a giant metal bath.

But we hadn't thought about how to heat the water properly.

We tried boiling the water on the woodstoves that we had set up,
but, even though the greenhouse itself was warm from catching the
sun, the water never held its temperature. The bath was just too big.
We stood around, quiet and angry, until Nuriya had another idea.
She asked her cousin Milyausha to see if she could get permission for
maybe a dozen more metal sheets. The very next morning she came

up from the refinery dragging five more sheets. Nuriya told us the plan. It was simple. Milyausha set to work straight away and welded the metal into the giant bath, crisscrossing the strips until eventually the whole thing looked like a metal chessboard. She drilled drains in the bottom of each bath, and Nuriya borrowed an old car engine from her husband's brother. She attached a pump to the engine to take the water out. It worked perfectly. There were sixteen individual tubs and, because they were small, we knew the water would stay warm. We laid down planks for gangways so we could walk from bath to bath, and then we hung a portrait of Our Great Leader inside the door.

We lit the stoves, heated the water, filled the baths. Everyone smiled when the water stayed warm, and then we took off our clothes and sat in the baths, drinking tea. All around us the glass was steaming and we were warm as soup.

Sweetness, said Nuriya.

That evening we went up to the hospital and told the nurses we would be ready the next day. They looked exhausted, black bags under their eyes. We could hear the soldiers moaning from inside the hospital. There must have been hundreds of them.

Nuriya pulled me aside and said: We will start right now.

We did only eight the first evening, but on the second day we did sixty and by the end of the first week they were coming up directly from the railway station in their bloody rags and bandages. We had so many that they had to wait in lines outside the greenhouse on long canvas tarps. Sometimes the canvas got sticky with blood and it had to be hosed off, but they were patient, those men.

While they were outside Katya wrapped them in blankets. Some of them were happy, but others cried, of course, and many just sat and stared straight ahead. The parasites were on them and the rot was setting in. You could see the worst of it in their eyes.

Inside, Nuriya was the one to shave their heads. She was quick with the scissors, and most of the hair was gone in a few seconds.

Without it they looked so different, some like boys, some like criminals. She shaved the rest of the hair with a straight-blade razor. She swept the hair up quickly because there were lice still crawling through the clumps. The hair was shoveled into buckets and placed at the door of the greenhouse, and the farm boy took them away.

The soldiers were so shy they didn't want to take off their uniforms in front of us. We didn't have any young girls working with us—most of us were thirty or more. I was forty-seven. And Nuriya told them not to worry, we all had husbands—which was true, except for me, I never had a husband, no reason really.

Still they wouldn't take their clothes off until Nuriya roared: Come on, you don't have anything we haven't seen before!

Eventually they shed their uniforms, except for the men on the stretchers. We used Nuriya's scissors for them. They didn't like it when we had to take off their shirts and undershirts, maybe they thought we were accidentally going to cut their throats.

The soldiers stood in front of us, hands over their private parts. They were all so skinny, poor things, they made even Katya feel fat.

We used the rotten uniforms for fuel but we made sure we took the medals off first, put them in little bundles until the baths were finished. All the men had letters and photos in their pockets, of course, but there were some strange things too—the spout of a teapot, locks of hair, bits of gold teeth. One of them even had a little finger, curled up and shriveled. Sometimes there were explicit pictures we weren't meant to see but, as Nuriya said, they'd been through a lot for our great nation, it wasn't our place to scold.

As the soldiers waited their turn, Olga sprayed them with a chemical that came in boxes all the way from Kiev. We used fertilizer tanks and mixed the chemical with water—it smelled like bad eggs. We had to cover the soldiers' mouths and eyes. But we didn't always have enough dressing to put over their wounds, so when we sprayed them it sometimes hit their open sores. I felt so sorry for them the way they howled. Afterwards they leaned against us and cried and cried and cried. We sponged down the wounds as well as we could. They dug their fingers into our shoulders and clenched their fists. Their hands were so bony and black.

When their wounds were swabbed, it was time for the bath. If one of them had lost his legs, it took four of us to lower him in the water and we had to be careful of the level so he wouldn't drown. If he had no arms, we propped him up at the edge of the metal sheet and kept ahold of him.

We didn't want to shock them so we kept the water lukewarm at first, and when they were immersed we poured kettles full of boiling water around them, wary not to splash. They said ooh and aah, and the laughter was contagious; no matter how many times we laughed in a day another man would make us laugh all over again.

The thing about the greenhouse was that it made the sound much bigger. It wasn't exactly an echo, it was just that the laughter seemed to bounce from pane to pane and back down to us, bent over the baths.

Olga and I were the ones to sponge. I didn't use soap to start with. That was a treat for the very end. I gave their faces a good scrub— they had such eyes!—and I cleaned very carefully, the chin, the brows, the forehead and behind their ears. Then I went vigorously at their backs, which were always filthy. You could see their ribs and the curve of their spines. I went down towards their bottoms and cleaned a little around there, but not so much that they got uncomfortable. Sometimes they would call me Mama or Sister, and I'd lean forward and say: There there there.

But most of the time they just stared straight ahead without a word. I went to their necks again, but this time I went much more gently and I felt them relaxing.

It was harder to do the front of their bodies. Their chests were often bad, because a lot of the time they had been hit with shrapnel. Sometimes, when my hands were at their stomachs, they hunched over very quickly because they thought I was going to touch them down below, but most of the time I got them to do that themselves. I was no fool.

If a soldier was really sick or had no spirit, then I had to wash him down there. Mostly he would close his eyes because he was embarrassed, but once or twice he still got aroused and I had to leave him alone for five minutes.

Olga wouldn't leave him alone. She carried a spoon in her apron and if a soldier got excited she bashed him there, and that was that. We all just laughed.

For some reason, I don't know why, their legs were the worst—maybe it was from standing around in those boots all the time. Their feet were covered with sores and scabs. Most of the time they could hardly walk straight. They always talked a lot about their legs, said they used to play soccer and ice hockey and how good they had been at long-distance running. If the soldier was a very young boy, I let him put his head on my chest so he wouldn't be ashamed of his tears. But if he was big and mean, I washed him much more quickly. He might say rude things to me about my arms, the way they wobbled, and for punishment I wouldn't give him any soap.

We washed their heads last and sometimes, if they were nice, we gave them a final rub of the shoulders.

The whole bath took no more than five minutes. We had to drain the water each time and disinfect the metal. With the hoses attached to the old car engine we were able to pump the water out quickly. In summer the grass died where the water jetted out, and in winter the blood made the snow look brown.

Finally we wrapped the soldiers in blankets and put new foot cloths on, hospital shirts, pajamas, even hats. There were no mirrors, but sometimes I saw the men wiping the steam from the greenhouse windows, trying to have a look at themselves in the glass.

When we were finished and they were all fully dressed, they were ferried up the road towards the hospital by horse and cart.

The men who were waiting outside the greenhouse watched the clean ones go away. The looks on their faces! You'd think they were at a picture show the way their eyes lit up! Sometimes children came up and hid in the poplar trees and watched, it was like a carnival sometimes.

When I got home at night to Aksakov Street, I was always exhausted. I ate some bread, turned off the oil lamp beside my bed and went straight to sleep. My neighbors in the room next to mine were an old couple from Leningrad. She had been a dancer and he was from a wealthy family—they were exiles now, so I steered clear of them. But one afternoon the woman knocked on my door and said the volunteers were a credit to the country, no wonder we were winning the War. And then she asked if she could help. I thanked her but told her no, we had more than enough volunteers. It wasn't true, and she was embarrassed, but what was I to do? She was an undesirable, after all. She turned away. The next morning I found four loaves of bread at my door: *Please give this to the soldiers.* I fed it instead to the birds in Lenin Park. I did not wish to be tarnished with their brush.

By the time it came to celebrate the Revolution in early November, there were only a couple of dozen soldiers to bathe each day, stragglers coming in from the front.

In the afternoons I began to visit the hospital. The rooms were crammed full of men. The beds were stacked five high, nailed to the walls like shelves. The walls themselves were splattered with blood and grime. The only good thing was the children who came in to perform on occasion, and also the music that came through the loudspeaker— one of the nurses had set up a system where they could play the gramophone from the front office. The music could be heard all over the hospital, lots of wonderful victory songs. Even still, the men moaned and shouted for their sweethearts. Some of them were glad to see me, but a lot of them didn't recognize my face at first. When I reminded them, they smiled, and one or two of the cheeky ones even blew me a kiss.

Of all the soldiers there was one boy I remember best—Nurma-hammed, from Chelyabinsk, who had lost his foot to a mine. He was just an ordinary Tatar boy with black hair and high cheekbones and wide eyes. He hobbled in on crutches made from tree branches. We sprayed him down, and I unwrapped the bandages from around the top of his stump. He was bad with the parasites, so I had Nuriya take good care of him. She swabbed the wound well while I got the bath ready. I checked the water temperature with my wrist, and then three of us supported him, walked him across to the bath. He was silent the whole time. I washed him down, and finally he said, Thank you.

When he was clean and dressed in hospital pajamas he gave me a strange look and began to tell me all about his mother's vegetable patch, how she spread chicken manure to make the carrots grow, how they were the most wonderful carrots a person could want in his life, how he missed those carrots more than anything else.

In my lunch box I had some leftover martsovka. Nurmahammed put his face to the food, smiled up at me, kept smiling while he ate, his head rising up from the plate as though making sure I was still there.

I decided to go up to the hospital with Nurmahammed. We got on the back of a horse wagon, the animals clopping their way forward.

All sorts of things were going on that day because of the celebra-tions—a special food truck had pulled up to the hospital kitchens, red flags were flying from the windows, two commissars had arrived to pin medals on the soldiers, a man sat on the steps playing a bal-alaika, and children were walking around in Bashkirian folk-dancing costumes.

"The Song of the Fatherland" came over the loudspeakers, and everyone stood still while we sang it together.

I squeezed Nurmahammed's hand, and I said: See, everything will be all right.

Yes, he said.

Usually the men were pushed around the hospital in wheelbarrows, but to our pleasant surprise there was a wheelchair for Nurmahammed that day. I helped him with the paperwork and wheeled him along the corridor to his ward. It was noisy in there, all the men shouting under a big cloud of cigarette smoke. Some of the soldiers had gotten hold of a huge vat of methylated spirits and they were dipping cups into it, passing them along the bunk beds.

Everyone wore bandages—some of them were wrapped from head to toe—and things had been written on the walls by their beds, names of girlfriends, favorite soccer teams, poems even.

I pushed Nurmahammed on through to D368, halfway down the ward. His was the second of five bunks. He used his one leg to prop himself on the edge of the first bed. I pushed from below, but still he couldn't heave himself up. Some men came and got their shoulders under Nurmahammed's weight. He flopped down on the bed without even lifting the sheets, lay there a moment, smiled down at me.

Just then the big troupe of children came into the room. There must have been about twenty of them, all in costumes, green and red, with caps. The youngest was maybe four or five years old. They looked so nice and clean and scrubbed.

A woman in charge made an announcement for silence. For a moment I thought it was my neighbor, but thankfully it wasn't, this woman was taller, sterner, no gray in her hair. She made a second announcement for quiet, but the soldiers were still roaring and laughing. The woman clapped her hands twice, and the children began dancing. After a few minutes a sort of hush came over the room—a slow wave, like a good thing being whispered through a crowd.

In the spaces between the beds the children performed. They twirled and reeled and went under bridges of arms for a Tatar folk dance. They sank to their knees, and then they rose and shouted and clapped their hands and sank to their knees once more. A tiny girl crossed her arms and kicked. Another child with red hair got embarrassed when his laces came undone. They wore big smiles and their eyes shone; it could have been their birthdays, they were so beautiful.

Just when we all thought they were finished, a small blond boy stepped out of the line. He was about five or six years old. He extended his leg, placed his hands firmly on his hips and hitched his thumbs at his back. He bent his neck slightly forward, stretched his elbows out and began. The soldiers in their beds propped themselves up. Those by the windows shaded their eyes to watch. The boy went to the floor for a squatting dance. We all stood silently watching. The boy grinned. Some soldiers began clapping in rhythm but, just as the dance was about to end, the boy almost fell. His hand slapped the floor and broke the impact. For a moment he looked as if he was about to cry, but he didn't, he was up once more, his blond hair flopping over his eyes.

When he finished the ward was full of applause. Someone offered the boy a cube of sugar. He blushed and slipped it into the top of his sock, and then he stood around with his hands in his pockets, rolling his shoulders from side to side. The stern woman snapped her fingers, and the troupe of children moved to the next ward. The soldiers began whistling and shouting and, when the troupe was nearly gone, the men lit up their cigarettes and dipped their cups once more into the vat of spirits. The blond boy peered over his shoulder to take another look at the ward.

Just then I heard the sound of a bed creak. I had forgotten about Nurmahammed. He was staring down at his one leg. He moved his lips as if he were eating something, then took a couple of deep breaths and reached down to his stump, ran his hands up and down along where the shinbone used to be. He caught my eye and tried a smile. I smiled back. There was nothing to say. What could I say? I turned away. A couple of soldiers nodded at me as I left.

From the end of the ward I could hear poor Nurmahammed sobbing.

I went back down to the baths. The sun was going down and it had gotten cold, but there were a couple of early stars. A wind whipped at the trees. Some balalaika music sounded from the hospital.

I closed the doors of the greenhouse and kept the lanterns turned off. There was a pile of uniforms and some kindling on the ground. I stuffed it all into the stove and fired it up, then filled a pail of water and waited. It took a long time for the water to boil and right there, in the greenhouse, I thought to myself that of all the good things in the world, the best is a hot bath all alone in the darkness.

❖

He wakes beside his mother in the morning, head tucked by her arm. Already his sister has risen to get water from the well to prepare breakfast.

His mother recently traded two picture frames for a single bar of soap. The soap smelled strange to him at first but now, every morning, when he rises from the bed, Rudik takes the bar from the pocket of his mother's bathrobe, hauls the scent of it down. There is, he has noticed, no soap in the hospital where he dances. The soldiers smell gruff and worn, and he wonders if his father will have a similar scent when he returns from the war.

His mother combs his hair and takes his clothes from the stove top, where they have been warming. She dresses him. Some of his clothes have been handed down from his sister. His mother has altered a shirt from a blouse—the cuffs lengthened, the collar stiffened with old cardboard—but still it seems ill-fitting to the boy and he squirms when she fastens the buttons.

For breakfast he is allowed the chair while his sister cleans the table around him. He hunches over his cup of milk and a potato left over from the night before. He can feel his stomach tighten as the milk hits the back of his throat, and he eats half the potato in three bites, tucks the rest away in his pocket. In school many of the other children have lunch boxes. With the war over, almost all the fathers have returned, but not his, and he has heard that most of his father's salary goes to the war effort. Sacrifices must be made, says his mother. But there are times when Rudik wishes he could sit at his school desk, open a lunch box to reveal black bread, meat, vegetables. His mother has told him that hunger will make him strong, but to him, hunger is the high feeling of emptiness when the trains emerge from the forest and the sound bounces across the ice of the Belaya.

During school he imagines himself out on the river, skating. On the journey home he looks for the highest snowdrifts in the city, so he can step high and be close to the new telegraph wires, hear them crackle just above him.

In the evenings, after listening to the wireless, his mother reads him stories about carpenters and wolves and forests and hacksaws and stars hung on nails in the sky. In one of the stories a giant carpenter stretches upwards and removes the stars one by one, distributes them to the workers' children.

How tall is the carpenter, Mama?

A million kilometers.

How many stars in each pocket?

One for everyone, she says.

Two for me?

One for everyone, she says again.

Farida watches as Rudik turns in the middle of the earthen shack floor, spinning on the heels of his boots. When he spins he raises dirt. So be it, let him spin, it is his joy. She will, one of these days, save enough money to buy a carpet from the old Turk in the local market. The carpets hang from twine and swing in the wind. She has often pondered what it would be like to have enough money to put carpets on the wall as well, to keep in the warmth, for decoration, to bring the shack to life. But before buying carpets she would purchase new dresses for her daughter, proper shoes for her son, a life away from this life.

Often Rudik's mother shows him the letters that have come from the German border, where his father is still stationed as a politruk, a teacher. The messages are short and precise: *All is well, Farida, do not worry. Stalin is powerful.* The words accompany Rudik as he walks through the rain with his mother to the hospital, where at the gate she lets go of his hand, taps him on the bottom, says to him: Don't be late, little sunshine.

She has rubbed goose fat on his chest to keep away the cold, now that the days are heading towards autumn.

The sick lift him in through the windows, already applauding. His appearance has become a weekly ritual. He grins as he is passed from one set of hands to another. Later he is guided from ward to ward, where he performs the new folk dances learned at school. Sometimes the nurses gather to watch. There are no pockets in Rudik's dance costume, and by the time he finishes so many cubes of sugar are stuffed lumpily inside his socks that the patients laugh about his legs being diseased. He is given vegetable scraps and bread that the soldiers have set aside, and he crams them into a small paper bag to bring home.

At the farthest wing there is a ward for those soldiers who have gone mad. It is the only place in the hospital where he will not perform. He has heard they have machines with electricity to cure madness.

This ward is full—faces against windows, tongues lolling, rows of fixed eyes—and he stays away, though at times he sees a woman who lumbers up from the greenhouses. She stands at the window of the ward, talking to a soldier whose pajama top hangs loosely on his shoulders. One afternoon Rudik notices the same soldier hobbling through the grounds on crutches, the bottom of the pajama leg knotted just inches beneath his knee, the soldier moving determinedly from tree to tree. The soldier shouts to him—something about a dance—but Rudik is already gone, scared, looking over his shoulder, out the gate, along the rutted dirt streets. As he runs he imagines himself ripping stars from the sky like nails. He returns home, hopping one-legged through the darkness.

Where've you been? asks his mother, stirring in the bed beside Rudik's sister.

In the palm of his hand he holds out the lumps of sugar.

They'll dissolve, she says.

No they won't.

Put them away and get to bed.

Rudik puts a lump between his gum and his cheek, drops the rest of the sugar into a dish on the kitchen table. He looks across the cabin at his mother, who has pulled the blankets high and turned her face towards the wall. He remains motionless until he is sure that she is asleep, then leans into the wireless radio and steadily adjusts the dial along the yellow paneling: Warsaw, Luxembourg, Moscow, Prague, Kiev, Vilnius, Dresden, Minsk, Kishinev, Novosibirsk, Brussels, Leningrad, Rome, Warsaw, Stockholm, Kiev, Tallinn, Tbilisi, Belgrade, Prague, Tashkent, Sofia, Riga, Helsinki, Budapest.

He already knows that if he stays awake long enough he will be able to turn the white knob to Moscow where, at the stroke of midnight, he will hear Tchaikovsky.

⁂

Well well well! His father stands in the doorway shaking snow from his shoulders. A black mustache. A strong chin. The voice raked with cigarettes. He wears a pilotka with the brims down fore and aft, so he looks as if he is both coming and going. Two red medals pinned to his chest. A Marx pin on the collar of his tunic. His mother hurries to the doorway while Rudik huddles in the corner beside the fire. Looking at his father is like looking at a painting for the very first time—he sees the painting exists, sees the colors and the textures, sees the frame within which it is hung, yet he knows nothing about it. Four years at war and another eighteen months in the territories. His older sister, Tamara, has long since made lace prints and jars of berry juice as homecoming gifts. She thrusts them into her father's arms, clings to him, kisses him. Rudik has nothing to give. Still his father comes across, knocks away the high-backed chair in his joy, picks Rudik up and holds him in the air, spins him twice, all wide cheeks, yellow teeth. What a big boy! Look at you! Look! And how old are you now? Seven? Seven! Almost eight! My! Look at you!

Rudik notices the large puddles his father's boots have left at the door, goes to the threshold and stands in the wet prints. My little boy! His father has a number of smells to him, not bad smells, a strange mixture, like trains and trams and the smell you get after wiping chalk from the blackboard with your elbow.

They walk in the street along the rows of cabins and wooden houses, into the late afternoon. Icicles hang from lampposts. Snow coats the rows of gates. The frost-hardened mud crunches beneath their feet. Rudik wears his sister's old overcoat. His father stares at the coat, says the boy should not be dressed in his sister's castoffs, tells Rudik's mother to switch the buttons from one side to the other. His mother pales and nods, says of course she will. They watch the wind rip the cardboard and sackcloth from the window frames of the wooden houses. Men drink vodka in an abandoned car. His father looks at the men, shakes his head in disgust, links his arm with Rudik's mother. Whispering, they seem as if they have years of secrets to tell each other. A cat wanders lean-shouldered along a crooked fence. Rudik flings a couple of stones at it. His father catches his arm on the second throw, but then he laughs, puts his pilotka on Rudik's head, and they chase each other down the street, hot breath steaming. After dinner—cabbage, potatoes and a special piece of meat Rudik has never seen before—he is held so tight to his father's chest that his head crumples the papirosy in the tunic pocket.

They spread the cigarettes out on the table and straighten them, stuff the stray tobacco back into the thin paper tubes. His father tells him that this is the dream of men, to straighten crumpled things.

Isn't that right?

Yes, Father.

Call me Papa.

Yes, Papa.

He listens to the curious highs and lows of his father's voice, the way it sometimes sounds torn, like radio waves when he turns the dial. The wireless, the only thing they haven't sold for food, sits above the fireplace, dark and mahogany. His father tunes in to a report from Berlin, and says: Listen to that! Listen! Music, now that's music!

His mother's fingers are long and thin, and they tap out a rhythm on the chair. Rudik doesn't want to go to bed, so he sits on her lap. He watches his father, a foreign thing. His cheeks are hollow and his eyes are larger than in the photographs. He coughs, a deep cough, a man's cough, and spits in the fireplace. Embers jump out onto the dirt floor, so his father reaches down and extinguishes them with his bare fingers.

Rudik tries it, but his thumb blisters immediately and his father says: That's my boy.

Rudik rocks against his mother's shoulder while he holds back the tears.

That's my boy, says his father again, disappearing out the door, coming back two minutes later, saying: If someone thinks there's no evil in this world, they should visit that fucking outhouse in weather like this!

His mother looks up, says: Hamet.

What? says his father. He's heard language before.

She swallows, smiles, says nothing.

My warrior's heard language, haven't you?

Rudik nods.

That night all four of them sleep in the bed together, Rudik's head by his father's armpit. Later he slips away and crosses to his mother, her smell, kefir and sweet potatoes. There is movement deep in the night, the bed slowly throbbing, his father whispering. Rudik turns very suddenly, jams his feet against the warmth of his mother. The rocking stops and he feels his mother's fingers on his brow. Towards dawn he is woken again, but he doesn't move and when his parents fall asleep, his father snoring, Rudik sees the light begin to finger the parting in the curtains. Quietly, he rises.

A handful of cabbage from the iron pot. The last of the milk, kept cold on the windowsill. His high-collared gray school tunic hangs on the wall. Dressing, he moves through the room on the balls of his feet.

His skates are hooked on the inside knob of the front door. He made them himself—filing down iron scraps from the refinery, embedding the metal into two pieces of thin wood, fashioning leather straps from scraps found behind the warehouses along the railway tracks.

He quietly unhooks the skates, closes the door, runs to the city lake, the straps joined around his neck, his gloves over the sharp steel so the blades don't cut his face. Already the lake is dark with movement. Sunlight kindles the cold haze. Men in overcoats skate to work, hunched, smoking as they progress, solid figures against the skeletal trees. The women with shopping bags skate differently, taller somehow, erect. Rudik steps onto the ice and breaks against the traffic, going the wrong way in the flow, people laughing, dipping, cursing him. Hey, boy. You! Salmon!

He bends his knee, shortens the thrust of his arm, quickens his pace. The metal blades have become slightly loose in the wooden slats, but he has learned balance and counterbalance and, with a small flick of his ankle, he persuades the steel back into the wood. In the distance he can see the roof of the *banya* where he goes each Thursday with his mother and sister to bathe. There, his mother scrubs his back with birch twigs. He likes to lie on the wooden benches and receive the slap of the twigs. He finds patterns in the tiny pieces of birch leaf that dot the length of his body. His mother has told him that the baths will make him immune to sickness, and he has learned to endure the scalding steam longer than any other child his age.

He jumps, turns, lands, feels the skates catch once more.

On the ice many patterns are etched beneath him, and he can already tell by the marks who is a good skater and who isn't. If he were to twirl for a long time in one place, he could get rid of everyone else, destroy their marks, be the only person ever to have skated there. A piece of litter catches beneath the blade, and he lifts his foot slightly, circles to crush it. Flecks of ice jump up from his boots. In the distance he hears his name called, the voice arriving from the edge of the lake, carried by the wind. Rudik! Rudik! Instead of turning, he leans on his right foot, and his whole body spins in the opposite direction to the shout. He knows not to swerve too hard, to lean just the right amount so he won't fall. Then he is off against a head wind, small specks of litter still clinging to the blade. Rudik! Rudik! He leans over farther, his body concentrating itself in his shoulders. Beyond the lake, on the roads, he sees trucks, motorbikes, even men on bicycles—their tires fat to deal with the ice. He would love to hold on to the rear bumper of a car, to have it drag him along like the older boys, careful with their scarves so they don't catch around the wheels, keeping an eye out for the brake lights so they can ready themselves to let go and travel faster than anything else on the road.

Ru-dik! Ru-dik!

He barrels in the direction of the road but is stopped by the sound of a whistle, a guard waving him away. He turns with one skate, the other foot high, makes a wide arc, and is forced around to the sight of his father, red-faced now, panting, on the bank, without skates. A wind rips along the lake, making the end of his father's cigarette glow bright. How small he looks, the smoke trailing away from his mouth.

Rudik, you're fast.

I didn't hear you.

You didn't hear me what?

I didn't hear you say Rudik.

His father opens his mouth to say something, decides against it, says instead: I wanted to walk you to school. You should have waited for me.

Yes.

Next time, wait.

Yes.

Rudik puts his skates around his neck and they walk together, hands balled into their gloves. The road circles past a row of old houses to the schoolhouse. Above the school wall is an arched iron insignia where four crows sit. Father and son make a bet on which of the crows will leave first, but none do. They stand silent until the bell sounds, and then Rudik tugs away his hand.

Education, says his father suddenly, is the foundation of everything. Do you understand me?

Rudik nods.

The bell sounds once again, and the children in the yard run towards the building.

Well then, says his father.

Bye.

Bye.

Rudik steps away, but then returns and rises to his toes to plant a kiss on his father's cheek. Hamet shifts his head slightly, and Rudik feels the edge of his mustache, wet with ice.

Rudik runs the gauntlet to the classroom. Blondie. Froggy. Girl face. Smaller than most, he is often beaten up. The boys push him into the wall, grip his testicles, squeeze them—pruning, they call it. They leave him alone only when a teacher turns the corner. Inside, flags on the wall, pennants, portraits. The wooden desks with their lifting lids. Goyanov the teacher on the platform, pasty-faced, calm.

The early morning call. *The Motherland is benevolent. The Motherland is strong. The Motherland will protect me.* The rustling of boys and girls settling down, the scratch of chalk on the board, mathematics, his name called, five times fourteen, you, yes you, five times fourteen, yes you, sleepyhead! He gets the answer wrong, and Goyanov strikes his ruler hard on the desk. Three more wrong answers and he is slapped on the palm of his left hand. And then, before the right hand is hit, a puddle appears on the floor. The other children laugh when they realize that he has pissed himself, giggle behind their hands, trip him as he walks the aisle. Seventeen steps from the toilets to the top of the noisy stairs, where the mosque and the blue sky hang together in the window frame. He roots himself there, touches the front of his wet pants. Beyond the mosque stand the chimneys, bridges, low smokestacks of Ufa. The sky is broken by the horizon's clean sharp shapes. Goyanov comes up behind him and takes him by the elbow back to the classroom, and he pisses himself a second time as he enters, all the children quiet now, hunched over their inkpots, dropping beads of black ink onto copybooks. He sits in his seat and waits, even through the lunch call, *Our Leader is powerful, Our Leader is great,* his stomach tight and knotted, until he is fully dry, and then he disappears to the bathroom once more, the mirror cracked, his face a thousand pieces, the rank piss around him, but it is quiet here, he leans into his reflection, the angle of the cracks distorting his face.

After school his father is waiting again, against the wall, coat collar turned up. Resting against his thigh is a muslin sack. In his other hand, a large bag with the bulge of a lantern. Hamet beckons him over, puts an arm around Rudik's shoulder and they walk silently towards the tram.

By the time they reach the foothills of the city, the sky is already darkening. Birch trees stand in armies along the ice-covered road. The last of the red light filters between the branches. They cross a broad rockslide threaded with the footprints of wild animals and snow falls in clumps from the trees. A cold wind huddles them together. His father takes a jacket out of his bag and puts it around Rudik's shoulders. They walk down a narrow gorge, and when they get to the small frozen mountain river at the bottom Rudik sees a line of fires along the ice where men are fishing in holes.

Trout, says his father. He slaps Rudik's back. Now go get some firewood.

Rudik watches his father stake out an empty ice hole. He re-breaks the ice and uses two thin blocks of wood for makeshift chairs, covering each with a blanket. Hamet sets up the lantern between the chairs and pulls a fishing rod out from the muslin sack. He snaps it together, runs a line through the eyes of the rod, attaches some bait to the hook, anchors the apparatus, stands over the ice hole clapping his hands.

Rudik waits near the trees, two large branches tucked beneath one arm and a handful of twigs in the other.

His father looks up. We need more wood than that!

Nudging his way along the tree line, Rudik dips out of view, clears snow from a rock, sits down and waits. He has never fished before. How can there be trout in a river that is frozen solid? How can they swim through ice? He breathes warm air into the openings of his gloves. A single star claws its way into the sky. No moon. He thinks about the warmth of the bed at home, how his mother nestles the gray blankets to his chin, arcs her arm to snuggle him. He is sure animals await him in the trees beyond the river, badgers, bears, even wolves. He has heard stories of wolves carrying children away. Other stars rise in the sky as if on a series of pulleys. He hears a plane but can see no moving lights in the sky. Sniveling, he drops the wood at his feet, runs back across the frozen river.

I want to go home.

You what?

I don't like it here.

His father chuckles into his collar, reaches out and takes Rudik's gloved hand. They step together into the trees and collect enough wood to last through the night. His father places kindling on the ice and says it is a mistake to create a single big fire, that is for idiots. Instead they make two small tepees and he instructs Rudik to squat over the fire whenever he gets cold, that the heat will rise through his body and spread, a trick Hamet learned during the war.

All along the river the other fishermen chat in low tones.

I want to go home, Rudik says again.

His father doesn't reply. He takes three of last night's potatoes and heats them in the embers of the fire, turns them so the skin doesn't scorch. They wait an hour for the first fish. When his father lifts it up through the ice, he takes off his gloves and the trout goes from living to gutted in seconds. He rips the fish belly open with his knife and, at the same time, follows with his forefinger, so that the innards come out in one motion. The guts steam in the air, and his father spears the body with a twig and holds it over the fire. They eat the fish and potatoes in the cold and his father asks him if he thinks it is delicious and he nods and then his father says: Do you like goose?

Of course.

Someday we'll shoot geese, you and me. Do you like shooting?

I think so.

For oil, for food, for fat. Geese are good for that, says his father.

Mama puts the fat on my chest.

I taught her that trick. A long time ago.

Oh, says Rudik.

It's a good one, isn't it?

Yes.

When I was away, says his father, pausing for a moment, I missed you.

Yes, Papa.

We've a lot to talk of.

I'm cold.

Here, put this jacket on.

His father's jacket is huge around his shoulders, and Rudik thinks that now he is wearing three jackets while his father wears only one, but still he puts his arms in the sleeves of the coat, sits there rocking.

Your mother told me you were a good boy.

Yes.

She said you've been doing lots of things.

I danced at the hospital.

I heard.

For the soldiers.

And what else?

School.

Yes?

And Mama took me to the big place, the Opera House.

She did, did she?

Yes.

I see.

Mama only had one ticket, but we got in and there was a big crush at the door and the door fell in and we almost fell but we didn't! We went down near the front, where they didn't come looking for us! We thought they were going to come looking!

Slow down, says his father.

We sat on the stairs and there were big lights and then it got dark and it started! They turned off the big lights and the curtain came up and the music was loud and everyone got quiet.

And did you like that?

It was a story about a shepherd and an evil man and a girl.

Did you like it?

I liked the way the boy saved the girl after the man got her.

And?

And the big red curtain.

Well that's good, says his father, pulling his tunic tight, checking the line in the ice hole to see if any more fish have been caught, his face flushed and his mouth red as if he himself has just been hooked.

And when everyone was gone, says Rudik, Mama allowed me to sit in the seats. She told me they were velvet.

That's good, his father replies again.

When the next fish comes his father takes out the knife, cleans the blade on an inside thigh of his trousers, leaves a streak of blood. He hands Rudik the small trout and says: You do it, son.

Rudik tightens his fingers inside the coat sleeves.

Try it.

No thanks, Papa.

Try it!

No thanks.

Right now, I said! Try it!

⚜

In a warehouse on Sverdlov Street—under the auspices of the Bashkirian Ministry of Culture—the new curtains of the Opera House are sewn by a crew of six women, the best seamstresses in Ufa. The special bolts of red velvet are forty-five meters long and fifty-eight meters wide and a single fold, when lifted and relifted, makes their arms ache. The women, in their hairnets, are not allowed to smoke or eat or drink tea anywhere near the cloth. They sit at the curtains for ten hours a day, shifting their chairs along the red sea of velvet. Each seam is supervised, and the lining where the curtains meet is restitched seventeen times before the supervisor feels that the proper nuances have been attended to. A running cloth, again of velvet, is made to order. The pelmets are carefully belled with white lace. The insignia of the State is embroidered on the curtains, at the center, so the two halves will meet at the beginning and end of every show.

When the curtains are finished, three representatives from the Ministry come to inspect them. They look the work over for an hour, running their fingers along the seams, gauging the height of the pelmets with their rulers, checking for consistency of color. They debate over the State insignia, holding a magnifying glass to the embroidered handle of a sickle. Finally they crack open a flask of vodka and each drinks a thimbleful. The seamstresses, watching through the blinds of an office window, touch each other's elbows and sigh with relief. They are called from the office, and the men from the Ministry line them up and speak in gruff voices of collective harmony.

The curtains are carefully folded and transported to the Opera House in a truck. Two carpenters are on hand, having designed a series of poles and pulleys to support the weight. A reinforced rope is threaded through the greased pulleys. Scaffolding is put in place to hang the curtains, and the cloth never once touches the ground.

The first night, before the show starts, one of the stagehands, Albert Tikhonov—from a well-known family of stilt walkers—hitches himself high onto his stilts, winks at his fellow stagehands, crosses the boards like a giant insect, wooden ends clicking on the stage floor, checking for flaws in the curtain. He finds none.

❊

The Motherland is benevolent. The Motherland is
strong. The Motherland will protect me. The
Motherland is benevolent. The Motherland is strong.
The Motherland will protect me. The Motherland is
benevolent. The Motherland is strong. The
Motherland will protect me. The Motherland is
benevolent. The Motherland is strong. The
Motherland will protect me. The Motherland is
benevolent. The Motherland is strong. The
Motherland will protect me. The Motherland is
benevolent. The Motherland is strong. The
Motherland will protect me. The Motherland is

benevolent. The Motherland is strong. The
Motherland will protect me. The Motherland is
benevolent. The Motherland is strong. The
Motherland will protect me. The Motherland is
benevolent. The Motherland is strong. The
Motherland will protect me. The Motherland is
benevolent. The Motherland is strong. The
Motherland will protect me. The Motherland is
benevolent. The Motherland is strong. The
Motherland will protect me. The Motherland is
benevolent. The Motherland is strong. The
Motherland will protect me. The Motherland is
benevolent. The Motherland is strong. The
Motherland will protect me. The Motherland is
benevolent. The Motherland is strong. The
Motherland will protect me. The Motherland is
benevolent. The Motherland is strong. The
Motherland will protect me. The Motherland is
benevolent. The Motherland is strong. The
Motherland will protect me.

❖

He hides the punishment lines from his father, but there is something about the crawl of the pen over the page that Rudik has grown
to like. He connects the letters as if each word were a piece of string,
never arranging the lines in columns, preferring their disorder, their
bump up against each other. This is contrary to how the teacher
wants it and sometimes the amount of punishment lines is doubled
or tripled the following day.

When his homework is finished he runs to the lake to check the
flags along the shore. If they are at half-mast it means someone
eminent has died, and this delights him since later Tchaikovsky will
be on the wireless again, uninterrupted, and his mother will lean into
it also.

They have moved to a new communal house on Zentsov Street—
one room, fourteen square meters, with an oak floor. A carpet from the
market hangs on one wall. His mother has placed the wireless against
the other wall so that the neighbors, newlyweds, can hear it if they
desire. Rudik clicks the radio on, tunes the dial, raps four times on the
wall so the couple knows to listen. The wireless takes a while to warm
up and, in that time, Rudik imagines the notes floating through as if
the air itself is in rehearsal. He positions himself at different points in
the room to find the angle at which the music arrives best. The notes
begin high and alien and scratchy and then settle down. During the
broadcasts his mother moves across the floor, soundlessly in slippers, sits
beside him, serious and appreciative. She tries to hold him back from
dancing in case his father comes home, but often she relents, tells him
not to make too much noise, turns her back as if she can't see.

His mother smells to him of the yogurt from the bottling plant
where she has found a new job. Just after his tenth birthday the paper
carries a photograph of her after winning a commendation for helping to double the production, the caption reading: *Labor as purpose:
Muskina Yenikeeva, Farida Nureyeva and Lena Volkova at the kefir bottling plant*. The clipping is placed on the window ledge beside his
father's medals. After two months the paper yellows, and his
mother patches some foil from milk-bottle caps, backs it onto the
newspaper cutting, makes a little hood over the picture to keep the
direct sunlight from ruining it.

His older sister, Tamara, uses the same technique for pictures of
male dancers she copies from books: Chaboukiani, Yermolayev,
Tikhomirov, Sergeyev. Rudik studies the drawings, how the dancers
hold their heads, the dip of their feet. Tamara stands in the courtyard
and encourages him to imitate the pose. She laughs when he tries to
stand stock-still on one foot. He doesn't own a library card, but
Tamara is a senior member of the Komsomol and so is allowed
books from the library, which she brings home for him—*Dance and
Realism; Beyond the Bourgeoisie, The Form of Dance in the Soviet Union;*

*Choreographic Structure for a New Society*—all books that force Rudik into the use of a dictionary.

He writes lists of words in a notebook that he keeps in his school-bag. Many of them are French, so he feels sometimes like a boy of another country. In school he draws maps with pictures of trains moving across the landscape. His notebooks are covered with sketches of dancers' legs, and when his teachers catch him with the book he simply shrugs and says: What's wrong with that?

He has begun to acquire a reputation for himself, and sometimes he storms out of the classroom, shuts the door noisily behind him.

Later the teachers find him in empty corridors, attempting pirou-ettes, but he has no formal training, only folk dancing, and his moves are stunted. He is sent home with notes from the school's director.

His father looks at the notes, crumples them, throws them away.

In Hamet's new work there is the salvation of numbness. He is out early in the morning on the Djoma River with twelve other comrades, war veterans, on a barge. The smoke from Ufa's factories drifts over the boat and the deep smell of metal is a reminder to him of blood. Hamet and the other men use giant boat hooks to bring in the logs that have floated down the river from the mill towns up north—Sterlitamak, Alkino, Tschishmi. The hooks are spun through the air like miniature sickles, catching and digging into the errant logs. They are hauled by hand to the rear of the barge, where the men step out and tie them with chains, jumping from one to the other as the logs roll beneath their feet, hats on, shirts open, water splashing around their boots.

Rudik has asked if he can step out into the water and roll on the logs, but Hamet has said that it is far too dangerous and, indeed, over the course of two years, as foreman, Hamet loses five men.

Hamet follows a city directive that says he must classify the dead man as drowned; sometimes he dreams of them at night, remember-ing soldiers whose bodies were used instead of trees to build roads. In the winters, when the lake is frozen and logs no longer drift downriver, he tours the factories, giving political lectures to the workers, just as he did for many years in the army, and he never questions what any of it means, to hook these logs and men.

One evening Hamet catches Rudik by the ear and says: There is nothing wrong with dance, son.

I know.

Even our great leaders like dance.

Yes I know.

But it's what you do in the world that makes you. Do you understand?

I think so.

Your social existence determines consciousness, son. Remember?

Yes.

It's very simple. You're made for more than dance.

Yes.

You will be a great doctor, an engineer.

Yes.

Rudik looks at his mother in the ratty armchair across the room. She is thin, and there is a hollow in her neck that looks smoke-blue. Her eyes don't move.

Correct, Farida? says his father.

Correct, replies his mother.

The following day, on the way home from the factory, Farida stops momentarily outside a house on a rutted dirt road. The small house is painted bright yellow, the paint is peeling off in large flakes, the roof is sloped by weather and the wooden doorway sags. The carved wooden shutters flap in the breeze. A single wind chime lets out a note.

She spies a pair of shoes on the porch step. Old, black, unpolished, familiar.

She works her tongue around in her mouth, moves it against a back tooth that has been loose for weeks, pushes at the tooth with force, places her hand on the gate in order to steady herself. She has heard about an old couple who live here with three or four other families. She feels dizzy, faint. The tooth rocks back and forth in her mouth. She ponders that she has lived her life through a constant driving storm, she thinks, she has walked on with her head down, her jaw locked, her mind always on the next step, and seldom before has she been forced to stop and examine it all.

Her tongue pushes against the loose molar. She puts her hand on the gate of the house to open it, but in the end she turns away, a pain shooting through her gums.

Later, when Rudik comes home—the flush of dance in his cheeks—she sits beside him on the bed and says: I know what you're doing.

What? he asks.

Don't fool with me.

What?

I'm too old to be fooled with.

What?

I saw your shoes outside that house.

What shoes?

I know who those people are, Rudik.

He looks up at her and says: Don't tell Father.

She hesitates, bites her lip, then opens up her hand and says: Look.

A tooth rolls in her palm. She places it in the pocket of her house-dress and then lays her hand on the back of Rudik's neck, draws him close.

Be careful, Rudik, she says.

He nods and steps away from her, spins onto the floor to show her what he has learned, and he is confused when she doesn't watch, her eyes fixed firmly on the wall.

After the boy left, Anna put on her nightgown, worn at the elbows, and perched at the very edge of the bed. I was at my desk, reading. She whispered good night, but then she coughed and said she felt blessed, that it was enough in this life just to feel blessed from time to time.

She said she knew, even after just one session, that the boy could be something unusual.

She rose and shuffled across the room, put her arms to my shoulders. With one hand she removed my reading glasses. She placed them in the center spine of the book and turned my face to hers. She said my name and it pierced my fatigue in the most extraordinary way. As she leaned across, her hair brushed against me and it smelled like the days when she had been with the Maryinsky. She turned me sideways in the chair, and the light from the candle flickered on her face.

She said: Read to me, husband.

I picked up the book, and she said: No, not here, let's go to bed.

It was a book of Pasternak's that had survived all our years, open to a poem about stars frozen in the sky. I have always adored Pasternak, not just for the obvious reasons but because it has seemed to me that by staying in the rearguard rather than moving with the vanguard, he had learned to love what is left behind without mourning what was gone.

The book was fattened from being thumbed through so much. My habit, which Anna hated, of turning down the edges of my favorite pages gave it a further thickness.

I picked up the candle, the book, my glasses, and I stepped to the bed, pulled back the covers, got in. Anna dropped her wooden dentures on a plate with a little sigh, combed her hair, climbed in beside me. Her feet were cold as always. With older dancers it is often this way—having tortured their feet for so many years, the blood just refuses to journey.

I read to her from a cycle of nature poems until she fell asleep, and it didn't seem indulgent to let my arm fall across her waist while she slept, to take a little of her happiness—the old steal from each other as much as the young, but perhaps our thefts are more necessary. In years gone by Anna and I have stolen from each other ferociously and then lived inside the stolen moments until we began to share them. She once told me that when I was incarcerated she often turned down my covers, even rolled across and made a dent in the pillow as if I were still there.

I read more Pasternak as she slept and then quoted it from memory when the candle burned all the way down. Her breath grew foul, and I leaned in against her, pulled the covers high. Her hair had loosened and it fell across her face and, with the little breeze from the open window, the strands crossed and recrossed her eyes.

Sentiment is foolish, of course, and I do not know whether I slept that night, but I do remember thinking a very simple thought—that despite all the years I was still in love with her, and at that moment it didn't seem foolish at all to have loved her, or to go on loving her, even in all our wreckage.

The factory alarm blew shrill at six in the morning. Anna turned the pillow to find the cool side, and I was left with her back to me. When the light broke through the crack in the curtains, I cobbled together some tea and kasha that still tasted all right from the day before, a small miracle.

We sat at the kitchen table beside the bed, and Anna played Mozart low on the gramophone, so as not to disturb the old washerwoman in the room next door. Anna and I chatted about the boy and then after breakfast she dressed and packed her dance skirt and slippers. When she raised her head from her shopping basket, she looked to me as though she was stepping back into days that once had been. With the corps de ballet in Saint Petersburg long ago she was given a special carrier bag for her slippers—Diaghilev himself had passed the bags around—but she had lost it somewhere in our shuffles.

In the corridor our neighbors were already about. Anna waved to me and closed the door as if the movement were part of a furtive dance.

That evening she brought the boy home a second time. He ate his potato carefully at first, as if unbuttoning an unfamiliar coat. He had no idea what to do with the butter, and he watched Anna for guidance.

The room and us, we were used to each other, but with the boy there it seemed like a foreign place, not seventeen years lived in.

Anna dared some Stravinsky low on the gramophone, and the boy loosened a little, as if he were eating the music with the potato. He asked for an extra cup of milk but ate in silence for the rest of the dinner. Looking over at Anna, I was put in mind of a crow calling out to another crow over the head of a sparrow.

He was pale and narrow-shouldered, with a face both cheeky and angelic at the same time. His eyes were a mixture of green and blue, and they darted around the room, never resting long enough, it seemed, to truly take stock. He ate ferociously, yet he sat straight-backed in the chair. Anna had already drummed into him the importance of posture. She said to me that he had almost immediately mastered the five positions, that he showed a natural turnout, but still he was a little uncouth and forced. Aren't you? she said.

He held the fork at his mouth and smiled.

Anna told him he was to come to the school gymnasium every day except Sunday, and he was to tell his parents he needed at least two pairs of slippers and two sets of tights.

He paled and asked for another cup of milk.

We heard our washerwoman neighbor fumbling next door. Anna turned the gramophone a little lower, and we made the three short steps to the couch. The boy did not sit between us but wandered instead up and down the length of bookcases, touching the spines of the books, amazed that they were crammed four deep.

At seven o'clock he wiped his hand across his runny nose, said good-bye. When we opened the window to look out he was already running down the street, jumping over the cracks in the pavement.

Eleven years old, said Anna, imagine that.

We committed ourselves to the gray night with Pasternak once more. Anna fell asleep above the covers, breathing a sadness through her nostrils. I shaved—an old habit from the camps which used to allow me an extra moment in the mornings before the chill—and then carted my insomnia to the window, stars being infinitely more interesting than ceilings. It had begun to rain and the water funneled over the roof and sluiced down the gutter pipe, giving its acoustics to the city. Her breathing became so heavy it sang in my ears, and every now and then her body clenched itself as if dreaming of pain, but she woke cheerily, shifted herself into her housedress.

Sunday was our day to clean.

A few weeks before we had found silverfish in our photo album, moving through our tentative and uncertain smiles. All my military pictures had been destroyed long before, but we still had one or two others gnawed through at our feet—our wedding, Anna standing outside the Maryinsky, the two of us standing by a combine harvester in Georgia of all places.

Anna left the gray silverfish to me, and I squeezed them between my fingers. Over the years the silverfish had become fat with us, photos taken mostly in Saint Petersburg and mostly in sunlight for some strange reason. On the back of the photos we had scribbled little notes for ourselves, but we had written *Leningrad*, just in case.

There were some more recent photos from Ufa, but in their bitter little ironies the silverfish had spared them.

In the afternoon, after a merciful nap, I found Anna behind the changing screen at the foot of the bed, standing on the tips of her toes, wearing the outfit of her last dance, thirty-three years ago. It was a long, pale tutu, and she looked a bit like a footnote to her past. Embarrassed, she began to cry, then changed out of the costume. Her breasts swung, small, to her rib cage.

Once we had filled each other with desire, not remembrance.

She dressed and took my hat from the rack, her signal for us to go. I limped out, along the corridor, into the day, using my cane. The sun was strong and high, although the streets were still damp. The poplars swayed in a light breeze, and it felt quite fine to be alive even with the oil refinery dust still heavy in the air. At the bottom of the hill we stopped at the bakery, but for some reason the electricity had been turned off during the day and for the first time in weeks we weren't greeted by the smell. We stood by the air vent to catch any remnant, but there was none so we walked on.

Even the mad war veteran at the bottom of Zentsov wasn't around, so the day had acquired an unlived-in quality.

By the lake families sat with picnics. Drunks talked to their bottles. A kvass vendor busied herself at her stall. At the bandstand, a folk group struck up in hideous disharmony. Nothing in this world ever approaches perfection—except perhaps a fine cigar, which I had not had in many years. The thought of it made me wince with longing.

Anna was worried about my wheezing and tried to insist that we sit down on a park bench, but surely there could be no sadder or more ridiculous sight, old exiles on park benches, so we pressed on, down the streets by Lenin Park, through the archway, towards the Opera House.

He was there, of course, as if in some divine comedy, standing on the steps of the Opera House. He was wearing a shirt that was obviously a castoff and the rear of his pants was streaked with mud like any boy's. The back seams of his shoes were split, and the angle of his feet—in third position—accentuated the split. He held the position for as long as we held ours and, when we finally stepped forward to greet him, he acted as if the encounter was perfectly natural.

He bowed to Anna and nodded to me.

I am honored to see you again, he said.

There were bruises above his left eye, but I didn't ask, too accustomed to the miseries of beatings and the small silences we bear with them.

Anna took him by the elbow and led him up the steps. She dug her pass out from her handbag, and the guard gave a gruff shake of the head. It was only then that Anna remembered me, and she came bounding down the steps to help.

If I were eleven years old I'd be jealous, I said.

Oh you.

Inside the Opera House the carpenters were at work on a set for *The Red Poppy*, which had been renamed *The Red Flower*, and I thought to myself, Why not rename everything, donate to it all its proper inconsequence?

The scaffold was up, and my old friend Albert Tikhonov—indeed a quiet one—was on his stilts as usual, painting the backdrop. He was covered foot to hair in many different paints. He hailed me from on high, and I waved back up. Below him a young woman in a blue uniform was welding a leg onto a broken metal chair. The stage seemed ablaze with the sparks from the welding gun. I sat four rows from the rear and watched the drama, significantly more interesting, I'm sure, than any Red Flower, rose or poppy or michemalia.

Anna took the boy backstage, and when they reemerged after an hour he was carrying two sets of slippers, a dance belt and four sets of tights. He was ecstatic, begging Anna for the chance just to stand on the stage, but there was too much going on there, so she invited him to try out his positions in the aisles instead. He put on the new slippers, which were too big for him. Anna removed one elastic band from her hair and one from her bag, snapped them around the shoes to keep them intact. She worked with him in the aisle for half an hour. He kept grinning as he moved, as if picturing himself onstage. In truth I saw nothing extraordinary in him—he seemed ragged at the edges, overly excited and there was a dangerous charm to him, very Tatar.

As far as I could see he had little control of his body, but Anna complimented him and even Albert Tikhonov stopped working a moment, leaned against the wall to steady his stilts and gave a quick

round of applause. To console myself for my sloth I too joined in
with the applause.

I could tell from Anna's face that she had already told him about
dancing in Saint Petersburg and that the memory weighed on her
heavily. What monstrous things, our pasts, especially when they
have been lovely. She had told a secret and now had the sadness of
wondering how much deeper she might dig in order to keep the
first secret fed.

Still, I could see that the boy was good for her—her cheeks were
flushed and there was a high timbre in her voice that I had not heard
for years. She saw something in him, a light intruding upon the
shadows to make sense of all our previous gloom.

They worked on a few more steps until finally Anna said: Enough!
We left the Opera House and the boy walked home, the slippers
slung over his shoulder, his legs deliberately turned out from his hips.

It had grown dark, but Anna and I stopped at a park bench by the
lake, weariness defeating us. She put her head to my shoulder and
told me that she was not so foolish as to believe that Rudik would
ever be anything more than a dancer to her. Anna had always wanted
a son, even in our later years. Our daughter, Yulia, lived in Saint
Petersburg, thousands of kilometers away. For most of our lives we
had reluctantly lived away from her, and Anna had never had the
chance to teach her to dance. It was, we knew, a history wasted, but
there was nothing we could do about it.

That night I didn't read to Anna. It was enough that she stepped
across the room and kissed me. I was surprised to find there was still
a stir in my groin, then even more surprised to remember that there
hadn't been a stir in almost five years. Our bodies are foul things to
live inside. I am convinced the gods patched us together this disas-
trously so that we might need them, or at least invoke them late at
night.

The small mercies of life struck a couple of weeks later, when a package from Saint Petersburg managed to find its way to us—Yulia cleverly sent it through the university. Inside was a pound of Turkish coffee and a fruitcake. The cake was wrapped in paper and taped behind the paper was a letter, kept largely innocuous, just in case. She cataloged the changes in the city and touched on whatever was new in her life. Her husband had been promoted in the physics department, and she hinted that she might be able to send us a little money in the coming months. We sat back in our armchairs, read the letter twelve times, cracking its codes, its nuances.

Rudik came over and devoured a slice of the fruitcake, then asked if he could take a slice home for his sister. Later I saw him open the package halfway down the road and stuff the piece into his mouth.

We used and reused Yulia's coffee grains until they were so dry that Anna joked they might bleach—before the Revolution we often used a pound of coffee a week, but of course when there is no choice it is extraordinary what you adapt to.

My own afternoon walks—slow and careful because of my foot— began to take me to the School Two gymnasium. I watched through the small glass window. Anna had forty students all together, but she kept only two of them behind after class, Rudik and another boy. The other was dark-haired, lithe and, to my eye, much more accomplished, no ruffian edges. Together, if they could have melded, they would have been magnificent. But Anna's heart was for Rudik—she said to me that he was somehow born within dance, that he was unlettered in it, yet he knew it intimately, it was a grammar for him, deep and untutored. I saw the shine in her eyes when she berated him on a plié and he immediately turned and executed it perfectly, stood grinning, waiting for her to berate him again, which of course she did.

Anna found herself a new dance dress, and although she kept herself covered with leg warmers and a long sweater, she was still slender and delicate. She stood beside him at the barre and corrected his tendus. She had him repeat the steps until he grew dizzy, shouted at him that he was not a monkey and that he should straighten his back.

She even pounded a few notes on the piano for rhythm, although her skill on the keys left a lot to be desired. I was amazed to see her one winter afternoon developing runnels of sweat on her brow. Her eyes quite honestly sparkled, as if she had borrowed them from the boy.

She began working with him on jumps—she told him that above all he must create what his feet wished for, and it was not so much that he must jump higher than anyone else but that he should remain in the air longer.

Stay in the air longer!

Yes, she said, hang on to God's beard.

His beard?

And do not land like a cow.

Cows jump? he asked.

Don't be cheeky. And keep your mouth closed. You are not a fly swallower.

I'm in the circus! he shouted, and he began leaping around the room with his mouth open.

Anna developed a system with him. Rudik's parents were of Muslim stock and as the only boy he was not expected to do much. Buying bread was his only chore, but after a while Anna began to pick it up for him to give him time to practice. She lined up twice outside different bakeries, one on Krassina and one on October Prospect. I often went along to wait with her. We would try to keep our place by the bakery vents if we could—the great solace of queuing was the smell that hung in the air. I took the first batch of bread home while she waited with his family's coupons at the second bakery. The process often took a whole morning, but that didn't matter to Anna. At the end of his lesson he would kiss her on the cheek, put the bread in his shopping bag and run home.

One summer evening we took him on a picnic: pickles, some black bread and a small jar of berry juice.

In the park, by the Belaya, Anna spread a blanket on the ground. The sun was high, and it threw short shadows on the surrounding fields. Farther downstream a group of boys dove off a giant rock. One or two of them pointed in our direction and shouted Rudik's name. Anna had a word in his ear. Reluctantly he got into his swimming gear and walked along the riverbank. He hung around near the rock for a while, a deep scowl on his face. It was easy to pick Rudik out in the crowd—he was thinner and whiter than the rest. The boys jumped from the rock into the water, grabbing their knees in midair. Great jets of water splashed up when they landed.

Rudik sat down and watched their antics, chin on his knees until one of the older boys came up to him and started pushing him around. Rudik shoved back and screamed an obscenity.

Anna got to her feet, but I pulled her down. I poured her a glass of berry juice and said: Let him fight his own battles.

She sipped the juice and let it be.

A couple of minutes passed. Then a look of terror crossed Anna's face. Rudik and the other boy had climbed up to the very top of the rock. All the other children were watching. Some of them began to clap, slowly and rhythmically. I stood up and began to move my old cart horse of a body as quickly as I could along the riverbank. Rudik was poised, motionless, at the top of the rock. I shouted at him. It was a five-meter jump, next to impossible since the base of the rock was so wide. He spread his arms, took a deep breath. Anna screamed. I stumbled. Rudik spread his arms farther and flew outwards. He seemed to hang in the air, fierce and white, and then he dropped into the water with a huge splash. His head narrowly missed the rock edge. Anna screamed again. I waited for him to emerge. He stayed under a long time but eventually surfaced, a piece of river plant stuck to his neck. He flicked the plant away, shook his head, grinned enormously, then waved at the boy who was still standing at the top of the rock, frozen in fear.

Jump, shouted Rudik. Jump, asshole!

The boy climbed back down without jumping. Rudik swam away and came up to us, sat down nonchalantly on the blanket. He took a pickle from the jar, but he was trembling and I could see the fear in his eyes. Anna started to scold him, but he kept eating his pickle and finally she shrugged. Rudik looked up at her from under a stray lock of hair, finished his food, and came over to lean his head against her shoulder.

You're a strange child, she said.

He came to our room every day, sometimes two or three times. Some of our phonograph collection was proscribed. We hid it in a wooden bookshelf that had a false back, one of the few pieces of my carpentry that had actually worked, having survived visits by the Ministry. He learned how to remove the records from their sleeves and catch them sideways so he didn't leave fingerprints. He was always careful to take the dust off the stylus. It was like medicine to him when the gramophone gave out a couple of clicks and the sound moved into violins.

Walking around the room, he kept his eyes closed.

He came to adore Scriabin, listening while standing still, as if he wanted the music to repeat itself a thousand times until Scriabin himself stood beside him, feeding the fire with flutes.

He had this terrible habit of leaving his mouth open as he listened, but it seemed wrong to tap him on the shoulder and lift him out of the moment. Once Anna touched his chin, and he recoiled instantly. I knew it was his father. They weren't bad bruises, but you could see that he had been knocked around. Rudik had told us that his father worked on the river, hauling logs. It seemed to me that he was slinging down the old curse of fathers—wanting his son to take advantage of the things he had fought for, to become a doctor or a military man or a commissar or an engineer. To him dancing meant the poorhouse. Rudik was failing in school, his teachers were saying he was fidgety, spending his time humming symphonies and occasionally looking at art books his sister had borrowed. He had developed an attachment to Michelangelo, and in his notebooks he made sketches—they were adolescent but well-realized.

The only good report he got was from the Pioneers, where he spent Tuesday afternoons practicing folk dances. And on the evenings when there was ballet at the Opera House—*Esmeralda, Coppélia, Don Quixote, Swan Lake*—he would be gone from his home, sneaking in the stage door, allowed a seat by my friend Albert Tikhonov, the stilt walker.

It was when he got home and his father discovered where he had been that Rudik was beaten.

Rudik didn't whine about his bruises, and he didn't have the empty gaze that I'd seen in other boys and men. He was being beaten for dance and still he went on dancing, so the whole thing balanced itself out. The beatings came on the spur of the moment, including a dreadful one the day after his thirteenth birthday. I didn't doubt that Rudik deserved it—he could be terribly cantankerous— yet I could tell that by beating him, by refusing him the chance to dance, his father was giving Rudik the gift of need.

Anna talked about going to see his mother but decided against it. If you are wise you step through the darkness only one foot at a time.

I have always thought of memory as a foolish conceit, but as the gramophone crackled Anna began to tell him bits and pieces of her past. She glossed over her own youth and quickly settled into her years in the corps. How she yammered on! The costumes, the designers, the trains across borders! Saint Petersburg and the rain through the streetlights! The rake of the Kirov floor! The tenor aria from the last act of *Tosca*! After a while there was no arresting her— it was like the Dutch boy's dam, except it wasn't only the river that had burst but the ramparts, the bank, the weeds on the shore also.

I was grateful that she didn't lie to him, that she didn't pretend to have been one of the great dancers, denied by history. No. There was a lovely truth to it all. She told him about standing in the wings of the grand theaters, dreaming herself onstage. She remembered Pavlova in less striking colors than anyone else, perhaps because Pavlova herself was such an elemental part of the dance. I found myself adrift too, back at the Maryinsky, in the front row, waiting desperately for Anna to come on with the corps. In *Swan Lake*, when the curtain call came, the cry went up for *Anna! Anna! Anna!* I felt it was my Anna they were chanting for, so I chanted too. Afterwards I would meet her and we would walk down Rossi with her arm linked through mine and at her building her mother would be looking down from the fourth-floor window. I would guide her close to the wall and kiss her, whereupon she would touch my face and giggle and run upstairs.

How long ago it was and how strange, but all dead friends come to life again sometimes.

Rudik listened to the stories with a sort of rapt disbelief. It struck me later that the disbelief was born of a benign ignorance. After all, he was thirteen now, and he had been taught to think differently than us. Still, it was remarkable to me that he remembered the stories weeks later, sometimes quoting Anna exactly, word for word.

He inhaled everything, became taller and gangly, with an impish smirk that could silence a room, but he wasn't aware of his body or its power. If anything, he was shy and afraid. Anna told him that his whole body must dance, all of it, not just his arms and legs. She tweaked him on the ear, saying even his lobe must believe in movement. Straighten your legs. Spot quicker on your turns. Work on your line. Absorb the dance like blotting paper. He stuck to it all diligently, never quitting until he had perfected a step, even if it meant another beating from his father. On Sundays, Anna took him first to the museum and then to watch rehearsals at the Opera House, so they were together every day of the week. As they walked home, Rudik would remember the exact movements he had seen—male or female, it didn't matter— reconstructing the movements from memory.

He lay between us, like a long and charged evening.

Rudik began to develop a new language, not one that fit him, he was ill-shod for it. But it was charming to hear the rough provincial boy say *port de bras* as if he had stepped from a room full of chandeliers. At the same time, at our table, he would eat a piece of goat's cheese like a savage. He had never in his life heard of washing his hands before a meal. Sometimes his finger went into his nose, and he had a terrible affinity for scratching his private parts.

You'll scratch it away, I told him once, and he looked at me with the sort of horror reserved for death and pillage.

Late at night in bed, Anna and I talked until she fell asleep. It struck us that he was our new breath and that the breath would last us only a short while, that he would eventually have to move on. It gave us great sorrow, yet it also gave us a chance to live beyond any sorrows we had already accumulated.

I even went back to my garden patch to see if I could resurrect it.

Years ago we were given a plot, eight tram stops from our house. Someone in the Ministry had overlooked our history, and we were graced with a letter that said a plot, two meters square, could be ours. It was poor land, brittle and gray. We grew a few vegetables— cucumbers, radishes, cabbages, wild onions—but Anna also had a penchant for lilies, and each year she exchanged a couple of food coupons for a packet of bulbs. We put the bulbs deep in the soil, on the rim of the plot, sometimes used donkey manure for fertilizer, waited. We failed miserably with the flowers most years, but life deals us its strange little ecstasies, and that particular summer, for the first time ever, we had a patch of dark white.

In the afternoons, when she was at the gymnasium, I would catch the tram out there, limp up the hill and sit on a folding chair.

Often, on weekends, a short man with dark hair knelt over his plot, ten meters from my own. We caught each other's eye every now and then, but we never exchanged a word. His face was tight and guarded, like that of a man who had lived his life with his traps constantly baited. He worked on his garden with a fierce industry, growing cabbages and potatoes mostly. When it came time to harvest, he brought a wheelbarrow with him and filled it high.

One Saturday morning he arrived up the path with Rudik at his heels. I was surprised—not just because this man was Rudik's father, but because the boy was supposed to be at the gym with Anna and, over the course of a year, he had never once missed a session. I dropped my trowel into the soil and coughed loudly, but Rudik kept his eyes on the ground, as if there were terrible events lurking around each plant.

I rose to my feet to say something, but he turned away.

It struck me then that Rudik's genius was in allowing his body to say things that he couldn't otherwise express. It was simply the way his shoulders slumped from one side to the other and the angle of his head that gave him a look—even from the rear—that said any approach would not just impinge on him but wound him deeply. He was forever removed from his father, and yet he was forever removed from me also.

I could see that he was cut above the eye but that his father also had a large bruise on his right cheek. It was clear to me that his father was trying to reconcile all that had happened between them, but no reconciliation would be forthcoming.

His father troweled in the ground and spoke up at his son. Rudik occasionally gave a word back, but most of the time he said nothing.

I knew that there would never again be another beating.

I decided to leave well enough alone and put on my hat, went home, told Anna about what had happened.

Oh, she said, and then she went to sit at the table, curling and uncurling her fingers.

One of these days I'm going to have to pass him on to Elena Konstantinovna, she said. He's learned all he can from me. It's only fair.

I went to the cupboard to take out the small bottle of samogon that we had kept for many years. Anna wiped two glasses with a clean towel, and we sat down to drink.

I raised my glass and toasted.

She wiped at her eyes with the sleeve of her dress.

There was only enough in the bottle to get us to the stage where we wanted more. Still, we allowed our happiness to reach instead into the gramophone, Prokofiev, over and over. Anna said she didn't mind letting Rudik move on to another teacher, especially Elena. Elena Konstantinovna Voitovich had been a coryphée in Saint Petersburg and was now the mistress at the Ufa Opera House. She and Anna kept in touch, and they had exchanged memories and favors—Anna said it might be possible after a few years for Rudik to get a walk-on role, maybe even a solo or two. Perhaps he can go all the way to the school at the Maryinsky, she said. She even talked about writing a letter to Yulia to see if she could negotiate any favors. I knew Anna was recalling herself when she was there, younger, more pliant, still full of promise, and so I nodded, let her talk. There is only so much we can do, she said, teaching is elastic, and if we stretch it out it will only snap back on us at some later date. She explained that she would bring him down to the advanced classes on Karl Marx Street some time during the week. First of all, however, she would cook up a great feast to surprise him.

My hand slipped across the table to hers. She told me to go and grab a book and that maybe with the samogon warming our bodies we would both be allowed a generous night's sleep. It wasn't true.

She danced with him all that week. I watched through the window of the gym door.

She had certainly knocked the roughest edges off his movement. His plié was still quite unaccomplished, and his legs contained more violence than grace, but he could pirouette well, and on jumps he had even learned to hang a moment in the air, which delighted Anna. She clapped. He responded to her gestures by jumping again, moving diagonally forward with slow grands jêtés and sweeping arcs, then crossing the rear of the room with a series of bad sissonnes where he bent the second knee. He retreated and stopped suddenly with his arms looped in a garland above his head, having scooped the air and made it his, which was certainly not something that Anna had taught him. His nostrils flared, and I thought for a moment that he might paw at the ground like a horse. Certainly there was more intuition in him than intellect, more spirit than knowledge, as if he had been here before in another guise, something wild and feral.

On Friday she pulled him aside and told him the news. I excused myself and watched from outside the door. I expected silence, maybe tears or a puzzled sorrow, but he just looked at her, hugged her close, stepped back, and took the prospect with a vigorous nod of his head.

Now, said Anna, for your last dance I want you to drop a tray of pearls at my feet.

He went across to the bench and picked up the watering can and did a series of chaînés up and down the room, sprinkling the floor for grip. For the next twenty minutes—before I went home—he strung together all she had taught him, moving from one end of the gym to the other, his tights worn and stretched. Anna glanced out the window at me, and we both knew, at that instant, that whatever attended us in the future we would at least have this.

❈

In the hall on Karl Marx Street he is one of seventy young dancers. At fourteen he is given a whole new language: royales, tours jêtés, brisés, tours en l'air, fouettés. He stays late, practicing. On entrechat-quatres he beats his legs together like a barber's shears. Elena Voitovich watches him with her lips pursed and her hair pulled back in a severe bun. Once or twice her mouth curls into a smile, but mostly she remains uncertain. He tries to outrage her with a brisé volé but she simply scoffs and turns away, says that they would not tolerate form like his in the Kirov or the Bolshoi or even the Stanislavsky. She speaks of the ballet companies with a tinge of regret, and sometimes she tells him of Leningrad, of Moscow, of how the women dancers there work so hard their feet are bloodied at the end of their sessions, and that the sinks in the opera houses are tinged with the blood of great performers.

He carries the notion home, practices with the thought of red soaking through his slippers.

His sister Tamara has left the house to study teaching in Moscow and he now has room for a full-length bed. Taped to the wall near the bed he has scribbled notes to himself: *Ask Anna to patch slippers. Work on spotting so as not to get dizzy. Find walk-ons. Get good piece of oak for barre. Have interest only in what you can't do well. Beethoven was sixteen when he wrote the second movement concerto number 2!* No direct sunlight hits the wall but still he has hooded the paper with foil like his mother used to do. His father paces the house but ignores the notes.

One March morning Rudik awakes to hear Yuri Levitan, the state radio's chief announcer, interrupting a slew of solemn music with a bulletin: The heart of the Comrade Stalin, inspired Continuer of Lenin's cause, Father and Teacher, Comrade in Arms, Coryphaeus of Science and Technology, Wise Leader of the Communist Party of the Soviet Union, has ceased to beat.

Three minutes of silence is called for. Rudik's father moves out into the street to stand beneath the trees, where the only sound is that of the grackles. His mother remains at the window and then turns to Rudik, takes her son's face in her hands, not a word passing between them.

That evening, at the end of another broadcast, Rudik hears that Prokofiev has died on the very same day. He climbs through the window of the locked hall on Karl Marx Street and, in the bathroom sink, he scrapes the soles of his feet against the metal mouths of the taps so savagely that they bleed. He comes out, dancing for nobody, blood on his slippers, sweat spinning from his hair.

❋

It was just before the May Day celebrations. We hadn't seen each other in about four years. He knocked on the door of the electrician shop on Karl Marx Street where I was an apprentice. He looked different, more grown-up, hair long. We used to bully the little bastard at school, but he stood at the door now, as big as me. I had heard he was dancing, that he'd appeared at the Opera House a few times, mostly as a walk-on, but so what, I didn't care. I asked what he wanted. He said he'd heard I owned a portable gramophone and he'd like to borrow it. I went to close the door, but he put his foot in it and it bounced back at me. I grabbed him by the shirt but he didn't flinch. He got right to the point, said he'd like the gramophone for an exhibition he was giving in the basement canteen of the oil refinery. I told him to jump in the lake and fuck a few trout. But he began to plead like a little child and finally he said he'd give me some money. So I got him to promise me thirty rubles out of his one hundred. He said okay, as long as I got him some good phonographs to play. My cousin was high up in the Komsomol and he had some recordings, mostly army songs but some Bach, Dvorak, others. Besides, thirty rubles was thirty rubles. So I got the portable gramophone for him.

The refinery was a big area of pipes and steam and canals, with its own three ambulances that would pick up the dead or the injured when there was an accident. Sirens going off all the time, searchlights, dogs. You'd know a refinery worker just by the way he looked at you. The entertainment collective was run by a fat old babushka called Vera Bazhenova. Most of the time she showed films or bawdy puppet shows, and every now and then she stretched to a little folk dancing. But Rudi had talked her into letting him perform for one night. He was good that way, he could call an ass a racehorse and get away with it.

The canteen was dirty and it stank of sweat. It was six in the evening, just after the shifts had changed. The workers sat down to watch. There were about thirty men and twenty-five women—welders, toolmakers, furnace men, forklift drivers, a couple of office workers, some union representatives. I knew a few of them, and we shared a glass of koumiss. After a while Rudi came out from the kitchen, where he'd changed his clothes. He was wearing tights pulled up high on his stomach and a sleeveless top. A long fringe of hair was hanging down over his eyes. The workers started laughing. He pouted and told me to put a record on the gramophone. I told him I wasn't his little Turkish slave, he should do it himself. He came across and whispered in my ear that I wouldn't get any money. I thought, fuck him, but I put the record on anyway. The first thing he did was a piece from the *Song of the Cranes*, and just three or four minutes into it they were laughing at him. They'd seen plenty of dancing before, these workers, but this was the end of the day, flasks were being passed along the rows, everyone smoking and chattering, and they were saying, Get this shit off the stage! Get this piece of shit off the stage!

He danced some more, but they got louder, even the women. He glanced across at me, and I began to feel a little bad for him, so I lifted the needle from the gramophone. The canteen fell silent. There was a mean look in his eyes—as if he was all at once challenging the women to fuck him and the men to fight. His lips twitched. Someone threw a dirty rag up on the stage, which set off another great roar. Vera Bazhenova was red in the face, trying to get them to quieten down, it was her head on the block, she ran the collective.

Just then Rudi stretched out his arms wide and began a gopak followed by a yiablotshko, up on his toes, then slowly sinking to his knees, and then he moved into *The Internationale*. The laughter turned to some coughing and then the workers began to turn toward one another in their chairs, and then they began stamping out *The Internationale* on the floor. By the end of the performance Rudi was back to ballet, the *Song of the Cranes*, full circle, and the stupid bastards were applauding him. They passed around a tin cup, and he got another thirty rubles. He glanced at me and tucked it all in his pocket. The workers gathered around after the show and invited us for some more koumiss. Soon everyone in the canteen was shouting and drinking. A little red-haired man got up on the aluminum counter and gave a toast, then stood on one leg and extended his arms. Finally Rudi grabbed the man, steadied him and showed him how it was done properly.

When we took the tram home, both of us drunker than elephants, I asked him for some of the extra money. He told me I was a miserable Cossack, that he needed it to pay for his train ticket to Moscow or Leningrad, whichever would accept him, to go fuck myself, that it was him earned all the money anyway.

❋

He has rouged his cheeks with a red stone and darkened his eyes with black liner stolen from the Opera House. His eyelashes have been thickened with a paste and his hair swept back with pomade. At home alone, he smiles and then grimaces in the mirror, creates a series of faces. Stepping frontways to the mirror, he adjusts his tights and his dance belt: the mirror is tilted downwards so he can see no more than his midtorso. He stretches his arm high beyond the reflection, takes a bow, and watches his hand reentering the mirror. He steps closer, exaggerates his turnout, tightens the upper muscles of his legs, brings his hips forward. He removes the tights to unhook the dance belt, stands still and closes his eyes.

A row of lights, a sea of faces, he is in the air to great applause. The footlights flicker and the curtains are opened again. He bows.

Later he removes the rouge and the eye makeup with an old handkerchief. He shifts the few pieces of furniture—sideboard, armchairs, cheap wall paintings—and begins to practice in the dark cramped space of the room.

In the afternoon his father returns earlier than usual and nods in the manner of men grown accustomed to silence. His eyes rest for a moment on the row of notes Rudi has taped to the mirror: *Work on battements and accomplish proper order of jêtés coupés. Borrow Scriabin from Anna. Linament for feet.* At the end of one row of notes, the word *Visa.*

Hamet glances at the handkerchief on the floor near Rudi's feet.

Silently he steps past his son, pulls the armchair back to its original position near the door. Beneath his mattress, Hamet has enough money for the fare. Two months' wages, bundled in elastic. He has been saving for a shotgun. Geese and wild fowl. Pheasants. Wood-cocks. Without ceremony, Hamet takes the money from under the mattress and tosses it to Rudik, then lies back on the bed and lights himself a cigarette to argue against the scent of the room.

On the way to Leningrad—or rather on the way to Moscow, which is the way to Leningrad—there is a stop in the little village of Izhevsk where I grew up. I told Rudi he would know the village by the red and green roof of the railway station. If he wanted to, he could drop in at my old uncle Majit's house, sleep the night, and if he was lucky he might even get a lesson from him on stilt walking. He said he'd think about it.

I had helped Rudi try out the stilts once before in the Opera House, when he had a walk-on as a Roman spear-carrier. We had been cleaning up after the show. He was still in his costume. I thrust the stilts into his hands and told him to get on them. They were short, only three quarters of a meter. He laid them on the floor, put his feet on the blocks, tied the straps tight and then sat there, dumbfounded, finally realizing there was no way for him to get up from the floor. He said: Albert, you bastard, take this wool out of my eyes. He unstrapped the stilts and kicked them across the room but then retrieved them and stood center stage, trying to figure it out. Finally I got a stepladder and talked him through how it was done. He stepped up to the top of the ladder, and I gave him the most important pointers. Never fall backwards. Keep your weight on your feet. Don't look down. Lift your knee high and the stilt will follow.

I strung a rope across the stage at about armpit level so he could hold on to it if he fell. He tried to balance on the stilts at first, the hardest thing of all, until I told him that he needed to move and to keep moving.

He progressed precariously up and down the length of the rope, holding on most of the time.

When I was young, my uncle Majit used to practice in an abandoned silo just outside our village. He did it there because there was no wind and every other ceiling was too low for him. He had maybe twenty or thirty different pairs of stilts, all made from ash wood, ranging from half a meter to three meters. His favorites were the meter-high ones because he could bend down and talk to us children or rub the tops of our heads or shake our hands as we ran beneath him. He was the finest stilt walker I ever saw. He would build a new set and step onto them and right away find the sweet spot for balance. Within a day or two he'd be running on them.

The only time Uncle tumbled was when he was teaching us how to fall properly. Never backwards! he shouted, you'll crack your skull open! And then he would start falling backwards himself, shouting, Never like this! Never like this!

As he was toppling, Uncle would switch his weight and turn the stilts and just at the last instant he would fall forwards instead, landing with his knees bent and sitting back on his heels. He was the only stilt walker I ever met who never even tweaked his collar bone.

I tried working with Rudi's stilt technique over the last couple of evenings before he left, but his thoughts were elsewhere. Just the notion of going away was a walk in the air for him anyway.

I told him that if he looked out from the train he would see children beyond the fields, my nieces and nephews, their heads bobbing above the corn. And if he looked behind the station he might even see a group of them playing stilt soccer. Sit on the left-hand side of the train, I told him.

I'm sure he never did.

APRIL 15, '59

R—

The magic of a dance, young man, is something purely acciden-
tal. The irony of this is that you have to work harder than anyone else for the accident to occur. Then, when it happens, it is
the only thing in your life guaranteed never to happen again.
This, to some, is an unhappy state of affairs, and yet to others, it
is the only ecstasy. Perhaps, then, you should forget everything I
have said to you and remember only this: The real beauty in life
is that beauty can sometimes occur.

—*Sasha*

# | 2 |

## LENINGRAD, UFA, MOSCOW · 1956–1961

The railway platforms were wet from the passengers' shoes and their shaken umbrellas. The whole day seemed weighted under a subdued gray damp. Railway workers moved around in their dark boredom. A new symphony was being piped through the loudspeakers, some factory drill of cello and violin. I took a bench under the platform eaves and watched as a woman my age bid good-bye to two teenage children. I smoothed my dress, neither too solemn nor celebratory, trying all the time to imagine what he would look like.

My mother had sent me a photograph taken years before, while she was still teaching him in Ufa. He had the thin cheeky face of a peasant boy—high Tatar cheekbones, sandy hair, a cocked stare—but he was seventeen now and would surely look different. She said he was extraordinary and I would recognize him immediately, he would stand out from the crowd, he had even turned walking into a sort of art.

When the train finally arrived, pouring steam into the air, I stood and held out a hat that had once belonged to my father, a prearranged signal—it was patently absurd but I felt a vague thrill, waiting for a boy half my age to emerge out of the day. I scanned the crowd, but nobody matched his description. Walking through, I brushed against summer overcoats and suitcases, even went so far as to hail two young boys who, in their fear, thought I was an official and hurriedly showed me their papers.

The next train was not for another four hours, so I went out into a light rain. In front of the station someone had altered the face of Stalin, chipping out tiny, almost imperceptible pocks in the stone cheeks. The flowers beneath the statue had gone untended. The statue's defacement was foolish of course, if not outright dangerous, but it was shortly before the '56 Congress and we could already feel the thaw in Leningrad. It was as if a tiny crack had opened and light was spilling through, a cumulative light that would continue to spread, its existence becoming an undeniable fact of our lives. Black canvas tents stood over the tram tracks where they were being repaired. The price of radios had fallen. Shipments of oranges from Morocco were getting through—we hadn't seen oranges in years. Buyers pushed at one another down by the Neva's docks. Just a few months before, in an attempt to resuscitate desire, I had been able to buy my husband eight bottles of his favorite Georgian wine. We even had hot water piped into the apartment, and very late one night I had slipped into the bath with him, surprising myself, him even more so. For a while Iosif had brightened considerably, but when he finished the wine he revisited his policy of gloom.

Instead of waiting outside the station, I walked along the Neva, past the prison, down to the bridge, where I took a tram to the university. I rapped on my husband's door to inform him of the situation, but he wasn't in his office—probably working somewhere or dallying with one of the other physics professors. It was my first visit back to the university in quite a while, and there was a hollowness to the corridors as if I were walking through the belly of a drum that once formed the musical centerpiece of my life. I even toyed with the idea of going into the Linguistics Department, but I felt that it might rekindle old wounds, not salve them. Instead I dug an old pass out of the depths of my bag and put my finger over the expiration date so I could get into the canteen.

The food was grimier and more insipid than I remembered. The ladies behind the counter regarded me with a sort of disdain, and a man with a giant broom pushed bits of food and rubbish around the floor, moving slowly as if contemplating the deep mysteries of his sloth.

Feeling like an intruder into my former life, I left. Outside the sun had broken through the clouds and reefs of arctic light lay on the sky.

Back at Finlandia Station there was a hum and a bustle that had not existed earlier and the working men passed cigarettes back and forth. Inside, a huge banner hung from the ceiling, swaying in the breeze, a picture of Khrushchev folding and refolding into himself: *Life has become better, life is more joyful.* The sign had not been there earlier but it somehow made sense, illuminated by the sunlight from the windows.

I sat back down on a platform bench and waited, wondering what exactly it was my mother expected me to do with a seventeen-year-old country boy. In their letters they said they had been graced by Rudi—whom she affectionately called Rudik—but I had the feeling they were graced not so much by him as by the memory of what dance had once meant to them.

I had not grown up alongside my parents, and in truth, my time with them had wound itself on a modest spool. They were exiled in Ufa, but the foothold of their lives was in what they still called Petersburg—the palaces, the houses, the fencing duels, the side-boards, the inkwells, the Bohemian cut glass, the orchestra seats at the Maryinsky—but that had receded from them forever after the Revolution. My father had miraculously survived the purges over the years, arrested and rearrested, kept in different Siberian camps, finally deported to Ufa, where he and my mother were more or less left alone by the authorities. My mother had always insisted on living in towns close to my father and, for the sake of good schooling and an ancient family dignity, I was brought up by my maternal grandparents in Leningrad, took on their last name and patronymic. I married young, got a job in the university, and had seen my parents only a few times. Ufa was a closed city—industry, forestry, weapons manufacturing. It didn't appear on maps and was an extremely difficult place for which to get a visa. And so my parents, although they never receded from my imagination or my affection, occupied dusty corners of my days.

I heard the whistle of another engine approaching the station and I dipped into my bag to take a quick look at his photograph.

The crowd from the Moscow train surged past. I felt momentarily like a upstream fish, flapping from side to side, waving my father's hat in the air. Rudi did not show.

Alone and worried, I began to think I had slipped across a tiny line in my life. I was thirty-one years old, the author of two miscarriages. I still spent much of my time imagining my children at the ages they could have been. And now, with this young Tatar boy, I was saddled with the responsibility of being a parent without any of its joys—I fretted about whether something unfortunate had happened to him en route, if he'd lost our address, if he would have the wherewithal to find the tram, if he'd even arrive at all.

I left the station, cursing him, and returned to the heart of the city. I adored our crumbling room in the communal apartments along the Fontanka River. The walls were peeling. The corridors smelled of paint and cabbage. The window frames were rotted. And yet the place gladdened me. The ceilings were high and cornices were molded in the corners. The wood was dark and secretive, the door was intricately carved, and in summer the light streamed through the windows. I could hear the canal water when boats went by, waves splashing against the embankments.

For hours I sat at the window, watching the street. Finally Iosif came home, tie askew. He looked at me wearily.

He'll get here, he said.

Iosif ate his dinner, went off to sleep with a grunt, and I thought of myself then as a piece of china—a single saucer, perhaps, or a lid—decorative and useless.

I paced the room, twelve steps from window to back wall, six steps across. I had deadlines for poems to translate but had neither the energy nor the inclination to tackle them. I gazed at myself in the mirror obsessively, held my face at different angles. A hard feeling of dislocation came over me. We don't ever, I thought, grow sharper, clearer, or more durable. I had a feeling that any youth I once owned had dramatically fled from me. How piteous! How mournful! How ridiculous! I pinched my cheeks for color, pulled on my coat, and descended the rank stairwell, wandered the courtyard, hearing noises from neighboring apartments, laughter, anger, a stray piano note.

It was white nights, the pale blue of midnight, no moon, no stars, just a few clouds still straggling along. My father had once written to me saying that the stars were deeper than their darkness, and I stayed out for an hour pondering that line when a figure finally broke the shadow of the archway.

Rudi had not turned walking into an art at all. Instead he was slumped and his shoulders looked rounded. In fact he might as well have stepped out of a cartoon, hauling a suitcase tied with string, his hair sticking out at angles beneath a corduroy hat. He was quite thin, which accentuated his cheekbones, but when I moved up close I noticed that his eyes were complicated and blue.

Where've you been? I asked.

I'm honored to meet you, he replied, his hand outstretched.

I waited for you all day.

Oh, he said.

He cocked his head, gazed at me with a sideways innocence, testing my resolve. I came in on the morning train, he said. You must have missed me in the station.

Didn't you see me holding the hat?

No.

I knew it was a lie, not even a good one, but I let it go. He hopped nervously from foot to foot, and I quizzed him on what he had done the rest of the day.

I went to the Hermitage, he said.

Why?

To look at the paintings. Your mother told me that to dance you have to be a painter too.

She did, did she?

Yes.

And what else did she say?

She said it's a good idea to be a musician also.

She didn't say that to be a dancer you have to get your timing right?

He shrugged.

Do you have a piano? he asked.

There was a hint of impishness at the edges of his eyes and I had to hold back a smile.

No, I said.

Just then another piano note wafted out from the fourth floor, and someone began to play Beethoven, quite beautifully. Rudi brightened, said perhaps he could meet the owner of the piano, convince them to let him practice.

I don't think so, I replied.

He took the stairs two at a time, even with his suitcase. In our room I sat him down at the table and made him eat his dinner cold.

Your cooking's better than your mother's, he said.

I joined him at the table, where he flicked another quick smile at me before he buried himself in the food once more.

So you want to be a dancer? I asked.

I want to dance better than I already do, he said.

He had a fleck of cabbage on his teeth, and he scratched it off with his thumbnail. He seemed so young and vital and naïve. His upturned smile made him look sad somehow, which he wasn't, not at all. The more I studied him the more I noticed his extraordinary eyes, huge, untamed, as if they were independent entities that just so happened to sit in his head, searching the apartment, scanning my record collection. He asked for some Bach, which I played low, and the music seemed to move through him as he ate.

You'll sleep on the couch, I said. You'll meet my husband in the morning. He'll be up early.

Rudi stood and yawned, stretched his arms, went to the couch, leaving the dirty dish on the table. My back was turned, but I caught sight of him in a mirror as he undressed to his undergarments. He slid onto the couch, pulled the blanket high.

I love it, he said.

What?

This city. I love it.

Why's that?

*Oh don't trust that Nevsky Prospect, it's all lies and dreams, it's not what it all seems!* he said, quoting Gogol, surprising me.

Then he lay back with his arms behind his head and exhaled, long and happily. I drank my wine quickly, then stupidly burst into tears for no reason at all, which embarrassed him, so he turned away.

I watched him sleep.

I thought then of my parents, the few times I had met them. They had been comical together, my father just a little taller than my mother and almost as narrow in the shoulders. He had a gray mustache, wore old-time shirts with cuff links, and his trousers always hovered above his ankles. His body had been ruined from all the years in the camps—in Siberia he had chopped off his toe with an ax to prevent gangrene, so he walked with a limp. Losing his toe had in fact saved my father—in the camp infirmary he met a doctor who was also a poet. They secretly shared lines from the old masters and, in return, the doctor made sure my father was kept alive. My father was well-known in the camps for his ability to hear a line of poetry and never forget it and, even after he was released, he could recall things that ordinarily would have whittled away. But his heart was weak from all the punishment, and his foot gave him tremendous trouble. Although a dreadful insomniac, he maintained a defiant cheerfulness, as if to say, *You have not broken me.* My mother, too, had retained her beauty through the years, her body still taut from years of ballet, her hair in a tight bun, eyes bright and lively. They had a remarkable regard for each other, my parents—even at their age they still held hands.

I looked at Rudi tossing on my couch, thinking that he was the secret now joining them together. And yet I didn't feel jealous. I suppose one finally learns, after much searching, that we really only belong to ourselves.

I was still awake when the white night integrated itself into the morning. My deadlines for the Institute of Translation still gnawed at me, three Spanish sestinas so complicated that I doubted I could arbitrate their elegance. After breakfast I took a tram and carted my self-pity to the countryside, to a place I had gone since I was a child. There was a peculiar spot where the river seemed to bend itself against the land—it was a trick of the eye but the water seemed to go uphill. A grassy bank was filled with wildflowers and a trio of willow trees bent down to the river. I have always liked the tactile feel of standing, fully clothed, in running water. I went in up to my thighs, then lay on the riverbank and let the sun dry me off. I shaped one of the poems and set it in order, the six incanted words working haphazardly for me: *faithful, dead, candle, silence, nighthawk,* and *radiance.* When I had achieved a modicum of success, I closed my notebooks and swam in my underwear.

In truth I was still attractive then, having taken on my mother's body, her dark hair, her fair skin, my father's pale eyes.

I stayed by the river until late and when I arrived home my friends were already gathered around the table by the window, chatting seriously in the guarded language we shared. This was the normal routine—Monday nights were generally spent in the company of scientists and linguists I'd been friendly with since university. The evenings weren't so much a *salon*—the word disturbs me, reeking as it does of the unmistakeably bourgeois—more a simple relief, all cigarettes and vodka, philosophy, invective and half words. Larissa was a professor of French. Sergei, a botanist. Nadia, a translator. Petr dabbled in the philosophy of science, ranting about Heisenberg and the inherent uncertainty of our lives—he was the sort of red-faced bore who could sometimes shore up an evening. I was vaguely in love with another Iosif, a tall blond-haired linguist who, when he got drunk, would switch to Greek. My husband didn't participate at all, staying late most nights at his university office.

I entered the room quietly and watched a small drama unfolding at the table. Rudi was listening to the conversation, chin on his hand, somewhat taken aback, as if he'd just been presented with a great amount of words to swallow. The discussion centered on a new play reviewed in *Pravda* to great acclaim for its portrayal of striking workers in pre-Revolutionary Hungary. The talk spun on the phrase "linguistic dualism," a term that had occurred quite often in recent reviews, though its meaning seemed nebulous to everyone but Petr. I pulled up a chair and joined the group. Rudi had opened a bottle of my husband's vodka and had poured for everyone at the table, including a glass for himself. He looked close to being drunk. At one stage he leaned and touched my hand and said: Great!

When the evening finished he spilled out into the night with my friends and came home three hours later—Iosif had already returned and gone to sleep—saying, Leningrad Leningrad Leningrad!

He started dancing and looked as if he was checking the span of his wings. I let him be, moving around him to clean the dishes. Before I went to bed he shouted at the top of his voice: Thank you, Yulia Sergeevna!

It was the first time I ever remembered being called after my father, since I had always used the patronymic of my grandfather. I climbed beneath the covers and turned away from Iosif, my heart beating. My father's visage swam in front of my eyes and, in my fitful sleep, an idea for the last line of the sestina resurfaced. The next morning the other two sestinas came to life so effortlessly that their underlying politics—the poet was a Marxist from Bilbao—seemed a significant accident. I put them in an envelope and brought them to the institute, where money was awaiting me. I bought some Turkish coffee and returned home, where Rudi was waiting, despondent. His first day of dancing had not gone well. He drank three coffees and went outside to the courtyard—from above, looking down, I watched him practice around the ironwork fencing.

All that week Rudi auditioned at the school and at night he wandered the city, sometimes coming back as late as three in the morning—it was white nights after all, nobody slept—talking about the beautiful palaces, or a vendor he had met outside the Kirov, or a guard who had swung a suspicious eye on him on Liteiny Prospect. I tried to warn him, but he shrugged me off.

I'm a country bumpkin, he said. They're not interested in me.

There was something unusual in the clipped way he talked, a curious cocktail of rural arrogance and sophisticated doubt.

At the very end of the week I was hanging laundry in the communal kitchen when I heard my name being called from below. Yulia! I looked out the small window to see him in the rear courtyard, perched high on the ironwork fence, balanced precariously.

I got it! he shouted. I'm in! I'm in!

He jumped from the fence and landed in a puddle and ran towards the stairwell.

Clean your shoes! I shouted down.

He grinned and wiped his shoes with the cuff of his shirt, ran up the stairs to hug me.

I found out later that he had talked his way into the Leningrad Choreographic as much as he had danced. His level was still just high average, but they liked his fire and intuition. He was much older than most students, but the birth rate had dropped so significantly during the war that they were willing to audition dancers his age, even give them scholarships. He was to stay in a dorm with mostly eleven- and twelve-year-olds, which horrified him, and he pleaded with me to let him come along to my Monday evening gatherings. When I said yes, he took my hand and kissed it—he was, it seemed, already learning Leningrad.

After two weeks he had packed his case and was gone to the school dorms.

Iosif made love to me the evening Rudi left, and afterwards he padded across to the couch where he lit a cigarette and said, without turning in my direction: He's a little shit, isn't he?

All at once it felt as if my mother and father were surrounding me, and I turned to the pillow, said nothing.

It was almost three months before Rudi arrived back. He strolled in with RosaMaria, a girl from Chile. She was the sort of beauty who took the oxygen from the air. She wasn't consumed by her own attractiveness but managed instead to carry it like an afterthought. Her father was the editor of a newspaper in Santiago, and she was at the Leningrad Choreographic to learn dance. Rudi, perhaps by virtue of being with her, looked different already. He was wearing a long army coat and boots to his knees, and his hair had grown longer.

RosaMaria laid a guitar case in the corner and took a seat in the background while Rudi sat at the table, listening, hunched over a small glass of vodka. Larissa, Petr, Sergei, Nadia and I were all quite drunk and deep into an interminable debate about Heidegger, who had suggested that life becomes authentic when lived in the presence of death. For me the debate seemed to relate ultimately to our lives under Stalin, but I also couldn't help thinking of my father, who had lived his life in the shadow not only of his own death but of his former history too. I flicked a look at Rudi. He yawned and filled his glass again with a sort of theater, holding the bottle high in the air, so there was a deep splash against the side of the glass.

Petr turned and said: So then, you, young man, what do you think is authentic and inauthentic?

Rudi slurped his vodka. Petr pulled the bottle away and held it close to his chest. Around the table there was a quick blur of laughter. It was a delightful little showdown between a tired middle-aged man and a boy. I figured that Rudi would never be able to handle Petr, but he picked up two spoons, rose quickly, pushed his way past the rubber plants to the door, beckoned us all to follow. The simple strangeness of his action silenced us, although RosaMaria smiled as if she knew what was in store.

Rudi made his way down the corridor to the bathroom and sat down in the empty bathtub.

This, he said, is authentic.

He began to bash the spoons against the porcelain, reaching different notes where the bath curved, with longer, hollower notes at the base of the tub, higher notes where the spoons met the rim. The taps rang high metallic twangs, and then he reached to hit the spoons against the wall. He held his face perfectly serious, banging out a series of sounds that had no form or rhythm at all. It was pure circus.

Johann Sebastian Bach! he said.

He stopped and we launched into a drunken round of applause. Petr was momentarily shell-shocked but rescued himself admirably— instead of stalking away, he went to the bathtub, bottle in hand, poured a long measure of vodka down Rudi's throat.

Together they finished the bottle, and then Petr held it above Rudi's head and said: May you have as many troubles as there are drops left in this bottle.

I do not wish to get wet, laughed Rudi.

The evening grew wilder and drunker. We ate bread with horse-radish sauce—it was all we could find—until a friend of Petr's arrived with three hard-boiled eggs to share. RosaMaria took her guitar from its case and sang Spanish songs in a dialect I didn't entirely recognize. Rudi went around the room with a metal saucepan, and he hammered on the woodwork, the tiles, the floor, the sink, until the neighbors began complaining.

Just at that moment Iosif came home. I met him at the door, shouted: Let's dance! He shoved me away and I slammed into the wall. The room went silent.

Iosif yelled: Get the fuck out of here! Everyone! Get the fuck out!

My friends looked at me and began to stub out their cigarettes in the ashtrays in slow motion, not quite sure what to do. Out! shouted Iosif. He grabbed Rudi by the collar and dragged him into the corridor. Rudi was astounded, his eyes wide. But RosaMaria stood in front of my husband and—simply by keeping her eyes locked on his—she made him stare at the floor. Finally Iosif went downstairs to the courtyard, to smoke, chagrined.

The night began again. I was aware that something extraordinary had just happened, that RosaMaria had shifted a small axis in my life, if only temporarily, and I gave her a silent inner curtsy.

She returned the next evening, accompanied by Rudi. He made himself immediately at home, talking animatedly about a myth he had read in his world literature class that day. It had to do with the Indian god, Shiva, who had danced within a circle of fire. He and RosaMaria were arguing about whether the act of dance was one of construction or destruction, whether if by dancing you made a work of art or you broke it down. Rudi maintained that you built a dance from the bottom up, while RosaMaria believed that the dance was there to be torn apart, that each move was an entry into the dance until it lay all around in separate, splendid parts. I watched them, not so much with regret but as a mirror unto myself and Iosif ten years previously, remembering how we once had talked of physics and language in the same dark and concentrated manner. They held court together until Larissa came over and the talk veered off into science, the theory of uncertainty again, which clearly annoyed the young dancers.

When Iosif returned he actually sat at the table with everyone, and didn't say a word, all polite resignation. He looked closely at

RosaMaria, her dark hair, her wide smile, but then he pulled a chair next to me, even lit my cigarette. Iosif pronounced Chile to be his favorite country even though he had never been, and I sat pondering how rich I would be if every piece of horseshit that came from my husband's mouth could be turned into a sliver of gold.

RosaMaria began visiting more and more, even without Rudi. I was aware that she was probably being watched, given that she was a foreigner. There was an intermittent clicking on my telephone. We turned the music loud in case the place was bugged, but really there was nothing extraordinary about our conversations anyway. She told me about Santiago, for which she was dreadfully homesick. I had, years before, translated some Chilean poetry and had imagined doorways, lean dogs, vendors of saints, but the country she talked of was all cafés, jazz clubs, long cigarettes. She spoke as if there were a tambourine in her throat. She loved dancing for the act of it rather than the art and so she was miserable at the school, where she felt that a rigidity was being forced into her. She had to wear skirts all the time and said that she had brought a pair of tight orange pants from Santiago—the notion of it made me laugh—and she was itching to wear them just once. The only person who kept her sane, she said, was Rudi, simply because he allowed himself to be Rudi. He was in constant trouble in school, especially with Shelkov, the school director. He refused to cut his hair, fought in rehearsals, put pepper in the dance belts of rivals. By all accounts he excelled in the classes he liked—literature, history of art, music—but he detested the sciences and anything else that didn't suit his rhythm. He had stolen stage makeup, eyeshadow and a glaring rouge, and had worn it around his dorm. She said he had no respect for the other dancers but he adored his teacher, Aleksandr Pushkin, who had taken him under his tutelage. RosaMaria mentioned rumors that others had seen Rudi late at night, walking near Ekaterina Square, where perverted men were rumored to meet, a notion that didn't seem to bother her, which surprised me, since it had seemed they were wearing each other like outfits.

We're not in love, she told me one afternoon.

You're not?

She raised her eyebrows, making me feel like I was twenty years old, not her.

Of course not, she said.

With RosaMaria I began to feel that I had once again opened myself to the world. We brewed coffee late into the night. She tutored me in Chilean dialects and wrote out old ballads, which I translated—she knew more love songs than anyone I'd ever met. Through her connections I managed to get my hands on a new gramophone. I read whatever I could find, Gorky, Pushkin, Lermentov, Mayakovsky, Mao, a Theodore Dreiser novel, Mitchel Wilson, Dante's *Inferno*, Chekhov, even reread Marx, of whom I was very fond. I took on some more work with the institute and went on long walks with RosaMaria.

Every few months I sent my traditional package to my parents, including a letter to tell them that Rudi was doing just fine, progressing in his classes, that he had found a teacher who understood him.

My father replied, in the simple code we used, that the fruitcake hadn't nearly as many raisins as usual, meaning of course that the letter was scant. He said that Ufa was gray under gray under yet more gray, and that he and my mother would desperately like to make a trip away from the city.

He wondered if I could pull any strings—Saint Petersburg, he wrote, had always been famous for its puppetry.

❖

You see him on Rossi Street with his boots high on his calves and his long red scarf trailing the ground behind him; you see him with his collar turned up, his hands deep in his pockets, his shoes tipped with metal so that they raise a spark; you see how he stands in the canteen line with his head slightly angled as if he is dealing with a wound; you see him receive an extra ladle of soup from the canteen woman with the black hairnet; you see him lean over the counter and touch her hand, whispering, making her laugh; you see, when he lifts the flap of his shirt to clean his spoon, that his stomach has flattened and tightened; you see him eat quickly and wipe a rough hand across his mouth; you see the canteen woman watching him as if she has found her own long-lost son.

You see him in the attic studio, in the morning light, earlier than anyone else, intuiting a move that has taken you three days to learn; you see him jostling in the corridors wearing your brand-new leggings and when you confront him he says, *Screw a horse*; you see him without his modesty shorts; you see him preening; you see him elbowing forward to front and center, where he can properly look in the mirror; you see him counting impatiently as he watches others moving through their combinations; you see him drop a partner because she is a shade too slow and he doesn't help her up, though she is crying and her wrist might be sprained, and he goes to the high window to yell *Fuck!* out over Theater Street; you see him through the winter and the summer and each time he appears larger to you and you are at a loss to explain what is happening.

You see him dye his white slippers black and sew on buttons so that they look different to everybody else's; you see him take your dance belt, but you don't say a word until he returns it filthy, and you ask him to wash it but he tells you to go take a shit and put your face in it; you see him the next day and tell him you want the belt washed and he says, *You miserable Jewboy*; you see him walk away chuckling; you see him when he passes you on the street without even moving his eyes in your direction and you think maybe he is a little mad or lonely or lost, and then suddenly he is dashing across the avenue towards the Chilean girl, who has opened her arms to him, and within seconds they are running along the street together; you see them go, you feel empty, foiled, until you decide you will open up to him, you will become his friend, and so you join him in the canteen but he says he is busy, he has something important to do, and immediately goes to the woman behind the counter; you see him chat and laugh with her and you sit there glaring, wanting to ask him if he ever met anyone he likes better than himself, but you already know the answer so you do not ask.

You see him taken under Aleksandr Pushkin's wing; you see him reading constantly because Pushkin has told him that to be a great dancer he must know the great stories and so, in the courtyard, he bends over Gogol, Joyce, Dostoyevsky; you see him curl into the pages and you think that he has somehow become part of the book, and you think that whenever you read that book in the future you will be reading him.

You see him and ignore him but somehow begin to think of him even more; you see him tear a ligament and you delight in the news but then you watch him dance and you wonder if your hatred helped heal his ankle; you see him before class practice Kitri's variation, his feet in half high-pointe, everyone staring in amazement, he is dancing a woman's role and even the girls wait around to watch; you see him studying the original Pepitas, getting to know them inside out so he can show you any combination with his hands, the hands themselves a complicated ballet, tough and fluid; you see him respond to Pushkin with silence and respect, you even hear him call Pushkin by the familiar name of Sasha; you see him haul the other students short when they miss a step and you see the way he accepts their stares, their shouts, their small hatreds; you see him stride into the office and call the director a fool and you see him step away from the outrage smiling; later you see him weeping uncontrollably for he is sure he will be sent home and later again you see him doing a handstand outside the director's office, an upside-down grin on his face, until Pushkin emerges, having saved him once again from expulsion.

You see him refuse the Komsomol because it interferes with his training, something nobody has ever done before, and he is brought before the committee, where he leans across the table to say, *Excuse me, comrades, but what exactly is political naïveté?*; you see him nod and apologize, move away down the corridor, cackling to himself, never to attend the meetings anyway; you see him in the library copying the musical scores, the dance notations, his shirt splattered with ink; you see him rushing to the master's rehearsal simply to watch and afterwards he moves his body to the memory of the dance; you see him doing what you used to do; you see him doing it better than yourself and then you see that he does not need to do it at all because it has become him; you see him lurking in the wings at the Kirov; you see the older dancers beckon to him; you see him feigning no emotion at the bulletin board when he is given the role you always wanted.

You see him everywhere, on the footbridge over the canal, on the benches in the Conservatory park, on Gorky embankment near the White Palace, in the sun outside the old Kazan Cathedral, on the grass of the Summer Gardens; you see his black beret, his dark suit, his white shirt, no tie, and he haunts you, you cannot shake him; you see him walking with Pushkin's wife, Xenia; you see the way she looks at him, you are sure she is in love with him, you have heard rumors, but you're convinced that it's impossible; you see Pushkin himself say he might one day go straight to the Kirov as a soloist, even though you know—you know!—you are a better dancer, and you wonder where you went wrong, when it was that you slipped, because your technique is better, you are more accomplished, more sophisticated, you have a better line, your dance is cleaner, you know there's something missing, you're not sure what it is, you are scared and ashamed and you hate when people say his name; and then one day you see him— in class, in the hallway, in the canteen, in the fifth-floor rehearsal rooms, it doesn't matter—and you believe you are seeing yourself, you want to move but you can't, your feet are nailed to the floor, the heat of the day rises through you, it will not stop, and you think you have stepped into an acid bath, the liquid is above you, below you, around you, inside you, burning, until he moves away and the acid is gone, you stand alone and you look down and realize how much of yourself has disappeared.

⁂

Respected Comrade,

In response to your directive of last Thursday it must be said that indeed the behavior of the young man leaves a lot to be desired, but the nature of his talent is such that the rigidity of the program suggested might dampen his abilities, which are clearly prodigious if undisciplined. He hardly knows what he does and yet he strives not only to know but to achieve beyond what he knows. His sporadic nature is still malleable. He is after all only eighteen years old. I hereby formally suggest that he be allowed to switch residencies so that he come live with Xenia and me in the courtyard residence, at least in the short-term, whereupon the discipline he so sorely lacks will become his through a calculated osmosis.

As always, with great respect,

*A. Pushkin*

⁂

Shortly after getting my father's letter, I began to go down to the Big House on Liteiny Prospect to see about the feasibility of getting a reprieve for his exile. My mother could have visited Leningrad by herself, but she refused to do so—she would have felt one-footed without him. *Yulia*, she wrote, *I will bide my time.* In the past I had tentatively inquired about the process of getting them out of Ufa, but it had been fruitless, yet now with the thaw firmly in place the possibility seemed stronger. I pondered that they wanted to spend time with Rudi more than with me, but it hardly mattered—the notion of a visit from them set my spirit echoing.

At the Big House there were gray faces at the partitions. The wooden counters were scratched and scored where people had leaned too heavily with their pens. The eyes of the guards were glassy as they fingered their rifles. I found out exactly which forms my father should fill in, what he should say, how he should present his case, and sent letters to him with all the exact instructions. Months passed, nothing happened. I knew my actions were dangerous, perhaps more perilous than anything I'd ever done—it felt as if I were hanging my heart outside my body, hardly clever. I wondered if I'd compromised everyone around me, even Iosif who, despite all, had even more to lose than I.

RosaMaria said that her own father, influential in Communist circles in Santiago, might be able to do something, but I thought it would be far wiser for her to remain outside the fray. It was quite possible that the bureaucracy would catch up on my history, carbon copies revealing truths far different from the originals, as in some dark European novel.

But almost nine months later—while I was doing a translation of a Spanish poem for the State Publishing House—I received a telegram:

THURSDAY. FINLANDIA STATION 10:00 A.M.

I cleaned the room from floor to ceiling and bought whatever provisions I could find. Iosif made space by saying nothing.

When I arrived at the station they were sitting on the bench underneath the giant clock, having come in on an earlier train. At their feet was a giant wooden trunk with a crude lacquer pattern. The trunk was covered with labels, though most of the lettering had been scratched out. My father wore his hat, of course. My mother was in an old coat with a fur-lined collar. She was sleeping with her head against his shoulder, her mouth slightly open. My father touched the inside of her wrist, just beneath the sleeve, to waken her. She opened her eyes suddenly, shook her head. I went to hold her, and she felt unusually brittle.

My father rose from the bench, spread his arms wide and said in a loud voice: Look, I have been rehabilitated! Then he lowered his tone as if in conspiracy and added: Well, for three months anyway.

I scanned the station for guards, but it was empty. Mother shushed him, but he leaned towards her and said enigmatically: Until morning comes, we are not yet free of journeys.

My mother said: You and your poetry.

He grinned and pointed to the suitcase. Yulia, my darling, he said, carry us.

On the trolley bus he didn't want to sit. Instead he clung to the pole with one hand and to his cane with the other. He grimaced as the bus moved, but his eyes darted around. Most of the time he seemed wounded—his city was largely lost after the Blockade and the rebuilding after the war—but every now and then he shut his eyes as if he were closing his whole self to a memory, and once he quietly whispered: Petersburg. His smile flickered, moving like a wavelength to my mother and then to me, so that his memory had a sort of domino effect.

Just off Nevsky the wire jumped from the trolley pole, stopping the bus in the street. My father went to the door to rejiggle the wire back into place, but the buses had been redesigned and he was standing in the wrong place, utterly lost. The conductor glared at him. The other passengers turned around, and I saw my father's face flush with fear.

My mother beckoned him to sit down. He put his hand on hers and remained silent the rest of the journey.

Iosif greeted my parents expansively. My mother held his shoulders and examined him. She had only ever seen photographs. Iosif blushed and hurried to open a bottle of vodka. His toast was long and formal. In the room my mother touched things, the butter dish, my husband's Party bulletins, the books I had half-translated. We had a fine meal together and afterwards my mother went down the corridor to the bathroom, ran the hot water tap, took a bath, while Iosif excused himself to the university.

When she returned my mother said: He's not as tall as I had imagined.

My father stood at the window and said: Ah, the Fontanka.

By mid-afternoon my mother had fallen asleep at the table. I managed to move her to the couch. My father propped up her head with his overcoat. He stroked her hair while she slept, and even in his slight frame he seemed to surround her with his generosity. Soon he was sleeping also, but fitfully.

Early in the evening Mother woke to prepare for a visit from Rudi. She brushed her hair and put on a dress that smelled as if it had been hanging in a wardrobe too long. Father took a long walk down to Nevsky, desperately wanting a cigar, only to find that the stalls were closed, but a neighbor gave me two, and my father sniffed the length of them, quoted some line from a Lithuanian poet about the deep mercy of strangers.

Rudi arrived late, of course. He was without RosaMaria. He wore a double-breasted suit and a thin black tie, the first I'd ever seen on him. He had wrapped a single lilac in notebook paper, and he presented it to my mother as he kissed her. She beamed and told him that he'd already grown beyond what she could have dreamed.

For the next hour they were like two cogs clicking together. She listened and he talked rapid-fire, endlessly, in a perfect pitch and rhythm—the slope of the school's floor, the sweat stains on the gymnasium barre, the rumor of a certain move once done by Nijinsky, the books he was reading—Dostoyevsky, Byron, Shelley—and how he had switched dormitories to live with the Pushkins. He said: I am hanging in the air longer, you know!

My mother seemed lost. Rudi placed his hand on my her trembling fingers for a moment. The problem was that Rudi had learned too much and he wanted to tell her everything. The old teacher was being taught, and she was confused by it. She nodded and pursed her lips, tried to interrupt, but he was unstoppable: the routine for his classes, the Dutch masters at the Hermitage, a step that Pushkin wanted him to learn, a fight with the director, his fondness for Rachmaninov, rehearsals he had seen at the Kirov, nights at the Gorky theater. He seldom slept, he said, needing only four hours a night, and the rest of the day was packed with learning.

To control her trembling hand my mother twirled her wedding ring and it struck me how thin she had become, the ring slipping easily along her finger. She seemed extraordinarily tired but she kept repeating: That's right, dear boy, that's right.

Finally my father had a quiet word in her ear and she put her face to his shoulder, stood, tottered a little, apologized, said she had to rest. She kissed Rudi on the cheek, and he stood there, silent.

You've done well, my father said to him. You've made her proud.

But at the door Rudi fingered his jacket and asked: What did I do wrong, Yulia?

Nothing. She's tired. She's been traveling for days.

I just wanted to talk.

Come back tomorrow, Rudi, I said.

I have classes tomorrow.

The next day then.

But he wasn't back the next day, or the next week. I had set up a screen to block off a corner of the room, put down the mattress for my parents, while Iosif and I slept on the floor. They talked about trying to find a room for themselves, somewhere to live, perhaps in the suburbs, the sleeping quarters, but first they had to sort out their residence permit, their pension papers and State bonds. Their visas were valid for only three months. Mother grew more and more listless, and Father was unable to deal with the bureaucracy, so it was I who tried to handle the logistics. Each day when I came home my mother was on the couch, head slumped against a pillow, while my father limped restlessly from window to window.

Somehow he had acquired a map of Leningrad, a difficult thing to find; maybe he'd bargained for it in a market, or run into some old friends somewhere. It was best not to ask. At night he spread out the map on the kitchen table and occupied his time by identifying street names that had changed.

Look, he said to nobody in particular, Ship Street has become Red Street, how strange.

He marked all the changes, the post-Revolutionary places that had lost their history. English Embankment was now Red Fleet Embankment, Swimming Pool Street was renamed after the poet Nekrasov. Ascension Street naturally had been changed, along with Resurrection Street, where an Orthodox church had been converted into a department store. Small Czar's Village had become Children's Village. Policeman's Avenue was now the People's Avenue. Millionaire Street was gone. Christmas Street had been transformed into Soviet Street, which he found monstrous. Other lost names struck him as a great injury—Street of Little Mosses, Catherine's Canal, Nicholas Street, Coachman Street, Miracle Avenue, Nightingale Street, Savior Street, Five Corners Street, Foundry Avenue, Meat Traders Alley, Big Craftsman Yard, Counterfeiters Lane. My father's love of poetry made him find more than a political implication in the renaming.

One day they'll name a street after the renamers, he said.

I whispered that he should be careful of what he said, to whom, and certainly when he said it.

I'm old enough now to say whatever I want.

It wasn't that he had lost faith in his past, but it had become unrecognizable to him, as if he had expected to find the logic of his boyhood but found something else entirely. The old names seemed coded into his tongue and would never leave. His difficulty was that he was unable to move with the change, yet his good fortune was that he hadn't been punished again for such stasis.

He gave up his obsession with the map when he saw that my mother was growing sicker. She refused to acknowledge that she was ill, but we took her to the hospital anyway, late at night in a taxi. The doctors examined her gently—my mother, by her nature, commanded that sort of respect—but they could find nothing wrong, even after a series of blood tests. She insisted there was something in the air that was making her feel drowsy.

Take me back, she said.

In the room everything felt tight, hampered, lifeless. Iosif disgusted me with his vague politeness. We hardly talked to each other at all anymore. For a number of years we had insulated ourselves from each other, and we had once even tried to think up a Russian word for *privacy* since it existed in the other languages I had studied. To some extent it existed for Iosif as a notion in physics, an unknowable place, but now it seemed that all the places we operated in were themselves unknowable. When I unpacked the few belongings from my mother's hospital bag I felt, in a strange way, that I was unpacking my husband from my life also.

The only tangible link to an immediate past for my parents was Rudi—*Our dear Rudik,* my mother would say—but he had disappeared for quite a while, despite the fact that I had left notes for him at the Leningrad Choreographic, pleading that he come visit.

Eventually he did come around to announce that he was about to perform at a showcase in school. He stood stately in the center of the room, feet together, and it struck me that his body had now accepted dance as its only strategy.

I will be performing for just a few minutes, he said, but I'd like to show you what I've learned.

The idea of it brought the color back into my mother's cheeks. She was astounded by his choice of dance, some terribly difficult male variation from a ballet based on *Notre-Dame de Paris*. He claimed that he had been practicing it with Pushkin and that he would be able to perform it quite easily.

But you're too young, you can't do a role like that, my mother said.

He grinned and said: Come watch me.

I had the Victor Hugo book on my shelf, and in the days leading up to the dance my father read it to my mother. His was a beautiful sonorous voice and he captured nuances in the text that surprised me. On the morning of the concert my mother plucked a special dress from the suitcase and spent hours adjusting it, then stood in front of the mirror with an elderly radiance.

My father put on a tie and a black suit. What remained of his hair had been combed back and I noticed that he had put the second cigar in the breast pocket of his jacket. He wanted to take a droisky for old time's sake and could hardly believe that the horses and carriages were long gone. Instead we got on the tram, and my father gave my mother's hand a secretive squeeze as we passed the all-weather KGB command post.

The showcase was in the Leningrad Choreographic, but we stopped for awhile outside the Kirov, its fierce elegance.

Anna, said my father. Aren't we beautiful?

Yes, she said.

Two old fools.

Beautiful or fools?

Both, he said.

We were seated in an upper balcony that ringed the gymnasium. Most of the other spectators were teachers and students—they wore tights, sweaters, leg warmers. We were horrifically overdressed. My mother sat erect in a straight-backed chair. RosaMaria joined us and introduced herself to my mother in her broken Russian. They immediately conspired with each other, my mother and RosaMaria, whispering and smiling—it was as if they were parts of the same creature, living in different decades but linked through some odd emotional chain. My mother laid her hand on RosaMaria's arm as the showcase progressed. The applause was polite for most of the students, who seemed to me accomplished and polished, if without spirit. Rudi was second last. When he came out he looked up to the balcony and my mother's frame straightened even further.

There were mutterings around the room. He wore a belt cinched very tightly at the waist. His hair had been carefully snipped and combed, short at the back but long at the front, falling over his eyes.

Of course he danced perfectly, light and quick, pliant, his line controlled and composed, but more than that he was using something beyond his body—not just his face, his fingers, his long neck, his hips, but something intangible, beyond thought, some kinetic fury and spirit—and I felt a little hatred for him when the applause rang out.

It was RosaMaria who stood up first, followed by my mother and my father, who nudged me. Beneath us Rudi bowed and kept on bowing even through the appearance of the next dancer, who stood angrily to the side. At last Rudi swept his arm out and left the floor at a high trot. He was met by a small handsome bald man who clapped him on the back. My mother whispered to me: That's Pushkin, he's doing a wonderful job with Rudik.

To which my father said: You're Anna Vasileva and you did a wonderful job with Rudik too.

We left into the cool spring night. The city was quiet. Rudi was waiting outside, and we huddled together, congratulating him. His body odor was severe, but still I wanted to draw closer and inhale him, his energy. He leaned over my mother and asked her how he had done. She seemed to hesitate a moment but said: You were marvelous.

On the plié I think I was going too deep, he said.

Then he touched my father's shoulder in a manly gesture and was gone down the street with RosaMaria, holding hands.

Who would have thought? said my father.

He had lit his last cigar and was puffing the smoke towards the sky. My mother watched Rudi disappear. You know, she whispered, his legs do look longer.

That's easy, said my father.

He smiled and went, on his good foot, to his toes.

Just then Pushkin emerged from the studios. He wore a tan overcoat and tie. He was accompanied by his wife, Xenia, a woman I had seen before on the streets of Leningrad. It was impossible to ignore her, the depth of her beauty, her blond hair, the magnificence of her clothes, the way she seemed lit from the inside. They turned to us briefly and waved, and I thought what curious mirrors they were in the world: my parents, teachers of the boy, looking at the Pushkins, teachers of the man, and the man himself already gone down the street.

My mother said to the Pushkins with great formality: Good evening. May I extend my congratulations.

Pushkin turned: Rudi has often talked about you.

She smiled and said: My deepest thanks.

A month later my mother was dead. In my room she suffered a brain hemorrhage, which took her in her sleep. I woke up to see my father sitting quietly by her body, his hand at the back of her hair. I expected him to weep, but he calmly said that she was gone, would I please make arrangements to have her buried in Piskarovskoye Cemetery. Then he closed his eyes and tightened his grip on her hair and whispered her name over and over until it sounded like a prayer or a song, gently sung. Later that day, as was old custom, he spread her body out on the table and washed her. He used an old shirt of his, saying that it would be his final gesture to sentimentality. She looked terribly emaciated. He dipped the collar of his shirt in warm soapy water and bathed her neck and smoothed the cloth along her collarbone. With the sleeve he wiped her arm and with the body of the shirt he washed her small wizened breasts. It was as if he wanted her to wear the shirt in some way, to carry it with her on whatever journey she was on. He covered her with a sheet, and only then did I see my father cry, deeply, inconsolably.

He had left the water tap dripping, and there was a gurgling from the pipes as if the sadness was in the throat of the building. I went outside and left him alone. The air was hard and raw. By the time I came back he had dressed her and put traditional coins on her eyes.

It was noticeably sunny the day we buried her. At Piskarovskoye we were given a plot in a copse of trees not far from the mounds of those who had died during the Blockade. Light slanted through the trees, midges rose from the bushes, small birds darned the air with their wings. There was little or no ceremony. It cost us three hundred rubles to bribe for the plot and another hundred for the ground to be dug. Nearby a man on a tractor was cutting the grass on the mass graves, beautifully tended to, ringed with red roses. He respectfully turned his engine off and waited.

My father held his hat to his chest, and I noticed the little graph of sweat stains that appeared inside the rim. How many years had he worn that one hat and how many times had she put it on his head? He shifted, coughed and said he didn't feel in the mood for words but that, even in her leaving, my mother had left many signs that she had been here.

May her influence enter the air, he said.

With this he coughed a second time and gave the ground a little grimace, turned his face away.

In a distant corner, through the trees, I caught a glimpse of a Black ZIL limousine pulling up in the graveyard, flanked by a fleet of black cars. We were startled a moment, thinking there might be some important visitor, but then the cars pulled away to the far end of the graveyard and we were glad to be left alone.

Rudi and RosaMaria stood next to each other. At first Rudi held his lower teeth against his upper lip. I wanted to berate him, to slap him, to jog a tear from him, but eventually, and for no particular reason, he broke down and began to weep.

My father, for his part, threw a handful of dirt on the coffin.

When we turned to leave the small forest, I noticed that the man on the tractor had fallen asleep, but he had taken his hat off and it sat lightly in his lap, and I thought that my mother would have enjoyed such a moment.

Later that day we took my father to the train station.

I am going home to Ufa, he said.

There was irony of course in the way he said *home*, but it was where he had survived most of his years with her and there was an eloquence, if not a practicality, to his return. Iosif came with us to Finlandia Station. I asked for a moment alone with my father. I carried his suitcase through the crowd. Light came in shafts through the windows, falling on the grayness below. We stopped by a train window. An old woman in a headscarf glared at us. My father held me tight and whispered in my ear that I should be proud of myself, that I should do what pleased me, within reason of course. He touched my cheek and I sniffled stupidly.

Great billows of steam were suspended above the station, hanging there as they have always hung, as if to say that most of us spend our lives breathing in our breathed-out breath.

❈

Music sheets, Bach and Schumann. Piano lesson, Mali Opera. Talk with Shelkov re military conscription. Special salts for bathing feet. Postcard for Father's birthday. Scrounge portable radio. Shorten lunchtime for barre work on extension. Take empty room. Sasha: *Perfection is the duty*. Work work work. In difficulty is ecstasy.

*Every day I count wasted in which there has been no dancing.* Nietzsche. Yes! Elocution lesson. Visa for Moscow. Tell Shelkov to eat shit or to eat more shit than he already does, bring him a bucket and a spoon. Better still, ignore him completely, the ultimate victory. Shoes. Permit. Clothes cleaned for conservatory concert. The boy on the bus. Vigilance.

Sleep less. Morning routine. Take twice as long with each grand battement to build control and strength. Stand long in relevé for strength. Nine or ten on pirouette. Chaboukiani, I kiss your feet! Do cabrioles face-on to the mirror rather than sideways. Sasha: *Live inside the dance*. Out-think. Out-maneuver. Out-learn. Even the wig should be alive!

Triple assembles tours. Work on phrasing. The others like to take a bite to see if I am gold or brass. Let them. They will break their teeth either way. *L'Après-midi d'un faune.* Estrade Guerra says that Nijinsky's ballon was like seeing a hare wounded by the huntsman's shot, rising before the fall. Nijinsky said it is not difficult to stay in the air, you just have to pause a little while up there. Ha! Anna was correct after all.

Sasha says much of the ballon came from the strength in Nijinsky's back. Exercise: walk on hands to strengthen back muscles. Richter tickets. Boy at the Hermitage said he had contacts in the conservatory. Rumors about Xenia, but if you don't try everything your life is wasted. Find name of Ukrainian poet who said that nothing will ever be good until you learn to drink champagne from your boots!

Pas de trois from *Guyane* with torches, second act pas de deux from *Swan Lake*, *Corsaire* duet with Sizova. Read Byron for texture. Ask RosaMaria to patch tights. Cut fingernails to stop scratching Masha while lifting. Tell P. to stop counting out the phrases, her lips move when she dances. The pas de deux is a conversation not a fucking monologue. Forget all this talk of F. as a rival. Bullshit. Become a toilet bowl and you will see better movement. Demand five dozen pairs of shoes and maybe you will get a dozen, use the best maker, the Georgian woman with the lisp. Haircut: slant parting? Gorky says that life will never be quite so bad that the desire for something better will ever be extinguished in men. Yes.

Cloth hat left in the changing room. Letter from Bashkirian Ministry. Nineteenth birthday party. *Eugene Onegin.* Tchaikovsky score. In *Corsaire* achieve Byron's romanticism and defiance. Sasha: *The greatest artists are born to enrich their art, not themselves.* Toothbrush. Honey for tea.

Perform as if things have to be said all over again. Sasha says the known way leads us to the unknown. Also, it is the unknown way that will finally lead us back to what is known. *You are a dancer for only a part of your life. The rest of the time you are walking around, thinking about it!* Those assigned to watch me—ignore them and you will lose an eye, but bow to them and they will strike you blind.

Extra practice in Room 17. Fix radio and put in order for telephone. Degas exhibition—RosaMaria said he wakens the sleep in her. Photographs. Destroy Xenia's letters.

❋

There is a story my husband used to tell Rudi. He recounted it over and over, after classes, when they were both exhausted and we would sit, all three of us, by the fireplace in our courtyard apartment. Once or twice Rudi played the piano softly while Sasha talked. The story shifted and changed, but Sasha enjoyed the telling and retelling of it and Rudi, for his part, listened intently. Even long afterwards, when Rudi left our place for his own apartment—when Sasha and I were alone again—the story left its mark.

Dmitri Yachmennikov, my husband said, was a minor figure in the world of Leningrad ballet in the late nineteenth century. A thin little man, a patch of black hair on the dome of his head, given to eating shoots of asparagus, he was a choreographer in a hall north of Obvodnyi Canal. He worked closely with his brother Igor, who played the piano.

Together the brothers were kept alive by the good graces of the young dancers they worked with—at their door someone always left some bread so they never starved.

One late winter evening Dmitri's brother died, slumping face forward into the piano. Shortly after the funeral Dmitri went blind.

People said the double calamity was caused by the strong bond between the brothers—Dmitri had been shocked into blindness and nothing would ever heal him. He walked up and down the street from his house to the hall, seldom straying farther than the market for his bundles of asparagus.

Dmitri decided to continue his career in choreography since it was the only thing he knew. He returned to the hall, locked the door behind him. But he could no longer plot a dance—instead he crawled about on the floor on his hands and knees, feeling its texture, rubbing his hands over the grain of wood, sometimes even chafing his cheek against the boards. He brought in a number of local carpenters and quizzed them about the composition of the wood, the length and direction of the grain. Everyone thought him thoroughly mad.

He was seen walking home at night, the sprig of asparagus crooked in his mouth, feeling his way forward into the faintly lit doorway of his home.

On the anniversary of his brother's death, Dmitri opened up the doors of the hall and invited local dancers in for an audition, explained to them what he wanted. The dancers were curious at first—the thought of a blind man telling them how to move seemed preposterous—but some began auditioning anyway. Instead of using his brother's old piano Dmitri brought in a cellist and a violinist, and as they played, he sat in the front row. Finally he picked a group of dancers he wanted to work with. They rehearsed for several weeks, during which Dmitri said little, but then suddenly on a whim he started to scold them.

Without seeing them, he was able to tell that the timing in their pirouette was off, that a hip was not aligned with a shoulder, that a jump was at the wrong angle. The dancers were stunned—not so much because the choreographer was blind but by the fact that he was correct.

The show soon became a local success.

The story spread in the autumn of 1909, when an article

appeared in a local gazette. Dmitri was invited to larger halls within the community, but he refused. He fought off offers from factories, schools, and finally even a teacher from the Kirov who was perplexed by Dmitri's method. He did however organize one guest appearance for an aging dancer, Nadia Kutepova, whom his late brother had once adored. She came to the hall and performed a solo especially for Dmitri, with no audience present. On his insistence there was also no music in the hall. Outside a crowd waited to hear the result.

The pair came out after two hours, Dmitri's arm hooked through the crook of her elbow.

When asked by the crowd how the dance had gone, Kutepova pronounced that under Dmitri's tuition she had danced perfectly. He had given her direction to make every move exquisite and it was, she said, one of her finer performances.

For his part, Dmitri told the crowd that as Kutepova danced he had heard one of his brother's symphonies being played in the hall, that through her body the music had emerged, and that by the time she was finished he could almost hear every note his brother had ever created.

Dmitri Yachmennikov had been listening to the floorboards.

❖

It was a hot summer in Ufa, the city enveloped in smoke from the factories and ash blown in from the forest fires off the Belaya River. A thin film of soot lay on the benches in Lenin Park. I was finding it difficult to sit and breathe, so I finally plucked up the courage to spend the last of my money on the extravagance of the cinema.

Having not been there since Anna passed on, I thought I might be able to revisit her, twine a lock of her gray hair around my finger.

The Motherland cinema was located down Lenin Street, gone slightly to ruin, the beginnings of cracks in the magnificent facade, posters yellowing in their glass cases. Inside, fans on the ceiling were at full force in the heat. I hobbled in on my cane and, having forgotten my eyeglasses, sat close to the front.

Word had gotten around that Rudi was featured in the newsreel, and there was a noise in the air, his name being whispered by what presumably were old classmates, young men and ladies, some former schoolteachers. Yulia had written to say that in Petersburg young women had begun to wait outside the stage door to get a glimpse of him. She mentioned that he was even due to dance for Khrushchev. The thought was chilling and wonderful—the barefoot Ufa boy performing in Moscow. I chuckled, remembering the names Rudi had been called at school: Pigeon, Girlie, Frogface. All of that had been forgotten now that he was a solo Kirov artist—the arrogance had been taken from the air and put in the victory soup.

After the anthem the newsreel came on. He was featured dancing the Spaniard in *Laurencia*. The sight of him was an acute but pleasing thorn. His hair was dyed black for the role, and his makeup was garish. I found myself holding Anna's hand, and midway she leaned over to me. Rudi was being savage and exotic, she said. He was bringing a flagrant ruthlessness to his idea of dance. She whispered urgently that he was altogether too flamboyant, that his feet weren't pointed well, his line was slightly wrong, that he needed to cut his hair.

I thought: How wonderful—even as a ghost Anna didn't hold back.

I recalled the last time I had seen him, at Anna's funeral, the look on his face that his gift was no longer a surprise. Now he seemed generations removed from the boy with the runny nose who had stood outside the Ufa Opera House, bruises above his eye, feet turned out.

The newsreel ended. I felt faintly nostalgic and dozed briefly in my seat before being awakened by some crude Western fare, *Tarzan*, the main feature of the day. I went out into the last of the sunlight. The sun had baked potholes in the dirt roads. Ravens were out pecking around the shriveled weeds. In the distance the forests flared orange. A cello was being played in a tower block along Aksakov. I

turned onto my street, almost expecting to meet Rudi, his younger
self, with Anna trailing behind.

I had forgotten provisions, but there were a few leftovers in the
room, potatoes and cucumbers. The stylus on the gramophone was
worn down, yet it still managed a little scratch of Mozart.

Remembering Anna's old trick, I dented the pillow. My pro-
longed wakefulness had in recent times become almost unbearable
and so I was surprised upon waking in the morning, not at the fact
that I was awake but at the novelty of having slept at all.

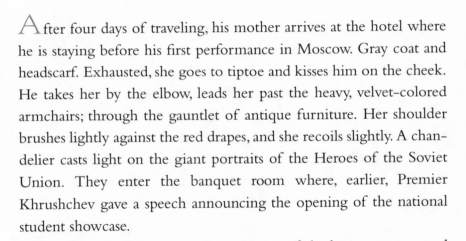

After four days of traveling, his mother arrives at the hotel where
he is staying before his first performance in Moscow. Gray coat and
headscarf. Exhausted, she goes to tiptoe and kisses him on the cheek.
He takes her by the elbow, leads her past the heavy, velvet-colored
armchairs; through the gauntlet of antique furniture. Her shoulder
brushes lightly against the red drapes, and she recoils slightly. A chandelier casts light on the giant portraits of the Heroes of the Soviet
Union. They enter the banquet room where, earlier, Premier
Khrushchev gave a speech announcing the opening of the national
student showcase.

At one end of the room, the remnants of the banquet are spread
out on the table.

I danced at the reception, he says.

Where?

On the wooden platform down there. Nikita Sergeyevich saw
me. He applauded. Who could believe it?

Look, she says.

Farida shuffles alongside the table: a splotch of beluga caviar on a
starched white cloth; a plate with a touch of duck pâté rimed to it;
the smell of sturgeon, herring, beef, truffles, wild mushrooms, cheeses;

krendeli biscuits in their broken figures of eight; a single Black Sea oyster on a glistening tray. She lifts a slice of salted meat to her mouth, decides against it, moves on, noticing empty silver ice-buckets for champagne, crumbs on the floor, cigar ashes on the windowsill, cigarette butts, lemon wedges in empty glasses, bent and broken tooth-picks, a display of red chrysanthemums in the center of the room.

Rudik? she says.

Yes?

She goes to the window, looks down at her boots, worn and salt-stained: Your father says he's sorry he couldn't be here.

Yes.

He wanted to be.

Yes.

That is all, she says.

Yes, Mother.

At the hotel exit a guard makes way for them as they step into the cold. He begins to skip down the street, the lining of his coat flapping. Farida smiles, quickens her step, feels a momentary lightness. Things spinning: snowflakes, boots, the chime of a distant clock. Watching people nearby, watching him, being watched.

Rudik! she says. Wait!

They spend the afternoon in his sister Tamara's room close to Kolomenskoye Park. Tamara shares a room with a family of six. Her corner of the room is small, damp, filled with rubber plants, knick-knacks, a fading print of a Tsiolkovsky, intricate rugs hung from nails. In piles on the floor she has arranged her books. The kitchen is dark and cramped. Recently her salary from the kindergarten has been curtailed and the shelves are empty. A heavy iron sits on the stove, beside the teakettle. No samovar. Down the corridor the toilet has overflowed, and the waft of it comes strong through the building.

Tamara makes tea and a fuss with a plate of biscuits.

This is like old times, she says.

She takes Rudi's shoes and polishes them. Later she fingers his coat and asks him where he gets his clothes made. He shrugs.

The afternoon grows lengthy as the light slants through the windows.

I have something, says Rudi.

He reaches in his suit jacket pocket, leans across, and hands them tickets for the following night's performance.

They're good seats, he says, the best.

Mother and daughter scan the tickets.

More tea, he says to Tamara, and she immediately climbs to her feet.

The next evening, in the Tchaikovsky Concert Hall, Farida and Tamara sit nervously as the seats fill up around and behind them. They gaze at the tiered chandeliers, the ornate cornicework, the gold carvings on the stems of the lamps, the magnificent curtain with repeating designs, hammers and sickles. As the dance begins their hands are clenched tight in their laps, but soon the women are gripping each other, amazed to see Rudi, not just the dance, but what he has become, whole and full and fleshed, patrolling the stage, devouring space, graceful, angry.

His mother leans forward in her plush velvet seat, awed and slightly frightened. This is my flesh and blood, she thinks. This is what I have made.

Yes! Chistyakova review from *Theater Moscow*, volume 42, 1959. "A dancer with excellent natural gifts." "Captivating us with the swiftness of his dance tempi." Sasha: *When at first you do succeed try not to look astonished.* Ha! Yes! Advice on how to handle the crowd— stand tall, fill out all the space with one huge sweep of the arm. Like a farmer in the field, he says, with his very last swipe at the hay. Or, more to the point, an executioner at the neck! See film shot by Lenikowski(?) Labrakowski(?) Photographs for mother. New shoes.

Wigs to get washed. Tailor the coat so it is short, up around the hips, give further length to me, oh shit I wish legs could grow! Access to special stores. Get leather bag with good strap if possible. Maybe sponge-soled shoes and narrow trousers, if possible. Tobacco for Father, heater that mother mentioned. Something for RosaMaria, jewelry box perhaps.

✳

He is told to hold position as if position is a thing that can ever be held on a floor like this, a sheet at his feet. He is in fifth, arms above his head. Earlier in the morning he landed hard on his ankle and can feel the throb of it now. The studio is bright and airy, light drifting in confident packets through the small windows. The photographer has a cigarette which seems to cling to his lower lip. He smells of smoke and bromide. Also, the acrid whiff of the flashbulbs as they break with each emission of light. He has to change each bulb when it breaks, unscrewing it from beneath the white umbrella, using a padded glove. Rudi has already asked the photographer why he is bouncing flash light into the natural light—it seems to him to have no logic—but the photographer said: You do your trade, comrade, I do mine.

Rudi remains in position, his ankle pounding with pain, thinking that if he did his trade, if he really did his trade, the camera itself would not be able to catch him. There are other photographs on the back of the wall, ranged in careful order, dated and tagged. Dancers all, captured benignly and formlessly, even the great ones, Chaboukiani, Ulanova, Dudinskaya. The photographer has brought his ignorance to the job and there is nothing more Rudi would like than to break the air with movement in the second before the flash erupts, create a blur on the film. The photographer is using a Lomo which, because of its black weight, is propped on a tripod and what stupidity to smoke while taking a photograph, but Rudi needs the photo for the Kirov, so he breathes in the pain. He is surprised by the ache, that by remaining still his body is more violently active, so he concentrates his rage on the photographer, more precisely on the series of fat rolls at his neck. The flash causes Rudi to blink, leaving a single bright image on his retina.

And again! says the photographer as he unscrews the bulb, pauses a moment to put a lighter to the end of the cigarette which has extinguished itself.

No, says Rudi.

Pardon me?

No more, he says.

The photographer smiles nervously. One more, he says.

No. You're an imbecile.

The photographer watches as Rudi descends the stairs, his black hat at an angle, shading one side of his face. At the bottom of the stairs Rudi bends, checks the swelling on his ankle and loosens the bandage minutely. Without looking back he waves at the photographer who is leaning over the banister, incredulous.

Send them to me, shouts Rudi. If they're no good I'll eat them and shit them and return them to you in an envelope.

He walks to the studios of the Kirov, where he rehearses through the pain with the master class. An older dancer tries to edge him out from the mirror. Rudi fakes a fall and slams his shoulder into the dancer's knee, half-whispers an apology, climbs back into his dance. There is a muttering in the room, but Rudi aligns himself in the mirror, hair down to his eyebrows, his shoulders muscled. In the middle of the floor he pirouettes beautifully. His partner, Sizova, gives a calm nod of her head, comes across and says: You're injured, don't show off.

Rudi nods and does the move again. At the window he sees Xenia, elegant in a beautiful coat and headscarf. He whisks his hand in the air, waving at her to go away. When she doesn't he turns to the front of the studio where she can no longer see him.

Later, with Sizova he works on the finishing touches for a duet from *Les Sylphides*. His ankle swells further but he dances through the pain, plunging it in a bucket of cold water at the end of the three hours. Then he rises again and puts in an extra half hour. Sizova watches the mating ritual in the mirror, not so much with himself as with the dance. Too exhausted to practice any more, she tells him she must leave to get a few hours' sleep.

As she goes down the corridor she passes Xenia smoking on the steps, her long blond hair covering her face, her eyes red and swollen.

Far behind, in the rehearsal room, she can still hear Rudi cursing to himself: Your legs are still not long enough, asshole.

❖

When I was a young girl in Santiago, there were games my brothers and I played when the day of the dead came around. My mother would fix up a basket of bread and corn fritters. We'd walk, with my father and brothers, to the cemetery, where other families had already lit up candles in the darkness. Hundreds of people crowded the graveyard. We had a humble family tomb under the oaks. The adults drank cheap rum and told stories. My parents talked of dead grandmothers who had baked wedding rings into bread, grandfathers who had held their breath in underwater caves, uncles who had received signs in their dreams. We, the children, played at the vaults. I put my favorite dolls on tombs and my brothers rode around on stick horses. Later we lay down on the cool stones and played at being dead. Even then, at the age of seven, I wanted to dance. On the tombs I sometimes thought I could feel the satin against my feet. It was the only night of the year we were allowed in the cemetery—our parents watched and made hot chocolate for us, and later we fell asleep in their arms.

It all returned to me like a dream on my last night in Leningrad.

A small farewell party had been held at a function room in the

Kirov, hors d'oeuvres and Russian wine that tasted vaguely like hand lotion. My room was three kilometers from the Kirov but, instead of getting the tram, I walked, taking it all in, following the curve of the canals, a final gesture to the city. It was a warm white evening. Three years in skirts. I wore my orange pants. Girls giggled and waved. The wine had made my head a little woozy. The straight lines of the architecture were gone, the palaces were blurry, the wide streets narrowed, and the bronze statues of the Anichkov bridge seemed to sway. I hardly cared. My spirit was already home in Chile.

When I got to the apartment block I ran up the stairs. Inside, Rudi was sitting on my bed, cross-legged.

"You left the door open," he said.

He had been at the party earlier and had already said a theatrical good-bye, but I wasn't surprised to see him. My bags were packed but he had opened them, removed the copies of *Dance* magazine that had beaten the censors, and they were spread out on the bed, open to pictures of London, New York, Spoleto, Paris.

"Make yourself at home," I said.

He grinned and asked me to take out my guitar. He sat, then, on the floor with his head against the bed, his eyes closed, listening. I thought of Mama, the way she had sung to me at night beneath the murraya branches. She said to me once that a bad voice came from a good life, a good voice came from a bad life, but that a great voice came from a confusion of both.

After his favorite song Rudi stepped across to me. My head was still spinning from the wine and he put his finger to my lips, took the guitar from me, laid it against the wall.

I said, "Rudi, no."

He touched the buttons on my cardigan, circled them with his finger, his fringe of hair against my forehead. He ran his hands across my waist, moved his fingers up my arms and on to my shoulders, his touch uneasy yet precise. I laughed and slapped his hands away.

"You're leaving," he whispered.

My buttons were open. His hands rested on my back and his legs trembled against mine. I had not slept with anyone since my arrival in Russia. I bit my tongue, pushed him away. Rudi gasped and lifted me, put his mouth to the ridge of my collarbone, thrust me against the wall. I slipped against his shoulder, caught the scent of him, said: "Rudi, no."

I turned my face to his. "We're friends."

His mouth touched my earlobe. "I have no friends."

"Xenia," I whispered.

He drew back sharply from me. I hadn't meant to invoke her, the name had slipped off my tongue. I immediately felt sober. He had been sleeping with Pushkin's wife for a while but the affair had ended abruptly. Although Rudi had dismissed her, she still watched him rehearse, cooked for him, cleaned his clothes, attended to his whims.

He went to the window, his hands cupped low, embarrassed by his arousal.

I laughed nervously, not meaning to shame him, but he stepped backwards and slammed his fist into the wall.

"For this I missed rehearsal," he said.

"For this?"

"For this."

He was so close to the window his breath steamed the glass.

At the bathroom sink I poured cold water on my face. He was still at the window when I returned. I told him to leave and come back when he was Rudi once more, his ordinary self. He had his own apartment now, eight streets away. But he didn't budge. The child in him seemed to reflect off the glass while he watched me in his own reflection. He had often told me that he loved me, that he'd marry me, that we'd dance together around the world—it had become our joke in the few moments when we found ourselves with little to say, but now the silence parted us.

He pouted in a charming way and I thought about the days we had spent together: massaging each other's feet, skating, sunbathing by the canals, the evenings with Yulia. Perhaps the wine was still in me, I don't know, but finally I said to him, "Rudi, come here."

He turned on his toes, brushing his feet as if in ronde de jambe. "What?"

"Come, please."

"Why?"

"Unbind my hair."

He waited, fidgeted, then came across to remove the clips, fumbling and tentative. He held the weight of my hair and let it drop. I pressed against him, kissed him, my mouth filled suddenly with his breath. I whispered that he could stay with me until morning, or until 9.30 A.M. exactly, before I left for Pulkovo Airport, to which he smiled and said that his head had run rudderless thinking of me and we should sleep together, yes, make love, since we would never see each other again, spoken like hard fact or the first piano note of the morning.

His eyes were intense and narrow as if a phonograph needle had stopped just at the point of a trumpet blast.

His hands slipped down my spine, drew me against him, his fingers then at the small of my back, my hips, my thighs, moving slowly. I arched and closed my eyes. He yanked hard at the back of my hair, pulled me closer, but then all of a sudden he turned his face to the pillow and remained motionless.

"Sasha," he said into the pillow.

He began to say Pushkin's name over and over again. I knew then that we would not make love. I stroked his hair and the night thickened, we pulled a blanket over us, the sensation of our toes touching. He fell asleep with his eyelashes fluttering and I wondered, What dreams?

I awoke during the night, disoriented. Rudi was sitting on the floor, naked, his feet curled into his stomach, staring at photographs, finally noticing me, gazing up, pointing at a picture of Covent Garden, saying: "Look at this."

He was studying a picture of Margot Fonteyn in her dressing room, her hair pinned back, her face serious, her eyes deliberate. "Look at her! Look at her!"

I propped myself up and asked if he had thought about the Pushkins during the night, if they'd appeared in his dreams, but he dismissed me with a wave, said he didn't want to talk of trivialities. He immersed himself in the pictures once more. Feeling useless, I patted the bed. He climbed in beside me and began crying, kissing my hair, saying, "I'll never see you again, RosaMaria, I'll never see you, I'll never see you, I'll never see you."

For the rest of the night we slept beside each other, arms entwined.

In the morning we left the room, carrying my suitcases. Outside a man in a dark suit was sitting on the low wall, smoking. When he saw us he stood up nervously. Rudi went over to him, whispered something in his ear. The man stuttered and swallowed, eyes wide.

Rudi started leaping down the street.

"I don't give a shit!" he said. "Fuck them! All I want to do is dance! I don't care!"

"Rudi," I said. "Don't be foolish."

"Fuck caution," he said.

He was going soon to Vienna to perform at the Stadhalle, and I said they would surely withdraw permission for the trip if he kept drawing attention to himself.

"I don't care," he said. "All I care about is you."

I looked at him to see if this was just another of his mood swings, but it was hard to tell. I told him I loved him, that I'd never forget him. He took my hand, kissed it.

We put my bags into a taxi. The driver recognized Rudi from a performance of *Les Sylphides* the previous week and asked for an autograph. Fame fit Rudi like a curious coat, new but oddly snug. In the taxi he closed his eyes and rattled off the street names as we passed them, each note in the right place. I kissed his eyes. The driver coughed as if in warning. Behind us a car was trailing.

At the terminal in Pulkovo there was a group to see me off. I felt light-headed, blissful at the thought of returning home—already I was taking the white dustcloths off the mirrors and the furniture. I could taste the dust in the room.

Yulia was at the airport in all her loveliness. She smiled her subversive smile. Her long dark hair was draped around her shoulders. I had given her some clothes a few days before, and she was wearing a bright purple blouse of mine, which set off her dark skin, her eyes. Her father had written a letter from Ufa and in it had enclosed a small note for me. He said I'd made his wife, Anna, happy with my spirit when we met and that he appreciated my attendance at her funeral. At the very end of the letter there was a rather oblique reference to the deserts of Chile—he said he had always wanted to see the Atacama, where it had not rained in four hundred years, and if I ever got there I should throw some earth in the air in his honor.

I kissed Yulia good-bye, shook hands with the others.

My flight was to Moscow and then onward to Paris and then New York, where I was to make the final leg to Santiago. I wanted to say a final farewell to Rudi but he had disappeared. I pushed through the pockets of people, called his name, but he was nowhere to be seen among the passengers and guards. I called his name again and still he did not show. I turned towards the glass wall that led to passport control.

Just then I caught a glimpse of the top of his head, distant in the crowd. He was engaged in serious and animated conversation with someone—at first I was sure it was the man who had been spying on us, but then I saw it was another young man, dark-haired, handsome, with an athlete's body and a pair of denim jeans, a rarity in Leningrad. The young man was touching Rudi gently on the inside of the elbow.

The call for my flight came through the loudspeakers. Rudi strode across and hugged me, whispered that he loved me, that he could hardly live without me, he would be lost, yes, rudderless, please come back soon, he would miss me terribly, we should have made love, he was sorry, he did not know what he would do without me.

He looked around over his shoulder. I turned his face back to mine and he smiled, a strange and chilling charm.

❈

### Incident Report, Aeroflot, Flight BL 286, Vienna–Moscow–Leningrad, March 17, 1959.

Due to circumstances beyond the airline's control, there were no meal or beverage carts provided for this flight. Passengers were so advised at the airport. Upon boarding, however, the Subject, a People's artist, was noticed to be carrying a case of champagne. The Subject at first seemed to exhibit a severe fear of flying but then became rowdy, complaining about the lack of food and beverages. Midway through the flight, unbeknown to flight attendants, he took a bottle, shook it, and sprayed the contents around the cabin. The Subject then walked the aisles, offering champagne to passengers, pouring the alcohol into paper cups. The champagne soaked through the paper cups and leaked. Fellow passengers complained about wet seats and clothes. Others began singing and laughing. The Subject took out additional bottles from the same case. When confronted he used foul language. The Subject remarked that it was his twenty-first birthday and began gesticulating and shouting about being a Tatar. Late in the flight the plane hit turbulence and many of the passengers experienced bouts of violent sickness. The Subject seemed increasingly frightened but continued to shout and sing. When asked to calm down by representatives of the ballet company with whom he was traveling he used another epithet and sprayed the final bottle of champagne around the cabin just prior to landing. After the landing in Moscow a warning was issued and the Subject calmed. On disembarking in Leningrad he made a comment to the Captain of the flight, the nature of which remained undisclosed. Captain Solenorov reported in sick for the return flight.

❋

He goes to the edge of the bed, pulls his shirt over his head, undoes the button at the top of his trousers, stands naked in the light. He says to the pilot: Close the curtains, keep the light on, make sure the door is locked.

❋

Late at night in Ekaterina Square, in the antique dust of Leningrad, when the streetlamps were turned off to save power and the city was quiet, a scatter of us would come from different parts of the city to walk beneath the row of trees on the theater side of the park. Quietly. Furtively. If stopped by the militia we had our papers, the excuse of our jobs, insomnia, our wives, our children at home. Sometimes we were beckoned by those we didn't recognize, but we knew better, we moved quickly away. Cars passed on Nevsky, catching us in their headlights, obliterating our shadows, and it seemed for a moment that our shadows had been taken for questioning. We imagined ourselves on the jump seat of a Black Maria, whisked away to the camps for being the *goluboy,* the blue boys, the perverts. The arrest, if it came, would be swift and brutal. At home we kept a small bag packed and hidden, just in case. The threat of it should have been enough: forests, mess cans, barracks, bunks, plank beds, five years, the crack of metal on frozen wood. But there were nights when the square was silent and we waited in the fog, stood against the fence, and smoked.

A tall thin boy picked at the springs of his watch with a penknife, carving time. The watch was on a chain, and he let it swing to his hips. Two brothers arrived each Thursday from the pedestrian underpass, fresh from the factory baths, their dark hair preceding their scuffed shoes. An old veteran stood under a tree. He was able to whistle many of the great Liszt rhapsodies. He was known to say aloud: *Why earn your joy only when you are dead?* He continued until morning, when the distant sound of the river steamers whistled him out. Sometimes the curtains of the rooms across the square opened and closed, figures appearing, disappearing. Black Volgas moved away from the curbside and went down the dark streets. Nervous laughter rang out. Cigarette papers were rolled and licked. Snuff-boxes were unfurled. Nobody drank—drinking would loosen our tongues and give to the living the breath of the dead. Sweat stained the rims of our collars. We stamped our feet, blew warm air into our gloves, moved our bodies beyond ordinary wakefulness, and beyond that once again, until at times it felt as if we would never sleep.

The night went by, our desires hidden, as if sewn inside coat sleeves. It was not that we even took our coats off, it was the touch, the shiver of recognition when our sleeves met as we lit each other's cigarettes. Hatred too. Hatred for such similarity.

The theater doors swung open late, allowing actors, dancers, stagehands out. Sometimes they walked all the way from the Kirov, twenty minutes. They leaned against the ironwork, wrapped in their scarves, gloves, leg warmers. A sandy-haired boy swung his foot into the air and propped it on a prong of the fence, stretched, his head to his knees, his breath steaming, his leather cap tipped backwards on his head. His body had an ease to it, his toes his feet his legs his chest his shoulders his neck his mouth his eyes. His lips were extra-ordinarily red, and his mouth was made more red again by the eyes. Even the leather hat seemed shaped to the way that he pulled it on and off. Most of the time he didn't stay long in the square, he was privileged and there were other places for him to go—basements, cupolas, apartments—but once or twice he remained, kicking his foot to the top of the fence. We passed, inhaled the smell of him. He never said a word to us.

We waited for him to reappear in the square, but he became more recognizable, his face in the newspapers, on posters. The thought of him lay with us.

When the rumor of morning arrived, the streetlights flickered briefly and we would part. We unraveled into the streets, some look-ing for the boy with the pocket watch, or the factory brothers, or the dancer with the sandy hair, the print of his foot on the damp pave-ment, his overcoat parted by walking, his scarf flying out from the back of his neck. Sometimes, by the stone steps that descended to a canal's black waters, the light of the moon was broken by a shadow's stride and we turned to follow. Even then, so close to morning, there was always the thought that water might hide its flowing under ice.

# | 3 |

*LONDON* · *1961*

Every Friday the drunks roll past, loud and foul with whiskey, reeking of piss and dustbins, and, as he has done for years now, he reaches
out the window, handing each of them a shilling, so almost every
tramp around Covent Garden knows that the place for a little money
is the factory on the far side of the Royal, where the middle-aged
man, the bald one with the spectacles, at the second to last window,
open, but only on a Friday, leans out and listens to the stories—*my
mother's caught up with consumption, my uncle lost his wooden leg, my aunt
Josephine got her knickers in a twist*—and, no matter what the story, he
says to the drunks, *Here you go, mate,* shilling after shilling, much of
his wages, so that instead of taking the Tube back to his room in
Highbury he walks all the way, to save the money, a good five miles,
stooped, his flat hat on, nodding to ladies and paperboys and more
drunks, some of whom recognize him and try to charm another
shilling from him, which he cannot give because he has calculated
exactly enough for lodging and food, he says, *Sorry, mate,* tips his hat
and walks on, a shopping bag banging against his calf, all the way
through Covent Garden and Holborn and Grays Inn, along Rosebury

Avenue, up the Essex Road onto Newington Green, the sky darkening as he goes, and he turns left on Poet's Road, walks to the redbrick lodging house, number 47, where the landlady, a widow from Dorchester, greets him airily at the front door, by the mock-ebony clock with the two pawing horses, and he bows slightly to her, saying, *Evening, Mrs. Bennett,* and makes his way up the stairs, passing the pictures of ducks on the wall, straightening them if another lodger has bumped against them, sixteen steps, into his room, where at last he removes his shoes, thinking he must polish them, and then he unloosens his tie, pours himself a Scotch from the silver flask hidden behind the bedstead, just a nip, sighing deeply as it hits his throat, opens the shopping bag, sets the shoes out on his work desk, just finishing touches—a shank to be trimmed, a wing block to be extended, a drawstring that requires threading through, a heel to be cut down—neat, precise, and when he is finished he wraps them each in plastic, making sure there are no creases in the wrapping, since he has a reputation to maintain, the ballerinas, the choreographers, the opera houses, they all seek him out, sending their specifications,

a foot so wide at the toes and so narrow at the heel he must stretch the shoe to accommodate it,

the fourth toe abnormally longer than the third, something he solves with the simple loosening of a stitch,

the shoe that needs a harder shank, a higher back, a softer sole,

he is well-known for his tricks, they talk about him, the dancers with their difficulties or those just simply fussy, writing him letters, sending him telegrams, sometimes even visiting him at the factory—meet your maker!—especially those from the Royal Ballet, so delicate and fine and appreciative, most of all Margot Fonteyn, his favorite, who once got an amazing three performances out of one pair of toe shoes, her requirements being terribly intricate, a very short vamp, a low wing block, extra paste at the tips, wide pleats for grip, and he is the only maker she ever deals with, she adores him, she thinks him the perfect gentleman, and in return she is the only ballerina whose picture hangs above his worktable—*To Tom, with love, Margot*—and it makes him shiver to think how she handles his shoes once she gets them, shattering the shank to make it more pliable, banging the shoe against doors to soften the box, bending the shoe over and over so it feels perfect on her feet, as if she has worn it forever, a thought which prompts a little smile as he puts the shoes away neatly on his bedroom shelf, steps into his pajamas, kneels down for two quick prayers, goes to bed, never dreaming of feet or shoes, and when he wakes he shuffles down the corridor to the shared bathroom, where he soaps and shaves, the whiskers grown gray in recent years, fills a kettle with tap water, returns to his room, puts the kettle on his stove, waits for it to whistle, makes himself a cup of tea, having put the milk on the windowsill overnight to keep it cool, then takes the stack of shoes from the shelf and sets once again to work, and he works all morning long, although Saturdays aren't considered overtime, he doesn't care, he enjoys the repetitions and differing demands, the women's toe shoes so much more intricate and difficult than the ballet boots for men, the French with more of an eye for flair than the English, the softer leather pads demanded by the Spanish, the Americans who call their shoes *slippers,* and how he detests that word, *slipper,* like something out of a fairy tale, he often thinks of the violence a shoe takes, the pounding, the destruction, not to mention the tiny incisions, the surgery, the gentleness, the tricks he learned from his late father, who worked the same job for forty years,

if you're adjusting the vamp and it's too stiff just use a little Bryl-creem to soften it,

soap the satin clean of dust not only before but during and especially after the making of the shoe,

think of yourself as the foot,

and the only thing that disturbs the rhythm of his shoemaking is the soccer match each Saturday, he makes the trip half a mile down the road to watch Arsenal, and on alternating weeks he supports the reserves, a red-and-white scarf wrapped around his neck, standing in the terraces, for which he has built himself a special pair of shoes that give him another four inches, since he is a small man and he wants to watch the game over the other fans' heads, *Arsenal! Arsenal!* the sway of the crowd as the ball is swept around the pitch, the spin, the dribble, the nutmeg, the volley, it is perhaps not entirely unlike ballet, everything in the feet is what matters, not that he would ever see a ballet, a notion inherited from his father

stay out of the theaters, son, don't ever go watch,

no point in seeing your shoes ripped to pieces,

tune your shoes, that's all,

and at halftime he finds his mind drifting back to the shoes in his room, how he can improve on them, if the shank was too tight, if the box could have been toughened, until he hears the crowd roaring and sees the teams trotting out onto the pitch, the referee's shrill whistle, and the match begins again, the ball tipped on by Jackie Henderson, taken down the wing by George Eastham, and then swung across into the center for David Herd to head home, and the shoemaker jumps in the air on his false shoes and rips his hat from his head, revealing his baldness, and after the match he walks home with the singing crowd, swept along, sometimes he is pinned against a wall for a moment by the bigger men, though it is not far to the house, and he is embarrassed if he meets Mrs. Bennett at the door, she has not yet figured out how come he is taller on Saturdays, *A cup of tea, Mr. Ashworth? No, ta, Mrs. Bennett,* up to his room to look at his work, to trim the cardboard where there is a bump invisible to any normal eye, or to feather the shank down with a skiv, and then he lines the shoes up by his bedside table, so that on Sunday, after a sleep-in, they are the first thing he sees, pleasing him no end, even thinking of them while in church, walking heavy-footed back down the aisle after services, among the ladies in hats and veils, out into the sunlight, a deep breath and a sigh of relief, away from the church grounds, past the suburban gardens, taking the remainder of Sunday as a day of rest, a pint of bitter and a spot of lunch, reading the paper

in the park, November 6, two days past his forty-fourth birthday—
*Hague Agreement to Be Altered, U.S. Charges Cuban Spy, Soviet Dancer to
Arrive in London*—a story he knows well, since the sketches of the feet
came in last week, he is due to start work on the shoes first thing in the
morning, a thought that occupies him as he prepares for bed, and ten
hours later he emerges at Covent Garden in the sunlight, walks towards
the shop, keen to get going, Mr. Reed the boss slapping him on the
shoulder, *Good morning, Tom oul' son,* and he leaves the toe shoes from
the weekend in the front office, enters the shop, takes off his overcoat,
puts on his large white apron, fires up the ovens, seventy degrees—hot
enough to harden shoes but not melt the satin—and then he goes
downstairs to the leather room, wanting to find a number of good
sturdy hides before the other makers arrive, smells the leather, rubs his
hands over the grain, then straight upstairs with the hides and a bucket
of glue beneath his arm, to his work desk, the makers arriving, all
cricket and wives and hangovers, nodding at him, he is the best of
them, they have a deep respect for him, coming as he does from the line
of Ashworths, the greatest makers of them all, craftsmen, the insignia on
their shoes down over the years a simple

*a*

a little more intricate than those of any of the other makers, who all
have their own flourishes—a squiggle, a circle, a triangle—placed on
the sole, so the dancers know their makers, and some of the fans even
go to the dustbins behind the theaters to rescue the ruined shoes, to
see who made them, the Ashworths being coveted, but Tom isn't
troubled by the pressure, he gives himself to his work, spectacles on
the bridge of his nose, studying the sketches of the Russian's feet, the
specifications in from Paris,

    the size, the width, the length of the toes,

    the angle of the nails, the ball of the foot, the way the ligaments
come to the ankle,

    the spread of the heel, the blisters, the bone spurs,

and just by the sketches alone he knows the life of this foot, raised in barefoot poverty and—from the unusual wideness of the bone structure—bare on concrete rather than grass, then squeezed into shoes that were too small, coming to dance later than usual given the smallness yet breadth of the foot, 7 EEE, then a great violence done by excessive training, many hard angles, but a remarkable strength, and stretching back from his worktable, Tom Ashworth smiles, shakes out his hands, and then is lost in the work, silent as if in a trance, making one pair of men's boots in the first hour, three in the second, slow for him, the order is forty pairs, a full day's work, maybe even two if he runs into difficulty, for the Russian desires his shoes made with a reverse channel construction, meaning two large hook needles must be used and—even though it's a much easier proposition than making toe shoes for a ballerina—it requires time and intimacy, and he stops only when a shout goes up for lunch break, a moment he relishes, sandwiches and tea, the younger cobblers a bit cheeky, *How's the commie shoes then, eh?* to which he nods and smiles—when the other makers saw the sketches they shouted, *Defected my arse! Defective more likely! He's a bleeding commie ain't he? No he ain't, he's one of us. One of us? I seen him on telly and he looks a right bloody poofter!*—and when lunch is finished he's back with the sketches, afraid he has made a wrong move somewhere, the figures trilling through his head, keeping the inside-out shoes moist with wet cloths, his bald head shining, he stitches by hand, invoking the Ashworth spirit, then brings the shoes to the drying oven, which he checks again with the thermometer to make sure it is seventy degrees

after all, no matter who the shoes are for, or why, they always have to be perfect.

# | 4 |

UFA, LENINGRAD · 1961–1964

**August 12**

The wooden shutters on the windows blew open last night and banged until the morning.

**August 13**

Up before dawn with the radio, listening, but fell back to sleep. When I woke Father had already eaten breakfast. He said, *You must rest, daughter.* And yet he is the one feeling sickly. The past weeks have worn him out. I beseeched him to return to bed. Still he insisted on accompanying Mother and me to the market. Father does not talk to anyone when he goes out, for fear of what will be said, even though it has not been officially announced. He walks with his head down as if they have put something heavy on his neck, his forehead brought low with the weight of it. At the Krassina market we found three bundles of spinach. No meat. Father took both canvas bags at first. We switched when we got near the fountain on October Prospect. The stone wall has cracked in the heat. He was bent over with exhaustion. When he gave me the second bag he said, *You must forgive, Tamara.* And yet there is nothing for me to forgive. What is to forgive? I had a brother, he is gone, that is all.

### August 16

In his leaving he has forced me home. Moscow seems years away already. What am I to become? My anger boils over. I almost smashed Mother's teacup but held myself back.

### August 17

Father came home from the factory long-faced. We dare not ask. We cooked chicken broth to soothe him. He ate without a word.

### August 18

A white car in the street, traveling up and down, up and down. It is marked Driving School, but the driver makes no mistakes.

### August 19

At the Big House with Mother again. They believe she is the only one who can change Rudik's mind. They gave us tea, unusual for them, considering. It was lukewarm. I thought for a moment it might be poisoned. A half-dozen phones were set up on the desk. Four men and two women. Three wore headphones, two worked into dictation machines, the other supervised. Most of them did not look us in the eye, but the supervisor stared. He gave Mother a set of headphones and told me to sit in the corner. They finally got through to Rudik on the third try. He was sleepy since there is a time difference. He was in an apartment in Paris. (They said later that it was a place famous for its men with unnatural perverted instincts. They insist on using that phrase in front of Mother, to watch her face. She tries not to have her face betray her. It is important not to display emotion, she says.) There was a time delay on what Rudik said. Sometimes they bleeped it out. They got angry when there were exchanges in Tatar. Mother swore later that she heard the end of the word *happy* but of course what she really wanted to hear was *return*. We are to tell nobody about the betrayal, yet they go ahead and question the dancers in the Opera House, his friends, even Rudik's old teachers, how do they expect word not to get out?

**August 20**

I walked by the Belaya and ate an ice cream on the sandbar. Children were swimming. Old women sat in bathing suits and caps. The world goes on.

**August 21**

They have suggested a possible amnesty if he renounces what he has done, returns. What chance? It will be seven years hard labor at the absolute minimum, at the worst it is death. What would they do? Shoot him? Electrocute him? Would they hang him so that his feet would swing in the air, his last dance? These terrible thoughts.

**August 22**

The knowledge that he will never be here again makes him all the more present. I lie awake late at night and curse what he has done to us. They are always the same two people who sit in the Driving School car.

**August 23**

The bulb in the kitchen went out, there are no more. We are relieved only by the late hour of the setting sun and the beauty of the colors in the sky. Father said that the smoke from the factories makes the colors stronger.

**August 24**

We were coming home from the Big House when Mother's legs went out from under her on an oil patch near the statue in Lenin

Park. She caught herself on the base of the statue and then said to me, *Look, I am almost hanging on his toe.* She was immediately frightened by what she had said, but there was nobody around to hear. All the way home she was scratching her arms. Father found lime for the outhouse to stop the stench caused by the summer heat. I sat in peace and read the newspaper.

### August 25

Mother has shingles. She took to bed, although the sheets irked her terribly. Father sat by the bed and pasted her stomach with a tomato poultice, an old army cure, he said. The juice made her look red and bloody, as if she had been skinned from the inside out. Father and I took a tram out of the city and went for a walk in the woods near the river. He told me that he and Rudik went ice fishing once. He said Rudik was great at gutting the fish with one sweep of the fingers. Returning home, Father wished for his rifle when a flock of geese rose.

### August 26

I washed the sheets. They had an imprint of red tomato where she has been lying.

### August 28

The fire in her skin has cooled, thank the heavens. Father thumped his chest and said, *Tomatoes.* Mother took a chair and sat in the sunlight.

### August 29

Power failure in the oil refinery, and so the air was clean today. I went walking in the sunshine, found berries in the bushes behind the tool manufacturing yard. Came home and Mother made berry juice, her specialty, which made her sparkle. But in the late afternoon I caught sight of a wizened face reflected in a pane of glass. I was momentarily unsure who it was. It came as a shock to realize it was Mother, I suppose I haven't truly looked at her in a long time. The irritation is almost gone, but her face is still puffy. Perhaps that is the way of age. I have to remind myself that she is only a few years from sixty. These days her mouth is set in a little pouch, which turns downward. To think that during the war she lived without a mirror! The only way to see herself was in a window, but even then many of the windows were shattered. There was the story she once told of a girl who lived underground. When she came out she didn't recognize herself and wanted to go back underground again. We return to what we know. I spend my time wondering why I am here in this hellhole, how could I have given up my Moscow registration, am I mad, how much do they need me? Moscow. How I miss it, and yet how can I return? Father cut himself opening the window this morning. Bandaging his wrist, Mother said to him, *Perhaps Rudik will find a nice girl and come home.*

August 31

Have come down with a summer cold. Took gingerroot.

September 1

Father has been demoted, no longer politruk. It happened two weeks ago, but he refused to tell us. It is possible he will have to leave the Party. There has been no announcement of Rudik's betrayal, though the word is almost certainly in the air. Mother's friends have changed their time to go to the steambaths. I saw them walking down the street carrying their towels and birch twigs. Mother shrugged her shoulders and said no matter, she will go alone. She has great strength. If I have the time I shall accompany her. At the market on Krassina we found a delicious jar of sour pickles. Good fortune and joy. *My favorite*, Father said.

September 3

On the bus to the market the old woman said to her companion, *You think it's bad now, wait until tomorrow!* Her friend laughed. For some reason I remembered that in Moscow, Nadia, from the third floor, once said everything happens so fast that living it never made any sense to her. She could never catch up with herself. She had a theory about being in the past, looking ahead at a stranger living out a life. Of course the stranger was herself. I never understood until the bus journey this afternoon. I saw myself sitting there, listening to two old babushkas. I watched myself, watching them. Before I knew it I had become them. How easy this shift from young girl to old woman.

September 4

This journal writes of too many small disappointments. I must be stronger.

September 6

It is a strange mill that does not churn the river! The kindergarten on Karl Marx Street has accepted me, and it is a good job. I am almost a week late but I will catch up. Joy!

September 9

We cannot open the classroom windows, they are soldered shut. But the wind blows through the front door and gives us some relief. The late summer drags its good days into bad. Muksina drew a picture for me. Majit brought me a drink from cowberries, how refreshing. The school takes me back to my youth. When Rudik was here they pulled his hair and bit him and teased him terribly, called him names. The children still have a number of cruel games, one is called the Little Macaroni. They make a child rock his head to the left and right and someone strikes him on each side of the neck as he turns. Another is the Dandelion, where they bash him on top of the head. I could not help the bad thoughts that came while walking home. Perhaps all those years ago the bullying of Rudik was punishment in advance.

### September 11

A consignment of chalk and a new blackboard, the small mercies.

### September 13

The days seem to grow longer as they grow shorter. Mother worries that Rudik did not take his boots with him. Imagine.

### September 14

Another long day. Mother recalled that when Rudik danced in Moscow he bought her a long black coat and, at the Bolshoi, she was loathe to check it in. At the end of the dance, during his encores, she rushed down the stairs to retrieve the coat, afraid it would get lost, and she almost missed the cheers. Now she says she would be glad to check her coat in, she would check her very soul in if she could just see him home again. Yet in the end she must realize she would lose both soul and son. There was one relief. We went walking and there was a beautiful red sunset over the Belaya.

### September 15

The first cold winds have blown in. Mother says she has pain in her knees. Her old body is a weathervane, she can tell when a storm is coming. The bathwater was as dark as tea.

### September 17

Electricity problems in the kindergarten once again.

### September 18

Life begins with bread. There is none. Still, there is the radio for distraction, at least for Father, who turns it on immediately when he comes from work. He says that a desire to make the world better is not worth much, the question is how. Before he left the house this morning Mother put goose fat on his chest, but still he came home coughing. The sicknesses switch between them. He didn't even want the borscht that Elsa brought from upstairs. He is terribly thin, he keeps waiting to be expelled from the Party, which will surely break him completely. A conference is to be held some time soon. I heard him say something odd as we were waiting for the evening bus to the garden plot, *We can put a satellite in the air, Tamara, but we cannot run our buses.* It was almost as if Rudik was whispering in his ear, how dangerous. Only last year Father said we were living in a glorious time, another record harvest, Siberia open, nuclear power, Sputnik, the freedom of the African nations, and he had even almost reconciled himself to Rudik dancing—such a brightness in his cheeks then. Now the problem of being himself seems to exhaust him.

### September 19

Mother talks sometimes of Rudik not having any food. When she speaks to him in the Big House he says he is fine. She is sure this is propaganda. She keeps asking if they still throw glass on the stage. He says no, but she is not so sure. She knows how they feel about us in the West. Rudik says they only did that at the beginning and, besides, it was Communists. We puzzled over that for a while. It makes no sense. When Mother left I sneaked an ice cream in the park.

### September 20

Father's wages went automatically to the State bonds. And mine have not yet come through. How I regretted yesterday's ice cream. Mother scrounged together some kasha. Elsa shared her leaves, but drinking tea so late disturbs Mother's sleep. Father screwed in the double windows for winter. The look on his face was as if the cold was already here.

October 2

Fierce whipping winds. We must ration the oil in the school tanks.

October 10

I have been unable to write, such misery, I must arrest these bad thoughts. The children are terribly cold. Games must be invented to keep them moving around the classroom. This is not my strength. Sasha dislikes running. Guldjamal likes to sit perfectly still, wrapped in two coats. Nicolas dislikes standing. Khalim likes to perch on one foot, he says this keeps his warm. And Majit is such a nuisance! What to do? The rest of the children gravitate toward whoever will give them extra food from their lunch boxes. Such fights! After school I tended to the garden plot. The first layer of snow had fallen so there was nothing to do. An old man came up to me and asked about Father. He said they had met many times at the plot. I cut the conversation short but told him to call around to the house since Father could do with the company. The man tipped his hat. He had a slightly bourgeois tone. I went back to work. Tending to the plot is for the sake of ritual. On the way home a bus splashed slush onto my coat. While I was cleaning it I found a new hole in the inside lining which needs to be darned. Mother, with her problems of incontinence, says if we could darn our bodies she would get a job as her very own seamstress! On my return I stood at the gate and saw something red on the door. My heart pounded with the thought that it might be sealing wax over the keyhole in order to move us. But it was just a notice saying to go down to the Big House again tomorrow. The thought of talking to Rudik warms Mother. She misses the things he used to send her from Leningrad. She sometimes searches for the Voice of America on the radio, but of course it is impossible. Even in Moscow it was always scrambled and besides, it is pure Western propaganda. She is aware of that. How I detest their two faces, the joke they try to make of us.

October 11

A terrible mistake. The old man I talked to in the garden plot came over today to talk with Father. He is Sergei Vasilev, the husband of Rudik's old dance teacher, Anna. Naturally Father was polite to him, in fact he even seemed to enjoy himself. I tried to apologize to Father, but he waved me away, said he had met the man before and he was happy to spend time with him, the man was rehabilitated years ago. Father said to me, *If an undesirable wants the company of another undesirable, well then, so be it.* He cannot afford to think in this manner, nor give up hopes of remaining with the Party. That would pierce him. I washed his shirts to make him happy.

October 12

A raven bashed against the school window and broke the glass, then died in the children's hands, which made them cry. Mother said that Rudik is in Monte Carlo, where there is a palace and a beautiful beach. It is very odd. Why have I never seen the sea?

October 13

Sergei V. came over to visit. He brought a pot of jam, which I hate to admit was very tasty. He smoked half a cigar. Father coughed all evening.

October 15

A spoonful of raspberry jam to sweeten the tea.

October 16

Three tubes of toothpaste were bought at the market. One will be kept to give as a gift. It is Bulgarian. It tastes just as bad.

October 17

They still think Mother has the power to draw him back. The tapes they make are sent to Moscow, where they are examined and filed.

Rudik said to her in Tatar that he is afraid the secret agents will break his legs. They were not quick enough to bleep it out. Mother said, *I cannot sleep, beloved son.* He says he is well-fed and has lots of money and that he is doing very well, yes, he even meets theater stars and singers and he is due to meet the Queen of England. Mother says perhaps they have brainwashed him, filled him full of delusions. He said some other famous names, and even the stenographer's eyes opened wide. But in the end who cares, they are just names, they will die too. The supervisor slammed the desk when Mother slipped in a few more Tatar words and Rudik's voice went high with worry. He is surely home-sick. They told us Monte Carlo is full of gambling and perverted men, and also very violent, he could get stabbed or shot. That happens a lot.

October 19

Mother woke with terrible dreams about his legs. Later she said, *I am sure he will find himself a nice girl.*

October 20

The oven is broken. The school janitor says he will come to the house to fix it next week. Even these small things worry me. But he is as handy as a small pot and quite handsome too.

October 21

Father has been so tired, he has no strength for this. He'd prefer not to eat. There was a postcard from an acquaintance of Rudik's, but it was impossible to read with the black marks. Sergei came over again. It seems that neither he nor Father has anything else to do with their lives. I dislike this old fool. I worry about him being in our house but it is true he has been rehabilitated. And I don't suppose things could get much worse. He had more cigars, which made the room rank. They were cheap, he said, they came from Yugoslavia. He offered Father one, but Father said that smoking it would make him feel like a pig with a gold ring in its nose. They laughed and then had a long discussion about the weather on the radio. Father says he likes to listen to the weather in Chelyabinsk and then he knows what it will be, whereas Sergei listens to the weather from the east, something to do with the winds and a complicated idea to do with patterns from the mountains. And then he quoted poetry, as if poets were weather forecasters! Mother said why would we want to know the weather in advance anyway? All we have to do is to look out the window. Or, even better, step outside if your body allows it. Before Sergei left he saw the postcard and said there is a way to read the sentences underneath the black marks, that you must get a very thin sheet of paper and lightly rub the postcard with a pencil and that way the indentations will come out. Father was made nervous by this and asked Sergei not to say such things. Mother tried with the postcard but it was a complete and utter failure.

October 22

Mother says she is thankful for the small mercy of her body (even her varicose veins!) when she sees Father and Sergei together. She told me that they often finish their conversation chatting long and seriously about their bowel movements.

October 23

Father said, *What is there to think about, except the past, if you have no future?* I tried to remind him of things, but that was a mistake because it made him angry. I attempt to convince him that Rudik is an ambassador, one of goodwill, he can tell the world the truth about us, but Father just shakes his head, no. He continues to say, My son the traitor, how can I walk down Lenin Street? Nor does Father like his armchair anymore. The problem is that he used to be bigger and now, in these months, his smaller body has to lie in the big indent. And there is a coiled metal spring beginning to bulge that must be contained, perhaps tomorrow, tie it back with string so that it doesn't stick out and hurt his back.

October 24

A new consignment of oil for the school! And Ilya the janitor did indeed fix the oven! There was nobody home. We talked. He charged no money. What a wonderful day! I forgot of course to ask him to fix the chair, which he certainly would have done.

October 25

Illogical rumors of Rudik with Margot Fonteyn in different places all over the world. How can that be? We are not machines or robots or satellites. It has no logic, but perhaps it is how the West treats its artists, if art is considered at all. Such a world we live in. How many lies are holding him up? How many treacheries? If only to know the truth. The West is using him as a pawn. They will suck the life out of him and spit him out into their dump yards.

October 27

A comic from the London *Times* was reprinted today in *Izvestiya*, a drunken bear at the feet of Stalin's ghost. They attempt to make fools of us. If they could only admit the leaps we have made, but they cannot. They are scared since we will outlast them.

October 28

My birthday. I used to think that when I was older the world would be uncomplicated, but nothing seems to finish, nothing ever becomes simple. Father woke up sweating. Mother had knit a scarf for me using the wool from some of Rudik's old sweaters. It is warm and yet I am loath to wear it.

October 29

Ilya came over again to fix the armchair. We had tea and bread. When he's not at school he says that he adores skating. After a while he got to work. He cut the back of the seat open, reached in, and was able to get the spring and pull it back. He heard it had been my birthday and he asked me to meet him to walk by the lake some evening. He has thinning hair and very dark eyes. I am nervous but why live life at the bottom of an ocean floor?

### October 31

We went past the Opera House, where washerwomen were busy scrubbing down the stairs with soap and water. By the bandstand men were singing bawdy songs and people were folk dancing. I laughed a lot. Later I boiled Father's undershirts.

### November 1

The children threw paint on the schoolhouse steps. What have they become? Ilya cleaned it up immediately—he said he did not want the young children to get into trouble. They flock around him and ride on his shoulders.

### November 2

Preparation for celebrations of the Revolution. Ilya is very busy in school but he had time to take me to the park. The lake is his second home he says. He skated beautifully. Later he presented me with a small silver chain and a locket with the design of a fish. It is not my birth sign, but who cares. How handsome he looked as he waved good-bye. He says they play hockey late at night—they light fires on the ice and sometimes they carry burning bushels so they can see in the dark.

### November 3

Father seems to fall further and further down into his overcoat. Rudik's trial in Moscow, in absentia, will begin soon. Father has sent messages to Sergei through the young Turkish boy three houses down, asking him not to come over to the house, since he doesn't want things to be jeopardized or influenced in any way. Father sits and stares. I fear for him.

### November 4

Such beautiful drawings the children did for the Celebrations, we hung them along the corridor.

### November 8

Revolution Day, yesterday. I dreamt I was at a kiosk selling summer apples with Ilya.

### November 10

They have given Rudik seven years hard labor. We have no strength for this. Mother fell on the bed and put her face to the pillow and wept. A death sentence had been quite possible, so in truth she should have been relieved. But she wept. Father told me a story from Berlin about a soldier who got his foot caught in the tram tracks. A tram was approaching fast. Another soldier was walking down the street when suddenly he heard the screaming. The second soldier tried to pull the first soldier's foot from the track. He couldn't, so he tore off his overcoat and threw it over the soldier's head so he would not have to watch the tram bearing down, to spare him the agony. I have heard this story before somewhere.

### November 11

Am I the one who must throw the coat over Father's eyes?

### November 12

Mother worries about Father, and yet perhaps it is her we should worry about. Her neck is red and scratched raw, perhaps a recurrence of the shingles. Father says nothing, and I have no idea where I can get tomatoes, which seemed to work last time. Even if it was possible to get them, they would be far too expensive this time of year.

### November 13

Father sits, still unmoving. He must now choose whether to denounce Rudik to the Committee, not really a choice, since they will surely denounce him anyway. Mother spent the night counting the money she has kept over the years in the porcelain elephant. Her outbreak of shingles seems to have calmed even without the tomato cure. She recalled for me her first ever meeting with Father. She seemed briefly happy, as if the memory propped her up. It was in the Central House of Culture of Railroad Workers, when he put a pinch of snuff up his nose. He had been talking of Mayakovski, quoting "Glory be to our beloved Motherland." Then of course he sneezed in the middle, which embarrassed him terribly. She recalled how Father bought her the porcelain elephant the next day. I tried to ask him about it but he didn't remember. He shooed me away like a fly. I cannot wait to tell Ilya these stories tomorrow. He says he doesn't care about Rudik, that I am the only one who interests him. Happiness!

### November 14

They have once again delayed the committee meeting. We went to the Big House again. Rudik, in London, was weeping, and I felt momentarily sorry for him. He is convinced he has made a mistake. They put pressure on him, and every day he appears in the newspapers. He says he cannot walk down the street without a photographer jumping from the bushes. He kept mentioning a dancer's name—I believe he was trying to hint at something—but I couldn't make out what he was saying. The stenographer gave me a rude look.

### November 16

I have been working on a cardigan for the newborn next door. It is almost finished but not quite as good as I wanted it to be. It has four buttons but needs a fifth. A walk in the snow with Ilya. He mentioned how he would someday like to have children. I wondered what I would call a child. Not Rudolf certainly. Maybe after Father. And what if it was a girl? For school; prepare letters to be sent to Brezhnev for his birthday.

November 20

A knock on the door and it scared us so! Suffering birds! The woman was nervous. Blond hair. Finnish. She said she was a dancer. I believed it from her body. She did not give her name. She said she was a friend of a friend who had come in through Oslo, she didn't explain how. She asked to be let in but Father refused. Then she got desperate. She had driven all the way from Moscow! Two full days! She said that Rudik had made friends with ambassadors in different countries and they had been able to bring things back. She had some items for us. We were convinced at first it was a ruse. Father told her it was against the law of the land. She flushed bright red. Then Mother asked her to leave. We kept looking up and down the street for the Driving School car, but it was not there. The woman pleaded but still Father said no. Finally the woman left the large package on the doorstep. She was crying with fear. It was terribly dangerous. We left the package there but before dawn Mother got up in her nightgown and brought it in, a light coating of snow upon it.

November 21

The package lay on the table. We could not bear to leave it unopened any longer.

November 22

Father drank a thimble measure from the bottle of brandy. Mother wore her new fur-lined coat, though only in the dark since she did not want the neighbors to see. When she put her hands in her pockets she found a note which said, *How I miss you. Your loving son.* I pondered what to do with the dress he sent me. It was far too tight at the hips. At first I thought I might burn it, but why? I decided instead to let the waistband out and wear it to the Motherland cinema next week with Ilya.

November 23

Father remembered that the dancer had said we are due another parcel, perhaps in the New Year. Next time I am sure we will open the door to her. Unless it is a ruse. We will find out soon enough. Father felt a certain measure of guilt, but he knows returning the parcel would mean even more trouble. Mother said, *Yes, it is wondrous, but a new coat does not replace him.* She was sitting in the armchair rubbing the fur collar.

November 26

Father was nostalgic and raised a glass to Rudik, and for the first time I heard him say, *My dear son.*

❊

Hereby we report that on June 16, 1961, NUREYEV Rudolf Hametovich, born 1938, single, Tatar, non-Party member, formerly of Ufa, artist of the Leningrad Kirov Theater, who was a member of the touring company in France, betrayed his Motherland in Paris. NUREYEV violated the rules of behavior of Soviet citizens abroad, went out to town, and came back to the hotel late at night. He established close relations with French artists among whom there were known homosexuals. Despite talks of a cautionary character conducted with him, NUREYEV did not change his behavior. In absentia he was sentenced in November 1961 to seven years hard labor. Furthermore, it has been decreed that, following the January 21, 1962, public dis-

avowal by Hamit Fasliyevich NUREYEV, vehemently denounc-
ing the actions of his son, he will be allowed to remain a standing member of the Party.

—Ufa Committee on State Security

February 1962

⚜

Six months before Rudi defected, Iosif came home to our room
along the Fontanka, carrying a bottle of cheap champagne. At the
doorway he kissed me.

Yulia, he said, I have wonderful news.

He removed his spectacles, rubbed the black semicircles beneath
his eyes, and guided me to the table in the corner of the room. He
opened the bottle, poured two cups, drank one immediately.

Tell me, I said.

His eyes drooped, and he quickly drank a second glass of champagne, pursed his lips and said: We have a new apartment.

For years I had cultivated our communal home along the river.
The kitchen and toilet were down the hallway and our room tiny,
old, ruined, but it felt majestic: an ornate fireplace, an intricate
medallion in the center of the ceiling from which a yellow lamp-
shade hung as a reminder of other days. Imagining the history
of the chandelier that once hung there wasn't so much bourgeois
sentiment as a quiet nod to my father's life. I had fixed all the
window sashes and arranged the curtains so they didn't obscure
the view to the Fontanka. Most of all it was the sound of the
water I adored. In summer it gently lapped against its walls
as the canal boats passed with their wares and in winter the ice
crackled.

Where? I asked.

In the sleeping quarters, he said.

The sleeping quarters were in the outskirts of Leningrad, where tower blocks met tower blocks, a place where I'd always felt that our country housed whatever was falling apart.

Calmly I took a sip of my drink.

Iosif said: It has an elevator, hot water, two rooms.

My silence made him shift in his seat.

I got the permits through the university, he said. We move next week.

I startled myself by saying nothing, rose slowly from the chair. Iosif grabbed my hair and yanked me across the table. I attempted to pull away, but he slapped my face: You'll start packing tonight.

I thought about telling him that he slapped like an academic, but that would only have invited his fist. I watched as he poured himself another glass of champagne. As he tipped it back his double chin disappeared, and in a chilling way he looked briefly attractive.

Good night, I said.

I removed a scarf from the drawer and walked out into the corridor.

Patches of sunlight spun on the Fontanka. I thought for a moment that I might tumble over the low wall and get carried through the city, drawbridges rising as I floated on. Such elegant foolishness. I followed the river north and took a sidestreet towards the Conservatory, to the Kirov, palatial in the square. Outside there was a poster announcing Rudi's performance in *Giselle*.

When I returned home Iosif was still at the table. He didn't look up. I had hidden some rubles in an antique samovar next to our bed. I took out enough for a balcony seat, pulled on my cashmere sweater. Descending the stairs once again, I thought I could hear the echo of Iosif's slap still reverberating around the building. By the time I returned to the Kirov, the lobby was teeming.

It was the rule of the theater that all coats and jackets must be hung in the cloakroom before the performance. I contemplated checking my cashmere sweater, but it felt good around me, its warmth, its delicacy. I wedged in my seat between two rather large women. I wanted to turn to them and say something ridiculous like, *Ah ballet, the perfect antidote.* I began thinking that perhaps Iosif was playing a crude trick on me, that really we wouldn't have to move from our room at all, that things would stay the same, that I would still sleep at night to the sounds of the river.

The musicians entered the orchestra pit and began tuning up, a flute here, a cello there, and the notes, initially discordant, started moving in unison towards one another.

My neighbors in the seats were chattering excitedly. Rudi's name fluttered in the air, and their pleasure at owning him began to disturb me. I wanted to stand and shout, *But you don't know Rudi, I know Rudi, my mother taught him how to dance!* Yet I hadn't seen him in a long time, almost a year. He was twenty-two, he had his own apartment, food privileges, a good salary and in the corridors of fate his portrait hung high.

The lights were dimmed. When Rudi entered, exploding from the wings to a round of applause, he tore the role open, not so much by how he danced, but by the manner in which he presented himself, a sort of hunger turned human. I wanted to let myself slip away into the performance, but after the first variation I began to realize how terribly hot I felt. Without drawing attention to myself, I tried to fan air to my body. I grew hotter and hotter, and yet I didn't want to disturb my neighbors by wriggling around in my seat, or pulling the sweater over my head. The shrill alarm of Rudi's dancing was saying, *Look at me! Look at me!* but I was obsessed by my sweater and how hot I was becoming. The air was packed with intensity. My face flushed and sweat collected at my brow.

When the intermission finally came, I stood up quickly, only for my knees to buckle and my legs to fold beneath me. I came to almost immediately, but already I'd created a fuss—people were pointing at me, whispering, and I had an immediate vision of the next day's newspapers writing about the lone woman who had fainted during Rudi's performance.

With the help of a gentleman behind me I got back into my seat and removed my sweater. I desperately wanted to explain what had happened, but I could tell he thought I was simply overcome.

He's wonderful, isn't he?

I was just hot, I said.

He has quite an effect, said the gentleman over my shoulder.

I thought I would faint a second time, but I managed a deep breath, rose, and stumbled out along the aisle, down the staircase under the light of the chandeliers. In the bathroom someone held my shoulders as I vomited. I was horrified when I heard her suggest that I might be pregnant, an impossibility. I cleaned up and splashed water on my face. The mirror was smudged with fingerprints, and I had the strange feeling that someone else's ghostly hand was on my face. At thirty-six, I had acquired crow's-feet, and there were the beginnings of dark bags beneath my eyes.

In the bathroom I could hear women exclaiming over the extraordinary performance. A couple of girls were smoking at a corner sink, rolling Rudi's name around on their tongues.

On the second floor I bought an ice cream, and by the time the bell sounded for the second act I felt I had recovered sufficiently to take my seat.

I leaned forward and squinted at the distant stage, until the woman in front of me, annoyed that my hair was touching her, handed me a pair of opera glasses.

Rudi's body was a thing of the most captivating beauty—hard lines at his shoulders, his neck striated with muscle, enormous thighs, his calf muscles twitching. He took his partner in the air and spun her with remarkable lightness. I couldn't help thinking about the day he had first arrived, at seventeen, when I had seen him undressing in my room, the pale promise of his body slipping beneath the blanket on my sofa. I returned the glasses and tried to quell whatever emotion was overcoming me. I was holding the edge of the chair far too tightly, nails gripping the wood.

When the ballet finished Rudi extended his arm in the air and slowly turned his head from one side of the theater to the other. The ovation rang in my ears.

I ran outside and hurried along the Fontanka, then ascended the stairwell. When I entered the room Iosif was still sitting at the table, drunk. I put my hands on his shoulders and kissed him. Shocked, Iosif pushed me aside, filled his glass, downed it quickly, then stumbled across the room and kissed me back. I tried to guide him into making love to me against the wall, but he was hardly able to hold me, drunk as he was. Instead he pulled me to the floor and yet I didn't care, why should I care, the dancing still spun in me—Rudi had stood upon that stage like an exhausted explorer who had arrived in some unimagined country and, despite the joy of the discovery, was immediately looking for another unimagined place, and I felt perhaps that place was me.

I opened my eyes as Iosif was wiping the sweat from his neck. He went back to the table and said: Don't forget, you have to pack.

If I could stack the foolishness of my life in cardboard boxes I could make a monument of it—I packed.

The following week I was out in the sleeping quarters of Leningrad, having left my beloved Fontanka behind. The new apartment was large and dark. It had hot water, a telephone, a stove, a small fridge. The elevator squeaked outside the door. I listened to the high whistle of the kettle. I promised myself that I would leave soon, get enough money together, pay the taxes, negotiate a divorce, take on the enormity of finding another place to live. But in truth I knew I had caved in to Iosif, that allowing him to make love to me had only cemented his dispassion.

Six months later I was sitting on the eighth floor of the new apartment building—trying in vain to translate a Cuban poem about mystery and shadow—when my friend Larissa knocked on the door. She had taken a tram all the way out to the tower block. Her face was ashen. She took me by the arm and escorted me out to the soccer field beyond the towers.

There's a rumor, she whispered.

Pardon me?

Rudi has left, she said.

What?

People are saying that he defected to Paris.

We walked under the goalposts and looked at each other in silence. I began to remember moments that seemed like clues. How, during that first week, I had often caught a glimpse of him looking in the mirror, as if he was willing himself into someone else's body. How he had talked about foreign dancers, listened to RosaMaria's songs, rifled through my books. How, whenever he went to the Hermitage, he was drawn to the Italian Renaissance painters and the Dutch masters. How, when we sat around my table with my friends, he had always looked hungry, as if he were ready to pounce on a word or an idea. I felt a terrible guilt and a dread.

Paris? I asked.

We must keep this quiet, said Larissa.

That evening I sat with Iosif and heard the elevator's pulleys screeching in the hallway. When it stopped on our floor I could hardly shuck the thought that they were coming to knock at the door. I packed a bag with what I imagined I would need. It included a Gorky novel with money pasted beneath the cloth cover. I put the bag under my bed, had nightmares of being chained to a table.

Iosif said: The little bastard, how did he dare?

He rose and paced the room, whispering: How did he dare?

He looked me in the eye: How did he fucking dare?

The next day Iosif surprised me by saying I had nothing to worry about, that I had done nothing wrong, that through his connections he could make sure I would be left alone. I ironed his shirt for a conference and as he prepared his briefcase he assured me that everything would be all right. He kissed me brusquely on the cheek and set out for the university.

They came anyway, the following Monday morning.

I was alone when I heard the rapping on the door. I stuffed money beneath the insoles of my shoes, even took a slice of bread and put it in the pocket of my housedress. Trembling, I went to answer. The man was the traditional sort, beady, in a gray overcoat, but the woman was young and beautiful, blond hair, green eyes.

They drifted in without introducing themselves and went to sit at the table. I had the sneaking feeling that Iosif had maybe gone to see them in order to protect himself, that he had finally betrayed me in a tangible way, after all our tiny intimate betrayals over the years.

Am I being arrested? I asked.

They said nothing. I felt sure they were going to march me out of the room. Each lit a cigarette—taken from my pack—and blew smoke at the ceiling. They had perfected their drama. They asked me how long I had known him, if he had ever mentioned the West, who he talked about, why had he betrayed his people.

You know he's failing, don't you, Citizen?

I haven't heard anything.

Miserably.

Really?

They threw glass at him in Paris.

Glass? I said.

They wanted to rip his feet open.

Why?

Because he was terrible of course.

Of course.

I began to wonder how he had performed in Paris, since it was indeed possible that he had been booed or relegated to the corps. Perhaps Rudi's style of dancing was anathema to the French, and it was conceivable that he really had failed. After all he was young, just twenty-three; he had been dancing only a few years.

They kept examining my features, but I held my face tight. Eventually the talk got around to the gatherings in my old room.

Your salon, said the woman.

There was no point in arguing.

She closed one eye: We need the name, address, occupation of everyone who came.

I wrote the names down. It was a pointless exercise since they knew them all anyway—when I was finished they looked the list over and told me, with wry smiles, whom I had forgotten. They had been watching me, it seemed, for quite a long time.

Write it again, they said.

Pardon me?

Your list.

My hands shook. They had me write down a second series of names and addresses—all those people who had ever spent time in my house, whether or not they had chatted with Rudi. I ferociously protected the corner of my mind in which my father sat. I had a vision of him at home in Ufa, in the shadow of the refinery, limping to the door to find yet more agents and yet more trouble arching through his life. But they didn't ask about him. It began to dawn on me that they were trying to find out if I could exert any influence on Rudi—to perhaps phone him and convince him to return—but they already saw that it was doubtful.

Finally they asked if I was prepared to publicly denounce Rudi.

Yes, I said, without a moment's hesitation.

They seemed vaguely disappointed and lit themselves another cigarette each. The man tucked a pencil behind his ear.

You will write a letter to him.

Yes.

You will tell him that he has betrayed his Motherland, his people, our history.

Yes.

Do not seal the letter.

I won't.

Your behavior is very precarious, the woman told me.

I replied with a measure of dignity that I would certainly mend my ways.

Do not mention this to anybody, the man warned.

I nodded.

Do you understand me?

He was almost frightened—one foot wrong could have an effect on the rest of his life too, his wife, his children, his apartment.

Yes, I understand.

We'll be back.

The woman turned and said: As for me, I would not have spat on him even if he had been on fire.

She glared, waiting for me to react.

I nodded and said: Certainly.

When they left I stood with my back against the door and waited for the elevator to begin its descent, and then for some reason, rather than cry, I laughed until I was exhausted, laughed as the pulleys clicked through the system of steel and rollers, laughed as I heard the pneumatic hiss, laughed as I heard the final stop, laughed, all the time remembering that night at the Kirov and the notion of sleeping with Rudi, or having slept with him, through Iosif. It struck me that I hated Rudi the way you can hate someone who makes love to you and leaves, in other words, with a certain grudging admiration or envy for the fact of having left.

My friends were terrified to be seen with me ever again. Their political diligence and reliability had been called into question, and they would always, now, have files. They too would listen for the elevators. I thought about how my life had been pared down over the years, peeled away layer by layer.

One night I found Iosif staring at a bottle. He curled his upper lip into a snarl, told me he had six shirts drying on the balcony and they needed ironing.

No, I said.

Iron the fucking shirts! he shouted.

He lifted his fist to my face, and held it centimeters from my eyes.

At the window—when I hauled the shirts in from the line—I could hear him behind me, pouring another glass of wine for himself.

I took the only option I felt might clear my head—the train, to visit my father in Ufa. It was late September by the time I got my visa. The journey took three days because of the connections. Exhausted, I couldn't find a taxi, or even a horse and cart, so I walked through the city, asking people for directions. Tatar and Muslim women were out walking with their children. They glanced at me and looked away. I couldn't help wondering how a city like this could have made a dancer like Rudi.

I finally found my father's street. It was lined with old wooden houses where the bright shutters made an argument against the nearby tower blocks. I negotiated the muddy ruts, pondering how in the world my father managed such a difficult walk with his cane.

He came to the door and almost giggled when he saw me. He was looking remarkably well, although he had let his hair grow past his ears, which gave him a faintly mad look. He wore a suit and a tie with a few food stains. His shirt buttons were done up to the neck, but the tie was open as if it and the shirt had different intentions for the day. One of the earpieces of his spectacles was broken and he had looped a piece of string around his ear to keep them from falling. Still, the only real evidence of serious aging were the few capillaries that had burst in his face. Yet I thought the burst vessels looked oddly handsome on him.

When we hugged I could smell the mustiness of his hair.

We sat down to Beethoven, and he made tea on the tiny stove. There was a portrait of my mother by the bedside. My father had met a young artist who had copied a photograph of her, using charcoal. How diligent the artist had been to her beauty, I thought, and now it seemed she would remain forever beautiful.

He caught me looking at the portrait and said: It's our function in life to make moments durable.

I nodded, unsure of what he meant. He drank his tea. I hesitated to tell him about Rudi, knowing the news had not yet been made officially public, but finally I blurted it out.

Rudi's in Paris.

Yes, he said, I know.

How do you know?

He looked around as if there might be somebody else in the room. I have my ways, he said.

He shuffled to the cupboard: It calls for a small celebration, don't you think? I haven't yet celebrated.

I don't think so.

Why not?

They'll sentence him to death.

What? he said. They'll send a death squad to Paris?

Perhaps.

The thought of it sobered him up. He moved his mouth around as if he were tasting whatever idea it was that had come to him.

We're all sentenced to death, he finally said, with a certain amount of glee. At least he'll have a better one than us!

Oh, Father.

He always was a clever little cockroach, wasn't he?

Yes, I suppose he was.

From the cupboard he produced an old bottle of vodka, which he opened with a flourish, draping a white cloth over his arm for style.

To the clever little cockroach, Rudolf Hametovich Nureyev! he said, holding his glass in the air.

We cooked a small meal under the charcoal gaze of my mother. He recalled her days with the Maryinsky, saying she was robbed of her prime, that she could have been one of the greatest—he knew it was a lie but it was a good lie and it made us both feel warm.

I made a bed on the couch.

Just before I fell asleep he coughed and said: His father.

What?

I was just thinking of his poor father.

Go to sleep.

Ha! he said. Sleep!

Later I heard him sit down at the table with a book, leafing through the pages—a pen nib scratched across the paper—and I fell asleep to the sound.

He was gone early in the morning, worrying me, so I dusted the room and cleaned in the corners to occupy the time.

On the table, beneath a stack of poetry books, I found a journal. I flicked through. On the first page he had written the date of my mother's death. The paper was cheap and the ink had soaked through to other pages, making it difficult to read. His penmanship was ragged and spidery, and I thought to myself, *This is my father's life.* I willed myself not to read his words and began dusting what I had already dusted. He had allowed his plants to dry up, so I carried them to the communal bath and put them in an inch of water to see if they could be resurrected.

An old woman, a neighbor, came and watched me in the bath-room without saying a word. She was heavy but frail with age. She asked who I was, and when I replied, she returned to her room with a snort.

I sat at the edge of the bath. There was hair in the drain, and it did not belong to my father—it was a young man's hair, dark and vital. It seemed somehow offensive that my father should bathe in a place others used.

All the time the idea of the journal was burning a hole through me. I went back along the corridor, sat at the table, touched the jour-nal's black cover, finally turned to a section about a third of the way through:

*And yet it's true that—while I have never*
*believed in god, which on its own does not*
*make me a good Citizen—that perhaps, in the*
*end, it will endear god to me if he really does*
*exist. Most of my time in this life has not been spent living*
*in any real sense, more a day-to-day survival, going*
*to sleep wondering, What will happen to me tomorrow?*
*Then tomorrow arrives while I am still wondering.*
*And yet a landscape of sighs can come together in a*
*collective music. At this moment there are birds in the*
*trees, a dozen children outside my room window,*
*playing, even the sun is shining. And, I will tell you*
*this, since it is all I want to say: Anna, the sound of your*
*name still opens the windows of this room.*

He returned home at noon, startling me. I was still looking at the same page when I heard the door creak. I fumbled to put the journal back under the pile of poetry books he had left on the table, but they went tumbling. I got to my knees and started picking them off the floor. He saw me tucking the journal beneath an old copy of Pasternak.

He held a bunch of lilies in his hand. He put them in a vase by the window, where they nodded in the wind. I wondered how many times he had said my mother's name as he was cutting the flowers.

His face betrayed nothing. I thought about asking him whether he would let me read the whole journal but, before I could, he said in a strange voice: Did you know that his father never saw him dance?

I stayed quiet for a long time and then asked: How do you know?
Oh I went to visit.
Where?
At his house.
You're friends?

We talk.

What's he like? I asked.

Oh he's a good solid man.

My father turned to the window and spoke as if to the world out-side: I fear he will eventually be ruined.

He remained at the window, fingering the curtain.

And his mother? I asked.

She's stronger, he said. She will survive.

He made his way to the table, picked up his journal, rifled through the pages.

You can have this if you want, he said.

I shook my head and told him I had read a sentence or two, that it was beautiful.

It's balderdash, he said.

He touched my hand and said: Yulia, don't ever let them poison your life with narrowness.

I asked him what he meant and he replied that he wasn't quite sure, it was just something that he felt fated to say.

I clung to him those few days, clung to his spirit. Whenever he left the house I read his journal. What it amounted to was a song of love, and it bothered me that he didn't once mention me. The only people to appear were he and my mother. His recollections of their life were a jumble—the last days were nudged up against the first days and sometimes the later years seemed to have shaped the earlier ones—as if time had been gripped and squeezed formless. It struck me that, despite everything, my parents had lived their lives with a certain panache. They had been born into plenitude and lived with the knowledge that they would die in poverty, yet they appeared to have accepted everything that had happened to them—perhaps in some ways they were happier for the reversal, cementing them together.

I thought of my own small pleasures, having lived much of my own life avoiding difficulty. I went wandering around Ufa, the dirt streets, the factories, the few remaining bright houses. At a bird auction near the mosque I bought a goldfinch being sold as a songster. I declined the cage and took the bird in the cup of my hands towards the Belaya River. When I opened my hands it seemed startled a moment but then took off, surely to be captured again. I detested the fatuous self-pity I had sunk into, yet embraced it also, since in some ways it was healing. Foolishly I bought two more birds and set them free, only to realize that I had no money for the tram. I took it as an appropriate irony and walked back to my father's house.

I stayed for three more days. On the evening before my return to Leningrad I told my father that I was pondering a divorce. He didn't seem surprised, maybe happy even.

Go ahead, get a divorce.

I frowned, and he flung his arms out.

Or at least marry someone else!

What about the apartment?

Who cares? he said. We live with ourselves, not our rooms.

I sulked for a while until he said: Yulia, dear. Get a divorce. Stay in Petersburg. Live what you have left.

He sat back in his chair and smoked the butt end of a foul-smelling cigar he had kept hidden.

Later that evening he told me he had something special to do. He put his finger to his lips as if there were other people in the room and then fumbled at the gramophone. I thought he was simply putting on music, but he lifted the stylus and began dismantling the apparatus. In the belly of the gramophone he had hidden a small flat box. He handed the box to me and said it had been my mother's, she had always wanted me to have it.

I should have given it to you before, he said.

His voice trailed off as I tried to open the box. It had not been opened for a long time and the clasp was rusted. I took a knife and delicately began to pry it open. My father watched silently. I expected to find another journal, perhaps one she had kept before the Revolution. Or maybe some of their old love letters. Or some trinkets they had collected through the years. I went to rattle the box, but my father grabbed my wrist.

Don't do that, he said.

He took the knife and pried the clasp. Without opening the lid, he handed the box back to me.

Inside there was a tiny china saucer, no bigger than an ashtray. It was small and delicate and pale blue, with bucolic pictures of farmers and draft horses painted around the rim. It disappointed me at first, how light it was, how fragile, how it seemed to have nothing to do with either of them.

It's one hundred years old, he said. It belonged to your mother's grandmother. Your mother rescued it from a cellar in Petersburg after the Revolution. Along with many other pieces. She wanted to keep them all.

What happened to them?

They broke on our journeys.

This is the only piece left?

He nodded and said: Poverty lust sickness envy hope.

Pardon me?

Poverty lust sickness envy and hope, he said again. It has survived them all.

I held the tiny piece of china in my hands and wept until my father told me, with a smile, that it was time for me to grow up. I wrapped the saucer again and placed it in the box, then swaddled it between clothes in my suitcase, hidden deep so it would not be found or harmed in any way.

Make sure it's safe, he said.

We hugged, and he quoted a line about watching random fleets of night birds flying across the face of the moon.

I returned to Leningrad by train—the landscape speeding by— and on the journey I plucked up the courage finally to get divorced. It was a matter of saving enough money for the tax and waiting for the right time. Over the next eighteen months I cobbled together a number of translations and hid the money along with the china dish.

And then one evening, in the early summer of '63, I woke up a little disoriented, wondering whether it was morning or evening. The news blackout on Rudi had been lifted that day. For two years he had not been mentioned anywhere, but that day both *Izvestiya* and *Pravda* carried articles about him. They said he had morally debased himself and his country, which was amusing, maybe even true. There was no photo of Rudi, of course, but he still shone somehow in the vitriol.

Iosif had grown angrier over the past months. Twice he had slapped me. Stupidly I caved into the desire to ridicule him and told him that he slapped like a member of the intelligentsia, so he had punched me, hard, knocked a tooth loose. Since then we had seldom talked.

He was at the table, hunched over a bowl of soup, reading both newspapers, slurping his food with relish. He looked old to me, the bald spot at the top of his head illuminated in the globe of lamplight from above his head.

From the bed I examined him, but after a while I became aware of a commotion outside the window, a distant and muffled shouting that seemed to intensify as I listened.

There was another shout and a thud.

I said to Iosif: What's that?

Go to sleep, woman, it's just the hooligans playing soccer, he said.

I put my face to the cool side of the pillow, but there was something about the texture of the shouting that disturbed me. I waited an hour, until Iosif had gone to bed on the couch, and then got up, went to the window, pulled aside the curtain, looked down. I was tired—I had been working on several translations—and had to blink many times before my eyes adjusted.

Beyond the courtyard, out towards the soccer field, a few hooligans were clustered around mounds of freshly dug soil. There was some new construction going on, and the dirt was piled up like a series of small hillocks. The hooligans had found a couple of short white sticks and had shoved them into the ground as goalposts.

A middle-aged man who looked like a war veteran—he wore an old military hat tilted at an angle—was trying to get at the sticks, but he was being pushed back by the teenagers. He was screaming at them, but, from my distance, I couldn't make out his words. The hooligans were circling him and jabbing his chest, but he was holding his ground.

All of a sudden the man broke through their ranks and pulled both the short white goalposts out of the ground, brandishing them as weapons. He backed away, swinging the posts. The hooligans watched. Once he was about five meters away the man rushed off, clutching the white posts to his chest. The teenagers didn't bother following. Instead they laughed and went back to one of the piles of soil from the construction site. They picked through the dirt until they found a white ball and began kicking it.

With a dreadful shiver, I realized that it was a skull.

The floor seemed to sway. I grasped at the window ledge.

The war veteran had, by then, turned around. He saw them passing the skull back and forth at their feet. I could not see his face. He dropped the sticks—they must have been armbones or legbones—and ran across the field once more, weighed down by his frame, his jacket, his hat, his sadness.

Behind him, the bones lay crossed on the ground.

The words of a song returned to me, the dead turning into a soaring flight of cranes. I trembled, wondering whether the bones were German or Russian and then I wondered if it even mattered, and then I thought of my small china dish hidden away and wrapped. Beneath the window frame I sat and curled up against the abandon of what we had become.

I pulled the curtains together, watched Iosif snore. I was exhausted yet exhilarated, as if something terrible was dragging me down and at the same time shoving me forward. I wanted to wake Iosif, to say that we would survive, that we would get through this, we could transform, we could learn. I wanted him to do something soothing and kind for me, but I didn't wake him, nor did he stir, and I knew then that the opportunity was lost. I was thirty-eight years old and leaving.

I pulled the suitcase from under the bed and began packing: my clothes, my books, my dictionaries, the half-finished translations, the china saucer. I made enough noise for Iosif to waken but he didn't. It seemed to me that the sleeping part of him knew what the waking half would feel.

I thought about kissing him on the cheek, but instead I wrote him a note, quoting my father's line about the stars being deeper than their darkness.

By the time I had packed and was ready to leave, it was morning. Reefs of clouds had appeared in the sky. The hooligans had disappeared, but the military man was still in the field. He had a shovel in his hands now, and he was reinterring the bones and skull in an untouched part of the field. The sun was suspended between distant towers, and the apartment buildings on the horizon looked like children's playing blocks. As if by design, a flock of birds rose and flapped small against the heavens. I walked down the stairs, not desiring the claustrophobia of the elevator. The day was already warm and humid. My suitcase was not heavy.

In the field I passed the military man, who looked at the ground and then turned his back on me as if to say: Our wars are never over.

<hr />

JUNE 1964

Tamara,

You will doubt it, but the news of Father's passing hit me with the force of an ax and brought me to my knees. I was in Italy. They stupidly waited until after the show, and then they handed me the telegram, which was routed on from Paris, where it was sent by mistake. Hence the time it took for me to get in touch. Nothing else.

I went out alone in the streets of Milan and could not help but recall him and, although you will not believe this, it was with fondness. It is true that I spent much of my life in difficulties with Father, yes, but I have also felt the opposite. To hold such conflicting emotions is indeed a possibility—even the cheapest choreographer will tell you that. So it wounds me deeply to hear the things you say.

It is true that I danced the following night—but dance to me, as you know, is every emotion, not just celebration but death, futility and loneliness, too. Even love must pass through loneliness. So I danced him alive. When I went onstage I took flight and was released. You may choose not to believe this, but it is the truth.

The stories you heard about me celebrating in nightclubs are absurd. The photograph of me spraying champagne inside the dressing room at La Scala was taken on another day, not on the night of Father's death. Do not believe them when they lie. The notion is hideous. I am twenty-six years old. How could any-one possibly think I have become such an animal as to be dead to feeling? Am I frozen? Am I wood?

The truth of it is that I bleed as much as anybody, probably even more so.

You curse me, but I am, in fact, protecting you and of course Mother. You should be thankful. To be away from home is to be away from everything that made me. And to be away from everything that made me, when it dies, is my own death. Darkness touches darkness everywhere.

Perhaps you will choose not to understand this.

But you should listen to me when I tell you how devastated I was, especially for Mother, who is never more than a step away from my mind.

You choose to say that my life is a circus now. Nothing is simple, Tamara, not even your attempts at simplification. Why did I do it? It was never my intention to leave, I could have stayed, but if you tread water long enough it is possible you might never learn to swim. I meant nothing by it. Politics is for fat men with cigars. It is not for me, I am a dancer, I live to dance. That is all.

And you ask, with a snort, what is my life now? Yes I am fortunate. I have a house, contracts, masseur, managers, friends. I have danced on almost every continent. I had tea in the White House with President Kennedy before he was shot. Margot and I danced at the inauguration of Johnson. At the Vienna State Opera House we got eighty-nine curtain calls. The ovations often last a half hour. I am gloriously happy, but sometimes I wake in the mornings with an awful sense of it being over and never having meant that much. I have no desire to be served up as a sensation, a nine-day wonder. I go from country to country. I am a non-person where I became a person. I am stateless. So it is. And so it has always been, even I suppose since our days in Ufa. It is dance, and dance only, that keeps me alive.

Goethe says: Such a price the gods exact for song, to become what we sing.

Sometimes things fly across my mind with no real meaning or purpose that I can decipher. Do you remember the beer seller who used to operate her stall at the bottom of Krassina? She had a face like a mule. She had just three beer mugs, and she used to shout at the men to hurry up and drink. She slid the abacus beads very precisely. You took me there one afternoon and you told me that you could tell the time of day by however much of her had disappeared. I did not understand until you showed me the shadow from the umbrella, how it used to slice her. At midday she was dark since the sun was high in the sky. By the end of the day all of her could be seen since the sun was so low. You were able to tell the time by her shadows.

I will tell you this—I often envy the freedom that you had to marry Ilya. Yes, freedom. You must understand that I desire choice. And yet that choice is denied to me. My life is tied up in opera houses, hotel rooms, dining halls, luncheons, rehearsals. In any case I am indeed sorry that I missed your wedding celebrations. I have been to similar occasions in the West and have thought of you. You surely looked beautiful. Give my regards and congratulations to your new husband.

Of course I do not care that he is a janitor, why should that disturb me? You should have more faith in me. Without janitors, without electricians, without plumbers, the world would surely be taking a shit in a bucket in the dark.

At this moment I am at the country house of a friend for three or four days. It is the first time, except for when I have been injured, that I have neither danced nor rehearsed in ten years. I need the space, since I have not taken a breath in a very long time. My friends are kind—they give me great companionship. Perhaps I have changed, but it is only for the good. I do not suffer fools gladly. Most of all, and most important, my dancing is transformed. I have built a great coliseum on the foundation of what I laid in Leningrad. The success with Fonteyn has been staggering. She has gone through some very trying times in recent years, not least since her husband was crippled. Yet Margot, when she dances, is a genius. I have seen her coming down the steps of her own house on pointe. She constantly amazes me, despite her age. When she is onstage nothing touches her, and together we are hand and glove. The world is our witness.

Up to now I have worked relentlessly and the world has taken its toll, so it is time to briefly replenish. I am here to take stock.

The land is generally flat, although we are in the hills. In some ways I am reminded of the landscape of Crimea. A friend of mine looks after me, cooking meals, taking calls, keeping the journalists away. When I hear phones ringing, I think of Mother. I hope she is strong. At times my anger is unstoppable. I would speak my outrage to the world except I know what would happen. If I spoke up she would be further marooned.

And I will tell you immediately that what rumors you hear of me and other men are completely untrue. I have many friends—it is as simple as that. Do not believe those who try to derail me, miserable cockroaches.

You should be proud of me, and if I could talk to you face-to-face you would certainly dismiss all the lies that are told in my name. I recall long evenings in Ufa, sunlight, factory horns, the dirty air. You see, I have not forgotten my homeland, but I will not be sentimental. There are secret police who still follow me, and I live in fear, but I will not let it affect me, I'll live through it in order to say: I have lived through it.

I do not regret anything. Regret is for simpletons.

I dream sometimes of Mother and bringing her to the West, where she could live in comfort. (You too if you desire.) I have been in touch with politicians, but they say their hands are tied. I have employed lawyers to look into the possibility. They take the money, of course, but I fear it is useless. Bloodsuckers! We have to stand strong and not let fate be thrust upon us. As for Mother, I hope she is being strong. She once cut his fingernails in front of us, do you recall? He was embarrassed to be seen like this, having his nails cut, so he hurried her along, yes? She cut his finger and he wore a bandage for days. Then he hid the bandaged hand in his jacket pocket.

Tamara, if these words reach you, tell Mother that I think of her endlessly. Inform her that her son dances to improve the world. And whisper my name to the grass where Father is.

That is all.

*Rudik*

# BOOK TWO

1961–1971

*I desire this thinking body—*
*This charred bony flesh*
*Alive to its own span—*
*To turn into a street, a country.*

—Osip Mandelstam

Eleven hours of rehearsal, one hour of slow barre work. Impossible to achieve the correct phrasing. You must desire the patience of a stonecutter. Chisel away until everything fits. After dressing room nap, another hour rehearsal with Rosella. In performance nobody—nobody!—noticed, not even Françoise.

Twenty encores, but so what, who cares? Remember: Perfection is the duty.

In an interview Petit says there are certain things that defeat themselves if they are said. That dance is the only thing that can describe what is otherwise indescribable. Yes.

The note from Grace Kelly hung from the lightbulb above the mirror.

Edith Piaf was watching from the veranda. Jean Cocteau smiled from the shadows. Marlene Dietrich was stretched out on the divan. There was talk of Leonard Bernstein on his way from his hotel, perhaps even an appearance by Picasso. Someone began quoting lines from Proust. All for me!

Walked back to the hotel with the bodyguards and heard a roadsweeper on the quays, humming Mozart. I thought that nothing will surprise me anymore, not even my dreams.

The de La Rochefoucauld house—fifteen types of champagne, more caviar than ever seen before. Orchids on the tables. Gold candelabras. Everyone was whirling around, the room had no corners. The talk was of choreographers, critics, audiences, but it swung finally to philosophers, all Western, including Derrida, so they left me disadvantaged. There is much to catch up on. Otherwise they will buffoon me. My reply was based on Sasha's idea that dance says what nothing else can.

Dance with the balls. The brain follows the balls.

Lots of nodding heads. Snickers behind their hands. I left them alone when really I should have stuck my tongue down their throats to pierce their empty hearts.

Twenty-three years old. The constant (unrevealed) thought of being an impostor. But you cannot become a history of what you have left behind. No tea, no heirlooms, no weeping. No stale bread, soaked in vodka and tears. You must boot yourself down the boulevards of Paris in your white silk shirt!

Mother was weeping uncontrollably on the telephone. Later during the night there was the thought of her at the wireless, turning white knobs: Warsaw, Luxembourg, Moscow, Prague, Kiev, Vilnius, Dresden, Minsk.

Tamara said: You have betrayed us.

Menuhin played Bach at the Salle Pleyel: the heart quickened and almost forgot everything.

A bath. Honey in the tea. Rehearsal. The perfection is not so much in the performance as in the journey towards it. This is the joy. You must burn!

Each corner, each sculpture, each painting takes the breath away. It is like walking through a history book that goes on forever, refuses to meet its own back cover. It is a marvel, a seventh wonder, almost as good as the Hermitage (although half the size and not quite the grandeur).

Already the guards recognize me and one of them greeted me in pidgin Tatar. His family left generations ago. He was with the Impressionists, so I lingered.

Claire took me along the Seine away from the museum. She gave me a pair of giant sunglasses for disguise then pulled the brim of my leather cap down. Four people immediately shouted, *Nureyev!*

At a stall a bookseller was waving a signed copy of *A Farewell to Arms.* Only a few weeks dead and his books are selling at ridiculous prices. (Perhaps one should die in the middle of a dance, *en l'air,* have the performance auctioned, frozen, sold to the highest bidder.) Claire looked in her handbag, but the book seller said he didn't have change. She bought it for almost one and a half times the price. She was curious that I was so appalled. Later she showed me the workings of the bank account—such foolishness.

Rumors that they tortured Sasha, questioned Xenia, took Yulia and put her in a cell for a week. Surely this cannot be true.

A new hairstyle in Paris: the Noureev. In *Le Monde* some vulture said it has appeared as quickly as the Berlin Wall, but as Cocteau explained, it is just their desire to commodify me. Oh, to have a mind like Cocteau's. (He said that in a dream he was once trapped in an elevator listening to *Symphony Divine.*)

The bearded Jew walked east through the Jardins de Luxembourg, his long overcoat swishing at his ankles. He had his hands behind his back, holding a prayer book. Then he sat on a bench under a tree and picked his teeth. He might have been thinking, *Ah, Petersburg.*

Madame B. waited while the Algerian tailor measured. Then she bought the black velvet suit. She said I should take endless delight in new beginnings.

In the apartment the maidservant made a disgusting drink of minted tea. I sipped it and immediately spat it back into the glass. Madame seemed delighted, as if she had found the elemental savage.

She came to the divan, ran my suit lapel between her forefinger and thumb. I excused myself to the window. Down below, on the sidewalk, the men walked with their overcoats draped across their forearms and the women wore their hats as if something were alive on their heads. The traffic stalled. Bits of newspaper blew along the Seine.

Madame was at the window, trying to shout down to me as I walked away along the quay.

The wristwatches were all German handmade and they had no price tags. It was difficult to be nonchalant when Madame asked which one I wanted. She desires to smother me with her wealth, yet why should I say to a fountain that I am not going to drink from your water?

Later Madame pointed out that, when nervous, I pull my shirt-sleeves down over my knuckles. She said it was uncouth, the gesture of a peasant, but that time would fix it. She leaned back against the balcony railing, holding a long cigarette. Her chin tilted as if she had just said something very wise. I tugged at my sleeve again. She waved her cigarette in the air. *Oh, non non non, Rudi, mon Dieu!*

Then came the extraordinary look on her face when I flung the watch from the balcony down into the garden.

If you wish to wear your hat indoors, who is to tell you no? (She forgets that a bucket of shit is an easy thing to pour, especially from a spiral staircase.)

You cannot end up mad (Nijinsky) or complacent (Tikhomirov).

A fan was waiting outside the Palais in the rain. Hungarian. Said he escaped in '59. He stood in the spill from the gutter and said that until he saw me perform he did not know who he really was. Such an idiot. He held a newspaper above his head and the ink had run down his face. Also he reeked of cognac. Still, I signed his autograph book.

Maria took my arm. At dinner we talked about the great ones, Karsavina, Pavlova, Fonteyn, etc. Of course I put Maria top of the list. She blushed.

Later she suggested wisely that one must experience an older dancer as one would eat a lobster claw. She demonstrated quite nimbly, ripping the claw and noisily sucking it clean.

The fools put sequins along my sleeve so that when I lift her they scrape the inside of her thigh.

In the pas de deux there were tears in her eyes, and the streak of blood became apparent. It was dress rehearsal and the crowd was impatient. In the wings she was screaming in pain, *God damn, god damn, god damn, I am ruined.* She spat at the French costumier. Then she changed her outfit and the doctor patched her skin. All in the space of two minutes.

When she reappeared she had the same angelic smile as always.

The *Le Monde* critic said she had begun to feel immune to beauty but, after the *Bayadère* pas de deux, she wobbled out of the theater with tears of joy in her eyes.

Do not allow the critics to make you so good you cannot become any better. Correspondingly, do not allow them to rip the cartilage from your carcass. (Sasha: *Your duty is to disprove those who don't believe.*)

Truth: When criticized you go berserk, but in your defense remember that it is those who calmly listen who never change.

Madame arranged for the boy to come over. She said he was from a good family and is studying Russian at the Sorbonne. She answered the door to him. Her lips pursed tight when she brought him into the library. He walked brazenly across the room, tossed his leather jacket on the Louis XV furniture. Madame froze and winced at the sound of the zipper as it touched the arm of the chair.

She put on Stravinsky, then excused herself delicately. We sat looking at each other. He put out his hand and said: *Gilbert.*

Sometimes the least word breaks the spell.

Gilbert said they had put the silverware on the table in my honor. He watched me eat the melon. I ran my tongue along the fork for him to see and could feel his shivers all the way across the room! For dessert I left the spoon in my mouth an extra few seconds. His young wife looked out from under her thin eyebrows and then excused herself to bed.

On the drive out to Rambouillet, Gilbert licked the steering wheel of his roadster and began laughing. We watched the champagne cork bounce in the rearview mirror. I thought that hundreds must be out on the roads, happy, in the darkness everywhere.

At Dominique's his friends made a fuss. *Rudi! Rudi! Rudi!* Gilbert shouted a Cossack toast after stacking glasses in a pyramid. The émigré waiter sniggered at my accent. I threw my coffee in his face, splattering his fine white shirt. The manager came over and groveled, assuring me the waiter would be fired.

Gilbert laughed and kicked me under the table.

Afterwards in the club on rue d'Assis the boys in red halter tops broke into a cancan. The English actor with the black sideburns looked in my direction. Outside, the sun stung my eyes. We walked straight to rehearsal. Gilbert slept on the bench in the dressing room.

The man in the corner seemed familiar but I couldn't place him. His mustache and eyebrows were thick and gray. He was fidgeting and smoking. I racked my brains, nervous that he might be following me. He did seem Russian, yes, but it wasn't until he turned to pay his bill that I noticed just how cunning and disenchanted his look was. Then it became clear—he was the émigré waiter from Dominique's.

He ignored me, left the café, yet made a good deal of noise as he pushed back the tables. He stopped by a fire-eater performing at the corner and then made a show of flourishing a twenty-franc bill, dropped it in the fire-eater's bucket.

I left the café and kissed the fire-eater's cheeks (he did not flinch). The asshole waiter watched me from a distance and then finally scuttled away, probably to the rue Daru where he and the others could mourn their paltry existence.

Truth: I conceal my fear in loudness, including performances.

The ovations become more exhausting than the dance. Perhaps one day there will be a ballet of ovations. On mentioning this to Claire she said that any such effort would be very Artaud. I was lost—no idea. Sometimes it is impossible to conceal this blankness. She said it was all right, he's a French experimentalist, she will get me his books, he might be interesting, something about the theater of cruelty.

She also promised the Richter recording. With a portable hi-fi I could listen to him on the road.

I thought at first it was a joke. I almost cursed her in four languages. I realized it was indeed Margot and almost choked. She said the whole thing was arranged.

Outside Covent Garden. Taking off my beret elicits a roar.

Rehearsal is pure and unpolluted. Margot's fierce intelligence. She dances from the inside out. For the pas de deux she took tiny faltering steps, dropped them perfectly on stage like tears. She makes us see not only the dance but also what the dancer sees.

Afterwards she brought me to her home at the Panamanian embassy and made a lamb stew, laughed when I pulled my shirt over my head and inhaled the smell. (Over dinner she made a joke that she is the mutton and I am the lamb, but the two decades between us mean nothing to me.)

For the Savoy reception she dressed up fashionably, someone said it was very *Saint Moritz*, whatever that means. When we walked in all the heads swiveled.

The English claim to civilization is pure shit! They allow their reporters and photographers everywhere. The problem with them is that they see dance as an aperitif, not the actual bread of their lives.

The French critics say you are a god when you dance.
　　I doubt that.
　　You doubt the critics?
　　I doubt the French.
　　(laughter all round)

I also doubt the gods.

Pardon me?

I'd say the gods are far too busy to give a shit about me or anybody else for that matter.

Walked in the rain, past the National Gallery, the Tate. The bodyguard didn't understand my terror, near Kensington Palace Gardens, on seeing the Soviet embassy.

Then it clicked and he bundled me away, his arm around my shoulder.

At Margot's, she heated the leftover stew and made a bitter English tea. Tito was away at some Panamanian function. She wore a low-cut silk blouse. Her neck could have been painted by da Vinci at the very least. She asked about home, said she could imagine Mother in her mind's eye, she must have been a beautiful woman. Unsure how to answer, I got up from the table and went into the back garden. She came out to say that she hoped she had not offended me.

Margot has a projector set up, dozens of cans of film, arranged by dates, beginning in 1938(!). Sat up all night unraveling the cans of film until I found some of Bruhn. His glorious formality. I went to my bedroom, couldn't sleep, paced.

The vultures ask about Cuba. I will not let them rope me in. A particularly stupid headline in the *Daily Express*: *Che será será.*

Elephant and Castle: one expects a magical fairyland but simply finds another part of Kiev.

Manager, agent, accountant—Gillian claimed they are the holy trinity of any great performer's life. At the end of the meeting Saul suggested he might be able to squeeze five thousand dollars from the German TV company. A twenty-minute performance, which means two hundred and fifty dollars per minute! I pretended to balk and could see him sweating at the other end of the table. (Margot says: *Do not lose sight of the dance*.)

Erik arrived in the lobby of the Savoy. Tall and lithe. He wore all white, even the stitching and zipper teeth of his jacket were white. We circled for a while, out-complimenting each other. He had just spent an awful lot of money on a Miró and the conversation swung between Miró and Picasso—we were surely talking about ourselves (Erik as Miró of course, me as Picasso.)

After champagne we asked the bellboy to find tea and cigarettes for Erik. He sat chain-smoking. At two Erik left for his room with an apology and a tortured smile. He avoided the elevator. The thought occurred to me that the greatest (second greatest?) dancer in the world was taking the steps four at a time.

Together we did an hour of barre, then went to class. The light streamed through the Covent Garden windows.

In the Tate, beside the Turner painting *The Chain Pier 1828*, he touched my shoulder. Later, on Saville Row, he wondered how we would look in the suits and bowler hats. The clerk pretended to be busy. I grabbed the measuring tape from around his neck and whispered to Erik that he should check the length of my inside leg. We wore the new bowler hats through the city, laughing.

Into the cinema on Shaftesbury Avenue. Darkness.

Erik's tall silhouette by the window in the Savoy, rain outside.

The English shoemaker was so different from what I had expected. Bald head, dirty suit jacket, face like a Cossack. Above his desk he has a framed picture of Margot. I could hardly breathe in the factory, stink of cow hides and buckets of glue. But his work is glorious. He spent hours preparing the shoes, meticulously going over every detail. Simply slipping the shoes onto my feet seemed to give a new energy.

(The maker on Kaznacheiskaya could learn a thing or two.)

Afterwards in the dressing room, a light burned out in the row of bulbs above Margot's mirror. She came to my door, knocked a couple of times and grew frantic when I didn't answer. *Rudi, dear, make a wish!* (She is very superstitious. Sometimes she catches an eyelash that has fallen on her cheek or a petal from a vase, and she is convinced this will affect everything.)

In Edinburgh the snow came down, brought me back to Leningrad.

Clarinda and Oscar (under a pseudonym) are writing the account of my defection for a publishing house, which is altogether ridiculous but the only thing that interests people. They say it will sell books, that readers want to know what happened, how I defected, blah blah blah. (I can't even remember the date, July 17 perhaps, who cares?) But I will cooperate and rattle on about freedom.

Their Kensington home is spacious and warm and they invited me to stay a month or two. She promised to wash my clothes, cook meals, look after me, why not? It costs nothing and she's more cultured than a slave.

In the afternoons they like to listen to dramas on the radio, so very English. They make tea and scones, light a fire. I lie on the bearskin rug. At night they put more wood on the fire and make hot chocolate. Clarinda loves to listen to me play the piano. She says I am brilliant (which is quite a lie, even for her). Perhaps I am getting better, but how I wish I could stretch my fingers farther. To be my own orchestra.

Clarinda found the magazines and stacked them strategically under the three Ionesco plays. I felt like a naughty son, yet I kept my jaw solid, said nothing.

The hotel room was full of assistants, lights, wires, hairdressers, waiters with trays. The makeup artist whispered that Avedon was likely to make a flamboyant entrance. I watched the door, waited. It was a trick, a good one. In reality he was there all along, among his assistants, watching, getting to know me, preparing the angles in his mind. He told them all to leave and the champagne was opened. When I took my clothes off he said: *Me oh my.*

In the morning I awoke crazed with fear. Gillian called his studio and threatened to sue if he ever published the pictures. Avedon sent me a telegram: *Your (big) secret is safe with me.*

Erik lay back and fell asleep. (I recalled Anna making Sergei's imprint on her pillow.) His breath was uneven and stank of cigarettes. *Song of a Wayfarer.* I kissed him and packed.

Instead of coming through a tunnel the limousine driver wanted to cross the upper deck of a bridge. He said I should see the city lit up. My escorts thought it would be uninteresting, they said the bridge was old and decrepit, but I shouted: *Let's go across the fucking bridge!* The driver grinned.

The city was a crazed jewel. I stuck my head out of the window. One of the escorts kept repeating that fewer apartments were lit up as it was a Jewish holiday. (Another neurotic kike.)

I couldn't stand their chatter anymore so I switched seats and sat with the driver up front. On instructions he closed the glass screen behind us. He was listening to Charlie Parker on the radio. He says they called him Bird because he never had his feet on the ground.

(Nijinsky declined to come down at all. Perhaps every madman prefers it in the air.)

Walked up and down by the newsstand, watched people pick up their copies of *The New York Times*, thinking, I am *en l'air* in a million arms. The photograph caught me in perfect line.

Sasha! Tamara! Mother! Father! Ufa! Leningrad! Do you hear me? I am hailing you from the Avenue of the Americas!

Snow and not too much traffic. The fur coat drew laughter and a few smiles. Outside the Apollo a woman recognized me and a crowd gathered. Someone said: *Do a Sammy Davis!* I stood on a fire hydrant, pirouetted and they roared.

Back down St. Nicholas Avenue in the car. (Nobody believes me when I say there are no beggars in Russia.)

On *The Ed Sullivan Show* he simply couldn't pronounce my name.

He had no interest in ballet and he said as much. But he was a pure gentleman with perfect manners. Each hair combed into place. He said that dance was Jacqueline's joy, so for years he had been trying to develop an honest interest. He claimed that watching Margot and me on television had changed his perspective completely (a brazen lie of course and quite stupid).

He ushered us into the Oval Office. His suit was cut beautifully and his tie was slightly loose. He swung in his chair the whole five minutes. Towards the end of the pleasantries he looked at my feet, said I was a symbol of pure political courage.

Outside, on the lawn, the secret service agents were hovering. Later Jacqueline came in carrying tea and he had to excuse himself.

Walking Margot and me to the helicopter, Jacqueline hooked her arm in mine, said she hoped we would return, that she and her husband hold us both in the highest artistic esteem. In the helicopter we sat in an awed silence while the figures on the lawn grew smaller. (I was momentarily climbing a staircase in Leningrad and the police were chasing me.)

*Newsweek*: You seem to plow your soul under in order to seed your very own Albrecht.
    (a sudden panic imagining Father at the garden plot.)
    Pardon me?
    For Albrecht you successfully create a new persona.
    I am an actor.
    But surely you are more than—
    Oh no more stupid questions please.

In the room next door I could hear her, already awake. I went to greet her. She smiled and began stretching—neckrolls and leg stretches in a carefully timed sequence. Without thinking, Margot was able to put both her feet behind her head and carry on a conversation. The irony is she claims to be afraid of growing old.
    (Lesson: continue to work always for mobility.)

The cover of *Time* and *Newsweek*—in the very same week. Gillian was ecstatic.

November 22, 1963. The weeping started outside the windows in the late afternoon, but nobody told us until six o'clock. Margot turned to the pianist, asked her to play Bach, but she was too overcome by grief, her fingers shaking above the keys. We sat in silence, then sent a telegram to Jacqueline. Our performance was canceled. In the streets people carried candles.
    In the Russian Tea Room the maître d' asked for a minute of silence, disturbed only by some fool who knocked his fork from the table.

A letter came through from Yulia to say she is divorced. She has nowhere to live. Our shithole country.

Another twelve hours in preparation for *Raymonda*. It is strange that the corps is so surprised when they come to watch me rehearse or when I give class. They sit in the corridor, smoking foul cigarettes, which makes me want to kick them in the ass down to the Ministry of Labor, if there is such a thing. They are lazy shits, their weak legs, unworked turnout, careless feet, they need to be transformed, one and all. The trombones sound like sick cattle, the pianist even worse. Not to mention the stagehands, who threatened yet another strike because the parrots are real and their shit falls from the cages in the wings. The poor bastards complain because they have to mop up.

Margot could hardly talk, her voice quivered uncontrollably. She said the bullet entered Tito's chest and came out the other side.

In Stoke Mandeville Hospital, after the visit with Tito (lying in bed, saying nothing), we were guided around the wards. The fourteen-year-old girl paralyzed from the neck down said she often imagines being Margot and then her legs can move.

A beautiful eight-year-old had drawn a crayon picture, using her teeth. It was a picture of me dancing in a field, and the little girl had drawn herself watching from the perch of a flowering tree. There was a loveheart on the flip side, both our names in the middle, Oona and Rudolf.

I told her I would hang it in my dressing room. The child could barely move her head and there was spit on her lips, but her eyes were bright blue and she almost was able to turn her mouth into a smile. She said she didn't wish for much but if she ever got to heaven the first thing she would want to do is dance.

(Some asshole photographer caught me weeping in the corridor.)

Tito will never walk again so Margot must go on performing to pay the hospital bills. Of course she is so very English, she doesn't see the irony of this. (I am loathe to tell her that Tito deserves what he got.) Outside, she switched her handbag from side to side, dabbed a handkerchief at her eyes, then rushed back in to see him once more.

The telegram from Princess Grace for the opening night. Quite daring: *Merde! With love, G.* Other greetings, the King of Norway, Princess Margaret, etc. Twenty different bouquets in the room. Out the window the rain seemed to shine in a dozen colors. The hotel doorbell rang—a bouquet from Margot to say everything is all right, she wished she were dancing.

All Italy was there. Yet the presence of fame does not compensate for the absences in my performances. The *Raymonda* pas de deux was, of course, abysmal without her, but even the solo was a bucket of shit. Afterwards Spoleto seemed to have lost its magic, and the thought of the hotel room was depressing. I canceled dinner, dismissed everyone, remained all night to repair the evening's mistakes.

The stagehands found me in the morning, sleeping on their tarps. They brought me cappuccino and a corneto. I rehearsed again, found the temperament. On the second evening I danced with a fire in my hair.

Margot was waiting in the lobby. She held an envelope. Her face contained the story. The concierge lowered his eyes and pretended he was busy. The news had obviously arrived earlier in a telegram. I was convinced at first it was Tito. But with tears streaking her face, she said: *It's your father.*

On the phone with Mother, she was too saddened for words. Later: Rachmaninov's Piano Concerti 1 and 2, Sanderling and the Leningrad Philharmonic, taking me back to other days. Father's shoes being polished and his face being shaved, his coat on a wire hanger, his dirty nails.

Erik canceled New York.

The only sadness: Father never once saw me dance.

I told Gillian and Erik there will be no rain or grief. We popped a bottle of champagne and toasted.

Reading the translation of Solzhenitsyn, there was a brief flicker of light on the page. The desire to resurrect Father was suddenly overwhelming. (Tamara's letter sat in my pocket like a wound.)

Outside Café Filo in Milan a boy was singing an aria I had never heard before. Erik asked for the aria's name, but the boy shrugged, said he didn't know, kept unloading the bread. Then the boy caught a glimpse of my face and ran up the street after me, shouting my name. He handed me a fresh loaf. Erik fed the bread to the pigeons in the square, kicking at the birds as they crowded around his feet.

Margot's generosity with everyone but herself is stunning. This of course is the ultimate in kindness. Given all the fuss with Tito she is terribly tired. Still she managed to arrange a parcel for Mother and Tamara. (The realization that there would be nothing anymore for Father was a shock.) She asked which color scarves would suit. I had forgotten for a moment how they looked in my mind, especially Mother. All my photographs are ancient.

Margot packed the box herself, to be carefully sent through the Finnish embassy.

❈

On the table, between the window and the four-poster bed, stands a vase of white lilacs. The sea outside is a rare blue. Through the window, the wind is a cold fresh slap. Rudi has anticipated her desires: a view to the ocean, sheets laundered in lavender water, hot tea early in the morning, wildflowers on the tray. He has given Margot the east-facing room on the island since she is inclined to enjoy the dawn.

Yesterday afternoon, just for her, he flew a piano in all the way from the mainland. The helicopter broke the expanse of blue and circled the island twice, gauging the winds. Suspended by ropes and cables, the piano seemed to have a flight of its own. Soft padding was put on the tennis court so the piano would land gently. Seven islanders were hired to navigate it into place. Rudi himself took hold of one of the legs and Margot smiled momentarily at the thought of herself as the piano, held aloft. It was a crazed venture, the piano could have been brought by boat, but he wanted it instantly, wouldn't listen to her. At first she had felt a thinness of emotion, such a waste, but then she was surprised by an acute wedge of ecstasy.

Rudi wore a sleeveless shirt. He was stronger even than the islanders. Their caps blew off in the wind from the helicopter rotors. Later he paid the men and dismissed them with a wave of his hand. He tuned the piano himself and sat to play until late in the night. Even when she had gone to bed Margot could hear the notes floating, high, sirenic. She thought that a life like this would be intolerable if constant and yet, precisely because it was unusual it was precious.

It frightens her to think that she is forty-five and he is just twenty-six, his life occurring so soon. Sometimes, in the way he moves, she thinks she can discern a whole history of Tatar arrogance. Other times—walking along the beach, choreographing a move, adjusting a lift—he is bent into submission, her experience towering over him.

Through the window she sees the piano in the middle of the tennis court, covered with a sheet of plastic that is coated with dew-drops. She will scold him later, mother him into bringing the piano indoors, but for now the view strikes her as fabulous, unresolved, the tennis net lying flaccid beneath the varnished legs.

Margot moves to the edge of the bed, where she stretches, gently at first, until her palms touch her feet, and then she reaches further with her fingers, to the soles, noting the calluses. She runs a tub of hot water. In the bath she sands her feet with a pumice stone, easily working with circular sweeps. She examines a mosquito bite on her instep, touches the small red welt, and then, out of the bath, she rubs herbal cream over her feet. They have been rehearsing together for a run in Paris and her toes ache from the temporary floor he has installed in the basement. She feels the gradual warmth of the lotion as she massages it from ankle to toe, repeating the stroke.

The rise and fall of the waves outside is barely perceptible, a fine corduroy of foam lines turned red by the dawn. A few seabirds ricochet on the air currents and in the distance Margot sees a yacht, its yellow sails unfurling.

Her eyes stop suddenly on a rip in the landscape as an arm lunges from the sea. A flash of dryness in her throat. She holds her breath, but then another arm rises, complementing the first, and she exhales— it is simply Rudi swimming, his hair turned dark by the sea. She sits down on the bed, relaxes, begins to pull her right ankle high in the air, placing her foot behind her neck in a stretch, a morning ritual. She releases the foot, wiggles her toes, and pulls her left leg behind, adjusts herself on the bed and then brings both legs back simultaneously, her long hair over her ankles feeling cool.

Releasing the grip, she reaches across the bed to call Tito at the hospital, to tell him she misses him, she will soon return to take care of him, but the phone rings on, unanswered.

Loose from the stretch, Margot moves closer to the window.

She watches Rudi's slow rise from the water, head first, then shoulders, then chest, his tiny waist, his penis large even after the chill of the water, his giant thighs, the tough calves, the michelangelo of him. She has seen him naked many times before, in his dressing room, unperturbed as a child getting ready for a bath, and she could make a map of his body if she desired. She has, in dancing, touched every part of him. His clavicle, his elbow, the lobe of his ear, his groin, the small of his back, his feet. Still, she raises her hand formally to her lips, as if to compensate for her lack of surprise.

His skin is glaringly white, almost translucent. The lines of his body are sharp, a scissored cutout, as far removed from Tito as she can imagine.

With a pang of pleasure she watches him walk from the beach towards the long grasses beyond the rocks, stepping through the growth barefoot. She hears the piano's plastic cover tear against the wind and the quick run of Rudi's fingers across the keys. Beneath the sheets, she feigns sleep as he comes in to wake her, carrying hot tea upon a tray, saying: *You slept in, Margot, get up, it's time for rehearsal.* After he leaves, she smiles, not her stage smile, nothing regal or controlled, and then looks out to the sea once more, thinking that even if there was nothing else there will always be the memory.

❖

Cosmopolitan: *The world's most beautiful man.* One must confront the fact that the face will change and the body is vulnerable. But so what? Enjoy the moment. The *world's* most beautiful man! When I'm seventy and sitting by the fire, I will take the photos out and weep, ha!

Somebody stuck the cover on my mirror and added devil's horns. I wouldn't mind but the bastards ruined my eyeliner pen—it is probably the fat cleaning bitch who left in tears yesterday.

The fans slept all night outside in the cold in Floral Street. Gillian made several flasks of hot soup and convinced me to go along with her—she said it was good publicity.

When we arrived there was a sort of hush, but then came a high-pitched scream which unleashed all the others. They ran forward, asked me to sign everything—umbrellas, purses, leg warmers, underwear. Gillian had, of course, arranged for a photographer to be there. Before I left one of the girls reached forward and tried to grab my crotch. (Perhaps I should wear the leg-warmers over my cock for protection!)

As a choreographer he steals liberally from everywhere, from the Greeks to Fokine to Shakespeare, etc. He says: *In the end, after all, many hands touch the artist's brush.* Margot took his suggestions and remolded them beautifully, although at first I felt I was dragging a carcass across the floor.

Every hour she phones Tito. Imprisoned by him. (Now that he can fuck nobody else, he must fuck her, her life.)

The heart returns to Paris. There is some sort of sticky tar there. (Tell Claudette to furnish new apartment, find four-poster bed.)

The letter came, sealed with red wax. A momentary hesitation, perhaps it was a Soviet ploy. (You cannot put anything beyond them, acid on the envelopes, etc.) But the seal was Royal and the note was handwritten and it had been folded very carefully. I said to the housekeeper: *Oh shit, not another letter from Her Majesty!*

The new bodyguard (part-time) once protected Churchill. He told me he met Stalin at Yalta. Tried to explain that Stalin was very polite. (A train whistled in my mind, the hospital, watching from the trees as the old babushkas washed the soldiers—how many centuries ago now?)

Found the Derrida text in a secondhand stall along the Seine. Also found a treatise on Martha Graham at the same stall, what a coincidence. Both were water damaged and had their pages stuck together. I told Tennessee Williams about the books (he was drunk at the Desjeux party) and he said it was an obvious metaphor, though he didn't explain why, perhaps couldn't. His fingers and even his beard were stained with ink. He was astonished I'd read him in Russian. He put his head on my shoulder and said: *Oh such a nice child.*

He grew tiresome and spilled a cocktail on my suit and I told him to kiss my ass. He replied with a grin that he'd be enchanted.

Claire brought a tape with *Vengerov and Rostropovich* scrawled in crude handwriting on the case. The Violin Concerto number 2, second movement, brought me to tears. Once in Leningrad I stupidly told Yulia that I would allow Shostakovich to sit in the rain.

Smelled a plate of radishes in the kitchen at Lacotte's. Was transported back. Had to leave, much to Lacotte's displeasure. At the door he wagged his finger. Woke up dreaming of a white cloth being put over Mother's face.

Perhaps Margot is correct when she says that I dance so much—*too much*—in order not to think of home.

Such difficulty in talking to anyone about Mother. When the facts are in order the mood is wrong. When the mood is correct the facts are in tatters. *She worked in a weapons factory. She sold matrushka dolls. She was chased by a wolf.* Sometimes, in the same interview, I forget exactly what I've said, so it becomes even more tangled in fantasies. For the Austrian journalist she somehow turned into a seamstress in the Ufa Opera House.

The times I hate myself the most inevitably collide with the times I dance badly. In darker moments I think perhaps my best performances were in the Kirov. (The phantom feel of Sizova's hips against my hands.)

Erik ran into an acquaintance of Richter's who told him that when Profokiev died there were no flowers left for sale in Moscow. They had all been bought for Stalin's funeral. Richter played at the funeral, then walked across Moscow to place a single pine branch on Profokiev's grave. (Beautiful, but is it true?)

Mister Nureyev, your movements seem to defy possibility.
    Nothing is impossible.
    For example, when following on from the sharp flourish of your ronde de jambe are you aware of your body?
    No.
    Why not?
    Because I am far too busy dancing.

My desire to comfort the journalists is almost as strong as my desire to alienate them. Afterwards I can feel my heart ballooning with apology.

The true mind must be able to accept both criticism and praise, but in the *Saturday Review* he said I hold my hands too high in arabesque, that the movement looks bloated and uncontrolled. If I ever meet him again he will hold his balls too high in his throat and then we'll see who looks bloated and uncontrolled.
    As for Jacques, he is a typical *L'Humanité* shithead, another one of those socialist bastards with a vendetta. He said I was being too literal. But what does he want, my legs to deal in symbols, my cock to reel off metaphors? I would tell him to do something productive for his politics—commit suicide, perhaps—but the weight of his fat ass would probably bring the ceiling beam down to the floor.

In the pub in Vauxhall a picture of me was suspended from the staircase on a thin rope. I asked the bartender if it was Yesenin but he didn't understand. At the counter there was a hush when Erik and I took our seats. The bartender asked me to sign the photo, which I did, across my chest, and everyone clapped.
    All evening they expected some outrage, something Russian, some-

thing Nureyev. Smash glasses, kick bottles from the table. I drank four vodkas then took Erik's arm. We could almost hear the place moan.

There was another death threat waiting at the hotel. The police said the note had been clipped from the headlines of a Soviet émigré paper. Who are these assholes? Can't they understand that I am not their fucking puppet?

(Margot says to ignore them all, that the best way is to smile and be polite. *Unleash it all onstage*, she says. I haven't the heart to tell her she's talking rubbish. She, of all people, knows that everything I do is already sprayed with my blood.)

Secret wish: a house by the sea, children on the beach, a chamber orchestra on the rocks being soaked by the giant waves. I would sit in a deckchair, drink white wine, listen to Bach, grow old, though of course that too would become a bore.

*Wisdom Defending Youth Against Love*, Charles Meynier: $47,500.

In the beginning he presents himself to her without, at first, betraying his true feelings. He is acutely aware of how he must look at her, neither revealing nor unrevealing. He must play this game of emotional roulette, fastidious, until they break into each other and become the movement (ratchet up the pas de deux and extend the solo).

He must be reinvented, after all, otherwise the role is pure shit— he will be a cardboard figure, a cipher without vitality.

Conceive the role as a fantasy of the protagonist's mind. In the end he must suffer agonizingly and, in full consciousness, be aware that all is lost.

A perfect rehearsal! We took an afternoon off.

He must remain in the wings long enough for everyone to feel uncomfortable and then he must burst from the other side of the world, frighten the mundane lives out of all who watch. For her, keep the tempo slow. She must arrive cold at first. And then he must warm her into the dance. With every garment she takes off, it must look as if she is stepping into a future self. Finally she is spirited away from him, carried off, ghosts moving in diagonal lines, a moving vee. Light (moonlight) never quite touches the ground. Keep strings muted, do not allow the music to overwhelm.

"If and when Nureyev retires, it is obvious that his future as a chore- ographer is assured." *Dance* magazine, December 1966. Ha! "He does not create solely *for* the body, he creates *on* it."

Erik suggested that I am increasingly obsessed with Mother only because I am so far away. (As if he could talk, the ghost of that gray- haired Viking bitch still hanging over him.) After I slammed the car door and walked through the traffic it suddenly dawned on me that I knew none of the Copenhagen streets. I went back and sat instead in the front seat with the driver.

Later, crawling into bed, Hamlet (how he detests this nickname!) admitted his error. It is so difficult to drive him to anger, and yet he becomes voracious when ignored.

Boating on the lakes. Champagne. Fireworks. The Hamburg woman with the necklace: *You are a Rimbaud of the steppes!*

Mother's exit visa application was turned down again, but this time the butchers asked her to sign a document refuting her desire to leave.

Erik waited at the airport, wearing glasses and a hat for disguise.

Within hours we were on the dance floor. A boy wore a white silk shirt and silver platform shoes. Ah yes, Piccadilly! I followed him outside.

The horse's hooves chopped up the immaculate green park as the other guests played polo in the rain. Erik came up behind me and put his head on my shoulder, nibbled my ear.

At dinner (mousseline d'ecrivisse, poussin rôti aux herbes, salad, purée of celery) the Baron looked at us severely. I whispered to Erik that the Baron was certainly a fine horseman but probably unable to control his whip. Erik laughed so hard he spat his sherbet out on the tablecloth.

The hollow of his neck. We dozed.

A speedboat to Galli. Erik, Pablo, Jerome, Kenzu, Margot, Gillian, Claire and me. Margot spent the whole weekend on the phone to Tito. We decided to get an orchestra boated in from the mainland. They were a ragtag bunch and we dismissed them but paid handsomely to borrow their instruments. We took turns playing until four, then dragged the piano inside to save it from the dew. (Erik quoted Homer about the sirens. The champagne was flowing. Jerome suggested that I plug everyone's ears with wax and tie myself to Erik's mast!)

Pablo sat naked to play Shostakovich (badly) and his ass left a sweat stain on the piano stool.

Early in the morning Erik came to watch me swim. I made my way underwater to the rocks, surfaced and hid. He called my name and soon became frantic. He jumped up from the sand and began to scream for help. After five minutes he dived into the sea in his pajamas. How he hates the chill of the sea. He didn't notice me until a few meters away, then in Danish called me a cunt.

I told him I had seen a bright star move in the darkness. He said it was obviously a satellite looking down on me, perhaps Russian. He was getting his revenge, but the thought was chilling.

In bed we read Flaubert's letters from Egypt. Outside the sea crashed.

The pair of underpants hung on the bedpost. An exuberant flag.

The stewardess hardly seemed pleased when she told me to take my shoes down from the seat and I replied that it was a first-class cabin, would she prefer my foot somewhere else—up her enormous German arse for instance?

Jan. 6. New Year promise to Margot: I shall keep my mind free from attachments to everything but dance.

Valentina's classes: her movements are like prayers in a church. One feels almost shy in her presence.

A bad class and the day was ruined. Then at performance the lights were too bright and I was looking down more than usual, away from the glare, and my feet tangled. Arthur, in his high pitch, said: *We all have our nights.* The glass narrowly missed his head.

   (At times like these I hate myself. The idea of being a genius-madman is tiresome.)

At the gathering Bacon asked why dance? I retorted, Why paint? He dragged on his cigarette and said painting was the language he would give his soul if he could teach his soul to speak. Yes!

❈

Each night he waits for the cue, stretches, meshes his fingers. Onstage, Margot unspools a length of chaînés, sweeps, descends and is still. He touches his left ear for good luck, waits a moment beyond the quietness, breaks the wings, takes flight, is released.

Music reaches into his muscles, the lights spin, he glares at the conductor, who corrects the tempo, and he continues, controlled at first, each move careful and precise, the pieces beginning to fit, his body elastic, three jetés en tournant, careful of the landing, he extends his line, beautiful movement ah cello go. The lights merge, the shirtfronts blur. A series of pirouettes. He is at ease, his body sculpted to the music, his shoulder searching the other shoulder, his right toe knowing the left knee, the height, the depth, the form, the control, the twist of his wrist, the bend of his elbow, the tilt of his neck, notes digging into his arteries, and he is in the air now, forcing the legs up beyond muscular memory, one last press of the thighs, an elongation, a loosening of human contour, he goes higher, and is skyheld.

The audience leans forward, necks craned, mouths open. He descends, lands and is off again towards her, the wind rushing past his ears, a blur of unbroken energy, to where she is waiting, headbent. He plants his feet before her, she accepts him, he lifts her upward, she is light, she is always light, he stays away from her ribs, bruised from rehearsal. A bead of sweat spins out from his hair. His face against her thigh, her hip, her stomach. Both of them burning away, they are one movement, a body nation. He allows her down, a gasp from the hall, they are alive—a French audience, the good ones are always French, even in Lebanon, New York, Buenos Aires, Vienna, London, they're always French—and he can smell her perfume, her sweat, her approval, he moves stage left and off. She will control it now, her solo. Standing in the shadows, he regains his breath, tissues his face, dams the sweat, his chest rising and falling, begins to calm, ah yes this darkness an embrace.

He scuffs in the resin box for traction, waits as she receives her applause. Here it is now, take it, grasp it, explode!

He returns from the wings already in midair, moves through four cabrioles, keeping his line long until the sound catches up, an instant of conjunction, a flash of muscle and he sweeps the stage with his body, owning it, no limits. Eight perfect entrechats-dix, a thing of wonder, the audience silent now, no body anymore no thought no awareness this must be the moment the others call god as if all doors are open everywhere leading to all other open doors nothing but open doors forever no hinges no frames no jambs no edges no shadows this is my soul born weightless born timeless a clock spring broken, he is in flight, he could stay like this forever and he looks out into the haze of necklaces eyeglasses cufflinks shirtfronts and knows he owns them.

Afterwards in the dressing rooms there are exaggerated complaints to keep themselves going—you changed your perfume, you sweated too much, your chaînés were abysmal, you missed the cue, you stayed out too late, you pirouetted like a donkey, let's do it better tomorrow—and they exit the stage doors together, arm in arm, laughing, smiling, the crowds waiting, flowers and shouts and invitations, they sign autographs and programs and shoes, but as they walk away the dance is still in their bodies and they search for the quiet point the still point where there is no time no space only pureness moving.

---

The crowd outside the Sydney Opera house was boisterous, charged. Some protesters were shouting about Vietnam. Margot and I sent in a dummy limousine and drove ourselves to the entrance instead. The crowd cheered when they realised it was us.

Rock Hudson came to the green room, shirt ambitiously undone. He said he was shooting some movie somewhere and sat in the dressing room while I applied make-up. He mentioned that he had found a restaurant with the most perfect oysters in the world, he would see me after the show if I desired. I caught a glimpse of him in the audience. He was turned away from the stage, looking at someone through binoculars.

At the restaurant Rock was loath to pay the bill since I had brought fourteen people with me (ha!). He went to the bathroom and came back re-energized.

In the museum café we fought about the impulse for Albrecht. Frederic suggested that intuition was an excuse. He tried shoring up his plate of shit with a quote from Goethe who said that nothing belongs to Nature once the artist has chosen it as his subject. As if that is even mildly relevant!

I threw my coffee at him but later in the Sobel Hotel at the bottom of the Kings Road (yet another Kings Road!) I thought perhaps he was just frightened by the enormity of the task. I sent him a telegram, charging it to the hotel bill.

Such fine choreography. (At last he learned his lesson.) For the second act he showed us a photograph of a kingfisher tossing its prey in the air after stabbing it, both bird (alive) and fish (dead) gloriously turning in midair.

The Persian rug was worth eighteen thousand francs. The owner saw me admire it and then said it was mine—for free. Erik said the first thing I would do is set up a model train on it, which is not entirely true. The owner seemed disturbed, his great gift cheapened, so I said that a journalist from *Vogue* was coming to my apartment and I'd mention the name of his store. He beamed and took out his business card with great formality.

Outside I threw the card into the gutter. Erik was horrified to see the owner staring at us through the window.

The woman in the Jacuzzi complained about my feet, said they were cracked and anyone with an open wound was not allowed in. I told

her who I was and she smiled stiffly, sat up in the water, left shortly
thereafter.

Beckett was at the café counter. He nodded hello. He was pouring
his coffee into his cognac, rather than the other way around.

Somebody said I should smoke the marijuana cigarette, that even
Brigitte Bardot might seem humorous if I was high. Even then I had
no interest. Why lose the mind, even worse the body?

   At home I sought refuge in Richter. His mischief. It is said that
he can stretch his hands to twelfth.

Margot's ligament tore. Antony asked her how she felt: *Rather sore,
I'm afraid.*

The search for a replacement. Evelyn has been told in no uncertain
terms that her performance is shit, there is far too much marking in
her movement, that if she is to be worthy of Basil, if she is to dance
at all, she will have to learn to perform at least a half-decent grand
jeté. She warmed up for a full hour and then bourréed out onto the
floor. She soared high and arched her back so far that her nose actually touched her calf, like a scissor blade meeting the round thumb-
hole. It was as if she had no bones at all. Then she snapped her legs
together with wonderful violence. I could only applaud. She picked
up her bag (full of barbiturates?) to leave.

   She was so elegant throwing the scarf over her shoulder that I
offered to partner her for the rest of eternity, but already the elevator
door was closing, ah well. (Perhaps I really did feel something for
her, but the truth is we are apples and oranges.)

A call from Gilbert. The suicide notion. *If you don't come back
soon, Rudi, I will leave a gap between the floor and my feet.* His wife, it
seems, has taken to bed in distress.

I told Ninette that, as a Tatar, I had spent centuries contemplating the gap between floor and feet. She shot back that she was Irish and had already spent hundreds of years in the air.

Mrs. Godstalk is almost a perfect copy of Madame B., except she once danced with Balanchine and now keeps her old toe shoes in the freezer, as if she will one day dance again. She took me to Madison Avenue at eight in the morning, before the antique shops opened. She said she would buy anything I wanted, even put it on an airplane to Paris rather than shipping it.

I suggested the Russian library chair in the shop on Sixty-third. It cost perhaps four years or more of Soviet wages. Later in the afternoon the envelope arrived with confirmation of purchase. What an idiotic cunt she is! She phoned eight times in three days until I used a pay phone in the rehearsal corridor and said in a French accent that Monsieur Nureyev had run off with her white poodle to serve it sautéed to the corps, who were all broke and very hungry.

(Margot laughed so hard she began hiccuping.)

Later in a moment of stupidity I reduced the chair to kindling. I called Mrs. Godstalk to say it had happened when a box of books fell from the shelf, shattering the legs. She sighed, said she was not naïve but that it was all right, she understood the artistic impulse.

Truth: I rope them in, then lock the gate and walk away laughing. Not very human, but true. The other voice says: Fuck them, they have far more money than sense.

Another call from Gilbert. The suicide notion yet again. There was the thought of returning to Paris, fucking him, then lending him a rope.

Margot was so happy with her recovery, she was smiling to herself and saying how warm the night was and did I see the old man in the orchestra seats, that was Antonio Bertolucci.

The bewildered cockroach (it was New York, after all) crawled through the resin box. I nailed him with Margot's spare toe shoe. The orchestra was tuning up and it drowned out most of her screaming. But she managed to laugh when I flicked the dead roach under the curtain down into the pit near the contrabasses.

The doctor, Guillaume, said it was absurd and dangerous, but I danced through the fever anyway. Hard to believe, but even the stagehands interrupted their poker game to watch the solo, presumably waiting for me to collapse, but I danced better than ever, could feel the fever vaulting out of me. Afterwards my temperature was almost normal. Guillaume stood there perplexed. The stagehands brought me a bag of ice.

Pneumonia. Erik rubbed goose fat on my chest. A full recovery inside two days.

On the phone Mother's voice was old and sad, even when I told her about the goose fat. She was coughing. I went walking afterwards in Mendocino along the cliff face. The seals were hacking into the air. (Later Saul called to say he had almost doubled my money on the gold market. He interpreted my silence as joy.)

At first Erik was dancing like three buckets of shit, but then he braided his feet back and forth in the air beautifully, without losing any definition, and I thought, *We all keep certain secrets, don't we?* For the entrechat-huit (reversed, with the eight beats descending) he paused for a second midair. Glorious. One could feel the audience straining forward. (You can tell how good the work is from the way it shapes itself into the crowd.) I was first to my feet for the encore. The whole house followed. Erik smiled, took Violette's hand, and they bowed together.

Backstage he was listening to Liszt's Concerto number 1, Richter with Kondrashin and the LSO. We drank Château d'Yquem. It seemed like a perfect night but after taking off his shoes, he looked pained and began rubbing his feet ferociously, then said he thought he might have chipped a bone in his toe after a particularly big sauté. (Liszt once played piano with a slight fracture in his left hand and said he could literally feel the notes skipping from bone to bone.)

No breakages nor fractures, but at the hospital the doctor told Erik that his feet were ruined, he might not be able to walk properly as an old man. Erik shrugged and laughed. *Ah well, I'll just have to bourrée along instead.*

Erik says that increasingly after performances he feels distanced from himself. He sits in his dressing room alone and exhausted, still in character. He changes clothes, faces the mirror, sees only a reflection. He must keep looking long enough until he finally recognizes an old friend—himself. Only then can he leave.

A series of rare Bashkirian woodcuts: 8,000 francs.

The thought of them sitting in Ufa, plain bread and borscht, a glass of vodka, Mother darning her blue smock, Tamara coming back from the market. My guilt is overwhelming but what is there to do?

When Elena (how beautiful she is) first arrived in France, she made a living sewing wedding dresses for the bourgeois families who had come before her. Then she told the story of her boat trip from Kiev to Constantinople—the boat was full of people fleeing with their most precious possessions, ridiculous things, lamps, letter openers, family crests. She stayed at the bow for most of the journey, which took many extra days in bad weather, and she said—quite wonderfully—that ever since, she has always felt there was water moving in everything, most especially history and violins.

He is fair, narrow, young, boyish. Such beauty sometimes makes me look at myself, though I fear nothing, he is shit, dances as if weighted with lead.

He broke down in fits when (as expected) he didn't even make the corps. I thought of comforting him yet again, but I do not lead my entire life guided by my penis, whatever Claudette says. Well, not always! How to make him understand that he needs more ambition, that being in the corps is not enough, a molecule of air within a drum, condemned to make a small noise in a small space.

He sat with his hair over his eyes, in imitation no doubt. I promised to help him. In the rehearsal room he needed to be convinced of the importance of slow adagio to give enough control to land and still hold a clean position. And he still wouldn't listen until I climbed to the windowsill and leaped, landed, frozen solid. (How I detest that linoleum floor.)

I watched him fail time and time again. What is there to do? He has no salt or pepper in his spirit. He finally said: *I'm tired.* I told him that if he left now he would be cutting the branch he was sitting on but he left anyway, his finger hooked under the shoe straps.

He wants to write a biography but what do I tell him, he is a shit, he reeks of garlic, he has too much bacon on his belt, his brain is stunted, and his entry into the Museum of Shitheads is undoubtedly assured. After explaining all this to him (!) he told me how much better I would be if I were shy and listened properly. I replied that yes indeed I look forward to being dead.

(Gillian says that my use of bad language, in English French Tatar Russian German etc. has become a virus.)

I carried Yulia's letter to the Tuileries, sat on a bench. The letter had been folded and refolded many times and had taken many leaps, arriving first for Margot in London, forwarded to the Austrian embassy in Paris, and from there to Gillian.

Yulia's writing is grand and looping. She had been meaning to write for a year but had postponed it for several reasons, none of which were important anymore. Her father had been found dead in the house in Ufa. Sergei must have known he was on his final journey, since he was wearing his hat, which he never did indoors. Pen in his hand, notebook on his chest. He had left a letter for her: *Whatever loneliness we have felt in this world will surely become understandable when we are no longer lonely.* He said he was not at all scared of death, that nothing frightened him, why should it, he was about to join Anna, he had always loved her even in the terrible moments of darkness.

I sat on the bench, the sun beating down. Immeasurable remorse.

Ended the day with Richter's interpretation of Prokofiev's Piano Sonata number 2, third movement—Andante, Prague. What mood could Richter have been in to offer this gift to humanity?

God, if he exists, is surely a visitor to the new farmhouse in Virginia. In the morning the air is cool and fresh enough to make everyone hungry. The horses gallop and neigh. The light is dense and yellow, the trees old and gnarled. (This is not the America I imagined when young.)

I went for a ride. The brown mare bucked me and stood, poising one hind leg behind the other, almost in arabesque, then she dipped her head down. Her mane touched the side of my face. For no particular reason I called her Yulia.

At the party, having drunk too much, I was struck by the idea that, as life goes on, there is a double for everyone, no matter whom. (Perhaps this is a result of the sudden spate of difficulty.) I looked across the room and saw that Sergei was standing by the buffet, minus his hat. He was talking to Tamara (only she never would've been so well dressed). Father sat in a corner. I searched for Mother and found someone vaguely similar—Lee's old friend from Colorado, although Mother's hair would be grayer by now. An older Polish woman reminded me of Anna. (An eerie trip back and forth across the Styx.)

When I saw Sergei's double making his way towards Anna's double it raised the hairs on my neck. He had his overcoat draped over his arm and even carried a hat.

On searching for myself I realized there was nobody.

In the dressing room: a full kilo of Black Sea caviar and twelve bouquets, including a dozen lilies. Sergei, old man, I thought of you.

Onassis had hired two young men to wash the white trousers, white shirts, white hats, white socks, white underwear, white vests, white everything. The Greek boy smiled at me from the deck, said he would like to give me something personal for my birthday, he could hardly believe it was my twenty-ninth.

After the celebrations I excused myself below deck. The boy was at the end of the corridor, waiting, wearing only a T-shirt, cigarettes rolled up in the sleeve.

Check with Saul: Why pay taxes when my country is a suitcase?

At the interval at Porte-Saint-Martin, for Hair, she leaned across and asked quite casually if I'd heard what had happened to Gilbert.

He had used a pair of my old socks to stuff the exhaust and left the car running. His wife found him in the garage, Mozart at full blast, an empty bottle of sleeping pills at his side.

Jacques suggested he would much prefer a communist hell to a capitalist one—the communists would inevitably have a fuel shortage!

Later in the evening he came up with the idea of a ballet about the Berlin Wall. The wall was, he claims, built in a day (is this true?). A Russian mason who fell into the mortar was not pulled out and so his bones still shore up the wall.

He said the Russian mason's lover (call her Katerina) will move along the wall, feeling from brick to brick, trying to recapture the spirit of her dead sweetheart. Against her better instincts, she will fall in love with an American soldier on the other side of the wall. But to cross to the soldier she will have to break through the remains of her Russian lover's body. (To dance a wall and the terror on both sides.) In the end the young American will cross to her and will be shot dead while straddling the brickwork.

(No dying fall.)

A monstrous idea, but we were drunk.


There are rumors that Sasha has discovered a young genius in Leningrad. Erik said my face went pale. (What bullshit.) Anyway, if this *genius* ever comes west he will just fire me to even greater things.


Before Margot dies, she says she will ask for one perfect performance to repeat itself in her imagination, one perfect performance, one so astounding and beautiful that she can relive every step of it in her head.

She did not say which one it would be, maybe she has not even danced it yet. So far, she said, she could possibly choose from eight to ten.

For me, at least one would be at the Kirov. My legs still feel for the floor's rake. In a dream I was barefoot in the resin box.

❖

She is sitting in a darkened hotel room when a young girl enters, smiles and opens the curtains. *Good afternoon,* says the girl, *your appointments are here.* She places a bowl of cut flowers on the table and Margot waits for the procession to begin.

Out the window is another city, all sky and light and glass, although Margot can't quite remember which city it is. Her ankle has recovered, although she wears it bandaged. Earlier, on the telephone, she talked to Tito, who said yet again that it was time for her to retire, it has been three and a half decades, she should have quiet now, come back to the ranch in Panama.

Tito, the runaround. Tito, the flirt. Tito, the man she adores, wheeled around their house these days, reduced to eye movements and hand waves.

She recalls standing at the foot of the stairs a week ago when he told her he still loved her. When she said the same thing in reply his face seemed to shed layers, and they played catch-up on their lives. In bed Margot positioned him so that he snuggled against her neck. She hadn't been able to sleep and so she rose, stood for a while by the door listening to his raspy breath and found herself moved by the shape of his body. When she told Rudi about watching Tito sleep he understood, he was able to fathom how hushed and vulnerable she could become—it is at times like these, when Rudi is good to her, that he protects her and they dance well together.

The room begins to fill with promoters, publicists, a journalist. Sporadic conversation, elegant and well-meaning. But after an hour Margot declares she is tired—most of the morning was spent at class with Rudi—and when the room eventually empties, she pulls back the covers on the bed to take a nap. Her dreams are merciless and Tito-peppered, visions of pushing a wheelchair through a river but the current is too strong and the chair is fixed in one place.

A foghorn wakens her and she remembers now: Vancouver, late summer.

It is then, from the neighboring room, that she hears the sound of Rudi and another making love, the noises alarming, fierce, intimate. She is knocked off balance, they never normally share adjoining rooms, one of their rules, and so she turns the television loud.

Vietnam at first. Then a cartoon. She presses buttons, finds a soap opera—a woman strides lightly across a floor to slap another woman's face.

There is a pause in the program and she hears a moan from next door, then the jingle of commercials. In the bathroom she runs hot water and adds herbal powders. Margot has worked her body hard in recent weeks, beyond previous extremes. The violence tells in her everyday gestures, the way she checks the time on her wrist or brings a fork to her mouth. She is aware of how extraordinary it is, what the body does to the mind, and what the mind does to the body, one convincing the other it is in control.

Some days she recognizes the private graveyard of her body, the callused toes, the headaches from pulling her hair back all these years, the mangle of her knees, yet had she known as a young woman how her life would be she wouldn't have cared, she would have danced it anyway.

She slips into the bath, lays her head against the rear of the tub. The sounds from next door take on a new form, muffled yet amplified, more intense for their lack of clarity. She puts two pieces of cotton wool in her ears so the voices disappear. Years ago, with Tito, he would always open the windows when making love.

Later she wakes, someone shouting her name from behind the doorframe, *Margot, Margot, Margot!* She opens her eyes, sits up in the bath, and the water breaks in waves around her. She smells cigarette smoke, knows immediately who it is.

She takes the cotton balls from her ears and says: *I was just back in my good years, Erik. I was dreaming.*

But it is Rudi, not Erik, who steps forward with a bathrobe, holds it open. She rises from the bath as he places the robe around her shoulders and kisses her forehead. Behind Rudi stands Erik, smoking. She feels a flush of warmth, these two beautiful men spoiling her.

*We phoned*, says Erik, pulling hard on the cigarette, *but nobody answered. Rudi was afraid you were drowning.*

⁕

The clerk took one look, threw his arms wide and said he had a pair of red drainpipes that would suit me to perfection.

The disco lights spun. We took a booth, ordered a magnum of champagne, and how we laughed! Lara was funniest of all. She is aware of Erik but still she said my lips were sensuous to the point of irresponsibility! I told her I would marry her. Her joke about the French nurse: *Roll over, Monsieur, I have to jab you.* And then, when the others were dancing, she leaned across with her long hair in my lap and she tickled my balls in full view of everyone!

Her grandfather was from Moscow but emigrated before the Revolution, made his fortune, she said, selling paper clips. (This crazy country.) She now owns four houses and, bizarrely, six swimming pools. She whispered that she enjoyed nude bathing, as if I couldn't have guessed. She was so drunk she said she had an idea for a nude ballet—Orpheus Descends (!)—curtain comes up, gentle cellos, soft moonlight, and then swinging penises everywhere. I told her I would dance it except I didn't want to bruise my thighs. When I explained the joke (silly girl) she spilled her drink down the front of her dress.

She said being alive is the bread, yes, but sex is the yeast.

RosaMaria appeared at the door. I recognized her instantly. Red satin dress, white rose in her hair. Erik nudged my elbow as she ran across the room to me, arms open. I twirled her in the air and her foot briefly caught on a tablecloth, but she extricated it with perfect grace while still spinning, then kissed me.

Everyone watched, especially Erik, as we went out onto the veranda. The night warm with cicadas. *Tell me everything,* I said. But she wanted to talk about me, the success, the years gone by. I beseeched her and, after much cajoling, she told me that when she had returned to Chile in '59 she had married a young journalist, a Communist, who had ascended in politics until he was killed in a car accident. She had moved to Mexico City and that was it. She danced for six years until her ankles gave in. She said she would like to dance with me just one more time, and yet she was clever enough to know that it would be nothing more than sympathy on my part.

Erik came out holding three champagne glasses and we toasted. In the end RosaMaria was cornered by a handsome Mexican writer with gray hair who wrapped her up in his eyes. We bid good night and she wiped away a tear.

His raspy baritone, his tough face, the hair over his eyes. He woke and his name escaped me, though I remembered him saying he was amazed any man could live that hard. The whole day had been spent fucking, rehearsing, fucking, performing and then fucking again (once during intermission).

He got out of bed, jubilant, made me tea, five lumps of sugar, and prepared a scalding bath in a claw-footed tub with gleaming brass fixtures. He sat on the edge and sprinkled fragrant salts. Precision. I left immediately afterwards, still couldn't remember his name.

Erik had left a message at the hotel front desk. *You shit,* in very shaky handwriting.

Do you regret anything, Monsieur Nureyev?

When everything is said and done I would not swap anything I have either said or done. If you look back you'll only fall down the stairs.

That is very philosophical.

I can read.

On Fifth Avenue all the heads in the crowd turned like a field of sunflowers. Warhol shouted *Goddamn!* and hailed a car. He said that it was a gypsy cab and that the price was outrageous. He refused to tip. When we stopped, the driver spat out the window, almost hitting Warhol's shoes. Andy is a pompous ass, although he said he will sketch me some day.

In his office there was a consignment of cakes from The Erotic Bakery. He handed me a doughnut and then tried to take a Polaroid. I had to rip it from his hands. He would probably sell it for thousands. He ran all around the office trying to evade me, screaming wildly in his bright green trousers.

He ended up in a back room where there were two sets of giant black-and-white dice on the ground. There were words written on each of the six sides. The first said: *You Me They We Us Joker.* The second said: *Fuck Suck Kiss Finger Handjob Joker.* The object is to roll the dice and come up with matching words. *We Finger. You Suck. They Kiss.* With the Joker one does whatever one wants. Warhol calls it human poker. He said the permutations are endless but that at least eight people are needed to play or it can be boring.

I said he should choreograph the game. He screamed: *That's it, that's it!* and scribbled something in his notebook. The asshole will probably put it in a movie (without a credit).

When I slapped her the sound rang through the gallery and out onto Fifth Avenue. She was, after all, pestering me for an autograph and I was trying to look at the painting. The owner came over but I refused to budge. My hand stung for a whole five minutes. In truth I wanted so much to apologize but couldn't.

Gillian said I should get the totem pole out of my ass, that it was time for me to grow up. I fired her and she said: *Yet again?* She began painting her toenails bright red.

Thankfully the slapped girl was an aspiring ballerina and doesn't want to press charges for the sake of her career, but Gillian is adamant that we do damage control in case it gets into the papers.

The suggested design:

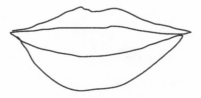

Jumping through the lips I needed six stagehands to break my fall. The *Post* said it was the most astounding exit ever seen in ballet. (Bullshit, of course.) The photograph was taken by some moron who caught me, back bent, out of line. Still, it sent the audience into raptures and they roared. (Polanski, Tate, Hepburn, Hendrix were there.)

The reviews were good, except for Clint, who called it all a diseased contrivance. (Asshole.)

A story appeared in the gossip pages, with a photo of me and Hendrix. *Rudi and Jimi pirouette.* His fingernails were blackened (perhaps with old blood) from playing guitar so hard. At the club he disappeared in a cloud of marijuana smoke but showed up later on the dance floor. I was surrounded by a dozen gyrating women. A tall black boy joined us, leather shirt and motorcycle boots. We removed ourselves to the courtyard and the party began.

The birthday celebration took place only to be forgotten. Thirty-one years old. Margot bought a beautiful crystal goblet and Erik gave me a Gucci watch. All I wanted was to walk along the beach. The stars over St. Bart's seemed almost as bright as those over Ufa when I went ice fishing, centuries ago.

Leopard skin boots! To the thighs! A là Twiggy! Backstage I was told they were deliciously wicked. At Le Bar I couldn't move for the gauntlet of erections. I spied one boy, he seemed two different people in one, a Janus, so that from the right he was beautiful but from the left he had a hideous scar. In the morning the boy kept trying to show me the good side of his face, which bored me, so I kicked him out.

Mother said that the snow over Ufa had deadened all other sound. Tamara says she wants to understand me, my life, but she is so foolish, how can she understand me? Nobody does.

Erik complains that I talk more and more shit each day. As if he doesn't. He says I should just do the one thing I know—that is, operate in my sacred space, onstage.

He detests my idea that dance makes the world a better place. *It is sentimental,* he says. I want to make a statement about beauty, but Erik (who spends his time watching the news from Vietnam and Cambodia) says that dance changes nothing for the monk who sets himself aflame and the photographer who watches through the lens.

*Would you set yourself aflame for something you believe in?* he said.

I asked if he would keep his finger on the shutter if I was burning. He would not answer at first but then he finally said: *Of course not.*

We fought until the alarm clock rang. I told him I had set myself aflame a long time ago, did he not realize this? He sighed and turned his back and said that he was sick and tired of it all, that he simply wanted a cottage by the sea in Denmark where he could sit and smoke and play the piano. I slammed the door and told him to go fuck himself.

He yelled after me: *Yes, that might be preferable.*

I said he certainly wouldn't get an encore.

The ice packs were not frozen and the Epsom salts had disappeared. I wanted to throw the small fridge out the window. The only deterrent was a crowd of cheering fans below.

Margot keeps threatening retirement. She is well aware of Bettina's power, for example, Joyce's also, even Alessandra's, perhaps even

Eleanor's. Yet every partner brings me inevitably back to Margot, her magnetism. On the phone she said she is torn. On the one hand, she says Tito needs her. On the other, she needs the money. (And she is afraid she will wither.)

Erik is correct although I screamed at him and hurled the flowerpot, just missing his head. I probably have, yes, been dancing terribly. Fuck!

The new masseur might well release me, however. He has suggested there are trigger points in the body where he can remove the tension. He manipulates it to other parts of the body where it dissipates. (Certainly on the beach I finally felt relaxed after six countries in just fourteen days.) Emilio has the strongest hands I have ever known.

I have grown to hate the standing ovations in restaurants, how infantile.

Victor is crazed and vulgar and lovely, a walking disaster (silk gown and ostrich feathers) and yet nobody makes me laugh more. The theme of the party he organized was Nureyev. He said the hairstylists all over New York were packed solid, that even Diana Ross had to bribe to get her hair done. (Later she told me that I was divine as myself.)

Quentin Crisp whispered drunkenly in my ear: *I am much too much every man's man to be the only man of any man.* (I'm sure he stole the line from somewhere.)

I told her that if she continued her career she would, at the very least, get to kiss the toad. She could be heard weeping outside the rehearsal and someone ran to get her a cigarette. Gillian said a cigarette will stop anyone crying. A thought: packages should be unceremoniously shoved into any available hole presented by hysterical women, dancers, lovers, accountants, stagehands, customs officers, etc.

The performance was full of error. Terrible. The movement is pure shit. He couldn't choreograph a Latin orgy. For the entrance I should blaze onstage as if it is the absolute beginning of the world. Open the body's windows and build the mystery from there.

Broadway, front row. The show was shit but Erik said we couldn't leave, people would gossip. I pretended to have a toothache and left, but returned for the party later. The lead actor asked if my teeth were okay so I bit his arm and said yes, they seemed to have recovered.

He went around all night with a bandage on his arm and his sleeve rolled up.

Gillian asked me how can I dance after fucking, and I could only reply that I could not dance without fucking. (One only wishes the intermissions were longer!)

Patrick uses the needle between his toes so nobody can see the marks. Before he goes onstage he cuts his finger and sprinkles salt into the cut (excruciating agony) to wake himself from his stupor.

In the bar on the corner of Castro I suspended myself from the balcony while the boy unzipped me and performed his quiet miracle. He was the same height as Erik and blond also. I almost pulled a shoulder muscle, hanging from the balcony so long. I suggested we return to the hotel for a friendly nap.

The Canova statue: $47,000. (Mrs. Godstalk!)

Warhol says the run-up to my thirty-second birthday will be like the final days of the Roman empire. He has ordered a red vinyl jockstrap for the occasion, which he may well wear outside his trousers. I couldn't help thinking that he will fade away into obscurity. His fashionability is waning. (Being around him is like inhaling one of those ridiculous poppers.)

At the post-party party the nude ice sculptures began to melt. There was a cake baked in the shape of an ass—marzipan dimples and creative icing. I blew out the thirty-three candles (one for luck) but then Truman Capote jumped up on the table in his frock coat, flung off his white hat, and planted his face into the cake, came up miming a pubic hair between his teeth.

Victor collapsed from exhaustion and was rushed to the hospital. Later he came into Studio 54 with the intravenous drip still in his arm. He guided the metal stand through the dance floor under the flashing lights. Soon everyone was cheering and applauding and whistling.

Victor bowed and took a booth in the far corner, readjusted the dripbag, and tried to buy everyone a drink before he collapsed once again. (He would have loved it if he could have seen himself being carried out by none other than Steve.)

Margot says, *Slow down.*

I told her that the countless small devils (sex, money, desire) mean nothing to me when stacked against the angel of dance.

Sasha fell in the park, it seems. Heart attack. Tonight I stayed late, sent everyone home, danced him alive.

Wandered into a courtyard where the last blacksmith in Paris was shoeing his first horse of the day. He allowed me to sit on the wall and watch him. The horse's leg in his hand and sparks at his feet.

Telegram and flowers for Xenia.

Fuck! The ankle just seemed to go out from underneath me. (Sasha all those years ago: *What, are you not friends with your body anymore,*

*Rudi?*) Three months recovery, Emilio said. In exactly four days I will throw the crutches into Central Park.

(three in fact!)

Two long weeks recovering on St. Bart's. No phone calls, nothing. It was so hot that the rain over the sea evaporated before it hit the water. Clouds of yellow butterflies rose from the trees. The world was far away and small.

The locals get up with the early light to work on their flower beds. Erik said the old men have a better life than the flowers—they have even less to do and can move to the shade when they desire. (Such a strange thing to say.)

After dinner he vomited in the bath. Food poisoning, he said. The housemaid cleaned him up. In his bathroom kit there were bottles of painkillers. In bed we turned back to back. He ground his teeth and kicked. By dawn the sheets were damp with sweat.

Photo from Tamara. Her heavy breasts, her stocky trunk, her abbreviated legs, how Russian she has become.

Twenty-four repetitions instead of twelve. Emilio has increased the weights and each day he measures the muscle. We walk the streets with the weight strapped to my ankle. The convict walk. Soon to be back dancing. Never before has he seen anybody recover so quickly.

Whole mornings doing massage. Hip extension. Torso twist. Hamstrings. Most of all my thighs and calves. He hangs my feet off the end of the table to prevent cramping and grows angry if I try to read a book on the special stand.

He says he can tell the plot of whatever I'm reading just by running his hands along my spine.

Perhaps the leg is stronger than ever before. The crowd in Verona, under the stars, give a twenty-minute standing ovation, even through a late drizzle. No word from Erik. The Chicago *Sun-Times* said he looked pale and, when he withdrew, the announcement was intestinal flu.

Margot has figured that we have danced together, in total, almost five hundred nights and she says to hell with it, she will go on, she will try for seven hundred, a lucky number!

Emilio's cure for insomnia: Pour water on your wrist, dab it gently with a towel, return to bed, warm your hands beneath your armpits.

Our final quarrel surely. Every piece of china was smashed except the teapot, which Erik cradled to his stomach. He lit a cigarette in the doorway, still holding the pot. When I turned away he dropped the teapot without even the hint of emotion. *Good-bye.* A stinging finality to it.

Gillian said it was inevitable. I slammed the phone down. I do not need to be told. Margot was with Tito in Panama. No answer. Victor came to listen, took a flight all the way. My head was reeling.

Tried getting through to Mother but all the lines were down.

It begins with scarves, dark ones bought at the Missoni store on rue du Bac; gradually, over the years, he gets to know the store owners so well that they open for him alone on a Sunday morning. The scarves become brighter, more patterned, until he is so famous they are an advertisement, unpaid for, some of them smuggled home to his sister and mother, who find them loud and gaudy. In London a Saville Row tailor makes him a high-collared tunic, a Nehru, not unlike the one he wore in school, except it is cashmere, and it is his joke to say that this is how he feels inside, *cash-a-mear*, spoken like three words accidentally met. In Vienna he buys a Rococo-style Murano glass chandelier with fifty-five lights and twenty replacement bulbs. In Cairo he finds a pair of antique Persian slippers. In Raizon he kneels on carpets made for him by a blind Morrocan man to whom he tells the story of the Leningrad choreographer who listened so intently to floorboards. The Moroccan loves the story so much that he repeats it to other customers, so the story shifts and changes as it makes its way through living rooms around the world, told and retold, the choreographer becoming a dancer from Moscow, or a Siberian musician, even a deaf-mute Hungarian ballerina, so that years later he hears the story, distorted, and he bangs on the dinner table and shocks everyone silent with the words: *Horseshit! That's horseshit! He was from Leningrad and his name was Dmitri Yachmennikov!*

He buys antique English bookshelves and folding tables. Romanian glassware hundreds of years old. An imperial dinner set from Austria. An Argentinean folding desk. Stained glass from a church in Bavaria. Iron crosses smuggled out of Czechoslovakia. A series of crucifixes by an artist in Vatican City. An intricately carved mirror from Chile, which he gives as a present to a stagehand from Santiago. He acquires musical scores handwritten in the 1930s for Vera Nemtchinova, pores over them late at night, teaching himself how to read the scores, how to hum them into his occasional insomnia. He orders maps drawn by a Soviet émigré in Mexico City, with the Republic of Bashkir firmly seated at the center, the town of Ufa finally finding a place for itself in cartography. One map is created for each of his homes, so eventually he has seven, a lucky number to him. The maps hang in gilded frames with a special nonreflecting glass. In Athens he buys a first-century Roman marble torso after the Diadumenos of Polykleitos, the body slightly chipped at the rib cage. His Virginia farmhouse has cabinet shelves that display precious carvings from Ghana. He buys Olga Spessivtzeva's slippers, shows them to his maker in Covent Garden, who learns a new stitch from them. On Madison Avenue in New York City he haggles over a Charles Meynier painting, *Wisdom Defending Youth Against Love.* He carries the painting back to his apartment in the Dakota rather than pay the extra hundred dollars for delivery.

Antique accordions, violins, cellos, balalaikas, flutes, fiddles, a mahogany grand piano from William Knabe and Co.: he surrounds himself with music.

In Stockholm he buys a glass case of rare fossilized ammonites. In Oslo, a cabinet made by Georg Kofoed Mobelfabrikant. In Rome he unfolds Chinese wallpaper panels depicting military scenes against a backdrop of herons, trees, temples. They are shipped to his island home on Le Galli near Capri. He makes a special trip to Nice to buy a series of Nijinsky photographs so he can study the poses, reset the steps, for which there is no written record. From Prague he orders hand-blown light fixtures from a glass craftsman. An Australian woman who deals in books sends him a steady supply of first-edition masters, mostly Russians. He rescues a grandfather clock from a trader in Singapore. From New Zealand he acquires a series of tribal masks. In Germany he buys a full set of dinner plates once used by a kaiser, the bone china trimmed with gold. From Canada he requests a cedar chest, since he doesn't like to use mothballs, he has heard there is a particular forest where the cedar is best. He has flowers flown from Hawaii to his London home. And in Wales, where there is a mastery and respect for the form, he has a train set built for him by Llewelyn Harris, a craftsman in Cardiff, the models so real that when he lays them out on the floor he can sometimes remember himself at six years of age sitting on the hill above Ufa station, waiting.

# BOOK THREE

*After the passing of irresistible
music you must learn to make
do with a dripping faucet.*

—JIM HARRISON, "DANCING"

# | I |

It is one of those heartless streets you find in parts of the city where the light is still tense with yesterday's darkness and even in the late afternoon it already feels like curfew and the spent trash of the day goes skidding along and pigeons sit gray on chain-link fences and the traffic is stalled and fume-blowing and the storefronts are dark and shadowy with filth and grime, Eleventh Street and C, Lower East, all smack and suicide, but Victor breaks it simply by moving down the sidewalk, making walking a form of dancing, beginning in the shoulders with a symmetrical roll not even the blacks have perfected, one oblong shrug of a shoulder and then the other, as if connected by synaptical cogs, first the left and then the right, but not just the shoulders, the roll moves down into his chest, into his rib cage, through the rest of his body, down to his toes—*god made me short so I can blow basketball players without ruining my knees!*—then up again to rest for a moment in his hips, nothing flagrant, no need to bring attention, the walk alone pays homage to his crotch, so if you are sitting on a brownstone stoop, high or hungover or both, you look up through the shit and the grime and the thousand other everyday torments too deep to mention and you see Victor coming along—looking like he's the first man ever to whistle—in his tight black pants and his neon orange shirt, his black hair swept back, his teeth white underneath his dark mustache and his body in a roll that isn't jazz or funk or fox-trot or disco, it's just pure Victor from head to toe, an art he must have managed since birth, laughing as he walks, a chuckle that rises high and ends low, a Victor laugh, on impulse, like his body just told him a little joke about himself, and the whole day slips away while you watch him, the clocks stop, the guitars tune themselves in unison, the air conditioners hum like violins, the garbage trucks sound like flutes, and you sit rooted to the steps as Victor waves to the other queens hanging out the windows, wigs and feathers and lust, while he crushes a cigarette or ties a shoelace or raps on a windowpane, using a silver dollar so it sounds out, and there are whistles and catcalls

Victor having become even more famous six years ago, after the '69 riots in Sheridan Square when he was arrested for violence and nudity—*nude violence!*—but then managed a hand job from a tall blond cop in the Sixth Precinct station, so Victor was talked about, laughed about, cheered in the bars baths backrooms of the city

and he moves on, in the empire of himself, taking a bow in front of the windowsills, Victor having learned every inch of the bow from his good friend Rudi Never-Off, holding the bend, arching his back, sweeping his arm to the sky, frozen for a second, grinning, then walking again, in the sequence of sun and shadow, down to the corner smoke shop, where he hauls deep on a joint with the pretty Puerto Rican boys who polish Victor's shoes with a white bandanna while he goes inside barefoot to tell the shop owner, *Man they should arrest the mass murderer who gave you that haircut,* his own hair so thick and slick that it shines under the shop neon, buying himself a packet of Lucky Strikes, his whole life a string of lucky strikes, from the streets of Caracas to the cockcrow of the new world, beginning as a carpenter, then a waiter, then a hustler, then a house painter, and, after Stonewall, an interior designer, *Yes, I'll design your interior!,* tak-ing only enough business to live the way he wants, knowing that the less a man works the more he is paid, one of the simple rules of New York City, and Victor has over the years proved many such simple rules to himself, his favorite being that if you live your life without falling in love you'll be loved by everyone—one of the great laws of love and fuckery—you take what you get and you move swiftly away, no looking back, so that even the Puerto Rican boys on the stoop can't hold him after sharing half their joint, he is gone once more, brightening the next street, and the next, hailed while shim-mying along, the dealers reaching into their tight yellow trousers for a couple of quaaludes, free of charge, saying, *Victor my man you tell those bluebloods where the real shit is at,* all the dealers hoping for Victor business later that night, since Victor business is good business, Victor might well guide a large troupe to your stoop, so you can wake up tomorrow slung alongside your sweetheart with your heart singing and a fat roll of twenties under your pillow, and Victor smiles as he takes the pills, saying *Gracias*—one of the two Spanish words he uses, *gracias* and *cojones,* both of them pronounced in three long syllables—like he's chewing for a moment on the childhood memory of Venezuela, the filth, the dogs, the soccer balls rolling towards the sewer pipes

when Victor was eight there was a statue said to have been sunk in the harbor at La Guaira near Caracas, a Virgin Mary, a story so vital to the townspeople that they brought pearl divers in, to no avail, they believed the Virgin would appear in a year of goodness and plenty, so when Victor was dragged out of the water, gasping for air, clutching the old and grimy statue, he was showered with money and gifts, and he took his mother and brothers to America, leaving a quarter of the money with the craftsman who had chiseled the statue for him, a perfect fake, so even then Victor knew that desire was just a stepping-stone to more desire

and he heads farther west through the Village, past a whore in hot pants wiggling her hips as if her body is on hinges, past the bums in bandannas selling the last of their *Occidental Death!* T-shirts, past the wheelchair beggars, past the black hipsters up against the railings on St. Mark's Place, past the farm boys high on their first taste of amphetamines, all the flotsam and jetsam of America, and on Second Avenue Victor drops some money in the cup of a young addict, she looks up to tell him she has never seen a groovier shirt, her eyes two puddles of mascara, and he drops another dollar in her smack cup, then skips around the spray from a fire hydrant, crosses Third Avenue, down the stairs at Astor Place, no logic to his skipping, two steps one step two steps three, waving to the clerk in the booth then jumping the turnstile while the clerk shouts, *Hey man, pay your goddamn fare!* and Victor nods to the passengers when he gets on the train, smiling, winking, never a lonely part of the city for Victor, not even on the subway, which he rides without sitting, without touching the metal bars or hanging straps, his legs spread wide for balance, as if preparing for the night in advance, jumping off the 6 train at Grand Central for four cigarettes and a cocktail in the Oak Room, vodka and grapefruit juice, a two-dollar tip to the bartender, *money is to roll that's why they made it round,* and then he weaves through the station against the rush of commuters, turning, zigging, zagging, down the litter-strewn steps to the Grand Central bathrooms—no place too nice for Victor and no place too nasty—already the rank smell of piss wafting through the t-room air, Victor announcing himself with the sort of composure that comes from a magazine, his lips pursed, his cigarette held high between his fingers, past the rectangular mirrors where a dozen men line up like a row of appetizers, Victor giving a nod to a pale-faced boy and a black man, tentative looks on their faces, unsure, he might be a cop or a queer-basher or a slicer, there've been some stabbings in recent years, but Victor reaches in his pockets, hands them each a quaalude, they relax and smile, down the pills, and all three dip into a stall, and soon they are laughing, touching, kissing, spooning, unspooning, until twenty minutes later Victor emerges to rinse his face and his neck and his armpits, other men watching, the rumor of Victor rippling among them, longing and jealousy in the row of mirrors since a blow job from Victor is currency in the city, a badge, an autograph, a nightclub rope suddenly lifted, *hey I'm a friend of Victor Pareci's,* but if you look around for Victor he is always gone, the sort of man you need precisely because he isn't there, always off somewhere else, his heart strung out on helium and all the valves have opened and he has been propelled elsewhere, out of your reach

to the underground room at the Anvil perhaps, or the Iranian embassy, where the great coke parties take place, or the rear basement in the Snake Pit, or a park-facing room at the Plaza, or the dark elevator to the Toilet, or the Algonquin for tea, or the pig parlor in the Triangle, or a table at Clyde's, or the rotten piers off the West Side Highway, the city in all its squalor and opulence belongs to Victor, he knows its streets, its avenues, its doormen, its bartenders, its bouncers, the distance it takes to walk from one joint to the other, and when it should be done, Victor never wears a watch but he knows the time of day anyway, down to the minute, no matter where he is, who he's fucking, what he's drinking, however stoned, however tired, however famous the company, because it may be time to move on, the cobwebs grow on you, who knows what might be happening down the block, the center of the world shifts and changes, and it is Victor's job to be there, *I'm the Greenwich Mean Time of Queerdom!*

and he is off on the express, the number 4, to Fifty-ninth and Lex, walking through the Upper East Side, the Jewish ladies with their poodles, or the poodles with their Jewish ladies, he can never tell which, Victor swinging his ass outrageously when he passes them on the sidewalk, hitting the leaves hanging from the curbside trees—*how bucolic!*—the light fading, streetlamps flickering into life, and he smokes with furious rolls and pulls, sending out plumes above him, another cigarette behind his ear for immediate firing, he smiles at the doormen in their white gloves, thinking there might be a new fashion in their regalia—Victor the door-whore, Victor the foot-man, Victor the man who invites you in!—and he skips across a marbled hallway, rather gauche he thinks, takes the elevator to the penthouse where the first cocktail party of the evening is in swing, a preballet affair, not exactly Victor's gig, he is seldom even out this early, but this is the house of a prospective client, he has been recommended by Rudi, and he has already given them a price, so he sashays into the mahoganied room where for an instant he stands beneath the giant chandelier and tries to announce himself with silence, but the room doesn't ripple towards him, there's no whispering over the rims of glasses, no awe, no clamor, *how disappointing!* so he pitches his bright shirt in among the dark dresses and the bow ties, leans over to deliver an exaggerated air-kiss, shakes a hand, picks a handful of hors d'oeuvres from a silver tray, the waiters slightly baffled by the sight of him, wondering if Victor is a gate-crasher or a celebrity—the sort of man who might pull the scaffold out from under the party or be the scaffold itself—but as Victor cruises the room a few heads turn in his direction, and, encouraged, he bounces on the soles of his feet towards the hostess, who surprises even herself by the size of her shriek, *Darling!* she snaps her fingers over the heads of three bow-tied men, the drink produced with startling speed, vodka and grapefruit, plenty of ice, and she takes his arm and brings him through the crowd, introducing him, the great Victor Pareci, a friend of Rudi's, delighting everyone he meets, just in the way he catches their eye or shakes their hand or touches their shoulder, a greeting that is genuine but fleeting, so his friendliness has no responsibility, nobody is forced to talk to him, yet they do

at least thirty invitations arrive each week to his Lower East Side apartment, and even the postwoman—with her hard Harlem accent, her tough beauty—arranges her shift so her lunchtime coincides with bringing Victor his mail, she likes to sit with him in his bright kitchen, opening envelopes together, regarding and discarding, *Victor honey you get more letters than Santa Claus!* she says, and Victor smiles and replies, *Ah yes, but that's because I know where all the bad boys live*

and Victor, more interested in the maverick corners of the party, where he knows there'll be a little outrage, breaks away from the hostess, kissing her hand as he leaves, and advances on a small group—an aging writer, a bored young artist, a fattening ballerina— who nod and smile as he sits on the floor beside a low glass table and says, *Excuse me while I practice a little resurrection!,* and from his pocket he produces a small bag, which he opens carefully, spilling the contents out on the glass, and then he chops out two lines with the blade of a tiny pocketknife, rolls a fifty-dollar bill, snorts the lines deeply, looks up at the ceiling, *Gracias!* and then doles out six more lines, places the rolled-up bill in the center of the table, *Ladies and gentlemen, start your engines!* and the young artist immediately leans across to scoop up the first line, then the writer, then the ballerina, who is somewhat coy but manages to snort more than anyone else, while the party swells with chatter, the hostess looking over and saying, *Oh that Victor!* and soon most of the room is looking in his direction, such delicious notoriety, he stands on the metal edge of the table and takes a bow, his throat tingling with joy, the small immediate hammer of energy through his body, he is just about able to balance on the table, a grin splayed across his face, finally jumping down to the floor to a little round of applause, knowing he has loosened the party enough so the myth will continue on the strength of this display alone, although Victor wishes Rudi were here, for nobody in the world can make an entrance quite like Rudi, everything quickly tense with possibility, charged, electric, Rudi ratcheting up his volume so he is twice as loud as anyone else, the night Rudi suspended himself naked from a million-dollar chandelier, the party where Rudi shaved his genitals with Andy Warhol's razor, Warhol later selling it to the highest bidder, the day Rudi prepared a meal for his friends and mixed a little semen into the hollandaise sauce and called it a secret Russian recipe, the gallery opening after which Rudi made love with three boys in a bathtub filled with lotion-slickened marbles

everyone with a Rudi story and each one more outrageous than the next—and probably untrue—so that Rudi is a living myth, not unlike Victor, cared for and coddled and protected by the mythmakers, a life not lived with any reason in mind, just an obeyance to light, or the lack of it, like a seed swelling in its own husk, both of them needing constant motion, since if they stay in one place too long they will become rooted like the rest, so that sometimes Victor thinks he too is dancing, always tapping his foot or shaking his head from side to side, his fingers twirling the end of his black mustache—*the reason I wear a mustache, gentlemen, is so I can smell last night's sins!*—and before you know it he has moved on, Victor ahead of himself, as if to say, *Oh look at me over there,* and no one can fill in the jigsaw, although there are rumors he learned all his movements from Rudi himself, that he sits in on rehearsal, watches constantly, which is another lie but one that Victor allows since it means people are talking about him, want to chat with him, own his recklessness for the night, and Victor obliges, half-listening but all the time watching the door until he sees the fur coats unfurled by the servants, hears the glasses clink, the excuses made, and Victor knows it is time to go, his rule, always be among the first to leave, down the stairs, not waiting for the elevator, and outside in the humid evening Victor follows a couple into their black limousine, the couple startled as he slides in behind them, chops out a line on the bar table, the woman is horrified, the man attempts cool, *Good evening, are you on your way to the Nureyev?* to which Victor winks, *Of course not, ballet bores me to tears,* and the man gives a smug grin, *Ah yes, but this is modern dance,* to which Victor responds, *Still faggots and divas, aren't they?* and the man recoils, wondering what sort of creature has crawled into his life, what faggot, what diva, and Victor, magnanimous to the end, offers the lady the first line, but she stares at him, her husband also refusing though not without a small wince, so Victor snorts the coke himself, grins, puts some on a handheld mirror, and shunts himself along the leather seat, leans forward to offer it to the driver, who shakes his head in bemused thanks, no, and Victor slaps a palm theatrically to his head and cries, *Oh! I'm so alone!* but then he kicks off his shoes and puts his feet on the opposite seat, saying, *But if you see Rudi, please say hi from me,* which the man thinks is a joke and he gives an extended chuckle, causing Victor to stare him down, until the man is so uncomfortable that he says, *This is our car you know,* and Victor says, *Of course it is!* and then turns to the driver, *Kind man! Drop me off in the Black Hills!* and the driver, clueless, is finally directed to the Dakota apartments overlooking the park and the couple are stunned not so much by the famous address as by Victor, the aura, the taste he leaves in the air, and he passes the driver a ten-dollar bill, hops out, feeling the charge of cocaine through his body, jumped up, sprung, loaded, waves good-bye to the limousine, and he heads straight to the gold-plated entrance

the first time he came to the Dakota, years ago, the doormen in their uniforms and epaulets directed him to the service entrance and Victor caused a fuss, until Rudi got on the intercom and shouted at the doormen to let his guest up immediately, but the next day, when Victor visited a second time, the doormen nodded austerely and allowed him to pass, so he went straight to the service entrance, his head hanging low, baffling the doormen, part of Victor's style, for, as Rudi says, remaining unknowable is the only true way to be known

and when he arrives upstairs in Rudi's apartment the preparations are under way, this is the first night of Rudi's run in *Lucifer* and a surprise party will be given in the seven-room spread, the last place Rudi would expect it, and Victor has offered his services free of charge, to choreograph the evening, to bend the flowers so they bow from their vases, to place the bowl of caviar at the just-reachable centerspot, to change the wattage in the lightbulbs, to scatter the chairs so there'll be no bunching, to smooth the creases in the velvet sofas, to adjust the drapes for the view to Central Park, to fold the napkins near the scented candles in the bathroom, to illuminate subtly the hand-painted Chinese wallpaper, all the etiquette of the evening, so the party will run like a drug or a dream or both, and Victor casts a quick look over the hired crew dressed in formal wear, then makes his way towards another group, the organizers, all society women, bejeweled, middle-aged, wealthy, powerful, reminiscent of beauty, skin tanned to tobacco color—oh what a row of elegant Lucky Strikes—and they are huddled, gravely going over arrangements, and when Victor breaks their ranks their faces change, both dislike and relief, the women are concerned, deeply so, since reputations are on the line, and it is exactly Victor's insouciance they can never achieve, although they try to draw it from him, while he shouts to nobody in particular, *Somebody please direct these beauties to the Valium!* and the women laugh, but Victor knows they are not just laughing, their laughter has another intelligence, the women have just relinquished control, and they lean in to Victor, having become his foot soldiers— he must use them like royalty and pieces of shit at the very same time—so he directs them to the kitchen, where the fridge has been liberally stocked with champagne, bids them to make a pyramid of glasses for him, fills the glasses with a flourish, says, *Let the bacchanalia begin!* and the women are forced to clink glasses, to forget all the crimes of the past, who threw a bigger party, who sat closest to the orchestra pit, whose hand got kissed by Oscar de la Renta, none of it matters now that Victor is in charge and, using his power, he tells them how wonderful they look in their Halston dresses, their sparkling Tiffany jewelry, their perfect maquillage, *I'd burn a thousand ships just to be around you!* and then he instructs them to watch the hired help, keep an eye on the waiters, be vigilant with the silverware, and— leaning so close now that they can see the dark outline of Victor's pupils—he seems as if he is about to reveal some fabulous secret, but pauses and says, *Ladies! the banquet table is in serious need of a face-lift!*

when Victor first moved in Rudi's circle he was surprised at the older women who crowded around, willing to do everything and anything, some of them even sporting boyish haircuts in the vague hope that Rudi would find them attractive, which he never did, but they continued to hope, although now that age is spoiling their bodies they are in search of a son to spoil instead, which makes Victor think of his own late mother, his one regret being that he wasn't with her when she succumbed, in the depths of the Bronx, to a strange liver disease, Victor at the time being so broke that he was unable to take her back to Venezuela, until years later he was on a trip with Rudi and they stopped off in Caracas for an afternoon, took a taxi to the hills, and spread her ashes at the foot of Mount Avila, watched her dust scatter, and it was one of the few times Victor cried publicly, he sat on the ground, put his head to his knees, wept quietly, then let out a howl, stood up and bid her good-bye, and it had shocked Rudi—this brute intimacy of grief—and the following night Rudi dedicated his dance in Caracas to her memory, stumbling once, but rising again in an elegant rage, which Victor, at the back of the opera house, thought a beautiful replica of his mother's life, the dance, the stumble, the anger, the applause, the encore, the curtain falling before she could limp to the wings

and Victor steps mock-angrily out of the kitchen, clicking his fingers at the hired help in their bad tuxedos, ordering them to assemble, it is a thin line he walks, for although he likes them, empathizes with them, respects them even, he knows what he must say, and soon the help are assembled in the kitchen, all twelve of them, high hair and bracelets, tattoos hidden beneath their sleeves, and Victor doesn't lean close but draws back for authority, speaking of the ladies, saying, *Those bitches have us over a barrel,* not a hint of a Venezuelan accent but still a sort of barrio bravado in his voice, as if this is the most important job they will ever do, and if they don't do it properly he will fire them even before Rudi comes back, since he knows what they want, everyone wants it, just to be near Rudi, just to say they touched him, but for good measure Victor turns up the heat a few notches, takes a deep breath, looks them each in the eye, says that if the work is not done well he will take every last man and string him up from the ceiling by his puny little cock and beat him like a fat white piñata—*you doubt me?*—and then he'll take every woman and thread the sleeve of his orange shirt through her orifices and swing her mercilessly over the trees into Central Park, where there'll be a dozen black boys waiting to gang-bang her, and the hired help are suddenly wide-eyed, until Victor breaks the tension with a long laugh, which becomes gentle, kind, full of tenderness, and he says if they do well there's an extra twenty-five bucks each, maybe even some nose candy, and now Victor is aware they are so thoroughly confused that he has them under his thumb, that the evening has firmly settled into place like a good carpentry job, the pegs snug, the legs squared off, thinking in fact that he has performed such a great job he might have time to dash into the park for fifteen minutes or so, make his way up towards the Rambles

oh the Rambles! all the scraddlelegged boys strung out in silhou-ette! all the tramping of weeds! all the faces shoved into brambles! all the bandannas in back pockets! all the drugs fermenting in all the bodies! what a human candy store! all the horsewhips and cockrings and lubricants and other chewable delights! all the winding paths! the soil indented with the patterns of knees! the moon out behind a dozen different trees! Johnnie Ramon with his shadow long on the grass and oh so tautly bowed! yes! Victor and the Rambles know each other well, and not just for nature walks, once or twice he has even accompanied Rudi there, because Rudi sometimes likes the tough boys, the raucous ones, the hot tamales who come down from the Bronx and Harlem

but instead of the Rambles Victor opts for an alternative dose of resurrection, ducks into the bathroom, cleans the top of the tank with pieces of wet tissue, chops out a line, snorts with great gusto, shakes his head and stomps one foot, and he is out once more, answering a sharp buzz from the intercom, saying, *Send them up!* and within moments the caterers are at the door with dozens of trays of

food, some of which he guides to the kitchen and the rest he has
lined up on the banquet table, all manner of delicacies, much of it
Russian, sliced sturgeon, beluga caviar in chilled bowls, horsemeat
pâté, krendeli, pirozhki, Black Sea oysters, meat salads, Stroganoff, the
women beside him fussing and fretting, he calms them by taking just
a tiny taste of the caviar on the tip of his finger, *Good enough for a
Queen!* then spends the next hour checking on the work of his
charges, the women watching the hired help, the hired help watching
the women, coordinated now like a song, so that Victor can do the
things he needs to do, tilting the paintings in the living room just the
tiniest bit off angle, especially the Meynier, his own little joke, *Wisdom Defending Youth Against Love*, and he turns the divan from the
window so that it will not be commandeered by some sad slouch,
arranges the ashtrays at a distance from the fine couches, adjusts the
dimmer on the lights, fans the tassels on the Persian rugs, lines up
Beethoven on the stereo to be followed by James Brown—*a little
musical anarchy please!*—all the time watching the clock, the evening
descending to the smallest details, the folds in the napkins, the position of the candelabra, the angle of the piano, the temperature of the
mushroom sauce, so that Victor becomes impatient, tapping his foot,
trying to figure out at what stage the dance is, if Rudi is finished yet,
how long the ovation will take, until the intercom buzzes and the
first guests of the evening announce themselves, so Victor bows generously to the organizing ladies, allowing them their kudos, barks
one final time at the bartender who has not polished the glasses to
satisfaction, *Beware, I will return!* for that is another rule of Victor's,
never be first at a party, even if he's in charge, and instead of taking
the elevator down he walks the stairwell, briefly pensive, almost sad,
Victor spending a moment alone with Victor, leaning his head
against the mustard-colored wall, breathing deeply, feeling the relax-
ation seep into his body, down to his toes, time for a quiet cocktail,
somewhere dark and anonymous, not a gay bar, not a club, and not a
Rambles cocktail either! somewhere he can rest temporarily, save his

energy for the remains of the evening, and he finds a seedy little joint on Seventy-fourth and Amsterdam, checks out the jukebox, wonders how Rudi will react to the invasion

it was way back in '68 when Victor was taken to the ballet by an elderly matron whom he was escorting, he sat in the best seats for *Romeo and Juliet*, bored at first, fidgeting in his pricey jacket, crossing and recrossing his legs, wondering how long it would last, how soon he could escape, but then something happened, Fonteyn gave Rudi one of those glances that seemed to change everything, Rudi lifted her, Fonteyn's face was glorious in the light, and the two dancers seemed to melt into each other, and Victor realized this was more than ballet, more than theater, more than spectacle, it was a love affair, a public love affair where the lovers did not love each other beyond the stage, which made Victor want to rise from his seat and perform, not ballet, but to move his body wildly and freely, and it was painful to watch such beauty without being part of it, he resented the look on Rudi's face, his energy, his control, so when the curtain fell Victor felt an inexplicable hatred, he wanted to go up to the stage and shove Rudi into the pit, but he stayed motionless, shocked that the world could reveal such surprises—this was ballet, ballet! for crying out loud!—and it made Victor wonder what else he was missing, what else was lacking in his life, and in the foyer afterwards while he waited in line to collect his escort's fur coat, Victor felt flush with heat and cold so that he shivered and sweated simultaneously, he had to go out into the night air, where a great swell of girls in widebottomed jeans shouted, *Rudi in the nudi! Rudi in the nudi! We want Rudi in the nudi!* some of the fans clutching photos of Rudi to their chests, clamoring for position, hoping for autographs, and Victor had to abandon his aging escortee, he jumped into a taxi and went downtown to dance and forget, to a club on the eighth floor of an old factory, lights blazing, boys on drugs, famous actors sniffing rags soaked in ethyl chloride, the smell of poppers, men in front of mirrors with their eyes closed, wearing pirate shirts, headbands, winklepicker boots, whistles around their necks, the music so loud that some boys walked around with blood leaking from their eardrums, and Victor felt better after an hour, having come home to himself, sweat-soaked and mobbed by men who desired him, but later, when he sat sharing champagne with a wealthy fashion designer, Rudi suddenly joined the table—*hey Rudi, this is Victor Pareci*—and Victor felt a pit of despair in his stomach as Rudi looked at him, they detested each other immediately, they could see the cockiness but they could also see the doubt, that volatile mixture, fire and vacuum, both men knowing that they were similar, and their similarities galled them, having stepped out of the dirty shanties of the world into the drawing rooms of the rich, that they were the edge of a coin and no matter how many times the coin was flipped they would always remain the edge, that the rich didn't understand this, but neither did the poor, and all this made their hatred palpable, and relief came only when they stepped away to opposite ends of the dance floor, but after a while they began dueling across the floor, seeing how many boys they could attract, and only Victor could live in a duel with Rudolf Nureyev, for this was Victor's turf even though Victor was short and dark and unfashionably Venezuelan—*short in stature, yes, but large everywhere else!*—he had been worshiped on the floor long before he was worshiped in bed, his hip roll exaggerated so his legs seemed detached from his body, his shirt twisted and knotted to show off his flat dark stomach, and it became a strange war between them, beneath the revolving lights, the air heated, a great caisson of drums and guitar and voice, until there was a blackout, not even a fizzle of electricity but a sudden plunge into darkness, the other patrons thinking it might be part of the routine—often the lights were shut off so the men could have sex—but Victor waited out the blackout, wrung the sweat from the flaps of his shirt, feeling whole and complete and invulnerable in the dark, hearing the fumbling and laughing and thrusting all around, and Victor felt proud of his abstention, flushed with a sort of ascetic glory as the room filled with grunts and shrieks, until the lights came on again, blazing, riotous, and who was there across the floor but Rudi, still and majestic, and as the music jumped back into life they grinned at each other and recognized at that moment that they had somehow crossed a chasm, they were standing on the same side of the divide, knowing with a deep certainty that they would never touch each other, never fuck or suck or finger or rim, and certainly never kiss, and the realization was a balm, a salve, an unspoken pact, they had no need for each other's bodies, but still they were inextricably tied, bound not by money or sex or work or fame but by their pasts and now, having met in a crosswind, they would duck out of it for shelter, and it was Victor who set out for the other side of the floor, staring at Rudi all the way, and the dancer put out his hand and they shook, laughed in unison, went to a table where they ordered a bottle of vodka and spent the hours talking, not about the world around them but the worlds they had come from, Ufa and Caracas, finding suddenly that they were talking about things they hadn't talked about in years, the corrugated roofs, the factories, the forests, the smell of air at dusk—*My street had a river of sewage running down the middle! My street wasn't even a street! My street smelled like two wet dogs fucking!*—and they could have been talking to mirrors, finding each other by finding themselves, the nightclub was forgotten, pure scenery, and they left at six in the morning, to the glare and envy of others, down the street for breakfast together at Clyde's, Victor rolling his shoulders, Rudi clicking his heels, the sun struggling up full and red over the warehouses and abattoirs of Manhattan's west side

and by the time Victor leaves the bar and returns to the Dakota, singing, *Take me back to the Black Hills,* the party is in full swing, he enters to a swirl of bodies—ambassadors balletomanes choreographers doctors engineers filmstars globetrotters highbrows imagemakers junkies kingpins leeches millionaires nighthawks oddballs producers quacks royals sexsymbols thespians underlings vamps wallcrawlers xenophiles yesmen zealots—all hyped up on the show, or the rumor of the show, a huge crowd in the corner around Martha Graham, telling her how wonderful! how provocative! how imaginative! how daring! how nouveau! how marvelous! how utterly groundbreaking! a look on Graham's face as if to say that if she swung a cat she would hit a hundred assholes, and Victor charges on, leaning over to kiss Margot Fonteyn, radiant, calm, precise, always friendly to Victor although she doesn't quite understand him, a ghostly quality to her goodness, he tells her she looks *Delicious!* to which she grins as if pained by the ongoing overload of compliments, and Victor spins away and hails Jagger in the corner, pinned to the world by his lips, chatting with a blond woman whose hair seems to totter on her head, and next to him Roland Petit gesturing to a group of young dancers, and across from Petit towers Vitas Gerulaitis, the tennis player, energetic and expansive, with a group of gorgeous young men—*Wash yourselves down,* shouts Victor, *and come to my tent!*—then he nods and winks liberally at everyone who's anyone, the Fords of the world, the Halstons, the Avedons, the Von Fürstenbergs, the Radziwills, the Guinnesses, the Allens, the Rubells, the Capotes, everyone, Victor flashing his high-wattage smile all around the apartment, but where the hell is Rudi? Victor casts his eyes quickly over the room, the designer rags and champagne glasses, where the hell is he? and he shakes more hands and air-kisses, all the time looking for Rudi, where the fuck is he? Victor has a tight sense of foreboding as he makes his way to the rear bedroom, where the party organizers are stationed outside like diplomats, talking seriously and guardedly, and Victor intuits the nature of the problem and barrels right through, although the women try to hold him back, to no success, and he snaps down on the gold-plated door handle, slams the door shut behind him, locks it, takes a moment for his eyes to adjust to the dark room, and Victor says, *Rudi?* but there is no answer, and Victor says this time, *Hey Rudi!* with a thrust of anger, and he hears a rustle, then a shout, *Get the fuck out!* a bedroom slipper coming for Victor's head, which he ducks, and then he spies a ball of disconsolate fury on the bed, Victor tries to figure what to do, where to stand, how to say things, but Rudi is suddenly off the bed and on his feet, screaming, *They say to me well done? Well done? Shit! They talk shit! Well done is for steak! They fuck up the music! They fuck up the curtains! They fuck up everything! Don't talk to me about well done! Leave me alone! This is the morgue! Get out! Who makes this party? I have never seen so ridiculous! Cunt! Out!* and Victor receives the tirade with a concealed smile, but he knows it's too early to laugh, he tries to look calm, not to reveal that his mind is whirling, going over all the endless permutations, the pulls and the sways of the evening, the quarrels, the ovations, the mistakes, the critiques, the depth of the manifold possible wounds, and in the end he says to Rudi, *Yeah, I heard you were dreadful tonight,* to which Rudi turns on him and screams *What?* and Victor shrugs, keeps tapping his feet on the floor, says, *Well, Rudi, I heard you were a piece of shit tonight, I heard your performance was really bad,* and Rudi says, *Who said that?* and Victor says, *Everyone!* and Rudi says, *Everyone?* and Victor replies *Every-fucking-one,* and Rudi twists his face savagely but doesn't say a word, yet his mouth reveals the hint of a grin, so Victor knows it's working, that the tide will turn, and he doesn't even wait, he just unlocks the door, shuts it gently, goes back out to the party, whispers to the women organizers, *No mortal wounds darlings! Back to battle stations!* and then he sees a man emerging from a doorway with his hand to his nose and his jaw grinding in the familiar way and soon he and Victor are tucked away sharing liberal amounts of cocaine

he once saw a doctor who was amazed Victor was alive let alone healthy, he should have been dead years ago, and Victor said to him, *A man's life, if it's a good life, is older than himself,* a saying the doctor liked so much he tacked it on the wall of his Park Avenue practice and gave Victor two hundred blank prescription sheets free of charge

and soon Victor is out of the bathroom and Rudi appears also, emerging from his bedroom as if nothing has happened, gliding through the living room in a beautiful white long-collared shirt, tight white jeans, snakeskin shoes, without even so much as a smile for Victor, but Victor doesn't care, he knows anything can happen now, all the heads are following Rudi's progress, and Rudi looks like a man who has just conceived the very notion of happiness, flicking his hair back from his eyes with a snap of his head, there is a sudden sense of magnetism in the room, Rudi seems attached to everyone, and Victor is one of the few who stands outside the performance, he settles instead into a moment of quietness, watching as Rudi gathers a group around himself, launching into some diatribe about dance as an experiment, all its impulses going to the creation of an adventure and the end of each adventure being a new impulse towards further creation, *If a dancer, he is good,* says Rudi, *he has to straddle the time! He must drag the old forward into the new!* to which his listeners nod and agree, charmed by what Rudi says, his accent, his mispronunciations, and Victor has seen this many times before, the way Rudi controls a crowd even off the stage, the way he swings from inanity to profundity and back again, *Good God he's not only beautiful but he's smart too!* and Victor loves to watch faces when Rudi is in full stride, it is one of the few stillnesses in Victor's life—to watch Rudi in his flux—and sure enough, without missing a beat, Rudi smashes six glasses in the fireplace in a row and then begins to play Chopin on the grand piano, an étude, the whole room hushed and tethered to him, and when he is finished he shouts, *Stop the clapping!* for everyone knows Rudi needs the praise but he hates it also, to him life is an ongoing series of failures, the only way to continue is to believe that you've never done your best, for Rudi has said before, *It's not so much that I love difficulty, no, difficulty loves me*

Victor once saw Rudi in his Paris dressing room before *Corsaire,* getting a warm-up rub from his masseur, Emilio, and Rudi was spread out on the massage table, the body perfectly sculpted, tough, white, coiled, a body that might make you stare unwittingly at your own, but what surprised Victor was not just the physique, but that Rudi had a special stand set up in front of the massage table and was reading a book by Samuel Beckett, signed for Rudi—*For Rudolf, all good wishes, Sam*—and Rudi was learning whole chunks of the book by heart, and later that night, at a dinner party in the Austrian embassy, he stood and performed a routine about stones in his pocket and stones in his mouth, quoted perfectly, syllable for syllable, to great applause and later still, while walking home, he quickened his pace towards the Seine and talked about how he had begun to believe that there should be no unity in art, never, that perfection embalms it, there has to be some tearing, a fracturing, like a Persian carpet with a wrongly tied knot, for that is what makes life interesting—*Nothing's perfect, not even you, Victor*—and at the wall of the river Rudi scooped up a number of pebbles, borrowed Victor's overcoat and stood precariously on the wall, launched into the speech once again, arms stretched wide, and Victor wondered what might happen if Rudi toppled into the water, if the Seine itself would dance

and Victor is delighted to see the party oiled smoothly now, everyone eating and drinking, a great buzz in the apartment, Rudi playing the perfect host, rounding the tables, chatting with guests, proposing a series of toasts, to his fellow dancers, to Martha, to Margot—*To dance itself!*—and Victor knows he must maintain the party's thrust so he hops quickly across the floor and pulls a Temptations record from its sleeve, arranges it on the turntable, drops the stylus, adjusts the controls, and then darts into the kitchen where he barks at the help—*I want every single plate back here in five minutes! Clean the whole fucking place! Get Rudi a drink! Get me a drink! Get everyone a drink!*—and the music spills into the room, jackets get tossed onto the backs of the couches, feet slip out from shoes, shirts are unbuttoned, there's a melting of reticence aided by the alcohol, a fat man in a fedora jiggles his flab near the stereo, a pretty actress raises the sight-lines of her skirt, Mick Jagger twists on the piano stool for a better view, Fonteyn throws her head back in laughter, Ted Kennedy shrugs off his tie, Andy Warhol enters in bright red pants, John Lennon comes down from his upstairs apartment with Yoko

Ono on his arm, and Victor can feel the electricity of the night, bodies sweating, drinks shared, ends of cigars suggestively licked, and soon a whisper of sex on the air—*Well, thank God for that!*—as if the place has been somehow laced with Spanish fly, strangers leaning closer, women clandestinely touching each other on the inside of the arm, men rubbing shoulders, and the moment stabs Victor with energy as he watches Rudi flit among the groups, charging them with eroticism, man or woman, it doesn't matter, Rudi sees it all as calisthenics for the hours ahead

eighteen months ago on vacation in Paris, at a club called Le Trap, in the upstairs room, lit only by red bulbs, Victor watched Rudi blow six Frenchmen in a row, stopping for a glass of vodka between each, only to hear that Victor had bettered him by two, *Such fine French cuisine! So deliciously tender!* so Rudi dragged the first three men he could find, lined them against the wall, *A veritable firing squad!* and went at them in the same way he danced, all elegance and ferocity, his sexual fame nearly equaling the renown of his dancing, Rudi was even known to take a break during performances for a quickie, and once in London he left the theater at intermission, pulled his overcoat over his dancing clothes, changed his shoes, ran down the street to the public toilets, where he entered a stall and was arrested for soliciting a policeman, *But you can't arrest me I have to perform in ten minutes,* to which the policeman sniggered and said, *Perform indeed,* and the intermission stretched out over forty-five minutes until Rudi was found by his manager, Gillian, who shouted at the cop that the whole of England was waiting, and the cop laughed at her histrionics but allowed Rudi out of the handcuffs, and Rudi dashed back up the street, burst through the side entrance, bounded onstage, fired up by it all, and danced brilliantly, the newspapers said it was one of his finest performances ever, and during encores Rudi noticed the cop standing near the rear of the hall, grinning and laughing while Gillian tenderly stroked his lapel

and the night bends itself further towards lust as Rudi nods across the room at Victor, and Victor nods back, a secret language, so Rudi begins to make a round of the party, thanking the guests, effusive, benevolent, whispering in ears, closing business deals, shaking hands, sashaying back and forth, kissing Lennon on the cheek, Yoko on the lips, slapping Warhol on the ass, doting on Fonteyn, kissing Graham's hand—*Good-bye, good-bye, good-bye!*—saying he has a late-night appointment at the Russian Tea Room, sorry, he must run, *Please excuse me*, a lie of course, but precisely calculated to begin to scatter the revelers, and Victor tidies behind the scenes, tips the hired help an extra thirty dollars each—*Buy yourself something pretty, boys and girls!*—and the party begins to splinter, on to other parties, nightclubs, even the Russian Tea Room, where the guests hope to dine once again on the vision of Rudi, but they won't, because he and Victor have something else in mind, they descend by the stairs and whistle for a cab—the night air pinning them momentarily with its humidity—and soon find themselves in new territory, jumping out of the taxi on Twenty-eighth and Broadway where they step on the word BATH engraved in the sidewalk outside, Rudi adjusts the brim of his well-worn leather hat, Victor rattles the door four times like a code, then shouts *Greetings!* to the young man who opens the door, and they slide their money across the counter, get their towels, head along the pine-paneled corridor, through the indefinite light, towards the lockers, where they change out of their clothes as the noise of the place begins to engulf them, the slap of bare feet, the dripping water, the hiss of steam, the distant shouts and giggles, and, wrapped only in their towels, with their locker keys around their ankles, Rudi and Victor head to the heart of the Everard, which is in its very own way a ballet—some of the greatest ass mechanics in the city plying their trade here—guys in earrings, guys in heels, guys with eyeshadow, guys in dresses looking as if they just stepped off the set of *Gone With the Wind*, guys still in their Vietnam undershirts, guys in aviator glasses, guys smeared with oil, guys who look like girls, guys who want to be girls, some at half-mast, some at full mast, some unfortunates at no mast at all, some squatting over the water jets for a quick enema, a shriek coming from the shower rooms, and everyone fucking, flesh sandwiches, fucking in the rooms and fucking by the water fountain and fucking in the shower stalls and fucking in the sauna room and fucking in the boiler room and fucking in the broom closet and fucking in the rest rooms and fucking in the baths, fist-fucking, toe-fucking, finger-fucking, cluster-fucking, not to mention rimming, a regular fuckfest, as if Victor and Rudi put the lust pill in the water, hallelujah and hail to the fuck tablet! come on down! join in! no matter who you are! short and fat! tall and thin! rich or poor! small or large! (preferably large!) come to the Ever-Hard! and Victor spies one man, all loaded up on adrenaline and amphetamines, wearing only a boxing glove, the palm filled with lubricant, yelling *Come and get it, come and get it, I'm a southpaw!* and another quiet in the corner, just watching, his wedding ring on, a different class of asshole altogether, Victor hates the married ones, their sly effrontery before they return home to their wives, but who cares, who needs them, who wants them, there is more than enough to go round, and he turns to Rudi and says, *All yours!* because they never operate together, they remain apart, different ends of the spectrum, and within moments Rudi is off to the other end of the corridor while Victor roams his own turf, testing the atmosphere, scanning the faces, the first ten minutes always a ritualized staking out, intent and serious, Victor never quite sure where to begin, a fact-finding mission—it is impossible, he knows, to dive right into the fray—and he washes his face in the drip from a pipe, then cuts through the steam, all the time carrying his towel at his hip, a gunslinger, lowering his eyelids to say, *No I don't want you, I will never want you, not even if you were the second last man on earth*, or holding them steady to say, *Perhaps*, or widening them to say, *Yes yes yes*, Victor darts his attention to an ass in the shower, or the hollow of a back, or the curve of a chestbone, or the arc of a mouth, or the turn of a hip, and he wanders until he feels his body revving up, blood boiling, desire rising, the steam shrouded over him now, yes yes yes yes, he gives a nod to a tall bearded blond boy who stands alone by the doorway to one of the rooms, blue-eyed, serious, and within moments they are meshed beneath the red lights, ignoring the sad sack of mattress on the floor, they go up against the wall instead, the slide of skin and the slap of desire, Victor allowing control, the man's breath hot on his neck, reaching back to tickle his paramour's balls, a rather pedestrian fuck, he thinks, choosers should never be beggars, and Victor composes himself when the man is finished, *Gracias!* and is off for more, deciding that he will be in the driving seat for the rest of the night, since that is the position he likes best, maximum locomotion, *Gracias! Gracias! Gracias!* a great incoming tide of fuckery, ruthless and merciless, first a boy, then a man, then another boy, with surely the most beautiful shoulder blades Victor has ever seen, he adores shoulder blades, he loves running his tongue along the high hollows in backs, then moving his mouth up along necks as the men shudder and moan, or running his teeth down the length of their spines, Victor never tires of fucking, he hopes he never will— the few straight friends he has, especially the married ones, don't believe he can actually fuck all day long and continue fucking the day after that, they assume he is lying when he says he has had more men than hot dinners, but it's the truth, the bare truth, *Hot dinners, my friend, are vastly overrated,* and he continues moving from body to body until finally he decides to take a small break, a temporary rest, and he approaches the baths, satisfied, happy, the hunt temporarily interrupted, he steps through the steam into the comfort of the water and soaks while the gymnastics around him continue—once upon a time the baths belonged to the Italians and the Irish, but since the late sixties, those glorious late sixties when flesh became fashion, the baths have belonged to the Victors of the world, the victorious, a risky business, raided occasionally by the cops, and Victor has spent nights in jail, where indeed the bathhouse tradition persists, such camaraderie! such affability! such jailhouse rocking!—and submerging himself now in the soothing warmth, Victor wonders how Rudi is getting on, but he knows there's no need to worry, Rudi is human flypaper, the men stay suspended on the mid-air of him, stuck to the memory of the moment, and they will whisper about it for years to come, *Well, I did my thing for the Cold War, yes, I got fucked by Rudolf Nureyev! And, let me tell you, he just hammered his sickle!* and the story will be appropriated and reappropriated, the size of Rudi's cock, the tap of his heartbeat, the feel of his fingers, the aroma left by his tongue, the sweat of his thighs, the imprint of his lips, and maybe even the sound of their own hearts breaking beneath their rib cages as he moved away

Victor has often said to Rudi that to love one man is impossible, for he must love all men, though at times Rudi has grieved and fulminated over lost love, which is not Victor's style at all, Victor believes in the roll and the spin, the gamble, and he can't quite understand how Rudi has been in love, in the past, how he can actually fall for one man, dedicate his heart to him, like Rudi did with Erik Bruhn for many years, the two greatest dancers in the world in love with each other, it seemed impossible, and it galled Victor the way his friend talked, as if a million tuning forks had all been struck at once in Rudi's chest, and Victor detested hearing about the dancers' small moments together all over the world, on yachts and in drawing rooms and fancy hotel suites and health spas high in the Danish countryside, Victor couldn't understand it, Bruhn seemed to him the antithesis of life, tall and blond and brooding, coldhearted, meticulous, *that fucking Viking!* it wasn't so much jealousy on Victor's part, or so he insisted, it was more that he feared Rudi being brokenhearted, that Rudi would get torn up by love, that he would lose everything in the same way married men disappear into the floorboards of their wives and children, and Victor dreaded being one of those people suddenly left by Rudi, forced to carry the sheer weight of having once been his friend, but he needn't have worried because in the end it was Rudi who left Bruhn, and Victor remembers well the night they finished—it was not the first time but it was the final time—Rudi on the telephone weeping in great heaving sobs that racked even Victor, and finally it transpired that Rudi was in Copenhagen—*it's so fucking cold here*—but was on his way back to Paris, he had broken up with Bruhn and wanted Victor to come over, and Victor packed immediately, went to the airport where a first-class ticket was waiting, and Victor couldn't help smiling a little at the quality of the journey, despite Rudi's heartache, and he laid back in the comfortable seat and wondered what he'd say to Rudi, what answers he could conjure, but when he got to the apartment on the quai Voltaire there was nobody there except the French housekeeper, and Victor sat by the window, momentarily happy for Rudi's misery since it meant another drama, but when Rudi walked through the door, his face long and haggard and carved by grief, Victor felt a huge stab of remorse, he could see the black lines of tears on Rudi's face, and Victor hugged his friend close, which he didn't often do, made tea with six sugars, then brought out a bottle of vodka, closed the curtains, and the two men sat in the darkness, drinking, talking not about Erik—which surprised Victor—not about the breakup or the misery or the loss, but about their mothers, feeling curiously like clichés at first, two grown men settling back into maternal solace, but after a while the yearning for their mothers became terribly real, and Rudi said to Victor, *Sometimes, Victor, my heart it feels as if it is under house arrest,* which sent a shiver through Victor, he knew that for years Rudi had been trying desperately to get a visa for her, even just for a day, so Farida could see him dance just one more time, share his world however briefly, sometimes it was harder for Rudi to be away than to be happy, he thought about her constantly, and Rudi had been in touch with everyone, presidents, ambassadors, prime ministers, queens, senators, congressmen, princes, princesses, but to no avail, the authorities wouldn't budge, they'd never give his mother a visa, and they certainly wouldn't give Rudi a visa, and Rudi was afraid Farida would die, and there was nothing in the world he wouldn't give just to see her one more time, and Victor downed another vodka and said he too spent his life wishing he could see his mother, resurrect her somehow, simply go back to Caracas to say that he had loved her, just to squeeze those three words together in tribute, and the conversation drew them so close that Rudi and Victor were able to sit in silence for an hour, more intimate than sex, without fraudulence, without mimicry, deep and soulful and necessary, never once mentioning Erik, instead recalling happier times, and finally both men fell asleep by the window to be awoken by the housekeeper, Odile, who brought coffee then left them alone, and Victor said to Rudi, *Perhaps you should phone Erik, maybe you need to talk to him,* but Rudi shook his head, no, and Victor knew then that it was definitely over, that Bruhn would become another milestone, and before they launched themselves into the day Rudi went to the mantelpiece to get a picture of Farida, she was standing in a factory with a white hat on her head, a wry sadness to her, the photo seeming incongruous among the fine art and furniture in the apartment, and Rudi held the photo close to his chest, as if tilted to the past, and later when the two men stepped out into the clean day they were slightly embarrassed, in the sunlight, by what had transpired in the dark, *Look at us Rudi, we're soaked in tears!* and yet they knew, even as the morning traffic threw its fumes along the Seine, that they had somehow arrived at the elemental litter of their hearts

the steam rising up around Victor now, thinking to himself that he shouldn't hit the pause button, that it rips him up too much, these memories, and he calls on a fellow bather for a cigarette and lighter, draws in the satisfaction of it, hears a murmur and sees Rudi settling down beside him in the water, a line of his hair from his belly button, his waist tiny and hammered into shape, no coyness at all, his cock with a sort of long satisfactory limpness like a traveler on a journey, and this amuses Victor, he needs amusement, thinking of all the cocks in the world being on journeys, some on package holidays, some in English gardens, some in stuffy Mediterranean rooms, others on Siberian Expresses, but some indeed, oh yes indeed, some would be Bedouin gypsies, ha! having been everywhere and back again to no peculiar purpose but the fulfillment of life itself—*Hey Rudi! You and me! We're Bedouin boys!*—and he explains the joke to Rudi and the two men lie back in the enjoyment of the moment, laughing, chatting about the party in the Dakota, about who wore what, who was with whom, and for half an hour they allow the water to surround them, the silence, the closeness, until Victor says with a grin, *Hey Rudi, what'll we do with the rest of our lives?* and Rudi shuts his eyes and replies that he should leave soon, he has to be up early, he has rehearsal piling up upon rehearsal, his life is like a never-ending practice for the real thing, that he has a series of big events coming up, all important, two charity galas, five photo shoots, a dozen television interviews, a trip to Sydney, to London, to Vienna, not to mention a screen test for a movie, it never seems to end, Rudi wishes sometimes he could just freeze it and temporarily step outside his life, there is so much to do, it takes away from the dance, he wishes he could just perform and not worry about a single other thing, and Victor stands up, sighs, raises one arm in the air and shouts, *Oh drown me in martinis! Buy me a Tiffany gallows! Prepare my last meal at Maxim's! Electrocute me in my Jacuzzi! Throw my platinum hand dryer in the bathtub!* and Rudi smiles, he knows he cannot play these sorts of games with Victor, and he nods to Victor who is now standing on the edge of the bath, taking a bow, so Rudi grabs him by the leg, pulls him back into the water, plunges his head down, *Watch my hairstyle!* and they laugh until they are exhausted, breathing hard, hanging on to the rim of the bath, two little boys charmed by each other, and suddenly another wicked gleam shines in Rudi's eye, he is out of the water, his towel draped around his neck, his body replenished, saying he is off for one final round, that William Blake would have approved—*The road of excess, Victor, leads to the palace of wisdom*—and there is another murmur through the baths, and Victor checks his own mental clock, thinking where to go next, where the best drugs might be, the best music, where another round of spontaneous sex might fuel the inner need, and he too rises from the water but steps in the opposite direction, ignoring a couple of handsome advances, a sacrifice indeed, and returns to his locker, sits on the wooden bench, pulls on his black pants and orange shirt, out of view of Rudi—*Time for another dose of resurrection!*—and after snorting the line he slips into his shoes, nods to the men in the corridors, walks around, looking for Rudi, but Rudi is nowhere to be found, perhaps he is shuttered away in some corner or is hiding or has left without saying good-bye, not unusual of course, just one of those things, Rudi owns the world so why say good-bye to any one part of it? and after checking the baths thoroughly Victor still finds no sign, so he steps out on the street, looks right and left, even jogs to the corner, but the avenue is curiously quiet and sinister, not a soul breaking its shadows, dangerous times, there have been beatings of gay men, but you live your life only as long as it lives you, so Victor starts to walk, rolling his shoulders once more, onwards and upwards—*Whoever brought me here, my friends, is going to have to pay the price!*—and he hails a cab driven by a handsome young Mexican man, Victor flirting with the idea of inviting him out for a drink at one of the downtown clubs, deciding against it when he sees the plastic Jesus bobbing on the dashboard, religion being nothing more to Victor than a worldly suppository, and he winds down the window to watch Manhattan glide by, its violence and gaudy neon, the West Side, flashing red yellow orange green wonderland, hustlers johns grifters whores, boys and girls ground down by the chemicals, Victor waves at them and they flip him off, so he waves some more as the taxi moves south to the Anvil, which is alive and throbbing now, especially alive at three-thirty in the morning, disco lights spinning, men in leathers and studs, men in denim jeans with the asses scissored out, men in country and western gear, men with steel nuts and bolts for zippers, a drag queen on a small stage performing with a six-foot boa constrictor, a group of go-go boys hanging from ropes, and Victor checks the bar just in case Rudi is here, but he's not, and as he looks around Victor realizes there's hardly a man in the bar he hasn't fucked, let alone a man's brother, and a good few of their uncles for crying out loud! not one of them ever holding a grudge against Victor, since fucking is as necessary as breathing here, maybe even more so, fucking is the bread and water of existence, and this bar is one of the hotter hot spots, tongues flicking into ears, hands wandering beneath waistbands, fingers circling nipples, the air itself smelling like sex, and before Victor knows it half a dozen vodkas with grapefruit have crossed the bar towards him, in grimy glasses, from different sources, like nighttime artillery, and he accepts them all with a bow, *More ice, gentlemen, please!* and he doles out the last of the free quaaludes, but still keeps a little powder for himself, a man has to be a little greedy, and he begins to dance, followed by a brood of admirers, all the anthems of summer moving through them, Victor resurrected again, like a migratory bird on the last leg of its journey, fighting on through whatever head wind the night might give him, wondering where in the world Rudi might have gotten to, if he really went home, when the two of them will get together again, and there is one final place, Victor knows it well, not too far from here, which may well be the night's resting point, the trucks! the infamous trucks! those dark rooms on sixteen-wheel axes! ah yes! the trucks!

a place that Rudi also likes, dark, anonymous, dangerous, a ditch of desire

and Victor debates it, whether to go down there or not, to the nightly row of vehicles in the meatpacking district, yes indeed, a lot of meat being packed, the last stage of the evening, and Victor—looking out over the dance floor—notices the drift has already begun, and he ponders that he does not want to become one of the hot-flush queens of New York, lamenting that he's now fucking boys half his age, no, not that, not ever that—*I have signed the charter of life! I will continue! I will roll on! Indeed I'll roll over!*—and with a wave of his hand and a few deft whispers, *Bring only five thousand of my most intimate friends!* he gathers up a flock, boys so far strung out that this may be the very end of their elastic, their eyes in the depths of their sockets, but a mania still there, traipsing behind the great Victor, a flotilla of yellow taxicabs waiting in the street, one of the few places in Manhattan at this hour where a cabby is guaranteed a fare, and Victor clicks his fingers while also kissing the bouncers good-night, and he and his cohorts hop into the taxis, some of them leaning from the windows, like cowboys on a urban drive, down the West Side, *Out with the lassos, girls!* telling the drivers they've just come in from Texas, that they're looking for a place to lay their sad-dles, *Cowboys make better lovers, my friend, just ask any bull!* the smells from the Hudson wafting in the open windows, the cobblestones shining from a recent rain, fires burning in oil drums where bums share cigarettes, the night air still chill with possibility, the taxis nego-tiating corners, until the trucks appear like mirages, silver and huge and shiny, a mill of activity, men in various states of elation and anni-hilation, some laughing, some sobbing, a couple attempting a waltz on the sidewalk, everyone so close to being broke that they are finally generous with the very last of their drugs, pills and poppers and powders they've been hoarding away for the dregs of the eve-ning, names being called from truck to truck, small cups of Crisco and jars of Vaseline being passed along, a man roaring about a pick-pocket, a drag queen screaming at a lover, young boys jumping down from the back tailgates, older queens being shunted upwards, all of it like a magical war zone, a human hide-and-seek, but Victor stands outside the commotion for a moment, holds the end hairs of his mustache between his teeth, scans the crowd, all sorts of familiar faces, and—just before Victor climbs into the rear of a truck, *Who knows, the world might very well end before sunrise!*—he looks up the cobblestoned street and sees a lone man walking towards the trucks, disturbing the globes of lamplight, moving with certainty and grace, the volume of the walk turned up so that Victor's attention is arrested, and instantly he knows, because he recognizes the leather hat, the bend of the brim, the lean of the body, and Victor feels a rush of emotion like wind over grass, causing the hairs on his arms to tingle, and Rudi shouts, *You Venezuelan turd! You left me there!* and he is laughing, his whole face worked into happiness, showing his fine white teeth, and a tremor runs through Victor's spine as he watches Rudi approach, thinking here comes loneliness applauding itself all the way down the street.

# | 2 |

LENINGRAD · 1975–76

In the winter of 1975 I walked around Leningrad, fretting over poems that were only half-translated. After divorcing Iosif I had moved to a communal apartment just off Kazanskaya. It was a bare, unadorned room with a linoleum floor, close enough to the Fontanka River to connect me to my old life. I rose early each morning to walk and work. The poets were socialist leftovers who still managed to rally and cry—in the beauty and space of the Spanish language—against the horrors of Franco. They had written to preserve what would have been forgotten, to give it a longer lease on life, and their words consumed me.

It used to be that I had gone to the countryside to think, to wade in rivers, but somehow Leningrad was a balm to me now. Barges moved slowly on the dark waters of the canals. Birds swooped above the boats. I still felt warmed by my father's notebook from years before, which I kept inside my coat pocket and read while I sat on park benches. My display of seeming leisure was questionable to some—another pedestrian would look too long in my direction, or a car would slow and the driver gaze suspiciously. Leningrad was not a city in which to be seen idle.

I began to carry a shawl and held an imaginary bundle in the crook of my arm, reached in to touch the emptiness, pretending there was a child there.

I spent my fiftieth birthday working on a single verse, a highly antifascist tract about a thunderstorm where small countries of light and dark rushed headlong over fields and gullies. It had obvious political resonance, but I began to think the poem related directly to me, having imagined a child of sorts for myself. My interpretation wasn't so much a wish fulfillment as a blatant mockery of how I had lived my early years with Iosif. Even after the two miscarriages it had been possible, when young, to be ambitious, for the Party, for the People, for science, for literature. But those ambitions had long been shut off, and the light that penetrated me now was the notion that I might become the sculptor of something human.

A child! I had to laugh at myself. Not only was I half a century in the world, but I had not met anyone since the divorce. I paced my room from wall to wall, mirror to mirror. I bought a box of clementines in the market as a birthday treat, but even peeling back the soft skin of the orange seemed to relate, however absurdly, to my desire. My father had once told me the story of how, when he was in the work camp, a truckload of giant logs was brought in to be chopped. He was on ax duty with a gang of twelve. It was a dreadfully hot summer and each swing of the blade was torture. He hacked at a log and there was the unmistakable sound of metal hitting metal. He bent down and found a mushroom-shaped chunk of lead embedded in the trunk. A bullet. He counted the rings from the perimeter to the bullet and found that they matched his age exactly.

We never escape ourselves, he said to me years later.

One spring morning I took a tram to the outskirts of Leningrad, where an acquaintance of mine, Galina, worked in a state orphanage.

When I sat in her dark office she raised an eyebrow, frowned. I told her that I was beginning to look for other work in addition to my translations. She hardly seemed convinced. The desire to be around orphan children was considered strange. Mostly they were idiots or chronically disabled. To work with them was a social embarrassment. On the wall above Galina's desk there was a print of an old saying she said came from Finland: *The crack of a falling branch is its own apology to the tree for having broken.* I had convinced myself that going there, even for an afternoon, was simply to get away from the poems. But I had also heard of certain women—women my age—who had opened foster homes, adjuncts to the *dyetskii dom,* the baby houses. The women were allowed to operate on a small scale, sometimes as many as six children, and they got a desultory pension from the state.

Are you no longer in the university? asked Galina.

I'm divorced now.

I see, she said.

In the background I could hear wailing voices. When we left the office a group of boys crowded around us, hair shaved, tunics gray, red sores around their mouths.

Galina showed me the grounds. The building was an old armory, brightly repainted, with a chimney stack that pierced the air. Prefabricated classrooms were propped on cinder blocks. Inside, the children sang paeans to a good life. A single set of swings stood in the garden where each child was allowed half an hour during the day. In their spare time the maintenance men were attempting to build a slide and the unfinished structure stood like a skeleton beside the swings. Still, three children had found a way to climb it anyway.

Hello! one of them shouted. He looked about four years old. He ran over and made a gesture to rub his soft fuzzy head, where his hair had begun to grow. The skull seemed too large for his tiny body. His eyes were huge and strange, lopsided, his face terribly thin. I asked his name.

Kolya, he said.

Go back to the swing, Nikolai, Galina said.

We continued through the grounds. Over my shoulder I saw Kolya climb the makeshift slide once again. The sunlight caught the dark stubble on his head.

Where's he from? I asked.

Galina touched my shoulder. Perhaps you shouldn't draw so much attention to yourself, she said.

I'm just curious.

You really must be careful.

Galina had been assigned the work in the orphanage after failing at university. The seasons had passed through her face and it struck me that they had now conjured themselves into one which had become bland and nondescript, not unlike myself.

But at a copse of trees Galina stopped, coughed then half-smiled.

It turned out that Kolya's parents were intellectuals from the far eastern stretches of Russia. They had been posted to a university in Leningrad where they'd been killed when their car smashed into a tram on Nevsky. There had never been any contact made with other relatives and Kolya, three months old at the time, had spent his first few years not saying a single word.

He's a clever child but ruthlessly lonely, said Galina. And he has certain behaviors.

What kind of behaviors?

He hoards his food and then waits until it's stale or moldy to digest it. And toilet things as well. He's not yet trained himself for the toilet.

We rounded a corner where a group of boys and girls were chopping wood, their breath steaming in the cold. Their axes glinted momentarily in the light as they raised them above their shoulders.

But he shows some promise as a chess player, she said.

Temporarily stunned by a vision of my father pulling a bullet from a core of wood, I said: Who?

Kolya! she said. He's already carved his own chess set from the slats of his bed. We discovered it one evening when he crashed to the floor. The pieces were tucked in his pillowcase.

I stopped on the path. An oil tanker had pulled up to the main building and Galina checked her watch. She sighed and said: I must go.

In the background I could hear the children laughing.

I suppose I can help arrange a job for you here if you desire, she said.

She shook her head and began to leave, jangling her keys.

Thank you, I replied.

She didn't turn. I knew what I wanted, perhaps what I had always wanted since a young age. Before I left I stood watching Kolya swinging from a monkey bar. A shrill whistle blew, calling the children in, while a guard swept a dozen more kids out into the grounds.

I returned to my room, to my dictionaries, my clementines.

At the Ministry of Education the following week I was told that all adoptions had been curtailed, and I concurred with the official that custody by the People was a far better thing, but then I plied her gently on the question of wardship. She gave me a fierce look and said: Wait here please. She came back carting a file and was rifling through it when suddenly she asked: Do you like dance?

There was only one possible reason that she could have asked the question. Rudi had been gone for over a decade. Talk about him had softened somewhat in recent years and there had been other high-profile defections that had taken the spotlight away from him. There had even been a review in *Izvestiya* of a tour in Germany that quoted Western newspapers saying how Rudi's touch had all but faded from the firmament. When Alexsandr Pushkin died in the early seventies the papers had mentioned Rudi briefly, but they had written that it was exclusively the teacher's genius, not Rudi's, which had made him an interesting dancer.

I tightened my fingers and waited for the official to clarify herself. She was looking closely at the particulars of my file. I felt that in my feverish haste I had dug myself a pit. Nothing had ever been stamped in my identity papers about the problem of having known Rudi, but obviously the files went deeper. I tried to mumble an apology, but the woman adjusted her glasses, peered over the half lenses.

She said sternly that she had seen a certain dance in the Kirov in the late fifties. The performer had danced beautifully, she said, but in later years he had disappointed her terribly. She was talking in half words, but it felt as if we had taken an irreversible journey together. She scanned my file further. I allowed myself a breath. She did not mention Rudi's name, but he lay in the space between us.

The truth was that I didn't really want Rudi in my life anymore, or at least not the sort of Rudi I had known years before. I wanted a Nikolai, a Kolya, someone I could help up from the slats of my own existence.

I may be able to help, Comrade, the official said.

I wondered what exactly I had allowed myself into. She said there was a provision under Article 123 of the Family Code for wardship, and there was a further provision under another law for Party members to have access to children of talent. I had been a member of the Party, but since leaving Iosif I had hidden low, afraid he might hunt me down. The thought even occurred that the woman at the Ministry was somehow connected to him, that she would betray me. And yet there was something about her that seemed honest, a display of simplicity that blended a sharp intelligence.

Does this boy show any particular talents? she asked.

He's a chess player.

At the age of four?

She made a note on a piece of paper and said: Come back next week.

I had often believed, to that point in my life, that friendships among women were fickle things, dependent on circumstances other than the heart, but Olga Vecheslova, as I got to know her, was extraordinary. She was younger than I and insecure behind her gold-rimmed spectacles. Dark brown hair. Dark eyes, almost black. She herself had been a dancer although there was no whisper of it in her body anymore—her hips were wide and her carriage bent, unlike my mother, who, even when sick, had walked as if balancing china on her head. Olga was unnerved but pleased by the notion of me having known Rudi. She disliked him of course, for betraying our nation. She also disliked him for his betrayal of the very thing we ultimately wanted for our own lives, the realization of desire. And in that hatred there was a need. It was a disease of sorts; we couldn't shake Rudi from our minds. Olga and I began to meet once a week, to walk along the canals together, aware that our actions could draw the wrong attention, but we forged on regardless.

Olga arranged that I be allowed to visit Kolya at the orphanage. Nearing the end of summer he seemed undernourished, his legs thin and spindly in his shorts. Terrible sores had erupted on his face. He had been punished for incontinence and there were welts on his back. At Galina's office I learned that he was actually six years old, not four, that his growth was stunted. I began to doubt myself, started biting my nails for the first time since I was sixteen. *I cannot handle a child like this*, I thought.

Even the bureaucracy of having a child would be a strategic nightmare, waiting in lines for schools, name changes, apartment applications, vaccinations, identity cards.

Still, I bought paint, a brush, a secondhand set of lace curtains for the one window, decorated the corner of the room blue, copied out pictures of chess pieces from a book, sketched them around the sill. On the shelves I placed knickknacks. The shelves themselves were made from orange crates. The main problem was that I had no bed for Kolya. There was a four-month waiting list in the government department stores for a new one and though I was translating more and more, money was still an anguish. Finally Olga managed to find a mattress which, when cleaned and patched, was quite presentable.

I looked around the room. It was still functional and drab. There were always plenty of birdcages to be found in Leningrad and so I hung one from the ceiling and inside I placed a porcelain canary, tasteless but delightful. At the market I managed to find a beautiful hand-crafted music box, which, when wound, played an Arcangelo Corelli concerto. It was an odd item which cost the price of many poems but, like the china plate my father had given to me, it seemed to resonate into both past and future.

When Olga was finally able to institute wardship, in late September of that year, nothing in my life, absolutely nothing, was better than that moment.

Kolya stood in my room and wailed so much that his nose bled. He scratched himself and an array of fresh cuts appeared on his arms and legs. I prepared a poultice, wrapped the wounds, and later that evening gave him a chocolate bar. He didn't know what it was, just stared at it, began unwrapping. He nibbled then looked up, bit a whole chunk, and tucked half of it under his pillow. I stayed up all night, nursing him through a series of nightmares, and even put some of the foul poultice on my own fingers to stop myself from biting my nails.

When he woke in the morning Kolya kicked out in fright but, finally exhausted, he asked for the other half of the chocolate bar. It was one of those simple gestures that, for no obvious reason, shores up the heart.

After a month I wrote to Rudi, telling him how life had quickened and veered. I never sent the letter. There was no need. I was a mother now. I gladly accepted the gray at the roots of my hair. I went down to the Fontanka with Kolya. He rode a bicycle we had found in the rubbish dump and he stayed close by my side, wobbling on the bike. We were on our way to the Ministry to file a report on his progress.

Watched *All in the Family* then cabbed to Judy and Sam Peabody's to see Nureyev (cab $2.50). Nureyev arrived and he looked terrible— really old-looking. I guess the nightlife finally got to him. His masseur was with him. The masseur is also sort of a bodyguard. And I didn't know this before I went over there, but Nureyev has told the Peabodys that if Monique Von Vooren showed up, he would walk out. He says she used him. But he's terrible. When he was so cheap and wouldn't stay in a hotel, Monique gave him her bed, and now he says *she* uses *him*. He's mean, he's really mean. At 1:30 the Eberstadts wanted to leave and I dropped them off (cab $3.50).

—*the Andy Warhol diaries,*
SUNDAY, MARCH 11, 1979

# | 3 |

PARIS, LONDON, CARACAS · 1980s

Monsieur was still sleeping and the city was quiet in the way I had
loved since I was young. I stood by the window and took in the smell
of the Seine, which was occasionally foul but on that morning quite
fresh. The pastries were baking in the kitchen and the two scents
merged together in the air.

At nine in the morning the bells from Saint Thomas d'Aquin
were carried on the wind along the quays. The kettle boiled for the
fourth time as I waited for Monsieur to wake. He generally did not
sleep in beyond nine, no matter how late he arrived home. I always
knew whether he had a companion with him since there would be
jackets and other clothes strewn on the chairs. On that morning,
however, there were no guests.

I took the kettle from the stove top and heard Monsieur rumbling
as Chopin came to life on the record player in his bedroom.

When I first began my duties, years earlier, it was Monsieur's custom to come out from his room wearing only his undershorts, but I
had bought him a white bathrobe for one of his birthdays, which, in
appreciation, he had begun to wear every morning. (He had dozens of

silk pajamas and many fine Tibetan robes, none of which he ever used, but he gave them to house guests who had not expected to stay over.)

I rinsed the teapot with a little hot water, spooned the tea, and put the kettle back on the stove over a low heat. Monsieur appeared and greeted me in his customary manner, grinning broadly. The simple things in life still pleased him, and there was seldom a morning when he didn't go to the window and take a deep breath.

I always thought that, for a young man of infinite means—he was forty-two years old at the time—there should be nothing but happiness, but he had days when the sky was indeed upon him and I would leave him alone to brood.

That morning, he yawned and stretched. I put the tea and pastries on the table, and Monsieur announced that he would be leaving the apartment later than usual. He said he had a visitor, a shoemaker from London, who he wanted to keep a secret as there were other dancers in Paris who might steal his time.

It was unusual to have morning visitors and I worried that perhaps there were not enough pastries or fruit, but Monsieur said he had met the shoemaker many times before, he was a plain man who would desire nothing more than tea and toast.

I knew about Englishmen since my aunt had for twelve years after the War kept house in Montmartre for a celebrated theater actor. The English had always struck me as polite, but I had grown to prefer the Russian way, demand and apology, which Monsieur displayed quite openly. He would, for example, raise his voice significantly over a meat dish that was overcooked and then afterwards express sorrow for his ill humor. I had even grown to enjoy Monsieur's tantrums, plentiful as they were.

Monsieur had laid a number of his old dancing shoes out on the floor when the shoemaker arrived. I answered the door to a small bald man who carried his overcoat draped over his arm, a suitcase in his other hand. He was about a decade older than me, in his late fifties at least.

—Tom Ashworth, he said.

He bowed and said he was here on instructions. I reached for his overcoat but he did not seem to want to part with it. He smiled apologetically and hung the coat on the stand himself. Monsieur paced across the floor and embraced the shoemaker who stepped back in embarrassment. His suitcase hit the coat stand and it rocked on its legs. I managed to suppress a laugh.

The visitor had a ruddy face, his eyebrows were full and bushy, and he wore crooked spectacles.

I retreated to the kitchen, leaving the door slightly ajar so I could see into the living room, where Monsieur and the shoemaker had taken their seats. The visitor fumbled with the lock on his suitcase and then opened it to an array of shoes. His demeanor loosened as he took the shoes out one by one.

I had guessed that, as an Englishman, he would take his tea with milk and perhaps sugar. I carried a tray out into the living room. I had forgone my own breakfast pastries in case he might want one, but he hardly looked up, so engaged was he by the shoes. They chatted in English, each leaning forward to hear the other. Monsieur had, it seemed, formed a deep attachment to certain older shoes and the tenor of the conversation was such that he wanted the old shoes to be repatched.

—They live on my feet, said Monsieur, they are alive.

Mister Ashworth said he would be delighted to repatch them to the best of his ability. I closed the kitchen door, began making an inventory of what I would need for the evening's dinner party: capon, spices, carrots, asparagus, butter, milk, eggs, hazelnuts for pudding. Monsieur had invited twelve guests and I would have to check the stock of champagnes and liqueurs. I generally cooked with a country flavor that had been passed down through my family. It had been for this reason that Monsieur had hired me, preferring, as he did, strong hearty meals. (Four generations on my mother's side had cooked in a country inn in Voutenay, outside Paris, but the inn was a victim of the victory in 1944, burned by the Germans in retreat.)

It was always my pleasure to travel to the markets around Paris in search of the finest ingredients. In general the freshest vegetables were found on rue de Bac. There was a butcher on rue de Buei whom I always visited for the best meats—he spoke a guttural Parisian that reminded me at times of Monsieur. For spices and condiments I had made the acquaintance of a Bangladeshi man in the Tenth Arrondisement who ran a tiny store in an alleyway off passage Brady.

I normally went on foot but that particular morning—since Monsieur was with the shoemaker—I asked whether I could use the car, which he had crashed and dented often. (He was a terrible driver and one of his crude New York friends, Victor Pareci, often made unpleasant comments about Monsieur's penchant for rear-ending.)

I accomplished my chores without difficulty.

Arriving back at the apartment with the provisions, I was surprised to see the shoemaker sitting alone. He had spread newspaper on the carpet so as not to soil it with glue. I greeted him in my faltering English. He explained that Monsieur had already left for rehearsal.

The shoemaker had arrived on an early flight from London, and, thinking he might be hungry, I offered an early lunch. He politely declined.

From the kitchen, preparing the evening's meal, I watched as he went about his work. He fitted the shoes on his hand like a glove and used a sharp knife to cut them. It seemed as if he were gutting a wildfowl. His stitching was confident and fast. At one stage, while waiting for glue to dry, he peered over his spectacles around the room. Monsieur was a connoisseur of fine art with a penchant for nineteenth-century male nudes. They appeared to disturb the shoemaker. He stood and examined the marble torso in the middle of the room. He tapped it with his fingers and was startled when he looked up and caught my gaze.

—Monsieur has a wonderful eye for art, I said.

The shoemaker stammered and retreated to his work. Thereafter he did not look up, but by mid-afternoon he was having some difficulty with one of the shoes. He grit his teeth and shook his head. I brought him some tea and asked if he were troubled. He looked at a watch which he kept in the pocket of his waistcoat.

—I've a lot to do, he said.

He had an odd smile which, as it spread across his face, seemed to relax him completely. He sat back and sipped his tea, consulted his pocket watch once more, then sighed and said he feared he would not get his work done before his flight.

—I don't suppose you know of an agreeable hotel? he asked.

—Monsieur will insist that you stay here.

—Oh I couldn't do that.

—There are two spare bedrooms.

He seemed quite undone by the notion of staying. He rubbed the back of his neck and repeated that he would prefer to stay in a small hotel, that he didn't want to intrude on Monsieur's privacy. He closed his suitcase and left for Montmartre where I had told him of a small pension.

Monsieur arrived home from rehearsal at five o'clock in the afternoon. I drew his bath for him. He adored it piping hot.

While changing out of his dance clothes, Monsieur asked about the shoemaker. He was unperturbed when I explained the situation and just went about his business.

While he bathed I cooked him a steak, almost raw, which he always ate a few hours before each night of dancing.

Halfway through his steak, he lifted his knife and pointed it at me.

—Phone Mister Ashworth's hotel and tell him that I will leave a ticket for the performance tonight and later he should join us for dinner.

It flashed across my mind that there would be thirteen people at the table. Monsieur had grown increasingly superstitious since I had known him, something he had acquired from Madame Fonteyn. I opted against saying anything since I knew it was quite likely that, as the evening went on, Monsieur would invite others to join him also. (I had providently bought enough capon to feed seventeen people.)

I made the call. The hotel clerk grumpily informed me that there were no phones in the rooms and that he could only take a message, since he was the sole person on duty. I beseeched him to go to the room, even invoking the name of Monsieur, but the clerk was unimpressed. There was nothing to do but go to the hotel myself.

I hurried through the last of the dinner's preparations, made a flask of hot tea with honey for Monsieur, took a taxi to Montmartre. It was summer and the day was still bright. A tiny park sat opposite the hotel and I glimpsed the shoemaker working in solitary comfort on the grass. I was a little taken aback, since he wore a hat and seemed very much younger than before. I crossed the street. He flushed crimson when he saw me approach and began gathering the shoes into a pile, stuffing the pair of scissors into his jacket pocket.

—Mister Ashworth.

—Tom, he replied.

—Monsieur has asked me to give you a message.

He flushed a further shade of red when I told him of the invitation.

—Oh, he said.

He removed the scissors from his pocket, took off his jacket, spread it on the grass, motioning for me to sit down. The fashion of the day was still towards short skirts but I was thankful that I wore a longer housedress, since nothing could be more embarrassing than sitting on the grass, on a man's jacket, wearing a short skirt, and trying to maintain good posture.

He stammered that he was honored I had come all this way to bring the invitation, that he would be delighted, if his attire was suitable, to attend the dinner, but for personal reasons he never went to the ballet.

—It has to do with a rule of my father's, he said.

I waited but he said nothing more. He stood up from the grass and extended his hand to help me up.

I returned to the quai Voltaire to prepare for the evening.

Capon is an exceedingly delicious bird when cooked correctly. I had learned the art as a young girl. To season it properly one needs nothing more than rosemary, thyme, and the juice of a lemon. One simply lifts the skin away from the breast, applies the seasoning, and allows the bird to do its work in the oven. To complement the dish I made scalloped potatoes and prepared asparagus to be lightly steamed.

The dinner was not due to begin until near midnight, but Tom arrived early. A crooked crease had been ironed in his trousers and his tie was knotted tightly on his neck.

—I am so sorry, but I didn't catch your name, he said.

—Odile, I replied.

He held out a bunch of daffodils for me and said: Well, Odile. It is already beyond my bedtime so you must forgive me if I appear a bit giddy.

If I am to speak honestly, I must say that at the time I simply thought him a nice man, free of pretension, not attractive in any traditional sense, but certainly interesting. I took the flowers, thanked him, and asked him to make himself comfortable until the other guests arrived.

While standing in the kitchen I kept the door ajar and watched him perch awkwardly on the couch. He said he was unaccustomed to wine and he held the glass as if it might damage him.

The usual two waiters, Pierre and Alain, arrived at eleven-thirty. They were aspiring actors. They took one look at Tom and, in their rudeness, discounted him immediately. They performed the last of the preparations, polished the candelabra, set the silverware, rinsed the wine goblets, while I put the finishing touches to the appetizers and dessert.

When the guests began to arrive I was disturbed to see that Monsieur was not among them. It was not unusual—often Monsieur arrived late to his own dinner parties—but my feelings were for Tom, who was distinctly ill at ease in the presence of the guests. The party was composed of a number of dancers, an Argentinean dance critic, a film star of some sort, a business manager, and a couple of society ladies, including Mrs. Godstalk, a New York woman who made sure she was quite a regular at Monsieur's parties. She was in her mid-fifties but she dressed in the provocative manner of a young woman, her bosom always spilling out from her gowns. She was, as far as I knew, married, but I had never heard her mention her husband.

She remarked on a painting she had bought for Monsieur, saying something about its formal balances. She mentioned the price and Tom shifted uncomfortably in his seat. The Argentinean critic agreed that the painting in question had perfect tonal components.

I watched poor Tom become the chair.

At midnight I decided to go ahead with dinner, even without Monsieur. The guests took their seats grudgingly. However, Tom, without my noticing, had grown terribly drunk. I had thought originally that he was nursing the one glass of wine all evening, but it seemed that the waiters in their petty spitefulness had been topping up his glass. Unused to the wine, Tom remained on the couch and proceeded to loudly regale the table with tales of a London soccer team nobody else was interested in. Mrs. Godstalk snorted while the men attempted to drown him out. Only the dancers seemed vaguely interested.

I suggested to Tom that he take a seat at the table and I guided him across. The only available chair was next to Mrs. Godstalk. I tried to take his glass of wine but he held on to it and spilled a little on the leg of his trousers. He tucked a napkin into his shirt collar with great difficulty and one of the ballerinas giggled.

I returned to the kitchen to serve the first courses.

As the dinner went on Tom's English accent grew stronger and louder as he waved his fork in the air, a piece of capon attached.

I watched from a crack in the kitchen door and finally decided that I'd need to take action. Tom had reached a point in his anecdote where his team was about to take a penalty kick. I waited for the appropriate moment to come out from the kitchen saying: Mister Ashworth! Mister Ashworth!

I quickly rattled off that the dishwasher had broken and, since Tom was a handyman, I would need his help, could the guests please excuse him from the table?

—At your service, said Tom, knocking his knee against the edge of the table, almost dragging the cloth with him.

He stumbled and I took his arm, sat him at the kitchen table, close to the wall in case he fell over.

—Odile, he said, slightly slurring my name.

Just then I heard the sound of Monsieur at the front door. Within moments there was some kind of altercation at the dinner table. Voices were being raised, Monsieur's loudest of all. Someone shouted back at him. I knew trouble was imminent—it was always so when Monsieur was confronted. I told Tom to stay where he was and I left the kitchen. All the guests were standing, fingers were being pointed, nails being chewed, cuffs being buttoned, and Monsieur, in the middle of the fray, was dispatching them one by one.

—Late? he was shouting. Me, late? Out! Out!

Some were dawdling, trying to ingratiate themselves with Monsieur, but he was having none of it. Mrs. Godstalk whispered in his ear but he brushed her away. Horrified, she kept saying his name over and over again. She tried to touch his forearm but he shouted: Out! The Argentinean critic was muttering at the door and he even managed to get in a complaint about the capon, but I was too caught up with thoughts of poor Tom to be annoyed. I wanted to get back to the kitchen before he too suffered Monsieur's wrath. I simply couldn't imagine what might happen if Monsieur found Tom sitting there, drunk—the furies of Hades would surely be let loose.

I hurried to get the guests' hands through the armholes of their coats, straightened their collars, all the time straining to hear sounds from the kitchen.

I finally shooed Mrs. Godstalk, the last of the guests, away.

Imagine my surprise when I found Tom and Monsieur in the kitchen, both liberally sipping from large glasses of red wine. Tom was telling Monsieur about a special pair of shoes he had made for himself for his soccer games. Tom was explaining that he had put platforms in his shoes to see over the heads of fellow supporters. But he had built the shoes so the platforms were unnoticeable and his landlady had never figured out why he was taller on days when there were soccer matches.

—My friend Victor could do with a pair of those, said Monsieur.

They spent the next hour in laughter. Monsieur took out some photographs that he kept in his wallet, one of his mother and one of his young niece, Nuriya, who had been born a few years previously to his sister in Russia. Tom held back a belch and said they were wonderful photographs, that he'd always liked Russian women.

He looked at me: Odile, even though you're not Russian, you're beautiful too.

His body finally gave in to the alcohol and he fell asleep at the kitchen table, his head resting against a slab of cheese.

Monsieur helped me move him into the spare bedroom. He even took off Tom's shoes and socks and wished him a good night's sleep. I rolled Tom over to his side and put a bucket beside him in case he should vomit.

For some reason I was inspired to kiss him, very gently, on his forehead. And then I went to bed.

The next morning broke with raindrops. I crawled from under the covers and went down the corridor. I was surprised to see the door of the guest room slightly open. I peeked inside. Tom was hunched over, trying to tie his shoelaces. His face was flush and his hair was askew.

—Good morning, Tom, I said.

He looked up, startled. His suit jacket hung precariously on the chair and his shirt was creased.

—I'd be delighted to press your clothes for you, I said.

—Thank you, but I really must be leaving.

—It would be no trouble.

—Many thanks, but no.

There was a catch in his throat. I left him alone since he seemed embarrassed. In the kitchen I prepared tea and coffee and set the table. I was cleaning up the remnants of the night before when out of the corner of my eye I saw Tom trying to leave the apartment on tiptoe.

—Mister Ashworth! I called out but he didn't reply.

—Tom! I said and he turned around.

Never before have I seen such fear on a grown man's face. His eyes were hooded and red, his lids were swollen, and he looked as if he was carrying the weight of an awful injury. He didn't say a word, just fingered the buttons of his jacket. When he was sideways to the door I could see that his eyes were glassy with tears. I ran up to him but he was already stepping slowly down the curving staircase.

I went after him. At the front door he hung his head, looked at his feet.

—I shamed myself, he said. Shoemakers in my family for many hundreds of years and I shamed them.

—There's nothing to be ashamed of.

—I made a fool of myself.

—No no no. Monsieur had a wonderful time.

—I'm a clown.

—Of course not.

—I have made my last shoe.

—Pardon me? I asked.

—Please give Mister Nureyev my apologies.

With this Tom bowed slightly and was gone, out the front door, along the quays. I watched as he moved through the rain. He pulled his suit jacket up over his head and rounded the corner.

Monsieur woke half an hour later and asked after Mister Ashworth. I told him what had happened. Monsieur stared into his tea and munched on a croissant. I stood at the sink and washed the last of the glasses. I couldn't help but feel empty. Monsieur must have intuited something because he asked me to face him, he wanted to see my eyes. I couldn't do it. I heard him rise from the table and then he came and touched my elbow. I stopped myself from crying or falling into his arms, but he took hold of my chin and tilted my face upwards. Monsieur had the kindest eyes.

—Wait, he said.

He went to his bedroom and came out, stuffing something into the pocket of his bathrobe, dangling his keys in the other hand.

Monsieur said: Let's go.

—But you're still in your bathrobe, Monsieur.

—It'll be a new fashion! he said.

Before I knew it we were driving the wrong way down a one-way street, with Monsieur shouting some crazy Russian love song at the top of his lungs.

Ten minutes later we pulled up outside Tom's hotel. Cars behind us hooted loudly. Monsieur jumped out and gave the drivers a rude gesture, then ran into the hotel but came out shaking his head.

—We'll try the airport, said Monsieur.

He put the car in gear and just then Tom appeared. He saw us, stopped, hesitated, then buried his hands in his jacket pockets and proceeded to the hotel entrance.

Monsieur shoved something down in the pocket of his bathrobe, jumped from the car and, at the bottom of the hotel steps, caught Tom's arm. A porter came out of the hotel to hold an umbrella above Monsieur's head.

Tom's eyes darted away from Monsieur. He cleared his throat as if about to say something, but Monsieur shook his head emphatically before Tom could say a word. From the bathrobe pocket Monsieur produced a pair of old dancing slippers. He flourished them in the air.

—Fix these, he said to Tom.

Tom's eyes locked with Monsieur's.

—Fix them, said Monsieur.

—Pardon me? said Tom.

—I want you to fix them. Since when do you not understand English?

Tom stood fidgeting, his face raw and red.

—Yes sir, he finally stammered, taking the shoes from Monsieur's hands. He held them a moment, and then said: You must forgive my foolishness of last night.

Monsieur hesitated: If you ever resign again I will kick you in the ass! Do you understand me?

—Sir?

—Nobody resigns on me! I fire them!

Tom bowed again, not a full bow, more a deep nod of the head. When he was upright he peered at me, his spectacles halfway down his nose.

❖

She had practiced her smile all through the years, her stage smile, the perfect smile, the smile that said, *I am in control, I am regal, I am ballet.* And she was smiling it now, Margot, across the table at Rudi. Indeed, everywhere the wedding guests were smiling. Still, Margot could sense there was something wrong with the day, mismatched, out of sync, she just couldn't put her finger on it.

Rudi, directly facing her, had his head thrown back in laughter, creased lines on his face, wrinkles around his eyes. Beside him was his friend, Victor, with his dumb mustache and a multicolored cummerbund. Margot wished she could seize Rudi's arm and shake him, say something to him, but what would she say? There was a thought at the back of her mind that she desperately wanted to communicate, yet she was only aware of its existence, not its content. So many days felt like this now. She had retired. Tito had passed on. She brought flowers to his gravestone in Panama City like a character from some nineteenth-century novel. She often stood at the edge of the field near the graveyard and found herself watching the wind move the grass. Or she found herself caught at a traffic light in London wondering just what sorts of lives were being carried in the cars that passed her. Or she would read a book and suddenly forget what it was all about. As a child, nobody had told her how the life of a dancer would be, and even had she known she never would have understood, how it could be so full and empty at the same time, seen in one manner from the outside but experienced differently on the inside, so that two completely dissimilar ways of living had to be held in unison, juggled, acknowledged.

Rudi had once told her they were hand in glove. She had wondered who was what, was she hand or glove, and now was she neither? Rudi was forty-three, maybe forty-four now, she couldn't remember. Yet he was still performing. And why not? She had gone on until she was sixty.

She watched the bride and groom begin their first dance. Tom with his old stiff body. Odile in her white shoes made especially for the occasion by her new husband. White satin rimmed with lace, no heels. Her thin legs. Her small hands. Tom lifted the train of Odile's veil and draped it over his forearm. Surely that must be the key, Margot thought, to live your life freely and honestly and *with love*. Her love had been dance. Rudi's also. It wasn't that they had been denied access to the other kind of love, no, that wasn't it at all, not at all— but theirs was a love of a different thing, bruising and public. Love had never quite happened to her in the way it happened to others. Tito, yes. But Tito was an impossible person until he became an impossible body. Tito saw her as an elegant armpiece. Tito had warmed other beds. And then Tito had been shot and became everything he had never been before, useless and good-hearted. Oh, she had loved him, yes, but not love in the sense that it hollowed her out whenever she saw him. Margot often wondered if she were naïve, but she had caught glimpses of real love and was catching one now, she was sure of it, Tom and Odile, the awkward way they handled each other's bodies, their shy courtesy, the sheer beauty of their homeliness.

Rudi had a champagne glass at his mouth. She had heard that he'd paid for the wedding ceremony, yet had not told anyone. His hidden generosity. Still, he seemed distant as the couple dragged themselves across the floor. People spoke of it as loneliness but Margot knew it was not loneliness. Loneliness, she thought, caused a certain madness. It was more a search for that thing beyond dance, a desire for the human. But what could be better, what could top the never-ending ovations, was there anything in life that had ever crested them? And then she knew. The thought had never struck her quite so clearly. She had danced until her body gave out and now she was loveless. The doctor had told her she had cancer. She would probably last quite a few years but it was cancer, yes, cancer, that was the full stop toward which her life was heading. She had not told anyone. She would not even tell Rudi for a while. But, still, there was something else she had to tell him, and she was searching her mind for the words. Dance. Cures. Pills. Sleeping pills and diet pills and pain pills and pills for life itself, pills for every illness, jealousy to bronchitis, pills in the drafty hallways where young girls sweated and wept for the roles they never got, pills for ruptured bank accounts, pills for backstabbings, pills for betrayals, pills for the broken way in which you walked, pills for the pills themselves. Margot herself had never taken the pills, but she often swept little white imaginary tablets through her mind to cure the pain. And now ovarian cancer. No pills to cure that. She felt the room closing in. She watched dancers on either side of her, tucking into their food, as they always did. Later the girls would throw up in the bathrooms. And the shoe-makers were raucous at the other end of the room. Beer glasses swaying in the air. Toasts. Later Rudi would sing his Vladivostok love song, his party piece. She could feel the evening creeping to its end, the inevitable farewell to the newly married couple, the envy she might feel. It was nothing she would ever make public. If any-thing, she was diplomacy itself. She had always been. And she was happy for Tom, happy he had found something beyond his craft. But what had she found, what had she discovered? A dark tumor in her body. She was not bitter, it wasn't that, she was just shocked to have been dealt such a hand. Surely she deserved more. Or perhaps not. Her life had been fuller than any other she had known. Death would probably arrive in a yacht, or a drawing room, or on a sandy beach.

What was it that she needed to tell Rudi? What was it in his grin, in his laughter, in his leaning towards Victor, in his consumption of the world that she needed to arrest, if only for a moment? What an exquisite life. They had, she knew, enjoyed the greatest years dancers could have. People thought they had slept together but they had not. They were too close for that. Yet they had thought of it, contem-plated an attachment beyond dance. To make love to him. It would have destroyed them. Dancing was more intimate, anyway. It was a mitosis, they became one. They had seldom argued. If anything she had been a mother to him, increasingly so over the years. But what Margot wanted to say had nothing to do with mothers or countries or other manifold myths. It had nothing to do with love or its atten-dant despairs. Nothing to do with dance. Or did it? Did it? She could feel her fingers trembling. Soon the bridal dance would be over and she would be forced to talk pleasantries, to bring out the Margot in her, to hold her chin high, to clap politely, perhaps even stand as if the married couple were to take an encore. She watched Victor whisper something in Rudi's ear. And then, with a wave of relief, Margot knew what it was. She knew she had to interrupt, she had to say this before she let it go, that it was the most important thing she could tell Rudi, the greatest piece of advice he would receive. She hesitated, laid her fork politely at the side of her plate, and reached for a glass of water to quench her thirst. She tried to catch Rudi's eye, but he was in another world. She would have to say this. She would have to tell him to give it up. It was that simple. He should pack it in and concentrate on his other gifts, choreography, teaching. Before he grew too old. She needed so desperately to say this to him. Retire. Retire. Retire. Before it's too late. She picked up the fork again. How to get his attention? She reached across and gently touched his outstretched fingers with the silver prongs of the fork. He felt the tapping and looked at her and smiled. Victor also smiled, but then Victor again whispered something to Rudi, and Rudi held up his hand to Margot as if to say: *Wait.* She leaned back in her chair and waited and the song ended, and she rose from the table to share her applause for Tom and Odile, and in the middle of the clapping, Rudi reached across the table to take her hand and say: *Yes?* She hesitated and grinned and then said simply: *Aren't they beautiful, Tom and Odile? Aren't they a wonderful couple?*

❊

Well, yeah, he wasn't a diamond cutter or nothing but he knew what he wanted and took all he could get.

So he pretty much got his money's worth, yeah.

You charged him more because of who he was, seventy-five quid was a good kill in those days.

You'd have to keep your mouth shut, no *Daily Mirror, Sun,* no *News of the fucking World.*

Besides, he was always doing this exam, like, checking out your arms and taking a look at your fucking neck, even between your toes, he was scared of junkies I s'pose.

You had to be fresh-faced, you know, with sleeveless shirts and tight trousers. But he didn't mind the smell of cigarettes, some of the trade didn't like cigarettes, but he wasn't like that, at least you were allowed a smoke afterwards.

He'd pick you up on Kings Road or around Picadilly.

Sometimes you'd go to the clubs with him if his mood was right.

Once or twice he'd go to Heaven over there in Charing Cross. Or the Colherne. But most of the time he'd go to the normal places, you know. The Roxy, the Perennial, Tramps, Annabel's, the Palais.

On the floor everybody was rightly fucked up on coke and booze.

People were shagging in the leather booths.

He was fucking weird, he'd take you to his table and he'd sit you down with his mates, all fancy pants and groupies. But then he wouldn't take you home, didn't want to be seen walking with you out the club.

Couldn't fucking figure him out.

But he was Russian and I s'pose if you shag your cousins for a hundred thousand years that's what happens, ain't it?

Sometimes he got his manager to drive you back, or a friend of his, or he'd get you a taxi through the club owner, they'd do anything for him they would.

So you'd be waiting outside his place, right? By the gate, just waiting. And all the neighbors could see if they wanted. But he didn't care about that. Figure that one out, then.

I was only there four times, he never remembered me or even asked my name.

I think I told him Damian or something. You never give your real name. Besides, I had a girlfriend and she had no fucking idea. She liked the money but.

I heard him on the telly one night. He was tossing on about dancing, some shit like, I don't know, like ruining your body for the pleasure of strangers, some shit like that.

And what the fuck did he think I was up to? Christ. For the pleasure of strangers.

He had his pleasure yeah, and then he had it again, and then he just rolled over and went to sleep and you'd think, fuck me, I should case this fucking place, I should nick all his weird fucking paintings, with lords and hounds and bugles and shit, just fucking skive out of there.

But five minutes down the road you'd be nicked.

One time I crawled out of bed and the housekeeper was awake, she made breakfast, scones and fruit, she kept looking over her shoulder at me.

Eerie little froggie chick, checking me out, making sure I wasn't running off with the silver. She'd rather put her head in the oven than talk to me.

I sat there quiet as could be and then she called a taxi.

The next night I was out in the Roxy again and he passed me in the club without a glance.

I'd already spent fifty of the seventy-five quid on a new shirt. It turned everyone else's head, but not his.

He had someone else in his booth all serious and close.

And then he got up and walked past me. He didn't even say a word. Cocksucker.

He's still performing with all his power. His genius is that he can bring out the child in all of us, just by watching him. He's heroic, he's dancing against the clock. Here is a man who will dance as long as he can, to the end, to the last drop of blood.
—JACQUELINE KENNEDY ONASSIS, 1980

What? Is that boy still dragging his bone all over town?
—TRUMAN CAPOTE, 1982

More than anything else he's a homebody. People don't realize that about him, but he is. When he comes to our French château the first thing he always asks for is a glass of wine and a little silence so he can sit by the fire and contemplate. And at our brownstone on Sixty-third and Madison he sits and looks at the art for hours on end, literally hours! His real passion is the Medievals. Not a lot of people are aware of that.

—RENÉE GODSTALK, 1983

Las Mercedes, Caracas
May 1984

Rudi!—

It is the beginning of the rainy season and I am stuck indoors having ingested some wonderful painkillers and I am sending this letter to my five thousand most intimate friends, ha ha, so please forgive the handwriting. I am practicing yoga, sitting on the floor in lotus position, my ass has never known such discomfort. Imagine what it must be like to be from New Delhi! I have changed humble abodes as you can see and now have a house here in the center of Caracas with flowers and vines and red tiles, which is slightly better than the Lower West Side, especially on Sundays after brunch when all the amateurs were lining Ninth Avenue, throwing up in the gutters. The jazz is worse, however. I used to think I missed Venezuelan music but there's a band that plays on the paseo every night, they sound like eight drowning rats, and the fact is there are only three of them. I came here with a friend who was in the buddy program, he took sympathy on me for a few months, he also happened to have a degree in Oriental medicine, but I brought a secret stash with me just in case, used up all my blank prescriptions, also sold my Warhol cock paintings, *et voilà!* here I am to spend all my money and die. Maybe they'll carry me up to the hills and cover me in cardboard. I am now alone since Aaron, my paramour, left with his Oriental medicines in tow, that's life I suppose, easy come easy go.

The city is not the place I knew, but who cares you won't exactly hear my heart breaking under the noise of the traffic. There's at least twelve hundred billion people in Caracas and highways and ramps and skyscrapers. They wear flared jeans and thigh-length boots (some of them I think must have raided your old closets!) and there's a boatload of rich gringos flushing out our oil. So, yes, the place has changed. I could not even find the hill where I grew up, if that's the word.

In the taxi from Simon Bolívar the driver made a detour to the Catia barrio to relieve us of the burden of our luggage. I somehow remembered the local slang for: *If you don't turn this taxi around I'll eat your dick for breakfast, you ugly cocksucker.* Such eloquence. He almost crashed into a light pole. He gave us the ride for free and then I tipped him outrageously so I now have a reputation, if my youth was not enough. Don't fuck with Victor he'd much prefer to fuck (with) you! Aaron did something terrible the first night. He threw all my Lucky Strikes out the balcony window and the young boys down on the paseo (all from the tin sheds in the ranchos) went wild. They tucked them under the sleeves of their T-shirts, à la Brando. Oh their brown arms, how it took me back. Be happy, go Lucky. One of the pretty little things (how pretty I used to be!) is an expert pick-pocket, I got to know him the next day when he came around for the cigarette ends. We struck a deal. He goes to the Hilton Caracas on Avenida Libertador, where all the businessmen stay, or the new art museum, where the tourists hang out, and he steals cigarettes for me. He gets an extra dollar if they're the right brand. He doesn't even need a knife to slice open pockets, his fingernails are so long and sharp that they cut any cloth, clever little thing. Sometimes I wonder what would I have been, apart from dead, if I had stayed here. Excuse me while I drag my carcass over to the table and ingest yet another tablet. We only live once.

I am doing yoga. I am doing yoga, Rudi. I hear you laughing.

Before he left Aaron taught me to meditate so perhaps this is the first time in my life that I've learned to cross my legs. The first time I tried it I swore I'd break apart, a bad Venezuelan pretzel. I always thought that if God (what a bore) wanted me to touch my toes he would have put them in my crotch, but He's not so benevolent, it seems. But the yoga's good for me. I tell myself over and over, *This is good, this is good, Victor, you are not a complete asshole, do your yoga, do your yoga, you are not a complete asshole, well perhaps just a tiny bit.* Before Aaron left (well, before I kicked him out) we used to wake early and go out onto the balcony, where we set up. Aaron was sad that it wasn't an east-facing balcony. We'd meditate for perhaps an hour and then we'd have breakfast. Orange juice, croissants and grapefruit, no vodka allowed! Aaron was a health food nut. He kept trying to get me to put on weight. The fridge was stocked with polyunsaturated margarine, pickles, yogurt, chutney, gherkins, peanut butter, coconuts, high-calorie chocolate milk shakes, everything. He was tall and sandy-haired and magnificent beyond compare. Rudi, my friend, his cock may not have been a poem but the cheeks of his ass certainly did rhyme. He saw you dance once in Connecticut, and said, I quote, that you were graceful, provocative and sublime—why do all the Anglo boys like their ridiculous words?

My doctor on Park Avenue told me that Caracas would be my death warrant, what with intestinal disorders, cheap medicine, bad hospitals, dirty air et cetera et cetera. But I have been here five months now and have steadily improved. What I do is I take a half-hour taxi ride to the coast. I sit on a deck chair

on the beach and meditate and in my head I envision the cells
and then I go blam blam you little fuckers blam blam, trying
to pretend they're the uptight bouncers who didn't let me in
free to the Paradise Garage at the end, blam blam, you're gone,
blam blam, you should work at Saints for godsake, blam blam,
look what ugly shoes you're wearing, blam blam, there's shit
on your lip. And then I open my eyes and there's blue water
(bluish) lapping up on the golden (yellowish) sand. What fun.
Then I verbally abuse my lesions and tell them to rot in hell. I
am a forty-two-year-old man playing games in his head. Why
not, life has played games with me. This morning, before the
rains, I went to buy myself a blanket and met a mestizo
woman who looked more like Mother than any other woman
on earth. Maybe, as you say, there's a double for us all somewhere. I went home, curled up on the chair and fell asleep
dreaming.

I miss New York and all the places and everyone and
everything and especially the Lower East Side, it was so disgusting, so wonderful. The only thing I regret is not having
enough regrets. For instance, not saying good-bye to the
garbagemen. I'd have loved to have seen their faces when they
saw my furniture out on the street. They must have sung an
aria. Oh this fabulous yellow divan! Goodness me, what a
pretty cock ring! Oh my, what a delicious-looking dildo, I do
declare!

My life has been one room after another (cubicles mostly)
and now I am more or less stuck in this one since if I go out on
the streets of Caracas it is quite likely I'll get rolled and not in
the desired way.

Oh Rudi, I feel tired with this medicine. When this rain
stops I will go out the door. I might even go out before, just to
feel it on my face. I suppose I'm not so afraid of dying, Rudi, I
wonder much more about what might have happened if I'd

lived it all in slow motion. Aha! One dexedrine, two dexedrine, three dexedrine, floor.

*Love—Victor*

P.S. I heard rumors there's a stallion called Nureyev that's making a stir in the horse world. Is this true? Ha. I bet he's hung like a Russian!

Kisses!

---

We landed later than scheduled so Monsieur was furious. He stormed out of the baggage area. We passed the line of armored guards and got into a taxi. Monsieur negotiated with the driver in broken Spanish. The afternoon heat was just as I had imagined. The green mountains rose in the distance but the city was full of smog.

I kept thinking of poor Tom at home alone in London.

The taxi swerved around potholes until we reached the older colonial district where we got stuck in traffic. There were white brick houses with laundry strung up between the windows. Old men were on the street in collarless shirts. Children played in front of cars and ran off when the traffic moved. A woman at a flower stall caught Monsieur's eye and he jumped out of the taxi to buy flowers. She wore a dress of yellows and reds. Monsieur gave her ten American dollars and kissed her on both cheeks and, when we pulled away, she caught my eye as if begging to live my life, sitting as I was in the backseat of a taxi with Monsieur. In truth, she could have had it. Monsieur was well aware that I was not happy to be accompanying him. To be away from Tom was very difficult, but Monsieur had pleaded with me to come, if only for a week or two.

—We need champagne, Monsieur said as the taxi inched forward.

The driver turned and grinned. With a complicated series of hand gestures he said he would be delighted to purchase champagne, that he knew a fine store. The driver swerved the car down a narrow laneway and pulled to a halt in front of a warehouse. Monsieur gave him money and he came out, moments later, carrying two large bottles. It was growing dim but the heat was still heavy and it made me sleepy, not to mention that the flight had been long and arduous. I had heard that Monsieur had made a fuss in first class, but now he touched my hand, thanked me once again for making the journey, apologized he wasn't able to get me a seat beside him on the plane.

—What would I do without you, Odile? he said.

At the house Monsieur tipped the driver generously, then walked up the driveway, pulled the bell rope. The ringing pierced the quiet but nothing happened. Monsieur banged on the tall wooden door. He was sweating and two ovals had appeared at his underarms. He let out a string of curses and said: I should have told him I was coming.

Between us we had a single fountain pen but no paper. Monsieur ran his fingernail under the label of the champagne bottle. Old trick, he said. He peeled the label off. It tore midway. He leaned against the wall of the house, sighed, and wrote: *Victor, I will find a hotel and come back. Rudi.* I folded the label, bent down to slip it in beneath the doorway, nudged it forward with my fingers. I stood and adjusted my dress, which had begun to cling in the heat.

A sudden blast of music came from the house. In fact, the whole place jumped to life. I went to the gate and called for Monsieur, who was already some way down the street. The door behind me opened.

A small figure stood in a silk dressing gown. His face was thin, a pair of headphones covered his ears, and the coiled black cord dangled down by his knees. He must have ripped the cord from the stereo when I pushed the note under the door.

—Mister Pareci? I asked.

He squinted at the torn champagne label. I had met him many times before, but he looked so different.

—Mister Pareci? I asked again.

He shuffled out onto the doorstep in an enormous pair of yellow slippers. He used the jamb to support himself, coughed once and looked down the street.

—Oh my God, it's Rudi, he said.

He stumbled back inside while I waved at Monsieur to return. He seemed annoyed at first but then pushed past me into the house.

—Victor! he shouted. Victor!

The house was a dreadful mess. Clothes were strewn all over the floor. Plates of half-eaten food had been left on the couch. Light trickled through the faded blue curtains. A ceiling fan spun. The mirrors were ornate but cracked. Vinyl records lay on the floor and Monsieur moved to lower the volume of the stereo.

—Victor! he shouted again.

The red light of the video player was blinking. A pornographic film was frozen on the television screen. I stepped over to turn it off.

—Look at you! shouted Monsieur.

At the top of the stairs Victor was trying to step into a pair of trousers. He had discarded the dressing gown. He had put on a bright red shirt, unbuttoned. His chest was thin and his skin pale. He coughed hard when his foot went into the trouser leg and he almost toppled over, but just managed to steady himself with his hand against the banisters. I felt a sadness for Victor but not enough to change my mind as to his true nature—I had seen him play the jester far too often.

Monsieur skipped up the stairs and kissed Victor on both cheeks. Victor let out a string of vile obscenities, saying: Where did you steal the flowers, Rudi? Where have you been? Tell me everything!

He sounded happy and tired at the same time, as if the happiness were trying to catch up with the exhaustion. They came down the stairs together, arms around each other.

—You remember Odile? Monsieur said.

—Oh yes, said Victor. Wasn't I at your wedding?

—Yes.

—Oh I apologize, I apologize.

At my wedding there'd been an altercation in one of the bathrooms with one of Tom's fellow shoemakers.

—You're forgiven, Mister Pareci.

—All I did was ask him to tie his lace, said Victor. I just couldn't resist.

He put his head to his shoulder like a naughty child, awaited my reply.

—Mister Parceci.

—Oh please don't call me that, I feel like such an old fart.

—Victor, I said, you are forgiven.

He kissed my hand. I told him it was my intention to make him comfortable and set him on the road to recovery while Monsieur found another housekeeper, a local woman, to take my position. I explained that it was not my desire to remain in Caracas forever. He blushed then, ashamed, and I cursed myself for my bluntness. He buttoned up his red shirt. Two more of him would have fit inside. He slipped his feet back into the yellow slippers and moved to a chair in the living room, flopped down, short of breath. He lit a long thin cigarette and blew the smoke to the ceiling as I made my way into the kitchen.

—Rudi, he shouted, come hug me.

Then, to include me, he added: You know, Odile, I'm the only person in the world who can order Rudi around!

I commenced cleaning, first the champagne flutes. There was no soap. Victor was living without scourers or washcloths or domestic cleaning appliances of any sort. I began to make a mental note of all the things I would need. I washed the glasses and placed the bottle of champagne on a tray, brought it out to the gentlemen.

—Oh, I'm so in love with you! shouted Victor.

Monsieur popped the bottle and I poured.

—Marry me this instant, Odile!

Monsieur began rifling through the records on the floor, looking for classical music. He looked up and said: You're a philistine, Victor.

—I'm all salsa these days.

—Salsa?

Victor began a dance, which winded him quickly, and he sat back down.

—Maybe you shouldn't have too much champagne, said Monsieur.

—Oh, shut up! said Victor. I have a cold, that's all.

—A cold?

—Yes, a cold. Tell me, Rudi. Will you spend the rest of your life here with me?

—I dance in São Paulo on Friday. Odile will be with you until I help you find someone local.

—São Paulo?

—Yes.

—Oh bring me with you.

—Maybe you should rest, Victor, take it easy.

—Rest?

—Yes.

—I'm dying! he shouted. Who wants to rest? Let's drink champagne! For God's sake let me see the label. I bet it's piss! He always buys piss, Odile! He's the world's richest cheap man.

Monsieur covered the half-label with his hand. Victor got to his feet unsteadily and went searching for the half that had been written on. He found it finally in his dressing gown pocket and sighed theatrically. He licked the back of the label and pasted it over his heart.

—Oh you've always been so cheap! said Victor.

I ran the tap to drown out the voices and cleaned the remaining glasses, held them up to the last of the sunlight. A vision of Tom flitted across my mind. He would be at home, watching television, repairing shoes. I missed him already. In the back courtyard the long-leafed plants were shivering in the breeze.

—Oh let's not talk shit, I heard Victor shout. You didn't come here to talk shit, did you? Tell me, Rudi. Are you in love?

—I am always in love.

—Love loves me, said Victor, in a voice that sounded curiously like Monsieur.

They laughed. The bottle was emptying fast. Victor held it in the air and read the half-label again.

—It's cat piss, he said in a fake French accent. They milk the strays on Boulevard Saint-Michel just for this.

Victor turned up the South American music on the stereo and in the room they danced briefly while I continued to clean. The dusk had fallen and the cool breeze of the evening brought some relief. I could hear Victor recovering from the exertion and finally, when I finished my chores, I excused myself to bed.

I was terribly surprised, after waking the next morning, to see Monsieur on the living room couch, sleeping, with Victor in a chair beside him, mopping Monsieur's brow with a white cloth. I had been sure it would be the other way around. Monsieur was suffering from a fever, it seemed. When he got up, however, he took some pills and the fever dissipated. He performed his morning stretches, said he had some phone calls to make.

—Reverse the charges, said Victor.

Monsieur had friends in every part of the world, including Caracas, and I was convinced he would find a housekeeper within a couple of days. The house was brighter with this knowledge and I managed to find enough food in the kitchen to prepare a breakfast of fruit and toast.

When the breakfast was finished, however, Monsieur announced that he and Victor would take a day-trip to the beach, and in the evening they would both go to São Paulo for the ballet.

—Please have our bags ready, said Monsieur.

To my surprise it was Victor who noted my sadness. He put his arm around my shoulder. He kindly drew a small map of the various marketplaces in the city and the location of a chemist shop where I could buy migraine tablets since I had forgotten mine. He stressed that I should not carry a lot of money. Then he rattled on about a delinquent boy who had long fingernails.

When they left I washed the sheets, hung them out on the branches of the pomegranate trees in the courtyard.

They returned after three days. Monsieur looked very tired, not his usual self. He instructed me that we would stay in Caracas for another week, until everything was sorted out for Victor. The thought of another whole week disturbed me greatly, but Monsieur said he genuinely needed my help. I continued to clean and cook. In the afternoons, while Victor slept, Monsieur was driven to the opera house since he wanted to work with the local dancers. Each evening he brought students, boys and girls, back to the house where they sat around, chatting and laughing. Victor was happy with all the clamor. In particular he latched on to a dancer named Davida, a very dark and handsome young man. In the evenings they took walks together. Later, while Monsieur slept, Victor and Davida curled up on the couch and watched videos. (The videos were shocking. I kept a stern face when I walked past the television set, though I must admit that on occasion I peeked.)

The time passed quickly and I didn't dwell on Tom's absence as much as I had expected.

At the end of the second week, just before our planned return, the three of us—Monsieur, Victor and I—were alone in the house. Monsieur had not yet found a new housekeeper and I had grown nervous that he had forgotten all about his promise. I began to fear the unthinkable, that I might even have to resign. I went to bed with a terrible migraine.

The following night I was cooking a local dish—empanadas—and Victor was instructing me on its intricacies, how to fry the cornmeal, how to spice the beans. He sat in the middle of the living room, directing from a distance, having taken his huge array of medicines. Despite the obvious toll the sickness was taking on his body, Victor was quite energetic, having slept most of the afternoon.

Afterwards they began drinking wine and telling stories but Monsieur seemed slightly more introspective than usual. I had noticed that Monsieur himself was almost at the end of his medicine but could find no other reason for the cloud that seemed to have descended upon him. He stood by the window, stretched, his head to his knee. He took his foot from the windowsill, tucked his hands between his elbows and his rib cage. Then, for some reason, he began recalling a moment long ago when he had received a letter from a lady friend in Russia. The story was long and detailed and Monsieur looked out the window as he spoke, until he was interrupted.

—You're not in love with women now, are you, Rudi?

—Of course not.

—You were about to disappoint me!

Victor poured himself another glass of wine. He coughed and said: Oh this cold. I guess I won't shake it until August at least.

—Will I continue the story or not? asked Monsieur.

—Oh, yes please, continue, please please.

—He died.

—Who died?

—Her father.

—Oh no! Not another story about death! said Victor.

—Wait, said Monsieur, his voice catching in his throat. When he died he was wearing a hat.

—Who was wearing a hat?

—Sergei! He always wore a hat but never indoors. In Russia that is rude.

—Oh! And Russians aren't rude?

—You're not listening to me.

—Of course I am.

—Let me tell you the story, then!

—The stage is yours, said Victor, and he blew Monsieur a kiss.

—Well, said Monsieur, the reason he wore the hat was he believed he was going to meet his wife.

—But you said she was dead.

—In the afterlife, said Monsieur.

—Oh God, said Victor, the afterlife!

—He was found in his house with a hat on his head. He was writing to his daughter. In the letter he asked her to say hello to me. But that's not the story. That's not the point of my story. It's something different. Because, you see, in his last words he wrote . . .

—What? said Victor. He wrote what?

Monsieur stuttered and said: Whatever loneliness we have had in this world will only make sense when we are no longer lonely.

—And what sort of bullshit is that? said Victor.

—It's not bullshit, said Monsieur.

—Oh it's bullshit, said Victor.

They were silent and then Victor's head drooped. He was like a balloon that had lost its air. He reached for a new packet of cigarettes and his fingers shook while he fumbled with the wrapping. He opened the package and took a cigarette out, got a lighter from his shirt pocket, flicked it into life.

—Why are you telling me this story? said Victor.

Monsieur didn't reply.

—Why are you telling me this story, Rudi?

Victor cursed, but then Monsieur knelt at the foot of Victor's chair. I had never seen Monsieur kneel to anyone before. He put his arms around Victor's knees, laid his head against the crook of his arm. Victor said nothing. His hand went to the back of Monsieur's neck. There was a muffled heave and I was sure Monsieur was crying.

Victor looked down at Monsieur's head and began to mention something about a bald spot, but the comment fell away, and then he gripped the back of Monsieur's neck even tighter.

Victor must have remembered me in the kitchen since he looked up and caught my eye. I closed the door and let them be. I had never before heard Monsieur cry in such a way. It made my hands tremble. I went to the courtyard where Monsieur's dance clothes were drying on the washing line. I could still see their silhouettes inside the house. They had their arms around each other and their shadows made them look like one person.

The following morning began bright and smog-free. I cleaned the house thoroughly and then arranged for the young dancer, Davida, to come over. He arrived in a pair of clogs and greeted me with a kiss. His hair was nicely combed back. He seemed to be an honest young man, so I took him aside.

—Would you look after him? I asked.

—I have a cousin who's a doctor, said Davida.

—No, I think you should look after him.

—Who will pay me?

—Monsieur will pay you, I said.

Over the next two days I prepared a week's worth of meals, crammed them in the small freezer for Victor and Davida. Everything was in order—Monsieur had promised to pay Davida and also to bring him to the Paris Opera House, in future years, where he could have classes and develop his talents.

Everything was kept secret from Victor but I had a feeling he knew what was going on. He walked around the house wearing his earphones even though they were unplugged.

On our last morning I packed Monsieur's bag and arranged a taxi to take us back to the airport. We sat around for a long time, waiting for the car to arrive. Victor talked a lot about the weather, what a great day it was going to be for the beach. He said he couldn't wait to put on a new pair of swimming trunks he'd bought in São Paulo.

—I'll look like I'm smuggling grapes, he said.

When the taxi drew up Monsieur and Victor shook hands and hugged at the doorway. As Monsieur walked down the driveway Victor reached into his dressing gown pocket. I heard the flick of a cigarette lighter. Monsieur turned around.

—You should stop that, said Monsieur.

—Stop what?

—Smoking, you asshole.

—This? said Victor, and he puffed on the cigarette, blew a big cloud of smoke in the air.

—Yes.

—Oh what the hell, said Victor, I haven't got my cough right yet.

# | 4 |

LONDON, BRIGHTON · 1991

Moderate rolling in of right foot on deep plié, severe on left. Mild right tibio talor and sub-talor, severe on left. Acute knocking of knee. Left lateral tipping of the hip. Arch in lower back, head dips forward. At the bottom of the plié the line is completely gone. Giveaway is the white knuckles on the barre. By twelfth plié he has overcome the pain. On examination, severe tension and contraction in left quadriceps, moderate in right. Acute fraying of the meniscus. Work in arnica to lessen inflammation. Cross fiber friction and twenty-minute effleurage at least. Lengthen quadriceps to allow bend. Rolling and broadening, hip extension, torso twist, scapula stretch etc. Bandage between rehearsal and performance. Figure-eight wrapping with cross on side to push left knee straight.

❖

I had no idea who to tell. It was impossible to think of anyone who might understand. I had not made many friends since moving to

Monsieur's home in London. There had always been Tom, but now he was gone.

It came out of the blue, like one of those winter showers that chills you to the bone. One day you're content and the next day it is all swept from beneath your feet. I looked around but couldn't recognize even the simplest items, the oven, the clock, the small porcelain vase Tom had bought for me. There was a note explaining his actions, but I could not bring myself to read beyond the first two lines. He seemed to be still present, as if I might turn around and find him sitting in his chair, reading a newspaper, yet another hole apparent in his socks. But he had taken his shoemaking equipment and a suitcase. For hours I cried. It was as if he had sent my whole life supperless to bed.

When I was a schoolgirl in Voutenay I was called Petit oiseau. I was small and thin, and adults always remarked on my hooked nose. I used to sit and watch my mother cooking in the kitchen, where we both took refuge in the simplicity of recipes and food. But there was nobody to care for. Monsieur was away and not even the gardener was around.

In the quarters Tom and I shared, he had kept a box near his side of the bed. Tom had been contemplating retirement and was making a final pair of shoes for Monsieur. For the presentation box he had used mahogany and nailed a brass plate on the front, although it had not yet been inscribed. I opened the box, took out the shoes and carefully snipped them apart with a pair of scissors. The satin cut easily and then I placed the pieces back in the box. I knew my senses were derailed but I hardly cared.

Monsieur always kept money in the bottom drawer of his bedroom cupboard. He used it to give to visitors who had run out of cash and were in need of a taxi home. I left a slip of paper saying I was taking an advance on my salary. My hands were shaking. I phoned the usual number for a taxi, checked the house to make sure all the lights were out, the windows were shut tight, the appliances turned off. Soon a loud beeping sounded outside the house. I tucked Tom's box under my arm, set the burglar alarm, and went out the front door.

I recognized the driver, a young man who wore an earring and a goatee. He rolled down his window and said: Who's the victim today then, eh?

He was a little surprised when I opened the door and slid into the backseat alone, placed the mahogany box on the floor. I had often escorted Monsieur's guests to their taxis but rarely took one myself. The driver tilted his rearview mirror, looked at me, and then turned in his seat and slid the glass panel open.

—Covent Garden, I said.

—You all right, love?

From my handbag I took a handkerchief monogrammed with Monsieur's initials. I dabbed at my eyes and told the driver I was fine, that I just needed to get to Covent Garden as soon as possible.

—Right-y-o, love, he said. You sure you're okay?

It was not rudeness that caused me to switch seats so he could no longer see me in the mirror, but that I simply couldn't bear the notion of the young driver watching me cry.

He drove quickly but the journey seemed endless. It was summertime. On the street girls wore tiny skirts and young men sported tattoos. The taxi lurched from side to side. Drivers behind us tooted their horns, furious they had been cut off. A motorcycle driver even kicked the side panel of the door.

By the time we got to Covent Garden the fare was in double digits.

I had recovered sufficient composure to ask the driver to wait for me outside the shoe factory. He shrugged. I stepped out of the car and was about to go inside when the thought of seeing Tom made my legs wobble. I had not felt this way since my graduation dance in Paris years before. What had I become? I was sixty years old and had just ripped up my husband's present to Monsieur. Surely, I thought, I was just suffering through a terrible dream.

I heard the whoop of a siren and turned around to see a police car instructing the taxi to move on. The driver was gesturing at me. Everything was happening in far too much of a hurry. I walked quickly along the outside wall to Tom's window and, without looking in, I left the box on the windowsill, turned around and climbed back in the taxi.

—Brighton, I said to the driver.

I could see the surprise on his face. Brighton? he said.

Behind us the police car siren whooped a second time.

—Brighton by the sea, I said.

—You got to be kidding, love.

He began driving slowly down the street.

—I'll take you to Victoria Station, you can get a train from there.

I opened my handbag and passed forward one hundred and fifty pounds. The driver whistled and stroked his goatee. I added another fifty and he pulled the taxi over to the curb. I had never before spent so much money so needlessly.

—You going for a little flutter then, love? asked the driver.

—Please, I said in my sternest voice.

He straightened up and got on his radio, talked to his dispatcher and within fifteen minutes we were on the main carriageway. I rolled down the window and, quite inexplicably, felt calm. The breeze drowned out the noise of a cricket match on the driver's radio. It seemed that I had carelessly stepped into a day not meant for me and soon it would be over.

In Brighton posters of Monsieur were tied to the lampposts all along the promenade.

Monsieur looked young in the photograph. His hair was long and he had an impish grin on his face. I wanted to walk up to the poster and embrace him. A young lady on the promenade held a stapling gun and was readjusting a few of the posters that had slid down the posts. It was Monsieur's final performance in England and there were rumors it might be his last.

I had asked the driver to find a nice bed-and-breakfast facing the sea. He stopped outside an old Victorian house and kindly offered to go inside to inquire whether there was a vacancy. I was glad to see that not all young Englishmen had lost their manners. He came out smiling and, after he had taken my hand to guide me from the taxi, he offered to return some of the money.

—You paid too much, dear.

I surprised even myself when I shoved yet another twenty-pound note into his hand.

—What I'll do is I'll buy the missus a nice dinner, he said.

He beeped his horn as he left.

It was certainly not his fault but I burst into tears.

The room was elegant, with a picture window that looked out to the sea. Children were laughing and kicking in the surf and I could hear a distant brass band playing in one of the pavilions. Still I was reminded of Tom, even in the simplest of items: the twin beds, the ornate vase, the painting of the piers. I had no explanation as to what had happened. Tom had, over the years, been mildly unhappy at having to live in Monsieur's house, but we had furnished our quarters to Tom's liking and he had seemed to settle in. He was not perturbed by the few occasions when I had traveled with Monsieur to other countries, nor even by the fact that I was sometimes called upon to look after Monsieur's needs in Paris. Indeed, Tom said he liked the time alone, he could get his work done. And while it was true that we were perhaps not as intimate as other married couples, there had certainly never been a time when I had called into question our devotion to each other.

I stood in the room. Perhaps the only word for my emotion was raw: I felt raw. I closed the curtains and lay down on the bed and, although it is not in my nature, I continued to weep aloud even while I heard other guests in the corridor.

I awoke thinking not of Tom, but of Monsieur's posters fluttering in the wind by the sea.

Monsieur was not due to dance in *The Moor's Pavane* until the following night. I thought about going to see him at his hotel but didn't want to compound his problems with my own. In recent times I had been angered by what the newspapers were writing about him. He had an ingrown toenail and a problem with his knees, but the newspapers never wrote about that. At one show some members of the audience had asked for their money back when his leg muscles cramped. In Wembley the music had stopped in the middle and they said Monsieur had frozen, waiting for the orchestra, but there was none since the music was taped. In Glasgow there was nobody to meet him at the stage door and a photographer had taken a picture of Monsieur alone and dejected, when, of course, that wasn't true to his spirit at all. Some of his steadfast admirers now refused to go to his performances, but his shows still sold out and the ovations were plentiful, even if the newspapers said they were addressed to the past. People liked to make sly comments behind Monsieur's back but the truth is that he was as dignified as ever.

The next morning I decided that, despite the circumstances, I would make the best of my day. I ordered breakfast in one of the seafront establishments. The waiter, a young man from Burgundy, made a strong café-crème especially for me. He whispered that the English may have helped win two world wars but they knew nothing of the coffee bean. I laughed and found myself doubling the tip. I felt strangely giddy when I thought about my rapidly disappearing money. Even so, I bought a sun hat and rented a deckchair, carried it to the strand, put the hat on in order to obscure my eyes.

Late in the morning I noticed a young woman standing near the water's edge. She was holding her skirt and dipping a toe in the surf. Her legs were long and beautiful. She went farther into the sea and stopped when the water reached to her thigh. Then she bent forward, whipped her long shining hair over her shoulder and soaked it briefly in the sea.

Then, much to my surprise I caught sight of Monsieur standing near the young woman. The waves were rolling up to him. I wondered who she could possibly be. Emilio sat close by on the beach, cross-legged, watching the proceedings.

I rose quickly to leave, but Emilio spied me and called my name. He stood up and his long ponytail swung. He greeted me with a kiss on either cheek and expressed his pleasure on seeing me in Brighton.

—Oh, I just wanted to see Monsieur's show, I said.

—I'm glad someone wants to, replied Emilio.

At that moment Monsieur spotted me and waved at me to join him. Emilio made a comment about the king summoning his courtiers and I had to smile a little. Emilio had resigned so many times from Monsieur's service that he had even put another masseur on call to work on those days between resigning and being rehired.

I bit my lip and went down to the water, where Monsieur was standing with the young lady.

—Let me introduce you to Marguerite, he said.

I realized then that she was one of Monsieur's dancing partners. She pushed her sunglasses up onto her head and smiled. Her eyes were a beautiful blue. I thought how wonderful it must be for her, at such a young age, to dance with Monsieur in the twilight of his career, but then I felt a sudden surge of anger since Monsieur had not even inquired after the reason for my appearance in Brighton.

—Odile will help solve your problem, I heard Monsieur say.

—Oh no, said the young dancer. I'll be able to arrange something.

There were children playing by the sea, using their shoes to scoop up water for sandcastles and moats.

—Odile wouldn't mind, would you?

Monsieur was staring at me. I mentioned that I had been distracted by the bright sunlight. He sighed and said the problem was quite simple. Marguerite, he explained, had invited some family members to the performance that evening. They were driving down from London. Her sister had an eighteen-month-old child and no-one to baby-sit.

I nodded and said: I understand.

—There, said Monsieur. Problem solved.

I flushed but stammered that it would be my honor to help.

—Six o'clock, said Monsieur.

Years ago an uncle told me that if I were to be a little bird, it would always be the one with the broken wing. That evening I had prepared a meal for a table of twelve and, even though I say so myself, the food was exquisite. The only variation was for my uncle's dish—I had laced it with spice and he spent the evening teary-eyed and coughing.

I wished at that moment to lace Monsieur's dish, to say something that would make him stand back and sputter. But he appeared sicker than usual. With his foot problems and other ailments, he was having difficulty walking, and the thought of him stepping onstage to dance, upset, was distressing.

—I'd be delighted to help, I said.

Monsieur nodded and hobbled away down the beach. The young dancer looked back over her shoulder, smiled, and mouthed her thanks. Monsieur whistled at Emilio, who rose and followed them.

The water lapped at my toes and I felt a migraine coming on. Beyond the promenade I dipped into a café to order a glass of water for my tablets. Only moments later did I realize I had also ordered a slice of Battenburg cake, Tom's favorite.

I left the cake untouched and returned to my room.

The sound of seagulls woke me and I saw on the bedside clock that it was almost six. I hurried to the hotel and pushed through the groups of admirers in the lobby waiting for Monsieur. I approached the front desk where, after a series of phone calls, I was directed to the penthouse floor.

Obviously there had been a mistake because when I knocked gently on the door it was Monsieur's voice I heard, loud and impatient, saying: What?

Emilio opened the door and I glimpsed Monsieur on the massage table. Emilio was wearing thin rubber gloves. I noticed even from a distance that there were welts on Monsieur's body and there was a little blood on the table's paper sheet, near Monsieur's feet. I stammered my apology, turned away, and the door closed quickly behind me.

I heard Monsieur curse.

—Lock the door! he shouted.

Downstairs, I was redirected to the young dancer's room. The child was sleeping, bottles of milk had been prepared, a change of clothes neatly laid out, and there was even a pram in the room so I could rock him back and forth if he woke. He was a beautiful little boy with thin wisps of dark hair.

I bade good-bye to the family and settled in one of the easy chairs.

I have always detested hotel rooms. I had no desire to watch television, nor to tune in the radio. I found myself thinking of Tom, how I had shredded the shoes and how he might feel when he opened the box. It was impossible to stop the tears. Feeling claustrophobic, I bundled the baby in a light blanket, put him in the pram and brought him downstairs in the elevator.

It was still bright outside. Many young lovers were on the promenade and some clairvoyants had set up along the beachfront. A few people stopped and cooed at the baby in the pram, but when someone asked me the child's name I realized that I didn't know. I hurried along with my thoughts of Tom.

I was convinced that there were no other women, although his old landlady still sent him Christmas cards. And there had been no alcohol involved. Maybe there was another explanation. I wished I had taken his letter with me and perhaps, I thought, my actions had been far too rash.

Down the promenade I heard some loud swear words. When I looked I found myself just yards from a gang of young troublemakers leaning against the seafront wall. Their heads were shaved and they wore Union Jack suspenders and red boots up to their ankles.

I considered turning the pram around and walking quickly back to the hotel but I feared they might see my panic and try to steal my handbag. I pushed the pram through but curiously they didn't seem to pay much attention. A few stars were out now and the sea was darkening. The baby woke and began to cry. I tried to soothe him and by the time he fell asleep again the darkness had descended.

I turned to see one of the young skinheads shimmying up a lamp-post. He reached into his rear pocket and I caught the flash of a knife as he began to cut the poster of Monsieur down. He was shouting something terrible about homosexuals while his friends laughed and pushed each other around. My heart beat fast. I looked for the sort of people I'd seen earlier in the day—men in boating hats and middle-aged women in sandals—but there were none in sight. There was no way to take the baby carriage along the pebbled beach, and to get up to the town there were a number of steps I would be forced to climb.

There was nothing else to do but walk back through. My legs trembled, my mouth felt dry, but I held my carriage erect and sang a nursery rhyme to the child.

The skinheads parted a little to allow me a passage. But the one who had torn the poster was jumping up and down and pretending to wipe his backside with Monsieur's image. I could hardly control myself. I felt my knees buckling. I pushed on until the pram got caught on a gap in the concrete and the wheel stuck. I wrenched the pram out from the crack but my feet tangled and I fell back on the ground, grazing my knee. The skinhead started laughing and dropped the torn poster near the wheel of the pram. I caught sight of half of Monsieur's face, his ease, his happiness. I scrambled to rise as one of the troublemakers called me a particularly nasty name. I was trembling, yet I grabbed the torn poster and stuffed it in the pram beside the child.

The skinheads shouted after me as I ran and ran down the promenade away from them. I stopped only when I could no longer hear their foul mouths. Then I leaned against the railing and tried to soothe the child who was screaming now, loud wrenching cries.

At that moment I knew that I hated my husband Tom more than any other person I had ever met in my life.

Two days later, when I got back to London, I found Tom dozing in a chair in our quarters with his hands in his lap. He looked wretched. His shirt was sloppy with stains and I could smell beer off his breath.

I ignored him and began to change into my night clothes, sat on the edge of my bed to remove my tights. Tom woke groggily and looked around as if unsure of where he was. But then he straightened when he saw the grazed cut on my knee. He didn't say a word, just went to the bathroom and came out with a damp tissue. He sat beside me on the bed and raised the edge of my nightdress and started to clean the cut. Little bits of the tissue tore off where the scab had begun to form.

—What happened, love? he asked.

I got into my bed and pulled the covers high, turned my face away. My knee stung from where he had tried to clean it.

Later I could hear Tom rummaging in the bathroom cabinet and then the kitchen. He came back into the bedroom with what smelled like a poultice. I pretended to sleep while he lifted the covers and applied the pungent mixture to my knee. I remembered then something Monsieur had said to me just after his fiftieth birthday—he had seen a photograph of himself standing alone onstage after receiving a curtain call, looking tired, and he had murmured: *Some day this hideous moment will be the sweetest memory.*

When he was finished, Tom pulled up the covers carefully and patted the edge of my bed. He said good night in a whisper, but I didn't stir. I could hear him removing his shirt and taking off his shoes, then lying down on his bed. The odor of his socks began to mix with that of the poultice. I smiled then, thinking to myself that, no matter what, his socks would have to be washed.

※

Ronde de jambe par terre to see range of motion of joints. Severe restriction. Erratic rolling. Hop is acutely pronounced and bones are jammed. Left foot can hardly brush the floor. Acute pain when metatarsals are touched, even when foot is held at central shaft. Key is to move metatarsals like fan, twist from side to side, effleurage gently between rays. Drain blood blisters and immediately remove welt between second and third digit on left foot.

# BOOK FOUR

**November 5, 1987**

The thought of plane touching down next week. Landing on the ice, finally skidding to safety. He might be arrested on his stopover in Leningrad. Ilya says there will be no scheming, yet I am not sure. They could take him away for his seven years and who could stop them? I woke up perspiring. After breakfast I put on my coat and walked to the department store on Krassina. Everyone was walking around in the warmth. There were rumors of a shipment of toaster ovens but none came. In the afternoon Nuriya showed me the painting she has made for Rudik—crows along the Belaya and a single white seagull flying above the cliff. She wrapped the painting in butcher's paper and said she would find a ribbon for it. She cannot contain her excitement, but at her age it is hardly surprising. Equal, I suppose, to my nervousness. Nuriya went to bed early and we could hear her tossing and turning. In Mother's room I tried to tell her that Rudik will be coming in a few days. For a moment Mother's eyes lit up with moisture as if to say: *But how could that be?* Then they fluttered closed again. How peaceful she looks when she sleeps and yet how terribly tortured when awake. The doctor has given her a couple more months. But what use is a couple of months when she has nothing to live for and no real body in which to live it out? Her mind continues to slip away. Ilya said perhaps Mother has stayed alive to see Rudik. Then he asked me if I am not old enough yet to forgive. Forgive? Does it matter? There is the simple reality that there is no soap and the handle of the toilet is broken.

### November 6

There is much to do: darn the tablecloth, clean the window ledges, fix the table legs, let down the hem of Nuriya's dress, boil Mother's nightgown. Ilya was asked to do odd jobs at the Opera House. It is good news. More money.

### November 7

Revolution Day. Blizzard across Ufa. The cold keeps us inside. The snow was three feet high in the graveyard and Ilya could not go out to prepare Father's plot. A forty-eight-hour visa seems worse than allowing Rudik no time at all. The flights alone will take a whole day.

### November 8

I watched Mother's lips. It is an effort in mind-reading. Perhaps Ilya is correct that she has kept herself alive these last few years just for one more look at him. But you cannot cure three decades in a moment. The thought is pure stupidity. We have heard they are arranging a special room at the Rossiya Hotel. It is said that they have refrigerators which make ice cubes. Who would want them? In the afternoon the snow relented. A trip to the department store yielded no new nightdresses, but the second attempt to boil Mother's was more successful. Deep in the cupboards I found an old gown with the faded imprint of tomato stains from the shingles. She has kept everything, even Rudik's shoes. The toes are still scuffed and the backs are broken from the way he always stuffed his feet in.

November 9

Even the nursery rhyme in school today seemed to have implication: *If you can't find your way back, why did you leave in the first place?* At the market we searched for sugar. Nuriya offered to barter the precious silver necklace we got for her fifteenth birthday. But still there was no sugar to be found. She cried. What is to be done? Ilya's salary is two weeks in arrears. What can we use to sweeten the cakes? Perhaps there will be some miracle at the market—truckloads of sugar will arrive just in time, herring, sturgeon, and we will celebrate under a large white tent, drinking champagne to the music of an orchestra. Ha! Ilya has, at least, managed to find the parts for the bathroom plumbing.

November 10

There were teenagers behind the mosque wearing leather jackets. Their hair was untidy and they wore badges on their sleeves. Nuriya said she did not know them. One can imagine this sort of thing in Moscow or Leningrad, but in here? People talk of another thaw, but do they not know that a thaw always brings a dirty stench?

November 11

Ilya says it takes great control not to tell anybody at the Opera House. The older workers have not dared speak Rudik's name for years. And some of the dancers have only ever heard it spoken with viciousness. Ilya says the younger ones are dreadfully rebellious. If they found out they might try to greet him at the airport. Nuriya is counting the hours until his return. The days pass too slowly for her. She keeps changing outfits and looking in the mirror. She has a photograph of when Rudik was a teenager. I hope she will not be shocked when she sees him. The good news: Ilya found a half-kilo of sugar this evening and a shipment of beetroot came in from the countryside. All is not lost.

November 12

He has arrived then surely! Leningrad tonight, no flight out to Ufa until early morning, so there he must stay. We have waited for a call but there is nothing. Ilya keeps lifting the receiver to make sure there is a tone for the operator to put us through. I am convinced a call will come in the moments between Ilya lifting the receiver and setting it down. No sleep. Mother seems agitated, perhaps she understands what is happening. Surely it would have been worse not to tell her. If only she could speak. What cruel fate. We are full of questions. Is he traveling on his own? Will they say terrible things to him? Does he still have friends in Leningrad? Will they allow him to walk in the city? Will the newspapers report his visit? There is a rash on my arm, similar to Mother's shingles. I am frightened beyond compare now, even the success of my banquet hardly matters. Ilya has finished the last repairs and he has found kumis for us to drink.

November 12–13, morning

The night turned slowly to day. The sky broke gray and the wind whipped outside. Snow piled up on the windscreen of the car provided to bring us to the airport. The driver refused to enter our house, so Ilya took him a steaming cup of tea. He flicked the windscreen wipers in thanks. The driver's face was red and shaven and stern. (He looked suspiciously like the man who used to pilot the Driving School car.) Nuriya fretted over her bitten fingernails. I allowed her to wear a dab of lipstick, she threatened a tantrum otherwise. We put on our coats. Mother slept through our preparations and then Milyausha arrived to look after her. I looked at Mother and wondered if she had any idea that her son was coming back more than twice as old as when he left. If he puts a foot wrong they will surely throw him in prison and he will have to live out the seven years.

The roses I had bought were beautiful but the air wilted them by the time we reached the airport. It was like holding money and watching it devalue. We were taken to a waiting room, a small gray box with three chairs, a window, a table, and a silver ashtray. Three officials waited with us. Their hard looks wilted the roses even more. I was flooded with the awareness that I had no need to apologize for what Rudik did in the past—they were not my actions. The officials seemed to relent under my gaze. They even offered Ilya a cigarette. The skies cleared and we mistook a flock of birds for the plane. My stomach clenched with nerves. The flock broke up north and south and moments later the plane broke through. It listed sideways and then our view of the runway was obscured. We were taken from the waiting room into the arrivals area. Twenty guards with machine guns were lined up against the walls. Nuriya whispered: *Uncle Rudik.*

I held my breath for surely the whole fifteen minutes it took for him to emerge through the sliding doors. How my heart skipped! Rudik wore a coat of a material I did not recognize, a colorful scarf, a dark beret. His grin reminded me of when he was young. One suitcase in his hand. He put the case carefully on the ground and stretched out his arms. How was it possible to ever hate him? Nuriya ran to meet him first. He lifted her in the air and swung her around. He kept his arm around her and came towards me, kissed me twice. A photographer came up behind us and bulbs flashed. Rudik whispered that the photograper was from Tass, that he would be accompanying us for the day. He said: *Pay no attention to him, he's a donkey.* I laughed. I had Rudik back, the true Rudik, dearest brother, not the one they created with so many lies. He held my face, stared into my eyes and took the roses from me, said they were wonderful. Then he pulled off my headscarf and I felt the deep shame of my grayness. He kissed me and said I looked beautiful. On closer inspection he too looked worn, there were deep lines on his face and crow's-feet around his eyes. He was a little thinner than I expected. He lifted Nuriya in the air again and clenched her tight and spun her and all seemed well. *I am home,* he said. He was accompanied by a large Spanish man, Emilio, who he said was a bodyguard and a medical person of some sort. He was a huge man but his hands were soft and his eyes kind. His hair was pulled back in a ponytail and tucked beneath his collar. Rudik met Ilya for the first time. *You are welcome to Ufa,* said Ilya. Rudik shot him a look but then smiled. There were also two French officials, hovering around, loath to leave Rudik's side. How strange it was to hear Rudik speak French as if born to it, but when he turned to me he switched to Tatar. He wanted to go see Mother immediately, but I said she was still sleeping and the doctor had advised a short visit in order not to tire her. *She is sleeping?* he said. He looked at a beautiful wristwatch: *But I have less than twelve hours.*

### Nine-thirty

The argument was settled by the officials who said it was necessary that he check into the Rossiya first. Nuriya, Ilya, and I accompanied him in the black ZIL, along with his bodyguard. We were squashed. For a moment I thought of apologizing to them that it was not a Western limousine, but I caught myself and felt a surge of anger. Rudik sat by the window, holding Nuriya's hand. She told him about a book she was reading. He seemed interested and even questioned her on the plot. He looked down at his watch, then took it off abruptly and stuffed it into Nuriya's hand. It was a double watch—it told the time also in a display of digital numbers. He said Nuriya should give it to a boyfriend. She blushed and looked at her father. *Can I keep it for myself, Uncle Rudik?* He said of course and she put her head on his shoulder. He looked out the window as we drove. *Look, the streets are paved.* Rudik didn't recognize a lot of the places, but when he did he shouted things like: *I climbed that fence when I was seven.* We drove past the lake where he used to skate. He commented on the flags: *Remember?* he said. He had a pair of tiny earphones hanging around his neck and when I asked him about them he reached into his pocket for the tiniest recording machine I had ever seen. He put the earphones over my head, pressed a button, and Scriabin filled the air. Rudik promised to give me the machine before he left. He whispered that he needed it for the rest of the day, it blocked out the noise of the Tass photographer who kept asking him ridiculous questions. He patted the palm of my hand: *I am so nervous,* he said. *Can you believe that I am nervous?* His voice sounded different. I wondered what he was nervous about? Being arrested, seeing Mother, or just being here? He said: *Everything seems smaller.* Then he turned to Ilya and talked for a while about how the seat latches on the flight from Leningrad didn't work. The tray, he said, kept falling in his lap.

### Ten-fifteen

The ZIL pulled up outside the hotel. The French officials ran from their car to greet us and the bodyguard stayed close to Rudik. But Ilya seemed a little despondent. He said there were still things to do at home and maybe it was best if he left to prepare them. He said that he'd get a tram back and see us later. Rudik shook his hand a second time. We went upstairs to his room. It was enormous but there was no fridge. He threw the roses on the bed where they landed in a heap. He paced, looking behind window shades and even the picture frames. He unscrewed part of the phone. Then he shrugged and said something about his whole life being bugged, it didn't matter whether it was the KGB or the CIA. Then he put his suitcase on the bed and opened it with a small key. It was not packed with his own clothes as I expected, but with the most unbelievable array of perfumes, scarves, jewelry boxes, brooches, all the most beautiful things. Nuriya grabbed his arm and put her face close to his shoulder. *I was only allowed to bring one suitcase,* he said, *and they took their cut at the airport.* Nuriya lay on the bed and touched everything. Rudik knew all about the perfumes, where they were made, who wore them, who designed them, the ingredients, and where they came from. *This is what Jackie O wears,* he said. He even had a bottle for Mother, a special gift from a lady in New York, wrapped in beautiful ribbons. A bottle of Chanel for me. Nuriya and I sprayed each other's wrists. Then he clapped his hands for silence, took a small box from the suitcase, gave it to me. Inside was the most gorgeous necklace I have ever seen, diamonds and sapphires. An immediate thought: *Where will I hide it?* He instructed me to put it on and wear it with pride. It felt cool and heavy against my neck. Surely it had cost him dearly. He kissed both my cheeks, said it was good to see me.

### Ten-forty-five

I suggested he rest before going to see Mother but he said: *Why?* Then he laughed: *There will be plenty of time to sleep in hell.* If he couldn't go home yet he wanted to drive around the city and see more sights. In the hotel lobby there was another long argument about scheduling and itinerary, but eventually it was agreed—we would drive in a convoy for a few hours. We drove slowly in the snow. The Opera House was closed; our old house on Zentsov Street had been knocked down long ago; the hall on Karl Marx Street was locked up; and the road to the Tatar graveyard was impassable. We parked the car a hundred yards down the hill from the entrance. Rudik begged the driver to find him some snowshoes. The driver said he had nothing except what he wore on his feet. Rudik looked over the seat. *Give me those.* He thrust some dollars at the driver. Rudik's feet were too small for the driver's boots but Nuriya offered him her socks which he stuffed in. The bodyguard wanted to accompany him, but Rudik was angry: *I'll go on my own, Emilio.* We watched from the car as Rudik negotiated the drifts and climbed the iron fence and disappeared over the hill. Only the tops of the graveyard trees appeared above the snow. We waited. Nobody said a word. The snow piled up on the windows. When Rudik finally returned—after trudging through the deep drifts—I could see that the sleeves of his coat were soaking wet, also the knees of his trousers. He said he had used a branch to clear some of the snow away from Father's headstone. I was sure he must have fallen somehow. He said he had listened to hear the thud of trains across the Belaya but there was none. We drove away. The light was glorious. It bounced off the snow everywhere. The wild dogs near the factory stopped barking and for a moment everything was still.

#### Twelve-fifteen

The bodyguard fished in his pocket for a small bottle of pills and Rudik took three without water. He said he had a flu, that the medicine cleared his head. Nuriya said that she too felt a hint of cold, but Rudik refused to give her any pills, said they would be too strong for her. At the railway station he bought sunflower seeds. *I haven't tasted them in years.* He ate two, spat out the shells, and threw the rest away. We passed Sergei and Anna's old house and slowed down. *I thought I might see Yulia at the airport in Leningrad,* he said. *Perhaps she is dead.* I told him I knew nothing of her. He said that she used to send letters to him but they had dried up over the years.

#### Twelve-thirty

At our house two more officials were waiting. Ilya sat by the banquet table but rose to shake Rudik's hand, their third handshake. Ilya looked into his eyes but Rudik was distracted. *Too many people!* He beat on his chest with his gloved fists and roared a terrible curse in Tatar. And then he began making a fuss with the French officials. He wanted to be left alone. I gathered up my courage and hushed him, then guided the officials out of the house. Rudik thanked me, said he was sorry for shouting, but they were nothing but donkeys, his whole life was surrounded by braying donkeys. He was terribly anxious to see Mother but first I had to explain to him all the difficulties, that she could not speak, that her eyesight was failing badly, that she might slip in and out of consciousness. He didn't seem to be listening. Outside the house we could hear the French and Russian officials arguing. Rudik was afraid they would insist on coming back in so he took a chair and slid it under the door handle. He told his bodyguard to stay by the door. How nervous we all were. He took off his overcoat, his colored scarf, draped it on the hatrack and entered Mother's room. She was sleeping. He pulled up a chair beside her, bent down, and kissed her. She didn't stir. Rudik looked up at me, pleading, wondering what to do. I gave Mother some water and her tongue moved to her lips. He held a beautiful necklace to her throat. Mother shifted but did not open her eyes. Rudik mashed his hands together like he was suddenly seven years old again. He whispered to her urgently. *Mother. It's me. Rudik.* I told him to give her time, that she would wake eventually, he must have patience.

### Twelve-forty-five

I decided to leave him alone. As I left I saw him slip the earphones off his neck as if they might muffle anything Mother might say. I stood outside the door. He continued to whisper, although I couldn't make out what he said. For a while it seemed as if Rudik was speaking a foreign language.

### One-thirty

He came out of Mother's room. His eyes were rimmed red. *Emilio,* he said, calling for his bodyguard. Rudik said that Emilio was a masseur with some knowledge of medicine, he might know of some way to make Mother feel better. His stupid Western ideas, I thought, how could his medicine be any better than what we had already given Mother? I hated that monstrous man as he walked towards Mother's room. What right did he have to interfere? I hissed at Rudik but he ignored me and slammed the door.

### Two o'clock

The bodyguard came out. He smiled at me and spoke in a broken English that was impossible to understand. Finally he made gestures in the air. It seemed he was telling me that Mother must once have been a beautiful woman. I changed my mind about him, despite his ponytail. He took many helpings from the banquet table and made sounds to say that things were delicious. And then he sat quietly for the rest of the day.

### Two-thirty

I entered. Mother was awake. Her eyes were fully open as if startled. Rudik was hunched over her and there were tears in his eyes. He was alternating between Russian and Tatar. Mother's lips were moving but it was impossible to make out her words. Rudik reached for my hand. *Tell her it's me, Tamara,* he said. *She knows your voice. She still doesn't know that it's me.* I leaned across and told Mother: *It's Rudik come back to see you.* There was a flicker in her eyes although I did not know whether she understood. *I will sit here until she recognizes me,* said Rudik. *I will not move.* I pleaded with him to come out and enjoy the banquet but he said that he was not hungry. I pleaded again. *No!* he shouted. And then I did something that I will never forget. I slapped Rudik once on the side of the face. His head turned in the direction of the slap and he stared at the wall. I could not believe myself. The slap was so hard that it stung my hand. Rudik slowly turned his head and looked at me for an instant. Then he bent down to Mother again. *I will come to your dinner table, Tamara, when I am ready*. I closed the door. A terrible feeling went through me when I stepped into the living room. Nuriya was staring at her new wristwatch, which was loudly beeping. She couldn't stop it.

### Two-forty-five

Ilya filled the bodyguard's plate once more. They drank kumis together. The bodyguard showed Ilya a game of sorts. The bodyguard plucked a hair from his head and then closed his eyes and told Ilya to place the hair between the pages of the book. With his eyes closed, the bodyguard started feeling the book with his fingers, lightly touching the pages. It was an old masseur's trick which helped him keep his touch. The bodyguard was so good at the game that he could feel the hair eight pages away. The snow blew against the window.

### Three o'clock

I created a plate for Rudik, pickled meat, cabbage salad, hard-boiled eggs. The door creaked when I opened it. I was surprised that he smiled at me. He seemed to have forgotten I had slapped him. There was something good in the air between us again, a distance had been bridged. Rudik did not eat the food but held the plate as if he might. Then he made room on the seat and I slid onto the chair beside him. We watched Mother's lips moving minutely. Her hair was spread on the pillow. *She's saying your name*, I said. *What?* he replied. I said: *She's saying your name, look at her.* His paused a long time but then he began to nod vigorously. *Yes, she's saying my name.* Just then he said something about the flags along the lake, about the radio and times when he would listen to music as a child. I couldn't understand him, he was talking gibberish. I took his hand. The chair was awfully small for the two of us.

### Three-thirty

I left the room. The bodyguard was fiddling with a book, feeling its pages. He asked for another helping of cake.

Rudik came out of Mother's room. He looked stiff, but his face betrayed nothing. He nodded at Nuriya and Ilya and went to the window. He parted the curtain where, outside, the officials were sitting in their cars. Rudik turned. He signaled something to his bodyguard. He was feigning happiness, I'm sure. The bodyguard opened his suitcase and Rudik handed out the last of his presents, more jewelry and makeup and chocolates. Then he flapped his arms to get warm even though the house was toasty. *Well,* he said. He dug down into his pocket and threw a sheaf of rubles on the table. It was a lot of money. Nobody moved. Outside, one of the cars beeped. The flight to Leningrad was due to leave soon. The snow was still falling. At the door he pulled his beret down, hugged Nuriya and shook Ilya's hand yet again. I stepped across to him at the threshold. *She didn't recognize me,* he said. I whispered in his ear: *Of course she did.* We repeated ourselves. *No, she didn't. Yes she did.* He looked at me and smiled a half-smile. *My face still stings,* he said and for a moment I thought he was going to slap me back, but he didn't. He twirled his scarf and then turned his back and went out to the car. We stood there with all our new possessions.

❖

Yulia, my dear, let me guess, you still don't have a piano?

He was panting somewhat from the five flights of stairs. I gasped, unaware that at my age such deep surprise was still a possibility. He smiled at his own little joke, introduced his companion, Emilio, and apologized for calling so late at night. He said he felt awful for bringing no gifts, but that he had already given everything away. I embraced him as he studied the darkness of the apartment from the vantage of the threshold.

Same old Yulia, said Rudi. So many books that you can't see the wallpaper.

How did you find me?

I have my means.

The electricity was off again in the building. I lit two candles and the light flared. Emilio stayed at the door and shook the snow off his shoulders. I invited him in and he was a little surprised at what he called my perfect Spanish. I explained that the language had been much of my life and he went to the bookshelf to look at my collection.

I pulled my dressing gown tight, then stepped behind the partition that divided the room. Kolya was sleeping. He grumbled at first when I woke him, but then he sat upright. Who? he said and he leaped out of bed, his hair tousled.

Put whatever food we have on the table, I whispered.

In the bathroom I rouged my cheeks with my knuckles, looked at myself in the mirror and laughed. The ghosts of my life had walked out to greet me at sixty-two years of age.

Hurry, called Rudi. I have only an hour or so.

Out on the table Kolya had spread a loaf of bread and some left-over cucumber salad. The bottle of vodka was already open but the glasses beside it were empty. The candles made nervous points against the darkness.

We're honored, I said.

Rudi waved his hand: They wanted me to go to a dinner at the French embassy, he said, but they bore me.

So they let you come back?

They allowed me forty-eight hours to see Mother. My flight was delayed. It leaves from Pulkovo in a few hours.

A few hours?

I didn't even get to see the Kirov. They managed the visit so that it would be closed.

Your mother? I asked. How is she?

Rudi smiled but didn't reply. His teeth were still strikingly white as if making an argument against the rest of his face. There was a short silence as he looked around the room. He seemed to be searching for other figures to come out from the shadows. Then he clasped my hands suddenly and said: Yulia, you have lost none of your beauty.

Pardon me?

Not a day older.

And you, I replied, are still a liar.

No, no, no, he insisted. You're still beautiful.

I am an old woman, Rudi. I have accepted my headscarves.

He reached for the vodka, poured out three small glasses, looked at Kolya, wondered aloud if he were old enough to drink. With his teenage gait Kolya went to the cupboard to get a fourth glass.

Your son? whispered Rudi.

In a manner of speaking, I said.

You are married again?

I hesitated, shook my head. They had been long years of poverty and struggle for Kolya and me. My translating skills were as good as useless: there was no longer such a call for foreign literature and many of the publishing houses had been closed down. I felt as if I were standing on the edge of a new life, already half-exhausted. I had begun to take on some menial cleaning jobs to put bread on the table. But my joy was in the fact that Kolya had grown into a good young man, tall, dark-haired, reclusive. Seventeen years old, he had given up the chess but he was working on becoming an artist—he had begun by drawing landscapes, solid and real, but he was branching out now, blurring the edges. He believed that change needed a reason, otherwise there would be no respect for the past: he wanted to paint through the traditions in order to find the new. He had done a series of portraits of Lenin, using milk. The paintings were history as parody—nothing showed up on them until held to a candle or a match. Kolya hadn't sold any but kept them under his bed and his favorite was one that he'd accidentally left near a heating pipe and only the nose had emerged. Above his bed he had written a quote from Fontanelle from one of my old books: *It is true that the philosopher's stone cannot be found, but it is good to search for it.*

What panicked me was that Kolya would soon be coming up to his military service. The thought of it was horrific—war closing off parts of him as they had closed off parts of my parents—and I often woke at night in a pool of sweat with visions of my son rounding a corner in a village in Afghanistan, a rifle strapped across his chest. Kolya, however, thought he had found a way to circumvent the system: when giving a urine sample, he said, he would prick his finger with a pin and allow a drop of blood to fall into the sample. If his urine showed an excess of protein he could skip the military. It often occurred to me that Kolya had somehow inherited my father's spirit, although he looked nothing like him, of course. He had the tenacity, the intelligence, and the temperament. He had taken an interest in my family history and was amplified by the echoes he had found— inevitably, through his questions, he had discovered Rudi.

I scanned Kolya's face for a reaction to the visit but he was, surprisingly, unruffled.

Emilio, I noticed, had taken a translation of Cervantes from my shelf. But instead of reading it he was feeling through the pages as if divining the words, his eyes closed. Rudi explained that he'd put a hair in the book earlier when they were alone in the room and now Emilio was searching for it, something Emilio liked to do to pass the time.

I surround myself with crazy people, said Rudi.

Rudi reached for the bottle of vodka and poured two more glasses. He smiled at me in our small and awkward silence. A quarter of a century had gone by and while the difference in age may have become less pronounced, a thin curtain of embarrassment had been drawn in the space between us. We began desperately talking around it. He sat forward, with his elbows on his knees, his chin in his palms, his eyes sparkling with the same old delight.

Tell me everything, he said.

He lifted the glass to his mouth, waited for me, and so I tried to unravel what I had thought had been firmly spooled—my apartment, my divorce, my street.

Do you still translate?

On the odd occasion, I replied, but I'd rather not talk about it, I'd rather hear about you.

Oh everyone hears about me, they always get it wrong.

Even you?

Yes, even me. But I get it wrong on purpose, he said.

On purpose?

Of course, nobody knows me.

It was as if, between the two of us, we were playing a bizarre form of chess, that we were each trying to lose all our pieces, to get down to the final king, topple it over and say: *Here, now, the board is yours, explain to me my loss.*

Just then there was a deep thump and the electricity came on again and the room was pooled in bright light.

Turn them off please, said Rudi, I prefer candles.

Emilio's hands lay in the center of the book.

Rudi said loudly: Medicine please.

Emilio closed the book, took out a bottle of pills from his pocket, threw it into Rudi's lap. Rudi took four pills in quick succession. There was a mist of sweat on Rudi's forehead but he wiped it away with a sweep of his hand. I wondered what it was that, on other days, Emilio found beneath Rudi's skin.

And are you still dancing? I asked.

They will put me down dancing, he said.

I couldn't help but believe him—one day they would exhume Rudi and find his bones set in an attitude of leap, or perhaps even a bow, rising up to say: *Thank you, thank you, please allow me to do it once more.* He had no idea what he would do if he ever retired, perhaps choreograph. He had made some movies in the West, but he said they were all nonsense, and besides he was not built for the camera, his was a stage body, he needed an audience.

An audience indeed, I thought.

Ah-ha! Rudi said suddenly.

He reached into his pocket, took out a wallet, and thrust it across the table at Kolya. There was no money in it but the wallet was beautiful, its edges trimmed in gold.

American snakeskin, he said.

Kolya stared at it: For me?

Rudi put his arms behind his head and nodded. For a brief moment the jealously of my youth returned. I wanted to take Rudi aside and tell him that there was no need to show off, that he was acting like a spoiled boy at a lifelong birthday party. But perhaps there was something deeper in the way he had given the wallet to my son. It occurred to me that Rudi wanted to be left with nothing, in the same way that he had left before. Kolya flipped through the empty wallet and Rudi slapped him playfully on the shoulder.

Watching them together slipped a knife between my ribs and hit my heart exactly.

Emilio continued his search in the book but after a few moments he began to doze. I went to the window. Outside, the dark brushed the city and the wind unleashed the snow. Down below three cars sat in the street. I pulled the curtain back further, saw a shadow and then a flash of light from a camera. A photographer. I turned away instinctively and closed the curtains.

How come they let you back?

Raisa Gorbachev, he said.

Have you met her?

He shook his head, no.

But she got you a visa?

He didn't respond but then said curiously: We have always absorbed our own disintegration.

I didn't know quite what to say, not sure if it was self-pity or pure nonsense. I almost laughed. But it was impossible to get angry at Rudi for becoming what he had become. Something about him released people from the world, tempted them out. Even Kolya had begun to move his chair closer. We poured a little more vodka and talked briefly then of my father's gramophone; my mother's lessons; the night Rudi arrived in Leningrad; his dances at the Kirov. He had seen RosaMaria once, he said, but had fallen out of contact with her. There was almost a second-handedness to our conversation, as if we had talked it all before, and yet that didn't matter: what we lacked was made up for by the tenderness of his visit.

We silently toasted each other and then he flicked a look at his wrist as if he expected to see a watch there, but his arm was bare.

Emilio, he said loudly, what time is it?

The Spaniard awoke with a start: We should leave, he said, closing the book shut.

Just a few more minutes, said Rudi.

No, we really must leave.

A few more minutes! Rudi snapped.

Emilio waved his hands in the air, a gesture he had surely learned from Rudi: Okay, he said, but we'll miss our plane.

He put the Cervantes book back in the space on the shelf. I had a vision of a day in the future, cold and rainy, when Kolya and I would take the book from the shelf and touch its pages to feel for a tiny bump.

Rudi sat back in the chair, perfectly calm, took a minute to become the focus of the room once again.

Then, without missing a beat, he stood up quickly: My drivers are downstairs. They'll think I have defected again.

He pulled on his coat and spun on his heels: Can you believe it?

What?

After all these years, he said.

He carefully screwed the bottle top back on the vodka and stared at the table as if gathering strength for something to say. He stepped across, held my shoulders, bit his lip and whispered: You know, my own mother didn't recognize me.

What?

She didn't know who I was.

I recalled my father's story about the workcamp and the bullet and how he said that we never escape ourselves. I considered telling Rudi the story, but he was already wrapped in his scarf, about to go.

Of course she recognized you, I said.

Why should she? he asked.

I wanted to come up with a perfect rejoinder, to bring him back to earth, to receive another thrilling smile, another surprise, but he was turning the handle. I went to hug him. He took my face in his hands, kissed me on each cheek.

Wait, I said.

I went to the cupboard and took out the china dish that had belonged to my mother. I opened the lid of the box. The dish felt cold and brittle. I handed it to him.

Your mother showed me this years ago, he said.

It's yours.

I can't take it.

Take it, I said. Please.

You should keep it for Kolya.

Kolya already has it.

Rudi blindsided me with a smile and took the dish in his hand.

Exits and entrances, he said.

Emilio thanked us for our hospitality and went downstairs to alert the drivers. Rudi followed slowly, his knees bothering him. I stood at the iron railing with Kolya and together we watched him go down.

So that's him? said Kolya.

That's him.

Not much, is he?

Oh, I'm not so sure, I said.

And as if on cue Rudi paused in the light on the third-floor stairwell, threw his scarf over his shoulder and performed a perfect pirouette on the concrete slab, the china dish clutched to his chest. He stepped slowly to the next landing, through the rubbish and broken bottles, stopped once again in the arc of light and his shoes sounded against the concrete as he spun a second time. No remorse. Kolya put his arm around my shoulder and I thought to myself: Let this joy extend itself into the morning.

In the lobby Rudi pirouetted one final time and then he was gone.

*Sale: The Rudolf Nureyev Collection, January and November, 1995, New York and London*

**Lot 1088:** Six pairs of Ballet Boots
Estimate: $2,300–3,000
Price: $44,648
Buyer: Mr. and Mrs. Albert Cohen

**Lot 48:** Costume for *Swan Lake*, Act III. Prince Siegfried, 1963
Estimate: $3,000–5,000
Price: $29,900
Buyer: Anonymous

**Lot 147:** Sir Joshua Reynolds: *Portrait of George Townshend, Lord de Ferrars*
Estimate: $350,000–450,000
Price: $772,500 (Record for the artist at auction)
Buyer: Private

**Lot 1134:** A French Walnut Refectory Table
Estimate: $22,500–$30,000
Price: $47,327
Buyer: Telephone

**Lot 146:** Johann Heinrich Fuseli, R.A: *Satan Starting from the Touch of Ithuriel's Lance*

Estimate: $500,000–700,000

Price: $761,500

Buyer: Anonymous


**Lot 1356:** Attributed to Théodore Géricault, *Homme nu a mi-corps (Man Naked to Waist)*

Estimate: $60,000–80,000

Price: $53,578

Buyer: Telephone


**Lot 728:** A Jamawar Long Shawl, Kashmir, late nineteenth century

Estimate: $ 800–1,500

Price: $5,319

Buyer: R. Ratnawke (made up)


**Lot 1274:** Pre-Revolutionary Russian China Dish in oak box (box damaged)

Estimate: $2,000

Price: $2,750

Buyer: Nikolai Mareneov


**Lot 118:** Felix Boisselier, *A Shepherd Weeping on a Tomb Erected to a Gnat*

Estimate: $40,000–60,000

Price: $189,500

Buyer: Private


All lots sold.

# ACKNOWLEDGMENTS

In this novel many changes in names and locations have been made to protect the privacy of people living, and also to give a shape to various fictional creations. On occasion, I condensed two or more historical figures into one, or distributed the traits of one person over two or more characters. Some of the attributions made to public figures are exact; others are fictional. For clarity's sake, I have not always used the diminutive and intimate form for first names commonly employed in Russian.

In the course of researching this book, I was privileged to read a great deal—fiction, non-fiction, journalism, poetry and Internet material—but the following title was invaluable: *Nureyev* by Diane Solway, which at the time of writing is the definitive biography of Rudolf Nureyev. For those interested in biography I would also strongly recommend the writings of Julie Kavanaugh and her forthcoming book on Nureyev. Other books and source material, including films, are too numerous to mention but a special thanks must be given to the staff of the New York Public Libraries, who run such a profoundly important system. Deep thanks must also be given to the American-Irish Historical Society, most especially Dr. Kevin Cahill, Christopher Cahill and Bill Colbert.

There are so many people I must thank for their kindness, help and vision throughout this process: Roman Gerasimov, who was my translator in Russia, Kathleen Keller, Tim Kipp, John and Beverly Berger, John Gorman, Ger Donovan, Irina Kendall, Josh Kendall, Joan Acocella, Lisa Gonzalez, Errol Toran, D.C, Nick Terlizzi, Charlie Orr, Damon Testani, Mary Parvin, Marina Staviskaya, Jason Buzas, Jaco and Elizabeth Groot, Françoise Triffaux, Brigitte Semler, Thomas Ueberhoff, Colm Toibin, Chris Kelly, Emily Tabourin, Alona Kimchi, Tom Kelly, Jimmy Smallhorne, Mikhail Iossel, Radik Kudoyarov, Nikolay Korshun, Ilya Kuznetsov and his friends at the Kirov, Galina Belskaya, Yanni Kotsonis and Myrna Blumberg.

A very special debt of gratitude is owed to all at Phoenix House, Metropolitan Books and the Wylie Agency, most especially Maggie McKernan, Riva Hocherman and Sarah Chalfant.

No thanks would be complete without deep gratitude to my family: Allison, Isabella and John Michael, and to our extended families on both sides of the ocean.

# ABOUT THE AUTHOR

**Colum McCann** is the author of four previous works of fiction, all published by Metropolitan Books. His books include *This Side of Brightness* and *Songdogs* (novels), *Fishing the Sloe-Black River* (short stories), and *Everything in This Country Must* (novellas). His writing has appeared in *The New Yorker, The New York Times Magazine, Atlantic Monthly*, and *GQ*, among other publications. McCann, who lives in New York City, has received a Pushcart prize, the Irish Hennessy, Butler, and Rooney awards, and was also an IMPAC finalist. In 2002 he won the Princess Grace Memorial Literary Award.